KT-417-353

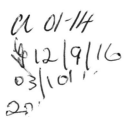

U 01-14
12/9/16
03/101
2n

Hello!

Just a note to say thanks for choosing to spend some time with me and my novel, *A Place to Call Home*. I hope you'll fall in love with the characters as I did when I was writing it.

This is a very special book for me and although all of my books are like babies to me and I shouldn't really have a favourite, it's definitely up there on the list of the ones I'm most proud of. During the writing process I found myself crying a bit, laughing a lot and really rooting for Ayesha, Sabina, Hayden, Crystal and Joy as they struggle to overcome their difficulties and make new beginnings in their lives.

To me, it's an uplifting story about what it takes to create a home and a family. Sometimes, particularly these days, families don't fall within the bounds of the 'conventional' arrangement but that doesn't make them any less of a family. Sometimes you have to take what's on offer and have the courage to work with it.

I hope you enjoy it.

Love, Carole ☺ xx

# A Place to Call Home

# Carole Matthews

sphere

SPHERE

First published in Great Britain in 2014 by Sphere

A CIP catalogue record for this book
is available from the British Library.

ISBN 978-0-7515-5219-5

Typeset in Sabon by M Rules
Printed and bound in Great Britain by
Clays Ltd, St Ives plc

Papers used by Sphere are from well-managed forests
and other responsible sources.

MIX
Paper from
responsible sources
FSC® C104740

Sphere
An imprint of
Little, Brown Book Group
100 Victoria Embankment
London EC4Y 0DY

An Hachette UK Company
www.hachette.co.uk

www.littlebrown.co.uk

To Ayesha and Sabina

# Chapter One

I stare anxiously at the clock. It's nearly two in the morning and my eyes are gritty from lack of sleep. In the bed next to me Suresh snores heavily, and I'm grateful that the sleeping tablet I slipped into his drink a few hours earlier still seems to be working well.

Even so, when I go to get out of the bed, I take care to lift the duvet cautiously and lower my feet quietly to the floor. I tiptoe across the room to collect my clothes from the chair in the corner. It's a bright night, the moonlight filling the room and illuminating me more than I would like.

For a moment I stand with my shalwar kameez gripped in my arms, watching the sleeping form of my husband of ten years. My heart's pounding in my chest and there's a sick feeling in my stomach, but I know that I have to do this. Whatever happens, I can no longer stay. It will be the last time I will ever be in this bedroom, in this house, with this man.

As soundlessly as possible, I make my way to the bathroom along the hall. Suresh's mother and father sleep at the back of the house, in the biggest room, which overlooks the garden. Thankfully, Sabina's room is at the other end of the hall to them. In the dead of the night, the only sound I can hear is my own nervous breathing.

I change my clothes in the bathroom, stripping off my nightdress and putting on the same shalwar kameez that I wore yesterday. I fold my nightdress carefully. That will come with me too. And my toothbrush. I'd like to freshen my mouth, but I don't dare risk running the tap. The walls are as thin as paper and I cannot risk doing anything that might wake anyone but Sabina.

The face that stares back at me in the mirror is thin and tired. This woman looks afraid. Afraid but determined.

Along the landing and I ease the handle on the door into Sabina's room. My child's pink nightlight fills the small space with a warm glow and I go straight to her bed, crouching down beside it.

I stroke my daughter's silky hair which is long and dark like my own. Sabina's hair, however, is tangled with sleep whereas my own hangs down my back in a heavy plait.

'Sabina,' I whisper in her ear. 'Sabina, my daughter.'

The child opens her eyes and gazes at me. The trust I see there is heartbreaking. For so long I've failed her, but not any more.

'Mummy is taking you on an adventure,' I murmur. 'We must be quiet though. As quiet as little mice. Can you do that for me?'

With sleep-filled eyes, she nods at me and I help to lift her out of bed. I put my finger to my lips. It's a needless gesture. Sabina doesn't speak. Not ever.

Quickly, quietly, I change her from her nightwear into her shalwar kameez. It's spring, but the nights are still cold, so while Sabina tiredly buckles her shoes, I get her coat from the wardrobe. My heart is in my mouth for fear of the door squeaking, but thankfully it's silent. I've done my best to furnish this room nicely. She has a pretty duvet cover, curtains and a lamp-shade that looks like a ballerina's skirt. But it's not enough, is it? The important things are love, affection, joy, and in this I've been so lacking.

Sabina, all buttoned up, sways sleepily on her feet, and I sit her down for a brief moment. Under her bed, tucked far into the corner, I have a bag already prepared for this event. It's taken me weeks to get to this point. Months even. We have a holdall that I bought cheaply from the market. It's very small, so that I could hide it adequately, and is filled with only enough clothes to last us until tomorrow. After that, I don't know what we'll do.

'We must go,' I say. My finger goes to my lips. 'Remember, very quiet.'

I take Sabina's tiny, warm hand in mine and I hope the contact comforts her as much as it comforts me. Leading her out of the room, we inch along the landing. Still I can hear Suresh's snores, and that calms me a little.

I don't know what my husband does for work, but I do know that it's not good. Sometimes he brings home men to our house and they laugh together until the small hours. Sometimes he doesn't come home at night at all. I never know which it will be, so I've had to wait a long time for this, the perfect moment.

On the stairs, I count our way down. The seventh stair creaks and I'm worried that it will sound out in the dead of the night, so I make sure that we step over it watchfully. Sabina is very slight for her eight years and, though I too am small, I lift her over it with ease. Her face is solemn, concerned. She trembles in my arms and I hold her tightly.

We make our way along the hall and to the front door. Lifting my coat from the peg, I slip it on and then pull my scarf over my hair. What will I do now if Suresh suddenly appears on the landing? Will I still be brave enough to bolt for our

3

freedom? Or will I return meekly to his side despite vowing that I would never do so? If he sees us he'll know, instantly, that we are fleeing. Fleeing from him, from his fists. When he attacks me, as he surely will, can I fight him off? Or will he decide that, this time, he must kill me once and for all? The thought makes me shake. What then would happen to my darling Sabina?

Looking down at my daughter's anxious face, I know that I have to do this. If not for me, then for her. I have to be a good role model. I have to be the best mother that I can possibly be so that my child will grow into a strong, happy and independent woman. All of the things that I'm not.

Staring at the holdall in my hand, I realise that I'm leaving with the same material possessions I arrived with from Sri Lanka all those years ago, to be, for the very first time, with my new husband. How full of hope I was then! I should reach deep inside myself and try to find that feeling again now.

I ease open the lock on the front door, the lock that I secretly sprayed with oil last week so that it wouldn't make a noise and give us away.

'Ready?' I whisper to Sabina.

She nods and we both step out into the darkness.

# Chapter Two

I stand with Sabina by my side and stare back at the house. It's featureless, identical to the dozen or more that are the same in our terrace. There's nothing to make it a home. No name, no pretty flowers in the garden. It's as cold and blank as the people who live in it.

I take Sabina's hand and we hurry away from the house. 'We must walk quickly,' I say to her. 'Can you manage that?'

She nods her acquiescence.

Normally I wouldn't use the underpasses in the city, especially not after dark, as they're a haven for muggers and drug addicts. But, as I haven't been allowed out at night for many years, there's a strange giddiness in having the freedom to put myself and my daughter at risk. The Redways are the quickest and straightest route to the Coachway and our escape, and I don't want to risk getting lost.

We don't live in a very nice area in Milton Keynes. Our house is right in the heart of the city, on an estate that has seen much better days. However, I'm grateful for that now as it isn't a long walk – about an hour, I'm thinking – to the Coachway and our ticket out of here. The train station is far away, at the other side of the city, and I'd have needed to call a taxi, which I couldn't risk. Too many of Suresh's friends drive cabs and he'd instantly hear of my departure. It's better to rely on my own devices.

'Are you all right, my child?' I ask Sabina. I can see my breath in the night air, a little puff of steam.

She nods again, but nothing more.

I'd give anything to hear her complain. If only she would whine about us walking too fast, or it being too cold, or demand to know about our destination. If only.

For months, I've stolen money from my husband's wallet as often as I was able. Just a little, as much as I could manage without him noticing – £5 here, £10 there. I kept it in an old Quality Street tin at the back of my wardrobe, underneath a pile of towels that we don't often use. Now I have £800 and my way out of here. It's in the bottom of my holdall, rolled and secured with elastic bands, £100 in each precious one.

We make our way in the darkness. Due to council cutbacks the streetlights are switched off, and it takes longer than I anticipated as I'm uncertain of the way. Sabina and I take a wrong turn and we walk for nearly quarter of an hour before I realise from the signposts that we're heading in the opposite direction to where we want to be. So we have to retrace our steps. Then, as I'm beginning to despair and the sky is beginning to lighten, I see the building of the Coachway ahead of us in the distance. I can hear the gentle thrum of traffic from the M1 behind it and it sounds like music to my ears.

'Not long now, Sabina,' I urge. 'We're nearly there.'

The building is modern, recently built, and the lights shine out harshly in the dissipating darkness. Hand in hand, we cross the final road to reach it – two conspicuous figures standing out in the emptiness of the night. I hope that Suresh hasn't woken and found us gone. I pray that he doesn't think to come look-ing for us in his car when we are so, so close to escape. My

6

hand tightens on Sabina's fingers and, picking up our pace, we walk faster.

The first coach to London isn't until half-past four and we have a little while to kill until then as, I'm relieved to say, we have made good time. With trembling fingers and my back to the waiting room, I slip some money from one of the rolls in my bag and buy our tickets from the machine, feeding in the crisp notes that I have stolen from my husband. At this hour, there are very few people here. A man in uniform carrying a clipboard lets his gaze fall on me as we pass. When I feel it linger, we go to sit in the corner furthest away from him, where a big plant in a pot obscures his view. The café is shuttered for the night and I've nothing to give my child but a carton of juice that's in the holdall.

'Do you want a drink, Sabina?'

She nods and I get out the carton of orange and fix the straw for her.

I check that my rolls of money are safely secreted once again in the bottom of the holdall and relish the comfort that they bring. Then I get the tickets out and clutch them to me. Two travelling to London Victoria. One adult. One child. One way.

As we sit on the cold wooden bench, I huddle my daughter to me and relief washes over me. We're not free yet, I think, but we've made it this far.

# Chapter Three

The sky continues to lighten and the coach arrives. Sabina and I board as quickly as we can. The driver wants to take my holdall and put it in the luggage compartment under the coach, but I cling to it. This is my lifeline, my future.

I find us seats and put the holdall by my feet, then settle Sabina next to me. Within minutes all the passengers are on board and we speed out of the coach station and turn on to the motorway. The amber lights of the road blur past my eyes and the anxious breath that I've been holding is finally released. We're on our way. Already Sabina's eyes are heavy with sleep and I cuddle her in to me. 'Are you comfortable?'

She nods at me and snuggles in to my side.

'Rest now,' I tell her. 'When you awake, we'll be there.'

Soon she sleeps beside me and, as I hold her close, my mind goes over what has led me to the point where I feel the need to flee for our safety in the middle of the night.

I've lived in this city for ten years, since I came here from Sri Lanka to meet and marry my husband, Suresh Rasheed, but I know so little of it now. It's changed so much and, for some time, I've gone only where my husband has taken me. Some weeks I wouldn't go out of the house at all. I wouldn't dare. If Suresh came home and found that I wasn't there, he'd fly into a rage. And I never knew when he was coming home, as he'd never tell me where he was going. Soon it was simpler not to leave the house at all. If there was shopping to be done or errands to be run, his mother would go, and take Sabina with her. I'd be left behind, anxious and fretting, to clean the house or to cook the meal. A prisoner in my own home.

I had no friends that I could turn to as, eventually, Suresh wouldn't allow me to see anyone other than his relatives. So the few women that I'd become close to had fallen away over the years as they couldn't bear to see the evidence of my controlling marriage. Now there's no one I can call on who isn't connected to my husband's family. I couldn't trust one of them to help me in case they should tell Suresh of my whereabouts and he'd find me and drag me back. I can't allow that to happen.

Yet it wasn't always like this. The first year when I came to England was a happy one. My husband and I took pleasure in each other's company. Suresh was never open or overtly affectionate towards me. He didn't like to hold my hand or kiss me, but he was considerate and a steady man. I thought that, in time, we could make a good marriage.

We rented our own house near to his parents, who had been settled in England for many years, since Suresh was a child himself. Our place was small but comfortable and I kept it clean and pretty. I did my utmost to make it a loving home. When, very soon, I became pregnant, Suresh was so pleased to find that I was with child.

Then he changed. Almost overnight. I'm still not sure why. It was many small hurts, I believe, that harmed his personality.

When my dear Sabina was born, he was delighted to become a father. Soon after, though, he became withdrawn, difficult. I feel that he was jealous of the attention I gave to my tiny, mewling daughter, but is that not what new mothers do? I knew from the moment I saw her that she was my life and that I would never love another human being more than this helpless bundle who clung to me for her every need. The whole of my heart was suddenly filled with her, and perhaps Suresh felt that there was no room left for him.

Within weeks, he was made redundant from his job, and that severely hurt his pride. Try as he might, he couldn't easily find work despite walking the streets and seeing all his contacts. Eventually we fell into financial difficulties; our bills weren't paid and we hid when men knocked at the door. We were forced to give up even our modest home and move in with his parents.

To start with my mother- and father-in-law were kind people, fun-loving, smiling. They tried their best with us all crammed together in their home and they loved their new granddaughter very much. But soon that changed too as their son became increasingly difficult to live with.

Before too long Suresh stopped looking for work at all and stayed in bed until late every morning. He'd never been a man of great faith but he no longer prayed at all. My husband started to drink heavily, and he fell in with the men who now keep him out at night.

It saddens me to say that my own faith is long gone too. At home we liked to embrace all faiths – sometimes we'd worship at the Buddhist temple, sometimes at the Hindu one. My mummy also liked to take us to the Catholic church sometimes, if there was a festival for the saints. 'It is better,' she always said, 'to keep one's options open.' Perhaps she felt one god would, eventually, turn out to be better than another. Now I'm not sure there's a god at all. My only instinct is survival. My parents would be disappointed in their daughter.

Sabina is close to her paternal grandmother – the only one

she's known. They would cook together in the cramped kitchen and she'd show my daughter the family recipes, as she did to me when I first arrived.

But she too is a woman who's now scared to speak. One day, as we prepared the evening meal together, I looked at my mother-in-law and saw my future self. That vision of my life began to make me anxious. She's a woman who clings to the shadows, who is intimidated by her own son. My husband's father, too, is frightened by what his eldest child has become and they've each retreated into their own shell. They don't speak up for fear of his wrath. They would stand by, powerless, while he hurt me. It's very sad and I'll miss the people they once were, but I must think of myself now and my child.

At first they tried to protect us, but soon they became frightened for their own safety. I'm frightened for them too. His mother would cry bitter tears for our pain, but that didn't stop the bruises I suffered. I came to realise that keeping Sabina and myself from harm was entirely down to me. I didn't dare tell them that I was leaving as I couldn't risk them knowing my plan. The less they were aware of, the better.

My daughter shifts in her restless sleep and I stroke her hair to soothe her. 'Hush, hush,' I murmur.

The bus is quite busy, but everyone is sleeping or in their own world, listening to music on earphones. No one pays us any attention, which is more than I could have hoped for.

A year ago, my husband beat me so badly in front of my daughter that she stopped speaking. I was curled into the corner of the living room while he rained blows on me and, as I looked up, my eyes met Sabina's. She'd come down from her bedroom when she heard the noise. It wasn't the first time that she'd seen her mother slapped or punched by her father, but this was much worse.

Sometimes she cried out and tried to intervene, and it tore my

11

heart in two that she should witness such things. As Suresh's fist made my head rock back, I saw her eyes wide with terror, her mouth frozen as if to scream, but no sound came out. The sight of her was so pitiful that it even stopped my husband in his tracks and I was able to hurry her from the room to soothe her, my own agony forgotten.

My injuries healed, my bruises faded, my broken bones mended, but my daughter's pain goes on. From that day to this, she's never uttered a single word. She hasn't laughed with joy or cried out with fright. Before that she was bright, articulate, clever for her age – and she was funny, so funny. It was a delight to listen to her childish chatter. Now she makes no sound at all. Not even when we're alone and there's no one else to hear. It's as if she can't forgive me, and I don't blame her. I can't forgive myself.

When she lost her voice, that was the very moment I realised that I had to get far away. I had to put a stop to this and I vowed to leave. How long would it be before I was unable to recover from the beatings? Would there come a point when the slaps and punches were aimed at Sabina too? There was no way I intended to let that happen. Already, she'd been hurt enough by this. I'd never wanted to harm a hair on her beautiful head and yet I'd allowed this terror to take her tongue.

The only way to right this wrong is to protect her now above all else.

# Chapter Four

We arrive at Victoria Coach Station just before seven o'clock and I realise straight away that London is the busiest place I've ever been to. In Sri Lanka I lived in a small fishing village by the coast near Kathaluwa, but that seems like a lifetime ago now.

When I first came to England I couldn't believe how many people there were in one place. I feel like that all over again, as if I've recently landed from abroad and know nothing. Surely in this vast metropolis Suresh will be unable to find us. There are thousands of people here. Thousands. All bustling back and forth like ants. Can we simply disappear here and live in peace as I want us to?

I wake Sabina, who thankfully has slept all the way. The coach was nearly full, but we sat quietly at the back and no one gave us a second glance.

When we come out of the coach station I look for a café that's open and find one that's a little way down the road. It's warm inside and smells strongly of fresh coffee. The place is worn round the edges but homely. I buy more juice for Sabina and a chocolate-chip cookie as there's nothing else I can see that she'll eat. I ask for a cup of tea and a croissant. The man behind the counter is kind and smiles at Sabina.

'She's a very pretty little girl, if you don't mind me mentioning it.'

'Say thank you,' I urge her. In return, she stares blankly at him. 'She doesn't speak,' I say apologetically.

He hands me my tea and wraps the croissant in a napkin, and I pay him.

'May I ask how to get to this place?' Out of my pocket, I pull my piece of paper with the address printed on it.

Some months ago, I made an excuse to my mother-in-law to go alone into the city, which was a nerve-racking experience. She lowered her eyes as I left and never asked me where I was going. The whole time I was out my stomach was knotted with anxiety in case I should turn a corner and find Suresh standing there, waiting for me. Thankfully he wasn't, and I reached my goal.

In the library, a kind lady showed me how to access the internet and how to surf. It was a whole new world. She assisted me in contacting a helpline and I was given the name of this women's-aid charity. The lady I spoke to said that they'll allocate me somewhere safe to go, a place that'll give me breathing space away from my husband so that I can think what's best to do for me and Sabina. So that's how I decided that London would be the place to go, and the women's-aid charity is where I'm heading for now. Their office doesn't open until ten o'clock so we have time to kill.

'Hop on the tube,' the man behind the counter says. 'Victoria Line, right up to Euston. It's easy enough. Won't take long at all. The place you want is right by the station. Ask someone at the other end.'

'Thank you.' I fold the paper carefully and replace it in my pocket. Though, if I'm truthful, the address is embedded in my brain.

In my holdall there's a colouring book and pencils for Sabina, and we tuck ourselves into a corner of the café on a worn leather sofa. I hope we can stay here for the next few hours until we must leave. While my daughter quietly busies herself with the business of colouring, I open a discarded magazine and flick through the pictures. I can speak English well enough, as I learned from an early age. I had lessons throughout my schooling and my village was popular with tourists who came to see the traditional stilt fishermen at their work.

We used to talk to the visitors and were sometimes cheeky enough to ask the people for pencils and sweets, even though our parents forbade us to. Yet I never imagined that one day I'd actually live in England. My ability to read and write in English, however, is now very poor through lack of practice, and Suresh would never allow me to attend evening classes to improve my skills. Instead, I've been learning along with Sabina and can read all of her books. I'm always sure to do her homework with her so that I can keep up with my child. No one wants a mother who is ignorant.

The pictures blur in front of my eyes and, in my coat pocket, my mobile phone tings. I take it out and, through my tears, I see a text from Suresh. My insides turn to water and my palms grow damp with fear.

I wonder what's happening at home now. He must have already risen to find that I'm gone and I've taken Sabina with me. My husband will be consumed with rage, I'm sure, and Suresh is a man who doesn't like to be crossed.

Reluctantly, I look at the message. *Where r u?* it says.

I don't answer, but simply stare at the phone in terror. Could he trace the whereabouts of my phone, I wonder, like they do on police television shows?

A moment later there's another one. *Come home or there will be trouble.*

My mouth is dry.

Then another. *I will hunt u down & find u bitch*, it says.

Perhaps he'll drive round in his car to look for us, but I don't think he'll go as far as calling the police. Panicky, I turn off my phone and walk as quickly as I can across the café to drop it into the nearest litter bin.

# Chapter Five

At nine o'clock we're standing outside the door of the women's refuge. We lingered as long as we could at the café, but I didn't want to waste money on tea that I didn't want to drink and I felt we were outstaying our welcome.

We're not the first, as there are two ladies already here queuing before us. One of them has a black eye and one of them has a plaster cast on her wrist. My heart goes out to them, as I've been there myself. The last time Suresh beat me he cracked my ribs and my jaw. They both look at the pavement, anxious to avoid conversation, and I feel the same. Sabina stands still by my side without complaining. It's warm already, a mild day for the time of year, and I'm hot, sweating in my coat. At ten o'clock, when the door opens, we're shown into a small waiting room and we do just that. Wait.

The other two women are seen before me and eventually Sabina and I are ushered into a small and rather scruffy office where two women sit at desks piled high with paperwork. We're offered seats at one of them. The lady looks up from the form she's currently filling in and smiles.

'I'm Ruth,' she says. Even though it's early in the day, she seems harried. 'Now then, how can we help?'

I tell her of my circumstances. I tell her that Sabina doesn't speak any more. I tell her that I cannot go back.

She sighs and then informs me that we're unable to go into any of the women's refuges they have as they're all full.

'I'm really sorry,' Ruth says with a frown. 'We've got several homes in the area and usually manage to squeeze everyone in somewhere, even if it's only for a couple of nights. Unfortunately, the two ladies before you have taken the last places.'

I have no plan as to what I'll do now. I thought that this lady, this Ruth, would help me. It seems as if I was wrong. I'm cross with myself, as we could have been here and waiting much earlier if only I'd known that help was offered on a first come, first served basis.

I sit still. So does Sabina. I'm not being difficult. I'm paralysed with fear. My plan was only to get myself to this place. If I stand up and leave, I'll have to go somewhere else and I don't know where that might be.

'You can never tell what's going to happen,' Ruth continues when she sees that I'm not going anywhere. 'But we're not expecting anyone to leave the refuges for at least a week or two. I'm not sure what we can do.'

Still I sit, unmoving. I feel that if I don't acknowledge that I've heard this then it will not be real.

Eventually, the woman sighs again at me, but it sounds kindly and not exasperated. 'I'll have a ring round,' she offers. 'See if I can find somewhere for you. Even if it's only temporary. It's the best I can do. We can't have you out on the streets, can we?'

No, I think. We cannot.

She tries several numbers while Sabina and I wait patiently. Each time she hangs up, the woman's frown deepens and my unease grows.

Shaking her head, she says, 'I've got one last place to try. An old friend of mine who might help me out. We used to work together years ago.'

Ruth jabs at the keypad and I see that she's gripping the receiver tightly. I fear she's more worried for us than she wants us to believe.

'Hi, Crystal,' I hear her say. 'Wondered if you could help me out, darling. I've got someone in desperate need of a place and I'm all out of rooms.' Ruth glances anxiously at me again. 'Even the B&Bs are chock-a-block. Can you put them up? Even if it's only for a few days?'

I can't hear what the other woman, Crystal, answers. But I realise that I'm holding my breath and praying to someone, to anyone, to help.

'It's a woman and her daughter. They're both very' – another glance – 'quiet.' There's a moment before she adds, 'Thanks, Crystal. You're an angel. I owe you one.'

When she hangs up, the relief is visible in her eyes and I wonder what my own expression shows. I believe that she's found somewhere for us to live. Somewhere safe. Somewhere that my husband can't find us.

'We don't normally use this house,' Ruth says. 'This is a big favour. Crystal and I go back a long way. I hope you won't be any trouble for her.'

'I don't think I will be.'

Ruth smiles at Sabina, but my daughter remains impassive as always. Ruth writes down an address and pushes it across the desk to me. 'It's a lovely house. You'll like it there.'

'Will I be safe?'

'Yes,' she says. 'Of course.'

I can only hope that she's right.

# Chapter Six

Suresh slammed his phone on the table. 'Where is she?' he shouted at his parents. Spittle flecked the corners of his mouth. They cowered together against the kitchen cupboards, still dressed in their nightclothes. He'd dragged them from their bed when he woke and realised that his wife, Ayesha, and their daughter were gone. 'You must know.'

His mother was first to speak up. Her voice shook and he was filled with loathing for her. 'My son, we don't know.'

'How could she leave without help?' His wallet was still on his bedside table and was stuffed full of notes. Why hadn't she taken that? He had her passport well hidden, so he knew she couldn't be embarking on some vain attempt to get back to Sri Lanka. 'Did you give her money?'

They both shook their heads.

'Then how has she got out of here? Where can she have gone? Did she have friends that I didn't know about? A man?'

'No,' his mother said. 'Nothing like that, Suresh. I am sure. She is a good wife.'

'Then why isn't she here?' He felt a surge of red-hot rage. They were so weak, so compliant, so spineless, he felt like shaking them. 'She's taken Sabina, my only child, and you've let her.'

'We heard nothing,' his mother protested.

'I don't believe you. One of you knows something.' He pointed a finger in his mother's face. 'When I come back, I'll find out who.'

Storming out of the house, he jumped into his car and gunned the engine. What time had she left? It was unusual for him to sleep so soundly. Why hadn't he heard a single noise? Not the closing of a door or the creaking of a floorboard? It was as if she'd vanished into thin air.

As he drove through the streets, heading aimlessly into the city, he wondered if there was any place that she'd be bound for. He racked his brains, but came up with nothing. She must have had a friend that he didn't know about. Well, when he found her, she'd pay for that. Ayesha shouldn't be keeping secrets from him, he was her husband. He'd make sure she couldn't stand up for a week, let alone leave the house. And the child too. She was getting to be disobedient, wilful like her mother.

Suresh couldn't go to the police, that much he knew. The less contact he had with the boys in blue, the better. Besides, what could they do? This was a family matter. It was best dealt with privately and he knew people who could help him.

He scoured the city centre, searching back and forth along the network of grid roads, his frustration rising as he got caught up in the rush-hour traffic. He trawled up Avebury Boulevard and then back down Midsummer towards the train station. There was no sign of her anywhere, but she could well have had a good head-start on him.

As he swung round, it occurred to him that he'd assumed she'd still be in the city. What if she'd managed, somehow, to get enough money together for a train ticket? Would she have the nerve to go away on her own? In all the years Ayesha had been here, she'd never done more than catch a bus to go shopping by herself. She couldn't drive, had no car. How far could she get?

He laughed to himself. She'd never have the courage to strike out on her own. She *must* still be here in Milton Keynes, somewhere not very far away, and *someone* was helping her. He'd find out where and he'd find out who. Tonight he'd give out her photograph to some of his associates, perhaps offer a reward. It would reflect badly on him that he couldn't control his own wife, but so be it.

Ayesha wasn't getting away. She was his and he'd bring her to heel. He'd make her pay for the pain and inconvenience she'd put him through. She couldn't have simply disappeared without trace.

As he'd promised in his texts, he would hunt her down and drag her back. The sooner the better.

# Chapter Seven

Ruth also gave me directions to the house. Which I believe I've followed very carefully. But as I stand outside this very large house in this leafy lane, I check the piece of paper again. Surely we're not to live here?

'This is nice, isn't it?' I say to Sabina. My daughter looks tired now and I'd very much like to give her a hot bath and put her to bed to sleep for an hour. She needs some proper food too. A chocolate-chip cookie won't sustain her.

We've come to the north of London, a place called Hampstead. It meant another tube journey, but it wasn't far. Just a few stops. I thought that all of London was dirty and busy, but this road certainly isn't. It looks like a very affluent place and, across the road from where I stand, there's an open park.

The house itself is pretty and painted white. It sits quite alone in a garden filled with mature trees. There's a tall wall at the front and high iron gates. A security camera regards us suspiciously. I look at the number again. Unless I'm very much mistaken, this is indeed the right one.

I'm not sure how we'll afford this house, but Ruth filled in lots of papers on my behalf and assured me that it will all be paid for. She promised that I'll also receive money from the government for myself and for Sabina to help us get on our feet again. She also said to me that I should consider whether to divorce Suresh and apply for maintenance money from him. I told her that it wasn't possible. That would mean making contact with him and he must never, ever know where we are. I'd rather be poor than have him find us.

Still, I can't stand here quaking all day. So I take my courage in both hands and press the buzzer on the gates.

A crackly voice says, 'Give the gate a good shove when you hear the click.'

Sure enough, it clicks and I shove. Opening the gate, we walk up the path, our footsteps loud on the gravel. I take a deep breath as we stand on the doorstep and wait to be admitted. What if this lady, Crystal, decides that she doesn't like us and turns us away? Then what will we do?

Moments later, Crystal opens the door. She's quite startling, with blonde hair, lots of it. It sits high on her head and tumbles to her shoulders in big waves. Her skin is very orange and her teeth very white. Her lipstick is so pink that it almost vibrates. She's wearing hardly any clothes. Just small white shorts and a pink top that's cropped to show her midriff. On her feet are very high shoes the same colour as her lipstick. I look at Sabina and her mouth has dropped open.

'Hello, sweetheart,' she says. 'You must be the woman that Ruthie rang about. I'm Crystal. Welcome to your new home. You both look knackered. Give me that.' She takes my bag from my hands and, before I have chance a to stop her, she whisks it away. 'Where's the rest of your stuff?'

'That's all I have.'

'Really?' She looks taken aback. 'Blimey. You know how to travel light.'

She clearly doesn't know of our circumstances.

24

'Come on then. Don't stand on the doorstep, sweetie.'

Anxious, I take my daughter's hand and we follow her inside.

The house is light, airy and spacious. Everything I can see in the large hallway is painted white. This is as different as it's possible to be from the home we've been living in, with its dingy, subdued colours and bleak atmosphere. Instantly it lifts my spirits, yet it seems to make Sabina more nervous as her grip on my hand tightens.

'I'll show you to your room,' Crystal says. 'Then I'll stick the kettle on. You look like you need a good, strong brew.'

She starts to go up the stairs ahead of me and I can see nearly all of her bottom. I almost put my hand over Sabina's eyes, but I feel it would be rude.

'I'm Crystal, by the way,' she says over her shoulder. 'But you probably know that from Ruth. I'm glad she gave me a call. I haven't seen her for ages and I could do with a good chinwag.' She pushes open a door and disappears inside. We follow. She waves her hand at the room. 'Here you go. Welcome to the madhouse.'

The room is big and there's a king-size bed. The bedspread is turquoise and the furniture – a wardrobe and a dressing table – is dark wood and looks expensive. There's a very large television on the wall.

'Like it?'

Warily, I cross the room to stand at the big bay window and look out over the green expanse of park across the road. Tears prickle my eyes. This is nicer than anywhere I've ever lived – even my family home in Sri Lanka.

'This is to be ours?' I venture.

'Sure is. Do you like it?'

'Very much.' I'm still looking round in awe. 'This is your home too?'

'Yeah. I'm on the next floor up.' Crystal slings my holdall on

25

the bed and then sits on it too. 'There's another lady called Joy. Miserable cow. Totally the wrong name for her. She's on my floor too. Then His Nibs is up on the top floor.' Crystal flicks her head upwards. 'Has it all to himself.'

'His Nibs?'

'Hayden.'

'A man lives here?' Ruth didn't mention this.

Crystal shrugs. 'It's his house. I had to give him a bit of chat to get him to agree to you staying here, but he's cool now.'

'He's a difficult man?'

'Hayden?' Crystal laughs. 'God, no. Troubled. He's a musician. A singer. Was a big pop star once. You know what these artistic types are like.'

But I do not.

'We all share the kitchen, and there's a ma*hoo*sive living room downstairs where Hayd has his piano. He hardly plays it these days, mind you. Likes to keep himself to himself. Sort of a recluse really. Goodness only knows why he has lodgers. Too much of a soft touch to say no, I suppose.'

Crystal barely pauses for breath and my tired brain struggles to keep pace with her.

'He's taken in us two waifs and strays – me and Joy – and now he can't get shot of us. He doesn't charge anywhere near enough either. That's why we both try to look after him a bit. He lets us pet him for a while, then we get on his nerves and he does a disappearing act. Takes himself off upstairs again, never to be seen.'

I must look worried as she adds, 'He's a poppet. Honestly. Just stay out of his way and you'll be fine. Don't let the kid run wild.'

'She won't.'

'What's your name, sweetie pie?' Crystal says to my daughter. Sabina stares.

'Sabina,' I answer for her. 'My daughter doesn't speak.'

'Wow,' Crystal says. 'Not ever?'

'No.'

'Was she born like that?'

'No,' I say. 'It is something that's happened recently.' I feel my cheeks flush. This loud lady must think that I'm a bad mother.

'Poor kid,' Crystal says. 'Pretty though. Takes after her mum.'

'I'm Ayesha,' I tell her. 'Ayesha Rasheed.'

'Pleased to meet you, Ayesha.' She jumps up and crushes me to her ample bosom. 'I hope we're going to be best friends.'

I don't think I've had a best friend before and I'd like that very much, but this lady scares me half to death.

# Chapter Eight

There's a bathroom attached to our room and it's very spacious. When Crystal has left us to go and put the kettle on, I run a hot bath for Sabina and she stands listless while I undress her. Sometimes I feel that I want to shake her, simply to get a reaction from her. Then I remember what it's like to be treated cruelly and I wrap my arms round her slender body, pulling her to me.

'I hope we'll be happy here,' I say to her. 'No one can hurt you now. I'll look after you and I hope that, one day, you'll feel that you can talk to me once more.'

She looks up at me with doleful eyes and I kiss her forehead. Helping her into the warm water, I wait for the contented sigh that should come, but it never does.

Her clothes smell stale and I should wash them tonight. Tomorrow I'll go to the shops and find us both something else to wear. I'll ask Crystal where to go, as she looks like a lady who'll know about shops. She looks like a lady who knows about a lot of things.

I catch sight of my reflection in the mirror and feel very drab in comparison to her. My shalwar kameez is dark in colour and covers my arms and legs. It doesn't hug the shape of my body. As is my culture, my mummy liked me and my sister, Hinni, to dress modestly. Once I was a married woman, so did Suresh. I've never worn make-up and I wonder how that shiny lipstick would feel on my mouth. I touch my lips, which are dry, parched.

When Sabina has finished in the bath, I dry her with the soft towels that are on a warm radiator. They're snowy white and plush. I don't know if these are ours to use, but I can't think why else they'd be here. This is, I think, more like a hotel would be than a home and I wonder how we'll fit in. Already I feel out of my depth.

I settle Sabina in the big bed. The sheets are soft, good-quality too, the duvet thick and fluffy.

'Stay here and sleep,' I say. 'I'm going to talk to the nice lady.' Sabina clutches my hand as if she doesn't want me to leave. 'I won't be long. Rest. It's been a busy day and I won't be far away.'

When I've made sure that Sabina is settled, I make my way downstairs and find Crystal in the kitchen. She's sitting at the table filing her nails, but she looks up and smiles widely when she sees me.

'Sit your bum down,' she says as she jumps up. 'Tea and biccies. The British cure for everything.'

Soon I'll have to go out and buy some sandwiches or something for us to eat as we have no lunch, no food.

I look round while she makes tea. The kitchen is also spacious. There's a big table in the middle and a huge cooker. It looks like the kind of cooker you might have in a restaurant rather than a home. I hope that I'll be allowed to use it as I love to cook.

At the end of the room there are French doors that open out on to a large, secluded garden that sweeps away from the house. It's fresh and blooming with a hint of the summer to come. It will be a nice place for Sabina to play.

29

'The garden is very lovely.'

'Joy looks after that. She's probably out there somewhere now.' Crystal opens the fridge. It's one of those big American ones like you see on television. 'Hayden gets milk delivered every day and eggs once a week so that we don't fight over them. Joy's got a veg patch out there, so there's always courgettes or tomatoes or something kicking about. We can help ourselves to stuff in the cupboards – rice, pasta, flour. Hayden sort of pays for that too. Joy usually tops it up when we're running low. We all have our own shelf in the fridge,' she says. 'Mine is the one with chocolate on it. Joy's is the one with yoghurt and fruit. Hayden's is the one with a dozen bottles of beer and nothing else.'

'He's a drinker?'

'No.' Crystal shakes her head. 'He just doesn't eat.'

She splashes milk into the mugs, then puts one down in front of me, and a plate of chocolate biscuits. 'I can't have any,' she complains. 'Watching my figure.'

I'm ravenous and have to force myself to be polite and eat with restraint.

'There are loads of rooms in this place,' she says. 'He hardly ever uses half of them. Some of them are full of decorating stuff where he started to renovate them and never finished. Apart from the ones that we have, they're mostly shut up. Those that do have furniture are all covered with dust sheets. Don't know why he doesn't sell up. But I'm glad he doesn't. He bought this house with all the dosh he made from his hits.'

I look at her blankly.

'Hayden Daniels,' she says. 'That's your new landlord.'

My expression doesn't change.

'Didn't you know?'

'No.'

'You've never heard of him, have you?'

'No.'

'Don't you watch *The Fame Game*?'

'No.'

She screws up her face, disbelieving. 'Have you been living in a cave?'

'Milton Keynes,' I say.

'Oh. Same thing, I suppose.' Crystal takes a biscuit.

Perhaps I should remind her that she's watching her figure, but I don't.

'It's a talent show. Ma*hoo*sive. On Saturday nights. *Everyone* watches it.' She shrugs. 'Anyway, he won it several years back. His song went straight to number one, so did his album. Then he had loads of hits and the money rolled in. That's how he ended up here. Now he can't stand it all and hides himself away like flipping Howard Hughes.'

I don't know who Howard Hughes is either, but I don't say that. Crystal makes me feel as if I know nothing.

'You'll like him,' she says. 'Underneath it all, he's very kind.'

I think I've forgotten what kind men are like.

'What's your story?' Crystal asks as she takes another biscuit. 'How come you've rocked up here with nothing but a titchy holdall and a kid in tow?'

I don't want people to know my business but, if I'm to be sharing a home with this lady, then she has a right to know. 'I've left my husband.' I hang my head in shame. 'He wasn't a good man.'

'Knock you about?'

Reluctantly, I nod.

'Tell me about it, sister,' she tuts. 'I've had more than one bloke who's been handier with his fists than with a tea towel. At least you've got away from the bastard now. Good for you, love.'

'I'm frightened that he'll find me.'

'Not here,' she assures me. 'You'll be safe in this house. We'll

31

look after you. Hayden can't stand people so he has this place done out like Fort bloody Knox. As well as the gate, there are CCTV cameras everywhere.'

I feel relieved to hear it. Tears well in my eyes. She puts her hand on top of mine and smiles kindly at me. 'You've landed on your feet, Ayesha. This is a nice home.'

'How long have you lived here?'

'A couple of years now,' she says. 'I met Hayden at a club after ... well ... He was having a bit of a rough time. We got on OK and he brought me home. We had one night of passion and then, well, I never quite left.' Crystal bites another biscuit. 'We're not, you know ...'

She makes a gesture, rubbing her fingers together, which I assume means that they're no longer having sexual relations.

'We're just mates now.' Crystal looks askance at the plate of biscuits. 'Good grief, they're all gone! You must have been starving.'

I think it would be impolite to point out that I've only had two biscuits and she's eaten the rest.

'I have no food,' I tell her. 'Are there shops near here?'

'Yeah,' Crystal says. 'Up on the High Street. Don't worry about that now though. There's plenty of food for tonight. I'll rustle something up later, if you like.' She puts a hand on my arm. 'You look all-in, sweetie.'

The kindness in her voice makes my eyes prickle with tears.

'Chill out for the rest of the day. Get to know the house. Put your feet up. There's plenty of stuff to keep you entertained. Tomorrow we can take a wander up to the shops together and get you anything you want.'

'I need to buy clothes too,' I say. 'But I don't have much money.'

'You literally left with what you're standing up in, didn't you?'

I bite down the tears that threaten to flow. 'Yes.'

'Then Auntie Crystal will take you shopping,' she says, clapping her hands together. 'You should change your image too, sweetheart. That way, if anyone does come looking for you, they'll find a very different woman.'

I look down at my shalwar kameez. It's very worn and dull. Then I look at Crystal's very small top over her very large breasts and I don't think I can trust this lady to give me style advice.

# Chapter Nine

Sabina looks much rested after her sleep and I snuggle up to her on the bed, enjoying the warmth of her small body spooned against mine. 'I think we'll be happy here, my child. I do hope so.'

When we've dozed together for a short while and she's starting to wriggle, I take one of her books out of the holdall and read it to her. As well as buying food and clothes, tomorrow I must find a school for Sabina to attend. I don't want her studies to suffer as she's a bright child and I want her to do well in life. The teachers at her last school understood her difficulties and I hope we can find somewhere here that will be as sympathetic.

'One day, I hope that you'll read out your books to me,' I say. 'I used to love to hear how clever you are.'

My child slips her thumb into her mouth and leans her head against my shoulder, but still she doesn't speak.

When I finish the book, I say, 'We should find something to eat. You must be very hungry.'

It's late now. Six o'clock. I like Sabina to be in bed by seven o'clock but it's been an unusual day and tomorrow there is no school to go to. Her tummy rumbles and that makes my decision. I get my Sabina up and dress her again so that we can go in search of food.

When we venture downstairs, Crystal is still in the kitchen, but has kicked off her high-heeled shoes. There's music playing and she's dancing around in bare feet. 'Hey, ladies.'

She grabs Sabina's hands and twirls her. My daughter looks as if she's in a state of shock and it makes me smile to see it.

'I'm a dancer,' Crystal says.

'Ballet?' I ask.

'Hmmm. Not that kind of dancer. More exotic,' she adds.

'You move nicely.'

'A lot of people tell me that.' She laughs raucously. To Sabina's delight, Crystal goes up on her tiptoes and whirls like a ballerina. Sabina copies her moves.

'My daughter has always wanted to learn to be a ballet dancer, but my husband wouldn't allow it.'

'Well, now she can,' Crystal says. 'She can do anything she wants.'

She can, I think. Yes, she can. The thought moves me to tears. Perhaps now I can start to take the simple things in life for granted. I can go out of the door when I wish, watch which television programmes I'd like to. Send my daughter to dance lessons.

'I must get a job.'

'All in good time,' Crystal advises. 'You've done a huge thing.' She looks at me with sympathy. 'I know what a big deal it is, believe me. Be kind to yourself for a bit. Chill out. Have you applied for benefits?'

I nod. 'Ruth helped me.'

'You'll get those through soon enough. It's not a fortune, but it'll be enough for now.'

Crystal gives Sabina a big final twirl and my daughter spins

35

across the kitchen like a top. I hope that she'll laugh out loud, that I'll hear the lovely sound of her childish giggle once more. But she does not.

'I want you to relax and enjoy your first night with us so, like I said earlier, I'll rustle something up for us to eat.'

'That's very kind.'

'I've got a black belt in cookery. One chop could be fatal,' she quips. 'To be honest, I'm not known for being the best cook in the universe. I've been known to burn water. I'm afraid you'll have to take your chances.' Peering into the freezer, Crystal says, 'I'll make us pizza. OK?'

'Yes. Very nice.'

'You can't go wrong with pizza.' She slides three pizzas out of the packaging and cuts off the plastic covering. A moment later and they're slammed into the oven. 'Easy.'

While we wait for the pizzas to cook, Crystal chatters away about nothing in particular. Her words drift over me as I'm too tired to concentrate. Despite her sleep, Sabina's eyes look heavy again too. She's been so very brave, my child.

Then, as Crystal is talking about something she's seen on television, I jolt back into the present. 'Can I smell burning?'

'Oh, crap.' Crystal bolts to the cooker and pulls open the oven door. Smoke billows out. The smoke alarm in the kitchen blares out and she grabs a tea towel, wafting it frantically in a well-practised move until it stops.

When the smoke has cleared, she lifts the pizzas out of the oven. They are blackened discs of charcoal.

She looks at the charred offerings despondently. 'We could scrape them a bit.'

Then we look at each other and laugh.

'I think they're perhaps beyond scraping,' I suggest.

We giggle again, and Crystal tosses the incinerated pizzas on to the counter with disdain.

'I could cook something,' I offer. Now my tummy's growling and I'm worried that Sabina hasn't eaten properly all day. 'What else have you got?'

She flicks the fridge open. 'We've got plenty of eggs and quite a bit of veg. There's rice and pasta in the cupboards. Any ideas?'

'Have you got any spices?'

'There's all kinds of bits and bobs here. No one ever uses them, mind.' Crystal flings open a cupboard to show me. There's cumin, coriander and a jar of dried chillies. 'Are you a good cook?'

I'm reluctant to boast. 'I think so.' It was the one thing my husband didn't complain about, so something must have been right.

'Then perhaps you can show me. God knows I'll never find the way to a man's heart with *my* kitchen skills.'

'I can make a vegetable nasi goreng, if you'd like me to.'

'You're on. Not a clue what it is, mind you, but it sounds all right to me,' Crystal says. 'I'll peel for you. Or open cans. I can manage that. What do you want?' She checks in the fridge again. 'There's a couple of courgettes, a red pepper and some onions.'

'That will be fine.'

'All of them?'

I nod.

'Wow. A feast!' Crystal puts the vegetables on the counter and pulls two knives out of the block. We stand together at the counter and chop them up. I realise that, for the first time in many years, I'm not tense while cooking. I'm not waiting for the front door to open, not waiting to see what mood my husband has come home in.

'We'll make enough for everyone,' Crystal says. 'Though it might be a bit spicy for Joy's taste. She's an old stick-in-the-mud, bless her. I haven't seen Hayden all day, so it's unlikely he'll come out of his room to eat. Sometimes he slides into the kitchen when no one's around and makes himself a pile of sandwiches. He stays in his room, holed up, until he runs out of grub. I'm guessing he must be having one of his funny days.'

I don't think she means the ha-ha type of funny and I feel a ripple of anxiety. The last thing I need is to be in the home of another difficult man. I push the thought aside and continue to measure out the rice, heat some oil in the pan and wait for Crystal to finish chopping the vegetables.

After a few moments I finally find the courage to ask, 'Why is he like that?'

'Long story,' Crystal says. 'Tragedy really. For now, let's just say the whole fame-and-fortune thing got to him. Sometimes it overwhelms him. Sad really. He should move on, but he can't. I'll tell you all about it one day over a bottle of plonk.'

I don't tell her that I never drink alcohol.

Then the back door opens and an elderly lady with short grey hair comes in. She's sturdily built and is wearing sensible clothing that seems to lack co-ordination, even to my untrained eye. On top she has a navy sweater with a checked shirt underneath, and brown, shapeless trousers. The lady looks out of sorts, her mouth turned down in a scowl, and she stamps her feet on the doormat as if she's making a point that no one else bothers to wipe their feet. She eases off her shoes and leaves them positioned neatly by the door.

'Hey, Joy,' Crystal says. 'Come and meet our new lodger.'

She looks at me and I'm sure that she recoils slightly. 'I didn't know we were expecting a new arrival.' She doesn't look pleased by it either.

'We weren't. Not until a couple of hours ago.'

'What does His Lordship say?' Joy casts her eyes heavenwards.

'He's pleased,' Crystal assures her. 'Glad to help someone in need.'

I wipe my hands and hold out one to her. 'Nice to meet you.'

'Mine are filthy dirty,' she complains. But when she eventually holds one out, it doesn't look too dirty at all.

'This is Ayesha Rasheed,' Crystal continues. 'And her lovely daughter, Sabina. This is Joy Ashton.'

Joy turns her scowl on us. 'I hope she's not noisy.' She nods towards Sabina.

'No,' I answer levelly. 'She's not noisy.' She is most *definitely* not noisy.

'Good. This is a quiet house.'

'Don't be so bloody miserable, Joy,' Crystal says with a laugh. 'It'll be nice to have a kid in the house for a change. It'll liven us up. We could all do with more fun in our lives. Right, Ayesha?'

I nod at that.

'How old are you?' Joy asks Sabina. When my daughter doesn't reply she says, 'What's the matter? Cat got your tongue?'

'My child doesn't speak,' I explain. 'She's not being rude.'

'Oh.' Joy purses her mouth.

'Sabina's eight years old.'

'She's very small for her age.'

'Yes,' I agree. She's also seen too much for her age.

'Are you having dinner with us, Joy?' Crystal brandishes the knife. 'Ayesha's making nasi goreng.'

'What's that when it's at home?'

'Rice and veg and stuff.'

Joy shakes her head. 'I don't like that foreign food. Not my cup of tea at all.'

'I could make you an omelette, if you'd like something more plain,' I suggest.

'I can do it myself, thank you very much,' Joy bristles. 'I might be old but I'm not incapable.'

39

'Lighten up, Joy,' Crystal tuts. 'Ayesha's being nice. She's only been here for five minutes, for heaven's sake. Don't frighten her away before she's even got her feet under the table.'

'Humph.' Joy stomps out of the kitchen.

'Don't mind her,' Crystal says. 'She's always like this. She's just lonely.' Then she looks wistful. 'Like the rest of us, really.'

# Chapter Ten

Sabina and I have dinner with Crystal. Mrs Ashton doesn't reappear to try my nasi goreng and neither does our landlord, Mr Hayden Daniels.

'You're one hell of a cook, Ayesha,' Crystal says. She pinches a little bit of fat on her tummy and frowns. 'You might have found yourself a new job.'

'I like to cook,' I tell her. 'I find it relaxing.'

'Don't let me stand in your way,' she says. 'I'll load the dish-washer. It's only fair.'

'Thank you.'

'I've got to go to work soon. Tomorrow we'll sit down together and sort out what you need to do. We'll get you some more clothes, and any special food you might want.'

'I must also find a school for Sabina.'

'We'll do that too,' she assures me. 'There's one near here that's supposed to be a good one. I don't get in until late though, so don't expect me around too early. Have you got enough with you to see you through tonight?'

'Yes,' I say. 'Thank you, Crystal. You've been very kind.' Then, I can't help myself: the strains of the day, our flight during the night, all of this catches up with me and I start to cry. Heaving sobs rack my body.

'Don't,' Crystal says. She strokes my hair. 'Don't cry. This is a new start. No more tears. Think only happy thoughts.'

I nod, though the tears continue to roll down my cheeks. She gets me some kitchen roll and I stem the flow. Sabina slides on to my lap and lays her head on my shoulder. I hold her tightly.

'You need to look after your mum,' Crystal says. 'She's had a really horrible time. But everything will be OK now.'

I mustn't cry. I have to be brave for both of us.

'I'm fine,' I sniff. 'Really fine.'

'Get an early night,' Crystal says. 'I bet you haven't slept a wink since yesterday. No wonder you're all tired and teary. Everything will look better in the morning. Trust me.'

So we clear our plates and, while we leave Crystal to load the dishwasher, Sabina and I climb the stairs. It seems strange that this is our home now, and I wonder if we'll ever feel comfortable here. Crystal's happy to have us, but I'm worried about Mrs Ashton and Mr Daniels. Perhaps they won't like us and will ask us to leave. Ruth said that it might be a temporary arrangement, and I have to be prepared for that. Perhaps she'll find us a cheaper place in a refuge and we'll have to go there instead. I hope not, because I think that I could really like it here.

In our room, Sabina changes into her pyjamas. We settle together on the bed and I turn on the television. It's only eight o'clock, but we struggle to find something that's suitable viewing for her. I've never been allowed to watch the soap operas that I hear so much about, but when I turn them on they just seem to be people shouting at each other, and I've had more than enough of that in recent times. In the end we settle on a cookery programme but, after only a few minutes, Sabina's eyes are rolling and she drifts into sleep.

I watch the rest of the programme, but take none of it in. My mind is whirring with all the things that I know I must do. I want to be strong for my daughter, but I'm anxious about our future. I may not have loved my husband in the last few years – for the most part, I didn't even like him – but he's controlled my life for so long that I'm concerned that I'm now unable to think for myself, and I want to do the very best I can for both of us.

Darkness falls and I turn on the bedside light, which makes the room look more cosy. In the bathroom I slip on my night-gown and fold my shabby shalwar kameez. It looks even more jaded in these crisp surroundings and I suspect that I may do too. This nightgown and ones similar have also been the cause of much trouble. It covers my arms and flows down to my ankles. My husband wished me to wear something more reveal-ing to bed, but I found that I couldn't bring myself to do it. I was brought up to be modest, and baring my body isn't some-thing I like to do. It was a source of many rows. I know that I didn't please him in the bedroom, but it's difficult to be intimate with a man who doesn't kiss you or show you love.

At the window, I look out over the street. There are a few cars parked under the trees now, but other than that it's very quiet and there's no one around. Then a taxi stops by the gate and for a moment my heart skips a beat, but then I hear foot-steps on the landing outside my door and going down the stairs. I remember that Crystal said she was going to work, though it seems late to be setting out, so I assume that she must work a night shift. Seconds later, the front door slams and I peep out to see Crystal tottering up the path. The gates swing open, she jumps into the waiting cab and it pulls away. I draw the cur-tains, closing out the night.

Lying down next to Sabina, I enjoy the soft comfort of the duvet. Yet, tired as I am, sleep won't come. I turn down the television so that it's providing background noise and let my thoughts filter through my brain, hoping that they'll finally start to make some sense. I should write to my mummy and daddy at home and tell them what I've done. In all these years, I've given them no indication that I was unhappy as a wife, because I never wanted them to worry about me; this will come as a terrible shock. But tell them I must. Tomorrow I'll get some paper and confess to them that Sabina and I are starting out on a new life. They'll be so saddened, but I also hope that they'll understand.

I must have drifted off as a noise startles me awake. I can hear the rhythmic clang of metal every few seconds. The bedside light is still on and I glance over at the clock. It's gone midnight and thankfully Sabina is still fast asleep. Straining to listen, all senses on alert, I think it's coming from downstairs. My heart begins to thump erratically. A new house is always full of unnerving sounds. In my old home in Sri Lanka, I could hear the sound of the waves on the ocean, the rustle of the palm trees in the breeze and the gentle whirr of the overhead fans. When I moved to Milton Keynes I had to get used to the blare of police sirens and clanking plumbing and the shouting of drunks coming home from the pubs and bars. This house is no different. The creaks and groans it emits are alien and worrying.

I listen again. Supposing Crystal has mistakenly left the back door open? It didn't occur to me to ask who'd make the house safe for the night. What if no one has locked up at all and someone intending us harm has come inside? My mouth goes dry. It can't possibly be Suresh. He surely would have been unable to find me so quickly. My heart sinks at the thought of him, but I must push this anxiety out of my mind. It can't be my husband but, despite the security cameras and the high gates, it may be someone who shouldn't be here. Perhaps Mr Daniels on the top floor won't hear them, and I'm frightened to wake him. Mrs Ashton, who is old and may have a hearing problem, may also be unaware. I could be alone in this.

The banging continues and I think that I can't simply lie here and do nothing. I'm a new woman now. The old Ayesha Rasheed would have remained in her room, cringing and afraid, but I'm not that person any more. I must be brave and see what the noise is. If it's a door banging, I must secure it. Despite the courage I have in my mind, I stay still for a few more minutes in the hope that it will stop and I won't need to investigate.

But it doesn't stop.

I consider dressing again, but instead I put on my coat over my nightdress and quietly let myself out of the room. The landing is dark and I've forgotten to acquaint myself with where the light switches are, so I stumble around in the darkness, feeling my way in unfamiliar surroundings.

As I creep downstairs, the noise is louder now. Clang, clang, clang. Relentless. It doesn't sound like a door banging any more, but I can't tell what it is. I could do with a weapon in case it's an intruder – an umbrella or golf club – but I look round me and find that in this house there's very little to be seen. On a table by the door there's a bronze statue of a woman and, failing to find anything else that might be useful to ward off a burglar, I pick it up. It feels cool when I wrap my sticky, perspiring palm around it.

Inching my way along the hall towards the kitchen, I realise that the sound is rising from beneath the house. There's a door under the stairs and I can see light shining round the frame. That's definitely where the noise is coming from.

Gingerly I open it, and it's definitely louder now. I take my courage in both hands and shout out, 'Hello?' My voice sounds more tremulous than I would like and fear constricts my throat.

There's no reply. So I make my way down the steps. One night Suresh made me watch a horror film with him when his

45

parents had gone to bed. He delighted in the fact that I was so terrified. It showed a woman making her way down to a basement much like this – except she had a torch, which kept flickering, and was wearing only her underwear. I take comfort in the fact that this basement is brightly lit and I have on my coat. But if the light were to suddenly fail, then I have no torch at all. So perhaps the heroine in the film, despite being in her pants, had an advantage.

As I reach halfway down the stairs, one of them creaks beneath me and the noise suddenly stops. Now I'm frozen to the spot and it takes me all my courage to go further. I pause at the bottom of the steps, heart hammering. Then I step out, little lady statue held high.

# Chapter Eleven

Just inside the room, there's a man pressed against the wall, weapon held high above his head. 'Aaaargh!' I shout out in terror and brandish the statue in the most menacing way I can think of.

At the same time, the man shouts out too. 'Aaaargh!'

When he sees me, he lets his weapon drop to his side. He looks at the dumb-bell in his hand and then he laughs with relief. 'You scared the hell out of me.' He puts his hand to his heart and puffs out a lungful of air.

I release my own breath, which I didn't realise I'd been holding. The basement is obviously used as a gym as it's filled with different fitness machines, but I don't know exactly what they all are. But I *do* now know that's what I could hear.

'I thought you were an intruder,' I tell him.

'I thought *you* were an intruder,' he counters, panting hard.

'I think we're both mistaken,' I venture. 'I heard the noise. The clanging of your machine.' I nod to the nearest one, which has a towel draped over the side. 'I didn't know what it was. I was worried that we may have had a burglar.'

The man laughs. 'I thought you'd come to brain me with my

Ivor Novello award.' He nods to the statue still raised in my hand.

I lower it. The room is mirrored all along one side and is brightly lit from many bulbs in the ceiling.

'I'm sorry to have disturbed you.' Now I feel foolish that I was worried. 'It's my mistake.'

'You must be my new lodger.' He puts down the dumb-bell, reaches for a towel from the bench next to him and rubs it over his hair.

I nod. 'Ayesha Rasheed. Very pleased to make your acquaintance.'

Surely this is my new landlord, Mr Hayden Daniels. I don't like to stare at him, but I think that Mr Daniels is a very attractive man. He's wearing grey sweatpants and a white vest which are damp with sweat but, strangely, no less appealing because of it. His skin is very pale, his hair very blond. He has a strong face – full jaw, high cheekbones – and his eyes are a most startling blue. I flush and lower my gaze. I've never seen a man like this before. The only man I've ever seen without clothes is my husband and he was soft all over, not firm like Mr Daniels.

I realise that I'm wearing my coat and I clutch it to me. Mr Daniels's eyes follow my hands and I flush under his scrutiny.

'Sorry. Excuse me,' he says, clearly aware that I'm now embarrassed. 'I would have liked us to be introduced in more pleasant circumstances.'

'Yes.' Then I can't help myself and boldly ask, 'Why do you do this in the middle of the night?'

He looks surprised at my question, but says, 'I don't sleep. I like to come and work out when there's no one around.'

'And now I'm disturbing you.'

'I didn't mean it like that. I was more or less finished here, anyway.' He glances at the machine he's obviously been using.

'Perhaps I might make you some tea. If you have camomile, that can aid rest.'

He hesitates for a moment and I think he might say that he doesn't want tea at all. Instead he smiles, just a little. 'No camomile,' Mr Daniels says, 'though I could kill for a cup of builder's tea.'

'I'll do that.'

I take in how tall he is. I'm not a good judge of heights, but he's head and shoulders above me. That, I think, is very tall. He's a muscular man too and my mouth goes dry again, but this time I believe it's not with fear.

'Let me jump in the shower and I'll be with you in five.' He looks me up and down. 'If you're staying, you could take off your coat.'

Now I look down and it seems silly to be wearing a coat in the house, but I'm glad that my nightgown is long. 'I have no dressing gown to cover myself. I left my home with very few of my things.'

'Crystal said you were in danger.'

I lower my eyes. 'I was.'

'I'm sorry to hear that.'

'I hope my child and I are safe now.'

'I hope so too.'

'I'll make tea.' I hurry out, glad to leave Mr Daniels to his shower, and make my way back to the kitchen. My heart is still beating like a drum even though I'm no longer scared.

Five minutes later, true to his word, he appears while I'm still searching in the cupboards for something called builder's tea.

Mr Daniels's hair is wet and there's a flush to his cheeks. Now he's not wearing a top at all, but quickly pulls a clean white T-shirt over his head. Not, however, before I catch a glimpse of his tummy, which is hard and rippled. I've never seen

49

a tummy like that before. He's also wearing black sweatpants and flip-flops, and there's a towel slung round his neck.

'I can't find what you require,' I tell him.

'Here.' He shows me the box of Typhoo. I'm aware that he's very close behind me and I can feel the warmth of his body as he reaches up to get it for me. 'This is builder's tea.'

'Oh.' I laugh. 'I'm sorry. I've not heard that expression before. I'm from Sri Lanka,' I tell him. 'If there is one thing I miss from home, apart from my mummy and daddy, it's the good black tea for which our country is known. Tea is very important to us.'

'I drink whatever's in the cupboard,' Mr Daniels admits. 'Crystal sees to it. She probably buys the brand that's on offer.'

'Then I must treat us to some good black tea. You'll see the difference.'

Mr Daniels doesn't seem to be very interested in what he drinks, but I'll buy some anyway. There's nothing as soothing as a cup of tea properly made.

He sits at the kitchen table while I brew the builder's tea. I make it strong, as I think builders would like that too. I make myself one, but not as strong.

When I take his tea to the table, Mr Daniels is holding the little lady statue. His arms look strong, well-defined, and are covered in a fine down of blond hair the same colour as his head. I'd like to run my fingers over it. Never before have I felt the need to stroke a man's arm.

'It's very pretty,' I say, nodding to the statue.

'Oh, this? Yeah. I got it for songwriting. Used to be quite good at it, back in the day.'

'You aren't good at it now?'

'I don't know,' he admits. Then his expression is sad. He puts the statue down on the table and pushes it away from himself. 'I don't do it any more.'

50

'Crystal told me that you're a very popular singer.'

'Did she?' He laughs. 'What else has Ms Cooper been telling you?'

'She said that you liked to be alone.'

'Ah, yes,' he says.

I don't think I should mention that she also told me that they were once lovers.

'She said that you eat only sandwiches.'

'Well,' he says, embarrassed now. 'I've never been much of a cook, and cooking for one is depressing.'

'I love to cook,' I admit. 'Perhaps you will try some of my food.'

'Perhaps,' he agrees.

But I'm not sure he means it.

'I'll try to be a good tenant,' I promise. 'I'll leave you alone. Sabina and I will be no trouble to you at all. This seems as if it's a nice house, and I should like my daughter and me to be here for a long time, Mr Daniels.'

'Hayden,' he says. 'No need for formality.'

'Hayden.' I try his name, but it feels strange in my mouth.

'I think it's probably time you went back to bed,' he says. 'You look worn out.'

'Yes.' In truth, I'm not tired now. I've pushed through it and am, quite probably, beyond sleep. I'd like to talk longer with Mr Daniels, but I feel that he wants to be alone again.

'Your daughter will be worried where you are if she wakes up.'

'She'll not be a nuisance,' I reiterate. 'There'll be no noise from her. She doesn't speak.'

'Really?' He frowns. 'Why?'

Though it's hard, I decide to be honest with him. 'Because she has seen too many bad things.'

He bites down on his lip. 'Then she and I should get along fine.'

I finish my tea. 'Goodnight, Hayden.'

'Goodnight, Ayesha.'

I head towards the door, but before I leave I turn back to him. 'Does it help?' I ask. 'Working out in the middle of the night?'

He shakes his head. 'No,' he says wearily. 'It doesn't.'

# Chapter Twelve

Hayden went through to the living room, taking his mug of tea and the statue he lovingly called Lady Novello with him. She made good tea, his new lodger, which was a promising sign. The strong brew soothed him.

He smiled to himself. What a way for them to be introduced. He hated to admit it, but he'd felt terrified when he'd thought that someone had breached the security measures. For a moment he'd forgotten that they'd got a new resident joining their enclave.

There was no way he'd intended to take in anyone else, but he was always a sucker for a sob story, and the result was that there was now someone new in his house. He'd put up a brief resistance to Crystal's begging that they take this woman and her daughter in, but in all honesty it was pointless. She knew he'd cave in at the least sign of pressure, and when Crystal set her mind to something she wasn't easily budged. That much he had learned about her over the years.

At the end of the day, it wasn't if they were short of rooms here. Would it really matter if one more were occupied? It was probably better than them standing empty, gathering dust. A house this size was ridiculous. He didn't know what had possessed him to buy it, but now he couldn't face the upheaval of moving out. Better to fill it with a rag-tag of wounded humanity.

He wouldn't need to have much to do with their lodger, she was Crystal's project. These days he rarely wanted to come out of his room. If he could work out a way to get his food fed through to him by a tube or something, he probably wouldn't ever do so.

It didn't look as if Ayesha was going to be a difficult tenant either, and Crystal had promised that it was nothing more than a short-term thing until the woman had got her life together. Days, she'd said. Weeks at the most. If he was honest, now that he'd met her, he felt sorry for her. She was a plain little thing, clutching her coat to her like a security blanket. Quiet. Timid. It didn't look as if she'd say boo to a goose. It wouldn't really matter to him if she stayed around for longer.

Being a soft touch was how he'd ended up with Crystal and Joy living here too. Crystal had been down on her luck when he'd first met her. She'd picked him up in a nightclub in the West End. He'd gone there at a particularly dark time in his life, thinking he could ease the pain, get blind drunk, hang with his old crowd once more. That night he'd found some relief, but not in the way he'd imagined. Crystal came back here with him in a cab. They were almost undressed by the time they arrived and he'd rushed her inside, desperate to lose himself in some anonymous sex. Yet by the time he got her to his bedroom he was more sober than he'd ever been. His body had gone through the motions, but his brain wasn't there at all. It made him realise that booze and sex weren't what he needed. However, Crystal had proved to be pleasant to have around and she didn't seem to bear a grudge that, after a promising start, he'd been a less than enthusiastic lover. They'd slept together once and it was fine. More than fine. But that was it.

The next morning she'd slipped on one of his shirts and stayed. When he woke, she made him breakfast. After that, she'd tidied the house, had filled the fridge, and had never moved out. He didn't eat all that much these days as everything tasted like cardboard, but she still insisted on cooking for him whenever she thought he was looking too thin. Then she forced a ready-meal on him, of lasagne or fish pie. He obliged her by eating it and making the right noises while simultaneously hoping that she wouldn't give him food poisoning. It was always a bonus if the dish wasn't either blackened or still-raw. Other than making him play occasional Russian roulette with her food, she never made any demands on him. Ideal company.

Then there was Joy. She'd been a neighbour in the same street, in a house just across the road from him, and had already lived in the suburb for half of her life when he'd bought this place. She'd complained vociferously about the renovation work, of course. Joy had come marching over, bristling with high dudgeon. He'd done his best to placate her and had sent her away mollified. Later, when he and Laura had moved in permanently, she'd complained about the paparazzi who used to be permanently camped outside his gates. She'd even turned her garden hose on them once. If he ever braved the photographers and ventured out to get a newspaper, she would always nod to him before turning back to tend her flowers. He couldn't say that they'd ever been close, but Joy was the only person in the street who came to see him after what happened with Laura. She'd held his hand and told him that she understood what it was like to lose someone.

Joy was widowed. Her husband wasn't snatched away from her in the prime of his life. He died after a long, debilitating illness, but that doesn't necessarily make it any easier. Instead of being well provided for, as she'd thought, he'd left her in thousands of pounds' worth of debt. He'd sunk money into a raft of shaky investments, the house was remortgaged a dozen times and there was nothing left. Joy had two grown-up sons – one working out in Hong Kong and another in Singapore – but she never saw them as she wouldn't get on a plane. Hayden had tried several times over the years to introduce her to the wizardry of Skype, but she wasn't interested.

Before she moved in, Joy had also complained a lot about Crystal coming and going in a taxi at all hours of the night and, in the course of the bickering, the two women had somehow struck up an uneasy friendship too. When Crystal heard that Joy was on the brink of losing her home, she'd asked Hayden if their neighbour could move in with them. Once again, he'd capitulated in the face of Crystal's begging and, in the end, he could think of no good reason to turn Joy away. Besides, where would she have gone if he'd said no?

It was getting on for eighteen months now that Joy had been with them. Perhaps longer. Time blurred these days. She still complained constantly, about everything, but with less venom now. It was just her way.

The people who bought her house drove huge, blacked-out Range-Rovers and had torn out all the flowers to have the front garden block-paved so they could get more cars on it. They cut down Joy's beloved apple orchard at the back that she'd nurtured with such great care, and put in a swimming pool and acres of plastic decking. Every time she looked out of the window and back towards her old home, she muttered, 'Bloody foreigners.'

She always kept her eyes averted when she went out of the gate, as if it was too painful even to look at.

Now Joy tended Hayden's garden. She pretty much kept the house in vegetables and wittered endlessly on about the delights of keeping chickens, which Hayden steadfastly tried to ignore. He might not be able to refuse waifs and strays, but he was definitely putting his foot down at the prospect of chickens.

The curtains were open and the moonlight lit up the room, falling on the piano and making it gleam. It was a baby grand that had once belonged to Elton John. He couldn't even remember now how he came to own it. There'd been a frenzy of rash purchases in the early days, before he'd pretty much lost all interest in material things. Most of them were now unused, covered in dust sheets in the upstairs rooms. Hayden put the statue down on top of it and stroked its gleaming surface.

He didn't come in here often these days. Mainly he kept to his room upstairs, where he watched what was going on in the world through the television – all of it profoundly depressing or banal. When he could stand the television no longer, he read. He used to prefer crime fiction, but now he couldn't read anything that involved death or violence so he stuck pretty much to biographies, most of which he found interminably dull. There were celebrities that were on their third volume of exposé – baring their souls, every aspect of their sordid lives, when they'd barely done anything to write home about. He'd been asked to do his own one on several occasions and had always refused point-blank. That hadn't stopped a dozen or more 'unauthorised' biographies about him being published, where some desperate author had written a work of fiction about him and had called it fact. He'd given up trying to sue.

Sometimes he even listened to music. But not often. And never his own songs. He couldn't stand to have the radio on now as he never knew when one of his hits might pop up, and that was simply too painful to bear.

When he used to go out, he'd be in a shop or a café and, quite unexpectedly, he'd hear his own voice. It sounded so strong, so hopeful, that he couldn't handle it and would have to leave. Only when he was back in the safety of his own home, behind his tall gates, would he stop shaking. It happened so often that eventually it was easier not to go out.

This room – which used to be his favourite – was long, the whole length of the house. Near the front bay window there were three cream sofas grouped together round a log burner. One wall was entirely covered in bookcases – a kind of library, which he must have dreamed up during a pretentious phase. Though, if you looked closely, it was mostly stocked with commercial fiction. There was a distinct lack of worthy, leather-bound tomes. There were a few classics, mainly stuff he'd read as a child. Perhaps one day he would buy a really good collection of worthy books to immerse himself in. Now he preferred stories that washed over him, chewing-gum for the brain. Novels that he didn't have to become emotionally involved in. The tacky stories of love gone wrong were Laura's choice. The grisly crime thrillers, once his own passion, were now nothing more than dust magnets. The biographies were a new and growing addition but he was tiring of them already.

The other wall was covered in his awards. Gold and platinum discs for this, that and the other. One was for his worldwide hit 'My For Ever Love', which largely funded this house and was one of those pension songs that normally come along once in a lifetime for a songwriter. He had churned them out on a regular basis.

Hayden hadn't decorated this place. He'd had a designer in while he was away on tour making sure the cash rolled in. The whole place was bland, inoffensive, lacking character. And had cost a fortune. The wooden flooring in here was something special, but he couldn't even remember what now. He did, however, remember gasping at the price, even then when he was spending money like water.

Now he was glad that the house was so minimalist, a blank

canvas. This was really the only room that held memories. He realised that he'd actually forgotten what it looked like in natural light as it was so long since he'd been in here during the day.

Opening the lid of the piano, Hayden tinkled a couple of the keys. The sound was wrong and loud in the still house, but he slid on to the seat anyway, even though it felt alien to him. He sat motionless and breathed deeply.

The moonlight shone directly on to the picture of Laura too. She smiled out of the darkness at him and he couldn't help but smile back. He did it so little these days that his cheeks felt tight and his lips stuck to his teeth. Even he recognised that was a bad thing.

'Hi,' he said to the photograph. 'It's been a while.'

Hayden had taken the photograph himself, out on Hampstead Heath, not far from the house. He'd bought a new camera and was trying it out. Something else that lay abandoned in a drawer. After what happened, he never wanted to take another photograph of a living being ever again. The bloody things should be banned from the earth. Some cultures believed that taking a person's photograph stole their soul. He was a firm believer in that now. Sometimes they stole more than that.

Every weekend, when he wasn't away on tour, he and Laura had liked to walk up on the Heath together. Until it became impossible. Once the paparazzi got wind of it, they were stalked whenever they ventured out for a stroll. They talked about getting a dog – but then they'd talked about lots of things that they never did.

His fingers moved over the keys again. Like an automaton, he played the opening bars of 'My For Ever Love', the song that was never far from his mind. He knew without even trying that the words wouldn't come out. His throat was closed tightly. Even sustained conversation was difficult. There was no song left in his heart. After a few more notes, his fingers stopped moving too.

The song had been written for Laura. She was the one who was supposed to be his for ever love. But she wasn't.

# Chapter Thirteen

'I am going to introduce you to the shopping experience of your life!' Crystal throws her arms wide.

We're standing on Oxford Street in front of a very large fashion store. The clothes in the window are so garish that they're making my eyes hurt. I have Sabina clutched tightly by the hand. If she's frightened of the crowds, she's giving no indication of it.

'Primark?' I say.

'Exactly!' She grins at me. 'Welcome to the first day of the rest of your life! This is a place of many wonders.' She links her arm in mine and marches me through the front door. It is, indeed, like entering a different world. The light's bright, glaring. Loud music pumps out and along one wall there's a display of video screens showing giant-sized women strutting about. Racks and racks crammed with every conceivable colour of clothing stretch out ahead of us.

'Have you been here before?'

'No,' I admit. And I'm a little bit frightened now that I am here, but I don't tell Crystal this.

'Good God, you have led a sheltered life,' she tuts.

'I haven't very much money, Crystal,' I remind her in a quiet voice. I think of all of our savings in the bottom of the holdall back at our new house. I've brought one roll of £100 with me, still bound by its elastic band, which seems extraordinarily extravagant. It's the most money I have ever had. I looked carefully at my funds this morning and know that they have to last me a long time.

'Let me worry about the cash today.' She pats my arm in a kindly way. 'Count this as my treat. I've had a good week at the club. Lots of tips.'

I didn't hear what time Crystal came home, but this morning she didn't rise until ten o'clock, which meant that I waited a long time for her, as Sabina and I were having breakfast at seven. Joy came down and said a cursory hello to us and took her two slices of toast into the garden as it's a sunny day. Mr Daniels – Hayden – didn't come down at all.

'I must leave some money to buy Sabina a school uniform too,' I remind her.

She dismisses me with an airy wave. 'You worry too much, girlfriend.'

Perhaps I do, but I think that I'm right to be concerned. There's so much to take into consideration in our new life.

This morning, after she had eaten breakfast, Crystal took me into Hayden's office which is at the front of the house, and telephoned the local school. She's made an appointment for us to go to see the headteacher and I'm anxious about it already. At Sabina's old school, they all knew her when she was a bright, chatty child and, when all that changed, they helped her, the teachers and pupils alike. I wonder what they'll make of my solemn, silent daughter at a new school. I'm frightened that she won't be liked or that she'll be bullied. What if they won't take her and she has to go somewhere different, for children with special needs? I feel sick at the very thought.

'Don't worry about that yet. School stuff is as cheap as chips in supermarkets,' Crystal assures me. 'You'll know that better than me.'

But I don't, as Suresh always gave his mother the money to buy Sabina's uniform. I have no idea how much these things cost, and that's what worries me.

'We'll go there as soon as we know she's got a place.'

'Thank you.'

'You, on the other hand, need a complete makeover,' Crystal says as we're swallowed up by the shop. 'Today's shopping is just for fun! You've gotta ditch all that drabness. You're a young, pretty woman and you look like a downtrodden old hag. In a nice way, obvs.'

Looking down at my shalwar kameez, I fear that she's right. I'm not that woman any more. At least, I don't want to be.

'We're going to modernise you. Get rid of those pyjama things. Whoever told you that khaki is your colour must be blind.'

'I'm used to dressing modestly,' I venture. I want to cast off my clothes to start my new life, but I don't want to abandon my culture.

'I've seen loads of women wearing those in fab colours with sparkly bits and looking a million dollars. We *could* go down that road, but you need to change your image completely so you'll be unrecognisable.'

'But I still wish to be me.'

'I get it,' Crystal says. 'No tits-out tops. No bum-skimming skirts. Though, to be frank, you'd look bloody great.'

Crystal is dressed more demurely today. She has on a tight white T-shirt and jeans. Her handbag, shoes and sunglasses are vibrant red. But it's still clear that she's a very curvy woman and has a lot of va-va-voom, as I heard someone say on an advert.

'I like what you're wearing,' I tell her. 'I wish I had the courage to be so bold.'

'Let's start there, then.' She ushers me towards the rails with jeans on.

Once she's assessed my size, she loads me up with different colours of denim – dark blue, pale blue. Then we spend a long time going through the racks of clothes and trotting up and down escalators in Crystal's wake while she piles T-shirts into my arms, until I have a higgledy-piggledy tower. She pops a couple of pretty little cardigans on top.

'What shoe size are you?'

'Three,' I say.

'Christ,' she mutters. 'Those are child's feet. Back in a mo. Get in the queue.' She disappears while, as instructed, Sabina and I join the long, long queue which snakes towards the changing rooms.

'Is this fun?' I say to my daughter. 'We've never been shopping like this before. Next it'll be your turn.'

She smiles at me and, for the first time in a long time, I think that it reaches her eyes. I squeeze her hand. With Crystal around, it's hard to feel sad.

Our new friend comes back, hands filled with shoes. Some of them look very high. 'Here you go, Beanie.'

She dumps them all into Sabina's arms and chases off again. This time she comes back with a little dress and two jackets.

'I don't think that I need all of these clothes.'

'A capsule wardrobe, sweetie,' she says. 'That's what Auntie Crystal is fixing you up with.'

I nod as if I know what she means.

'You should think about cutting your hair too,' she says. 'Bin that dreary scarf. Go for a sharp bob and maybe dye it. A nice plum colour would suit you.'

It sounds frightening to me. Perhaps Crystal is right though. If I did change my hair, my complete image, then it would take me another step away from my old life.

She lowers her voice until I can only just hear her over the blaring music. 'Have you thought about changing your name?'

'No.'

'I did. My real name's Christine, but who wants a lapdancer called Chris? Crystal is much more exotic.'

'I don't know what I'd call myself.'

'Maybe don't change Ayesha, that's really nice. But you could be Mrs Roberts or Richardson instead of Rasheed. Something like that. It would seem sensible. No need to do it formally. Stick to Rasheed for official documents, your benefits and stuff like that. Use Roberts when you're out and about.'

'Could I do that?'

Crystal shrugs. 'Don't see why not. It might give you an extra bit of protection. Just in case.'

Just in case Suresh comes looking for me, she means. Would he do that? I'd like to think that he could simply let me go, but he might feel differently about Sabina. He was never over-affectionate to her as a father, and a lot of our difficulties stemmed from the fact that he wanted a son and I was unable to give him one. That made me a failure as a wife in his eyes. Sabina is his only child and, as such, will he want to reclaim her like a prize? I can only hope that it'll be too difficult to find us in this big, big city.

'Right, we're on,' Crystal announces, and sure enough, we're at the head of the queue. 'Get in that changing room and show me what you've got hidden beneath that drab exterior!'

# Chapter Fourteen

Standing in the cubicle alone, I pull off my tired and dirty shalwar kameez. The small, timid woman who stares back at me looks worn down by life, and tears fill my eyes.

Well, all that is about to change.

Sorting through the pile of clothes that Crystal has pressed on me, I first try on some jeans with a T-shirt and a pair of heels that are not as towering as the others and look as if I may be able at least to stand up in them.

I feel self-conscious as I survey my new attire. I've never before worn clothes that are so revealing: Suresh would never have allowed it. It's as if I'm naked. The T-shirt says I WILL SURVIVE! in small pink letters in the middle of my chest. It's still quite loose compared to how Crystal wears them, but it shows off more of my boyish figure than I'd usually be comfortable with. I try very hard to like what I see, to look at myself thinking that I need to throw off the downtrodden woman that I was and embrace the new, modern me. I must become a woman who can take control of her life and know what she wants from it. Taking a deep breath, I try to connect with the strange creature who gazes back at me and wonder if I could grow to like her.

A few minutes later, when I've composed myself, I totter out from the safety of the changing room to where Crystal and Sabina are waiting to assess me. Our new friend is standing with her arm slung casually round my daughter's shoulders and I feel lucky that we have, by fate, landed in a house with kind people, with someone who has taken it upon herself to help us.

'What do you think?' I smooth down the T-shirt.

Crystal spins towards me and then stops dead. 'Wow!' Her eyes grow wide like saucers. 'Look at you.'

Other people turn to do so and I feel myself flush.

'You look bloody sensational!' she cries. 'Turn round. Give us a twirl.'

I hold out my arms and turn for her. As I do she smacks me soundly on the bottom. 'That arse is something else. Wildly jel.'

I get a flashback to a slap across my face. A slap that made my teeth rattle and my skin burn. A slap that was rough and not intended as play. I push away the memory. It will not spoil my mood today.

'This needs to go though.' Crystal pulls off my headscarf and, self-conscious, my hand goes to my hair. 'No more hiding this light under a bushel. This has to go too.' She grabs hold of my plait and slides off the restraining band, then runs her fingers through it to unbraid it. In my other life, I may have been offended by someone manhandling me like this. Now I feel lucky to have someone like Crystal to help me. I have a dear sister in Sri Lanka, Hinni, who I haven't seen since I moved to England, and I miss her keenly. She would treat me in this way. I like the way Crystal touches me. It's open and straightforward. It never occurs to her that it might make me anxious, and therefore it doesn't.

She fluffs up my hair, draping it round my shoulders. 'Get an eyeful of that, honey.' Crystal drags me to the nearest full-length mirror and positions me in front of it. 'I have to pay a fortune for extensions to get anywhere close to that lustrous mane.'

I've never worn my hair loose. Ever since I was a child, it's been held back in a plait.

'I thought you should cut it, but you look completely different with those clothes and with your hair down like that. That bastard husband of yours could be ten feet away from you and he'd never recognise you.'

I stroke my hair. 'You think so?'

'I *know* so.' She turns to Sabina. 'Isn't Mummy pretty?'

My daughter nods her approval, and there's a hint of a smile on her solemn face.

'Do you really like it?' I ask my child.

She nods again. Say yes, I silently beg. Please say yes.

But she doesn't.

'Try the dress on now,' Crystal instructs. 'Then it's your turn next, Little Bean.'

Sabina looks excited at the prospect.

So I go back into the changing room and, before I take off the clothes, I look at myself in the mirror once more. A weary sigh escapes my lips. If I were a different person, I could carry off this look, but I'm not. I know that I can't go out into the world looking like this. I can just manage it in the safety of my changing room, but not in public. I want to change my image, but I also want to remain true to myself.

Going back out to Crystal, I hang my head. I don't wish to seem ungrateful for her kind attention. 'I'm so very sorry, but I can't wear these,' I say. 'I'm uncomfortable. I must have a top that covers my arms, clothes that don't cling tightly to my shape.'

Her face falls. 'You know most women would die for a figure like that.'

I shrug. 'It's not who I am.'

'What else would you wear other than those pyjama things?'

'Sometimes a sari.'

'Is that a religious thing?'

'No. Not really. But it's my culture, I suppose.'

'You're not dressing like this as it's what that husband of yours wanted?'

I shake my head. 'I was brought up to be a modest woman. I can't change that.'

She tuts and rolls her eyes. 'I can do modest. Two minutes. Don't move. Let no one take that changing room. Lie down on the floor in it if you need to!'

Crystal dashes off and, sure enough, she's back moments later, arms loaded with more clothes.

'The definition of modest.' Crystal dumps her stash on to me. 'Give this lot a go.'

Back inside the changing room, I see that she's brought me a pretty smock top. It's white and embroidered with pink flowers. Another is a loose blouse in a pink and blue floral design. The trousers she has brought are white linen and loose-cut. Quickly I slip them on.

I smile at my reflection. This is much more to my liking. I feel modern, different, but not under-dressed.

Re-emerging from the changing room, I wait for Crystal's pronouncement on my appearance.

'Fabulous,' Crystal announces. 'You're right. That's much more you, sweetie. Now work your stuff!'

She pouts and preens in front of the mirror as if she's a model and, hesitant, I follow her moves. She grabs us all pink feather boas from a nearby stand and we strut up and down in Primark.

'We're supermodels,' she declares over her shoulder as she wiggles ahead of us. 'We don't get out of bed for less than ten thousand a day, dahling!'

The song playing says 'You don't know you're beautiful,' and Crystal sings along with it loudly, pointing at me. That makes me giggle and other women in the store stop to look at us but, for once, I don't care. I feel lovely. And silly. In this moment, my very being is lighter than air. Sabina hides her mouth with her hand and I hope that, behind it, she's laughing too.

'Is that better?' Crystal throws over her shoulder.

'Much better,' I say.

'Modest. Modest. Think modest,' she chants, and rushes off again.

When she comes back, Crystal has picked out a summery maxidress and a little cardigan to go with it. I like these too and we do more parading. Then they go on the pile of clothes deemed To Be Bought, along with the white linen trousers, the blouses and a white jacket.

'You want Sabina to dress in the same way?'

'Yes please,' I say. Our personal shopper scoots off again.

When Crystal returns, laden down, she ushers my slightly startled daughter towards the changing room with a pile of clothes. 'Now you, Beanie.'

I hold Crystal back while Sabina, barely visible above her clothes, takes a cubicle number from the lady. 'I must run an errand,' I whisper to her. 'It is Sabina's birthday tomorrow and I'd like to buy her a gift.'

'Tomorrow? Why didn't you say? We can have a party.'

'It isn't necessary.'

'She's a kid. Of course it's necessary.'

'Sabina has never had a party before.'

Crystal recoils in horror. 'What, *never*?'

'No.' Now I feel ashamed that she's never known this small pleasure. 'No one but family was allowed to come to our house. We never really celebrated birthdays.' Or Christmas. Or anything very much.

'What a miserable bunch,' Crystal says. 'Well, it's not exactly going to be a red carpet event at our place as you're new to the 'hood, but we should do something. Toast the start of your new life together.'

'I'd like that.'

'OK. You nip off quickly while I help Beanie. By the time she's changed, you'll be back.'

So Crystal follows my daughter into the changing rooms and, with only a moment's misgiving, I leave them to go in search of a suitable gift.

Minutes later, I've bought a Hello Kitty backpack for her. Not an extravagant purchase as she'll need this when she starts her new school, but I'm sure that she'll love it. My daughter may not speak, but in other ways she's exactly like any other little girl. Everything has to be pink and sparkly.

I'm back as they emerge from the changing rooms together. Sabina looks shyly at me. My daughter too has abandoned her shalwar kameez, and I can't help but stare at the modern girl who looks back at us in the mirror. She's wearing a loose-fitting floral dress and underneath she has on a white long-sleeved T-shirt. When she gets older, I will be happy for Sabina to choose her own way, but for now I'm very pleased with these clothes.

Crystal shows her how to walk up and down as if she's on a catwalk, and it makes me giggle to watch. Yet my throat is constricted and my eyes brim with tears when I ask, 'Do you like your lovely new outfit?'

She nods enthusiastically. I hope in her excitement that she'll forget herself and cry out. But I'm disappointed once more.

'Come. We'll try on your other things.' I take her back to the changing room and we work our way through the clothes that Crystal has chosen until we're both weary and in need of refreshment.

'We've earned a coffee and some cake,' Crystal says as we emerge for the final time. 'You look like you're flagging.'

Indeed we are.

She scoops up an armful of clothes. 'Let's pay up and get out of here.'

'Crystal,' I say. 'I can't afford all of this. We must choose just one outfit. Until I get a job, I must watch every penny carefully.'

'Not today.' She wags a finger at me. 'This lot is on me.' As I open my mouth to protest, she says, 'I insist. One day you'll do something nice for me. That's how it goes.'

From my limited experience, I don't think that's always true but I will always, most certainly, be very grateful to this lovely, brash, loud lady for bringing me and my timid daughter out of our shells.

# Chapter Fifteen

Hayden was lying on his bed listening to music on his iPod when there was a knock on the door. He didn't want to see anyone now, but then he rarely did.

'I know you're bloody well in there, Hayd.'

Crystal. Who else? Joy knew when the darkness had descended upon him and stayed well out of his way until it eventually lifted. Crystal wasn't cut of the same cloth.

'Open the door, you muppet.'

'Go away, Crystal.'

'No.' She rapped again. 'I'm not going to talk to you through a piece of wood either.'

Sighing, he pulled out his earphones. He'd get no peace until he found out what she wanted. When she first moved in here, she'd tiptoe around him, but that didn't last long. In recent months she'd certainly become more strident in voicing her opinions on his retreat from the world. The thing was, the less he saw people, the less he wanted to see them. He was much happier being alone. Less pain that way. But sometimes he couldn't avoid it, and he knew Crystal wouldn't go until she'd spoken to him.

Opening the door, he said, 'Yes?'

'We're having a party,' she announced. 'The kid is nine tomorrow and we're going to celebrate their new life with a few drinks and some cake.'

'Count me out,' Hayden said.

'No.' Crystal wedged her foot in the door before he could close it. 'You're going to get your arse out of that bedroom and come and play nicely with us.'

Hayden grimaced.

'We've forgotten what you look like while you're locked away up here, doing your Mae West thing.'

'It was Greta Garbo who wanted to be alone.'

'Whatever,' Crystal said and made a W with her fingers that she held in front of his face.

That made him smile and she took that as her cue to press on.

'They're nice,' she said softly. 'They've had a really crap life and deserve a bit of affection and fun. Ayesha's going to cook some Sri Lankan dishes too. You like a bit of curry.'

'I don't really do children.'

'There's *one*,' Crystal tutted, 'and she doesn't even speak, bless her. It's not as if the bloody Brady Bunch are coming to run riot in the backyard. It's just us.'

'When?'

'Tonight. Six o'clock. That gives you three hours to get your arse in gear. You need to have a shower and a shave. You look like shite.'

'Thank you.'

Sometimes he thought it would be easier to live completely alone. Ask both Crystal and Joy to leave. But something stopped him short whenever he thought of it. On the whole, it was better to have someone around rather than no one. Most of the time they let him be. Crystal did the shopping now, so he didn't really have to go out. Joy looked after the garden. If they didn't, he'd

74

have to get someone else in to do those jobs. The alternative was unthinkable. He might have to do them himself, and he couldn't even bear the thought. Paparazzi no longer camped at his gates as they knew he rarely ventured out. Yet if he did start to go out again, they'd soon be all over him. (Conversely, the less he went out, the more it was a story when he was star-spotted.) And to think, all he'd ever wanted to do was play his guitar and sing. He never appreciated the intrusion there would be into his life until it was too late to turn back the tide.

'Do it for me,' Crystal wheedled. 'Even for you – you don't come out much these days. It can't be good to hide away all the time like this, Hayd. Life goes on, you know.'

But does it? Does it have to?

He'd been happy once. Delirious. The days had been golden. He was adored, revered. His music was played around the world. He had fame, fortune, a woman he loved more than life itself. Who wouldn't want that?

Then the dark side of celebrity culture had reared its ugly head. He couldn't step out of the door without being followed by a crowd of jostling photographers. His life was no longer his own. The tender, romantic moments he tried to share with Laura were captured digitally and beamed around the world to appear in every newspaper and glossy magazine. Within minutes they were all over the internet. He attracted a dozen different stalkers, some more serious than others, and had eventually been forced to surround them both with a round-the-clock security team. What had begun as a golden life rapidly became a gilded cage.

'Hey,' Crystal said, snapping her fingers. 'Back in the room.'

He realised that his attention had drifted, as it so often did, his brain going round and round on the same old loop, going over things that he could have done differently. How his life would have been so much simpler had he never won *The Fame Game*.

'Say you'll come,' she begged. 'Don't be a miserable bastard. You need to come out of your room sometime. All this night-time stuff, Hayd? It's starting to freak me out. You're not a bloody vampire.'

He held up his hands. Resistance, he knew, was futile. 'I'll come.'

She grinned at him, victorious. 'Don't think of *not* turning up. Don't you dare be late either. Or I'll be back for you. I'm warning you.'

'I fully appreciate that.'

'Six o'clock. In the garden. If you look out your window, you'll see that the weather is fantastic.'

It shocked him slightly to realise that he hadn't actually noticed that. To cover his anxiety, he teased Crystal. 'Dress code?'

'Casual. But make a bit of an effort. The millionaire-tramp look is so last-year.'

'Point taken. I'll see you later.'

Crystal trotted away happily now that she'd bullied him into submission, and he listened to her clomping down the stairs in her ridiculous shoes.

He closed the door and went back to his bed. All he wanted to do was lose himself in his music again. He tended now to listen to jazz or heavy rock, anything but the commercial pop that he had been so famous for himself.

However, when he put his earphones in again he found he couldn't settle. Crystal was right: the sun was shining for all its worth out there, and he wondered how long it had been since he'd felt its warmth on his skin. Perhaps it would be nice to go out into the garden for once. A party, though? That was a whole other area of terror.

# Chapter Sixteen

It's very hard to find time away from Sabina now that we're sharing the same room, so, while she's showering for her party, I quickly rush downstairs and find Crystal in the kitchen.

'Can you write for me in Sabina's card please?' I'd normally feel ashamed by my failings, but already I know that Crystal will understand and I've no embarrassment in asking her to help me. 'I'd like to do it in English and my writing isn't good enough.'

'Sure.' She finds a pen in the drawer and comes to sit beside me at the table. 'Do you want to copy it?'

I shake my head. 'I'd love to, but I fear it'll take too long and I must have it completed before Sabina comes out of the shower.'

'OK. Shoot.'

'To my beautiful daughter,' I say as Crystal writes down my words. 'May your life be filled with love and laughter. May you be strong, independent and happy. With love always, your dear Mama.'

'That's lovely.'

'They're words that come from the bottom of my heart. I

hope that she'll find a man to love her as she should be loved and for who she is.' A man who won't squash her and beat her into the person that he thinks she should be. I don't care if he's black, white or green. Or if he's short, tall, thin or fat. I don't mind if he has a mop of ginger hair or a pate as shiny as a conker. I don't care if he's Buddhist, Muslim, Hindu, Christian or nothing at all. I simply want her to find someone who cares deeply for her.

'Shut up.' Crystal nudges me. 'You're going to make me blub.' When she's finished, she hands the card back to me.

'Thank you.' I lick the envelope and seal it. Then I hurry upstairs to wrap the Hello Kitty backpack.

This afternoon, we all visited the small primary school that's only a few streets away from the house. It's a pretty little school and the headteacher showed us around and then helped me to fill in the forms that were necessary. Now Sabina has to wait to see if the local authority will accept her, but the headteacher was very hopeful. She didn't seem to mind that Sabina is unable to speak any more, and I think that my child will be comfortable in that environment. Crystal – who's now self-appointed Auntie Crystal – says that we must keep our fingers and everything else crossed.

After that, Crystal took us to the supermarket and, again, insisted on buying all of the food for the party this evening. As soon as Sabina is able to start school, I'll be free to look for suitable employment. I don't know what I'll be able to do. My spoken English, I hope, is impeccable, but my writing and reading are of very poor quality. It's something that I must address or I'll only be able to do lowly work, and I want to make my daughter very proud of me. So proud that she will be moved to cry out, 'Mama, my mama, you are wonderful!' That's my dearest dream.

I spent the rest of the afternoon cooking up some of my

traditional dishes to serve this evening, and I hope that my new housemates will like them. I didn't risk anything too spicy, so I've steered away from the very hot devilled foods that we Sri Lankans are so fond of and have made a white chicken curry, fish koftas, aubergine salad, dhal, some fried potatoes and rice. My style of cooking has changed since I've been in England and is now mixed with both Indian and Western influences which I learned from my mother-in-law. I hope that they'll like it.

Sabina and I go down to the garden, where Crystal is already setting the table that's out on the patio. There are brightly coloured plastic beakers and plates. She's filled jars with pretty flowers that have been picked from the garden, but I don't know what they are.

'They look very nice.' Sabina, in her new dress and T-shirt, stares at them in awe. The evening is pleasantly warm and it'll be nice to sit and eat outside. Where I lived before, the garden wasn't attractive. It was small, overlooked by houses to the side and behind us. The grass was scrubby and unkempt. At the bottom there was a shed; an old freezer propped against it was all that kept it from falling over. It wasn't a place to sit out and eat in comfort. My mother-in-law wasn't a gardener. Neither can I profess to having green thumbs.

'You look great,' Crystal says, taking in my new outfit. I've worn the white trousers and floral smock that she chose, and my hair is still loose. It's nice to feel the warmth of the sun on my arms. One has been broken three times in the same place and is now pinned with a metal rod. When it's cold or damp, it aches terribly. 'There's one thing that both of you need though.'

She goes back into the kitchen and reappears with her hand-bag. 'Sit your bum down.'

I take one of the chairs and Crystal sits next to me. 'A bit of slap,' she says. 'Not too much.' She pulls out a make-up bag.

'I'm not too sure,' I begin to protest.

'Shut up, woman. Indulge me.' She proceeds to daub me with a variety of colours that she picks out seemingly at will.

'I've never worn make-up before,' I tell her.

'You don't really need it,' she says, tongue out in concentration. 'You're delish as you are. I'm adding a few highlights, that's all.'

Sabina is rapt.

Crystal's hands fly over my face with great precision.

'There,' she says, eventually. 'Beautiful.'

Sabina nods her agreement.

Crystal hands me a compact mirror and, reluctantly, I hold it up. I'm worried that she has made me look like a clown. But I need not have feared. True to her word, Crystal has put only a subtle touch of make-up on my face. My eyelids have been shaded with a shimmering powder and my lashes look longer and fuller. There's a pleasing blush to my cheeks and my lips are slicked with a bronze gloss.

'It is nice,' I tell her. 'Thank you.'

'Now you're hot to trot.'

'I think so.' Although I'm not entirely sure what that involves.

'Your turn,' she says to Sabina.

Before I can insist that my daughter is too young for make-up, Crystal winks at me. Expertly she waves the brushes over my child's cheeks and eyes and slicks her lips with a clear gloss. 'There you go.'

Sabina's delighted, even though she's been given the barest minimum of colour.

'Very pretty,' I tell her, and she preens in Crystal's small mirror, thoroughly pleased with what she sees.

Crystal applies some more gloss to her own lips, this one bright pink and not subtle at all. She puts away her make-up, clearly happy with a job well done. 'Right, now that we're all gorgeous, come and help me pick some more flowers, Beanie,' Crystal says. 'I've got two more jars to fill.'

I glance at my watch. It's nearly six o'clock. 'I'll check on our supper.'

'Need any help?'

'I think that I can manage, thank you, Crystal.'

She grins at me. 'You don't lack confidence in the kitchen,' she laughs. 'I couldn't knock up a dinner like that. You're right at home there.'

I blush. 'I love to cook.'

'Can't wait to tuck in. It smells heavenly.' She grabs Sabina's hand and pulls her away down the garden.

Turning back to the kitchen, I put on an apron to cover my new outfit. Everything is coming along as I want it to. I stir the chicken and taste the dhal before adding a little more seasoning.

Crystal and Sabina return with more flowers and arrange them in the waiting jars. My child has a crown of flowers fixed to her hair and she smiles like a little princess.

'You look very pretty,' I tell her. 'Did you make that yourself?'

Sabina nods towards Crystal. Please say her name, I think. But she doesn't.

Joy is the first to join us in the garden.

'I'll slap your hands if I catch you picking my flowers, Christine Cooper,' Joy grumbles.

'Take a chill pill, Joy,' Crystal counters. 'That's what flowers are for. Don't they look fab?'

'They're very pretty,' I agree. 'But I don't know what any of them are. The house I lived in before didn't have any flowers.'

'No flowers?' Joy looks as if she can't comprehend such an omission.

'None at all,' I confirm.

'Well, these are tulips,' she says, touching a pale pink head in the nearest border. 'You must know those.'

I shake my head and she tuts her disbelief.

'These purple ones are called snake's-head fritillary. The delicate yellow ones are *Narcissus pipit* and the arching white stems are *Spirea ajuta*.'

'You know a lot about flowers.'

Joy shrugs, but I can tell that she's pleased by my observation. 'Some.'

'Get a drink down your neck, Joy. Loosen up.' Crystal thrusts a glass of wine at her. 'Want some, Ayesha?'

I shake my head. 'A soft drink for me, please.'

She pours out mango juice for me and Sabina.

'A cocktail for the birthday girl,' Crystal says, and lifts her glass in a toast to Sabina.

'Oh, it's your birthday is it, little one?' Joy says.

Sabina nods.

'Tomorrow,' I say. 'She'll be nine.'

'She'll never speak if you always answer for her,' Joy notes, and I take a step back from the sting.

'Give her a break, Grumpy Knickers,' Crystal says.

'I've brought up two children,' Joy counters. 'I do know what I'm talking about.'

'Yeah, and you've got half a dozen grandkids too, but when do you see any of them?'

'I have five grandchildren and I'd see them regularly if they didn't live on the other side of the world.'

'Or if you'd get on a bloody plane.'

'I don't like to fly.' Joy gulps her wine.

I feel my chest fluttering with panic. I don't like it when people argue. One wrong word and it can escalate so quickly.

'Look, we're freaking Ayesha out. This is supposed to be a welcome party and a celebration of their new life and Beanie's

82

birthday. We're spoiling it by bickering like fishwives. It's just a bit of banter,' she assures me. 'Don't let it bother you.'

Now *I'm* unable to find my own voice, and simply nod.

'Is supper ready yet?' Crystal wants to know.

'I think so. I'll check.'

'Is His Lordship joining us?' Joy flicks her head towards the upstairs of the house as she always does when she refers to our landlord.

As I turn to go back into the kitchen, Mr Hayden Daniels appears at the French doors.

'He certainly is,' he says to Joy. 'Hope I'm not late.'

Hayden grins at Crystal, who looks relieved that he's come downstairs to be with us.

'Perfect timing.' She hands him a bottle of beer. 'Ayesha is about to serve.'

Hayden turns to me and does a double-take. His eyes widen and he rocks back as if someone has punched him. I don't know what to do with myself, I'm so embarrassed.

'You look so different,' he manages eventually.

'I hope that's a good thing,' I offer, but he makes no reply and continues to stare.

Perhaps Crystal has put on too much make-up after all and I look like a silly girl, not like a mother of a nearly-nine-year-old child. Perhaps he thinks my clothes are too young and don't suit me.

I feel myself flush furiously under his scrutiny. 'I'll get the food,' I say, and am glad to be able to rush indoors.

# Chapter Seventeen

I carry the dishes from the kitchen to set on the table while Crystal, Joy, Sabina and Hayden seat themselves.

'Sabina,' I say, 'have you washed your hands?'

She nods at me, but stands up and goes to cleanse them at the sink.

When I've laid out all of the dishes, I explain what each of them is.

'Looks fab,' Crystal says, already picking up a serving spoon.

Joy wrinkles her nose. 'Is there anything here that I can eat?'

'Don't be such a fussy cow,' Crystal admonishes her. 'It all looks wonderful.'

'I don't eat foreign food,' she says.

'Then you don't know what you're missing,' is Crystal's conclusion as she tries the chicken curry. 'This is well tasty.'

'I haven't made it too spicy, Joy, but I can cook something else for you if you don't wish to eat it.'

She sighs with resignation. 'I'll give it a go. If I don't like it, I'll get myself a sandwich.'

'That's another one of the reasons she won't go to see her

grandkids,' Crystal says to no one in particular. 'Because she won't eat "foreign" food.'

'It doesn't suit my palate,' Joy insists.

'Get over yourself,' Crystal says. 'It's delish. What do you reckon, Hayd?'

'Excellent.' He looks up and his eyes meet mine. I lower them quickly.

'And that's from a man who's happy to live on nothing but sandwiches,' Crystal adds.

When I risk a glance up again, Hayden's attention, thankfully, has returned to his food. Today he's wearing a black T-shirt and baggy jeans that sit low on his hips as, I understand, is the current fashion. He's wearing a black wool hat pulled down on his head even though it's warm out here. Outdoors, it's easier to see how pale he is. Sabina sits next to him and his skin looks very white against the creamy chocolate of hers. I don't think that Hayden can go out in the sun too often. I believe, though, that he's a very handsome man. I'm shocked at myself as I haven't thought like this since Hinni and I were silly girls giggling at the village boys at home.

I'm not sure if Hayden's enjoying the food or not. He's gripping the fork so tightly that his knuckles are white with tension and he seems to be eating automatically, his jaw tight. Hayden is very slender and I wonder if eating isn't a pleasure for him.

'Is it to your taste?' I venture.

He pauses with his fork to his mouth and seems suddenly aware of what he's doing. The next mouthful, he really seems to savour. 'Yes,' he says. 'It's fantastic.'

'I'm not looking for praise,' I say. 'I'm looking for your enjoyment.'

'You have it,' he assures me.

I may be mistaken, but I think that he releases his grip on his fork ever so slightly and his jaw relaxes a little.

'Give it a go, Joy,' Crystal urges. 'You don't know what you're missing.'

'It looks a little spicy for me,' Joy says, wrinkling her nose.

'How can you tell until you put it in your gob?'

'The chicken curry isn't hot,' I promise her, but she grimaces at the word 'curry' and I realise that I'm not winning the battle. 'I'll make you something more mild next time,' I offer.

'I'll make myself a sandwich,' Joy says, and she wanders into the kitchen.

Now I feel embarrassed that she doesn't like my food. I hoped when she saw it and inhaled the aroma that she might change her mind.

'Take no notice of her,' Crystal whispers. 'One of the reasons she won't go out to see her sons is that she's convinced she'd starve to death. Can you imagine?'

'That's a great shame.'

Crystal shrugs. 'She's too set in her ways by half.'

When we've finished eating, I clear the plates.

'Look what I've got,' Crystal says as she follows me in, bearing dishes. She opens the cupboard and inside is a birthday cake for Sabina. It's pink, with a picture of a little girl on it plus the word *Princess* in yellow icing.

'That's lovely. How kind of you. Sabina will be very happy.'

'Thought she'd like a surprise. It's only from the supermarket, but you've seen what I can do to a pizza. You wouldn't want to taste my baking.'

'I could show you.'

Crystal holds up a hand. 'My talent lies in opening packets. I'll leave the fancy stuff to you.' She lowers her voice. 'You might not have won Joy over yet, but that's the first time in two years I've seen Hayd eat a proper meal. It's nice to see. Well done.'

That gives me a warm glow of pride.

'I bought some candles for the cake too. Now, if I can find the matches, I can light them.' She rummages in the drawers until she finds what she's looking for.

Crystal fixes the candles in the cake with an inordinate amount of attention and then lights them. 'Ready?' She goes to hand me the cake.

'You take it outside. Sabina will like that,' I tell her.

So Crystal holds the cake aloft and carries it into the garden. Sabina's eyes light up when she sees it.

'*Happy birthday to you*,' Crystal sings. '*Happy birthday to you!* Come on, you lot, join in.' She waves her free hand at me, Joy and Hayden. 'Come on. Don't let me sing on my own.'

Crystal starts again. '*Happy birthday to you!*'

I manage to squeak out an effort, though I think it's terribly off-key. I've had very little reason to sing in a long time.

Joy also sings along, although her voice is croaky.

Hayden looks very reluctant to join in. Crystal glares at him. He opens his mouth but at first nothing comes out. Crystal pauses in the song and waits for him.

Eventually he sings out, '*Happy birthday to you!*'

The sound is pure and clear.

I gape in surprise and, when I look around, Crystal, Joy and Sabina are doing the same thing. This is why he was a popular singer. His voice is strong, soaring, and I realise that the skin on my arms has risen to goosebumps in delight.

'*Happy birthday, dear Beanie*,' Crystal continues, wavering slightly.

Then she falls silent as Hayden finishes alone: '*Happy birthday to you.*'

We're all still staring at him, agog, and now he looks embarrassed.

'Wow,' Crystal says eventually. 'You've not lost it, Hayd.'

'No,' he agrees, shyly. 'Apparently not.'

'You can have a big slice of cake for that!' Crystal starts us clapping and, under my guidance, Sabina blows out the candles.

'You know, I think I'll go back to my room for now. Leave you to it.' Hayden pushes his chair away and stands. 'Bit too much excitement for one day.'

'Don't—' Crystal starts, but he holds up a hand to stop her speaking.

He turns to me. 'Thank you, Ayesha. Dinner was very good.' Then to my daughter, 'Happy birthday for tomorrow, Sabina.' Giving a self-conscious wave, he leaves.

Suddenly, the garden feels a little cooler, and I shiver. We all watch Hayden walk inside and head straight up to his room.

'Is he going to be all right?' I ask, concerned.

'I really hope so,' Crystal says. She sighs and then turns to me. 'That's the first time he's sung a single note since his girl-friend has been gone.'

# Chapter Eighteen

Hayden drew the curtains even though it was still light outside and lay on his bed. He was shaking inside after his impromptu performance, brief as it might have been. It had been a big deal for him and he was shocked and surprised at hearing the sound of his own voice after so long. Crystal was right. It *was* still there.

There was no denying that he'd felt backed into a corner. How could he refuse to sing 'Happy Birthday' to the kid? Perhaps Crystal knew that. Perhaps he'd have words with her. Then again, perhaps he should be grateful to his friend.

Crystal had stuck with him through thick and thin. In the early times, there'd been some very dark moments. Moments when he'd thought it wasn't worth being here at all. Moments when he wanted to do nothing more than swallow some pills and down a bottle of Scotch.

He'd been with Laura since they were both sixteen. They'd met at sixth-form college when they were both studying art and he was spending every Saturday busking in Oxford to earn some extra money. They'd been inseparable ever since. Laura had been with him all the way as he'd clawed his way up the slippery ladder of his music career. She'd stood in pubs every weekend while he played to twenty, thirty, fifty people. She'd handed out flyers and taken email addresses to try to build up his following. When he'd had to work as a van driver or in a warehouse to supplement his income from playing, she was the one who never lost faith. Laura had been his one, his only love. Childhood sweethearts. Which, of course, the press lapped up. The fact that one of the hottest men on the planet – their description, not his – was a one-woman man sent them into a feeding frenzy. Of course, as a consequence, every time he was within ten metres of another woman, there'd be stories about him being unfaithful. Laura bore it all stoically. She accepted it as part of his life possibly more than he did. Hayden hated the attention. He'd wanted to be a singer, a musician, appreciated for that talent and that alone. It didn't seem long after he'd auditioned for *The Fame Game* that everyone – even him sometimes – had lost sight of the most important thing. The music.

There'd been a relentless round of interviews – *This Morning*, *Lorraine*, Jonathan Ross, Graham Norton. He'd been on all of their chat shows a dozen times. Every time there was a new single released he was wheeled out, smile plastered firmly in place. If you want to sell records, it has to be done, he was told.

Then he'd been pressured by his management company into doing an aftershave campaign. For months he'd appeared, barely clothed, in glossy magazines, on billboards and in every conceivable ad break on the television, spouting some pretentious nonsense. Even he'd got sick of seeing his moody, airbrushed face everywhere. Now, after all this time, the ads still popped up at Christmas and made him cringe. It had earned him a lot of money, there was no doubt, and Laura had found it amusing when the deluge of fan mail inevitably followed.

He'd had to employ two people simply to reply to them all, which meant he found it less so.

Their simple life, which until *The Fame Game* had involved nothing more complicated than long walks in the fields of Oxfordshire and nights curled up on the sofa watching movies, had been transformed overnight. He'd been required to go to film premières, red-carpet events, the opening of clubs, restaurants, shops. At first it was fun, but it soon became tiring to spend every night of the week with a glass of warm champagne, talking to people who he didn't know but who nevertheless wanted a piece of him. Laura enjoyed buying the dresses to wear and soon she was sent samples from designers, to be seen in them. She liked that.

Then they'd moved to this house because he felt it was the thing to do, convinced that he needed a London base. So they'd waved goodbye to the countryside and swapped it for city life. He'd had it renovated while he was on tour, ready for Laura to put her own stamp on it, to turn it into a home. Some of the rooms hadn't been started, some were still half done, and he doubted they'd ever be finished now. He'd just closed the doors on them all and never looked inside.

He and Laura had loved it here, until the paparazzi became permanently camped by the gates and they couldn't go out without being chased down the street by flashing cameras. They couldn't go for a walk, a pizza, a drink without being followed. Every private occasion became gossip-page fodder for glossy mags and internet chat rooms. Sometimes the lenses were a distance away, but they still recorded every detail. Sometimes they were pushed right under your nose. Whichever way, they were intrusive. Now he couldn't even walk to get a newspaper. If he ever went out, it was under the cover of darkness. It was no wonder Elvis Presley had, in his last years, lived an upside-down life, sleeping all day and going out at night. As Crystal had noted, he wasn't very far away from that himself.

In an industry that was brimming over with inflated egos, Laura had been his haven. She kept him grounded. At eighteen, they'd rented a damp flat together in Oxford which they could barely afford. It was at Laura's insistence that they moved when the black mould that decorated the walls started to affect his voice. It was Laura who'd always given him the belief in himself. They never had two pennies to rub together, and it was getting to the point where he needed to make his work pay as a musician or he'd have to find another, more steady job. You couldn't buy a home, raise a family, living from hand to mouth. For years he'd soldiered on, coming close to record deals, the promise of bigger venues, being taken on by reputable management. They were all floated, but nothing seemed to come of them and he never quite got the breaks.

As a last-ditch attempt to make the big time, Laura had encouraged him to fill in the online form for *The Fame Game*. At first he hadn't wanted to sell out to a talent show. He'd seen them force artists to be something they weren't, only to dump them when they became one-hit wonders. Then he'd come to realise that there was no other way he could do it. Time was running out and, with much reluctance, he signed on the dotted line. After that his life was no longer his own. He wondered now if either of them would have been so keen if they'd been able to foresee how it would turn out.

When he'd made it big, all their plans had been put on hold while they rode the crazy wave of fame. But as soon as they hit their thirties, they'd talked again about getting married, settling down, him stepping out of the limelight. Both of them wanted children, but neither of them wanted to bring them up in the glare of the spotlight. It was time. They knew it. The last five or more years had been crazy and Hayden had made enough money to last them a lifetime. A couple of times they'd taken a helicopter down to Cornwall, Devon or Dorset for the weekend and had looked at property there. He'd liked Dorset the best – the secluded coves, the rugged cliffs. He'd spent a lot of happy childhood holidays in that part of the country and there was always something that pulled him back. Wherever they ended up, getting out of London and retiring to the quiet seclusion of the seaside had seemed very appealing.

He'd bought Laura an engagement ring, as a surprise. His personal assistant had arranged a VIP after-hours consultation at Tiffany's. He'd managed to slip her favourite ring out of the house for size comparison, and commissioned one accordingly. He'd wanted to buy the biggest diamond in the shop, but he knew Laura would want something more modest and he'd settled on a classy, princess-cut solitaire. They were going to their favourite restaurant, somewhere that appreciated their need for privacy and would put them in a shielded booth right at the back, away from nosy customers and photographers. The last thing Hayden wanted was anyone to catch the moment when he went down on bended knee. He'd ordered champagne on ice and arranged for Laura's favourite flowers to be on the table.

He'd told Laura where they were going, but not why. For once, he'd advised the security team that they'd go alone. Sometimes he just wanted to remember what it was to be normal, and there were some moments in your life when you simply didn't want an audience. Even if they were on your side.

But things hadn't worked out as planned. What in life ever did? Laura had left him alone and she never got to see the beautiful engagement ring he'd bought for her.

# Chapter Nineteen

Sabina is exhausted when I've finally cleared up and taken her to bed. I tuck her in and softly sing 'Happy Birthday' to her again as if it's a lullaby. She falls asleep almost instantly.

It's a little bit difficult, us both being in the same room, as I don't want to switch on the television and disturb her. This would be an excellent time to read, but I've only Sabina's childish books and I've gone through them both with her a hundred times.

Unlike my daughter, I'm not tired. I'm what I think Crystal would called 'wired'. Perhaps it's due to my new 'trendy' image, which is taking some getting used to. Perhaps it's a sugar rush from Sabina's birthday cake. Or maybe it's because I cannot get the sound of Hayden Daniels's beautiful singing voice out of my mind.

I sit in the darkness for a while, enjoying the silence of the house. It's simply nice to know that there's no one who will come home to me, greedy with marital demands or ready with his fists. I push away the memory. Nothing will spoil this nice evening.

I know that counselling is the thing to do nowadays to get through such a crisis, but I could never bring myself to talk to a stranger about the things that have happened to me. I could never bring myself to talk to anyone. Not even Crystal, who seems to have a way with her that encourages confidences. Instead I must lock my memories, my thoughts, deep in my heart, keep them to myself and hope that, one day, it will feel as if it all happened to someone else. I don't wish my past to blight the future of my daughter.

I hear Crystal's shoes clomp down the stairs and glance at the clock on the bedside table. It's nine o'clock and I don't know where the time has gone. A moment later there's a gentle knock on my door and I go to open it.

'You're not sitting here in the dark by yourself?' she says.

'Sabina is asleep,' I whisper. 'I don't like to put on the television.'

'Go and make yourself comfy in the living room for an hour. Beanie'll be all right here on her own for a while. No one else ever uses that room. There's a big telly, an iPod and loads of books.'

Books? My interest piques at that. 'Perhaps I will.'

'I'm off to work now.' Crystal nods towards the front door. 'I'll see you in the morning. Just wanted to say thanks for a really smashing meal.' She massages her tummy. 'I'm going to have to take up running while you live here.'

'Thank you,' I counter. 'It was a very kind thought to have a party for Sabina.'

'Poor kid looks like she could do with a bit of fun.'

'Yes.' I don't want Sabina to be thought of as a 'poor kid', but there's no doubt that her life has been lacking in lightness up until now – but all that is about to change. Our lives will be about brightness and levity. I'll make sure to tell her every day how very much she is loved.

Crystal kisses my cheek. 'See you, sweetheart. Whatever you do, enjoy the rest of the evening.'

She clomps down the rest of the stairs and I hear the door close behind her. Joy, I think, will already be in her room, and unless Hayden decides to have a nocturnal workout, I'm unlikely to bump into him either. He seemed in a terrible rush to be alone again, as if he could only cope with company for a very short time. I know what Crystal means now when she says that he's a troubled man.

Checking that Sabina is still sound asleep, I let myself out of the room, quietly closing the door behind me. I wonder if I'll ever grow accustomed to the fact that this sumptuous house is my new home, and I hope that we'll be allowed to stay here for a long time. It's early days, I know, but I still feel something of an intruder here.

I go downstairs and let myself into the living room. It's dark now, so I turn on the light but keep it dimmed right down. The room is a little chilly, but I feel unable to switch on the fire to warm it. I should like to request permission to do so, and there's nobody to ask.

A large television is fixed to the wall, remote control on the shelf beneath it, but I don't feel like watching television yet. There are books too, lots of them. So many that I feel over-whelmed. How can one person own so many? I could read a book a week for the rest of my life and still never run out. I browse some of the titles, running my fingers over the spines, but I don't know where to start. Some of them have words that are too long for me to understand, and I hate this feeling of ignorance. My eyes light on a couple of rows of pretty covers – pinks, yellows, pale blues. They look bright and welcoming. I'd like something fun to read, not a book about murders or crime. There's one called *Bridget Jones's Diary*. Perhaps this will help me to learn about what it is to be a modern woman. I lift the book from the shelf, hoping that no one will mind, and clutch it to my chest.

There's a sofa with a reading lamp next to it where I can sit, and I turn it on. It provides a warm glow to a little patch of the cushions. However, before I settle there with my chosen novel, I peruse the room. The walls at one end are covered with gold and silver records, in picture frames like a gallery. I look closer and am not surprised to see that they've all been awarded to Hayden Daniels for a variety of songs and achievements. There are pictures of him with various celebrities – some of whom even *I* recognise, and I'm the first to admit that I've led a sheltered existence.

On top of the piano there's a pretty girl with blonde, flowing hair and skin that's creamy white. I wonder if this is the girl-friend who's now gone? He must have loved her very much to have been so badly affected by her departure. It's a shame that Hayden doesn't sing any more. From what little I heard, it seems as if he well deserves all of these accolades.

There's an iPod slotted into a player and I think that it would be nice to hear some music for company. Without my daughter, I always feel so terribly alone. I flick through the playlists, a luxury I was never afforded at home, so I don't really know what I like.

I scroll through the names of various artists, but none of them means anything to me. And then I see a playlist of Hayden's own songs. 'My For Ever Love', 'The Miss You Years', 'Everything About You'. To my shame, I must say that I don't know any of these songs either.

Pressing the screen, I make my selection. 'My For Ever Love' starts to play. It's a haunting song, a ballad. I keep the sound low so as not to disturb the household.

Hayden's voice is mesmerising, moving. Tears spring to my eyes as I listen to the bittersweet lyrics and I start to sway. When I was Sabina's age I loved to dance, but I can't remember when last I did. My body feels stiff, as if it's fighting the rhythm rather than flowing with it. My muscles, my spirit feel clenched and tight. I'd like to sense these notes in my veins, but I don't know how. I put down my book and attempt to move my arms in time to the music. Closing my eyes, I tilt my head back and try to let the sounds wash over me. Risking a twirl, I finally start to pick up on the mood and my rigid movements start to soften. This feels good. So very good. I must add to my list of Things To Do in my new life: dance more.

# Chapter Twenty

Turning over, he reached out for Laura but, as always, the other side of his bed was empty, and that was enough to jolt him awake. Hayden sat up and ran a hand through his dishevelled hair. His mouth was parched, his pillow wet where he'd cried in his sleep. He must have dozed off, but when he woke, he was still thinking of Laura.

It seemed as if every time he closed his eyes he went through this. All this time and he still hadn't learned a way to block it out. Without even trying, he could see every second of that fateful day play out before him as if it was happening all over again.

He and Laura were happy, hand in hand, as they left the house. Her blonde hair swinging in the sunlight, pretty laughter on her lips. She'd insisted on driving, thoughtful as ever. Hayden had been in the recording studio the night before until late and she'd said she thought he looked tired. He didn't feel tired at all. He felt elated, almost giddy with excitement. He was going to ask the woman he loved to marry him, and he couldn't wait. The restaurant wasn't far, ten minutes away at the very most, so, at Laura's insistence, he'd settled into the passenger seat next to her.

They'd both put on dark glasses ready to swing out of the drive, and Hayden had pulled down his customary wool hat. The ring was nestled in his pocket and he got a buzz of excitement as he thought about how Laura would react. She'd love that he'd been so clever, so secretive. Especially when it would have been so easy for someone to snap him coming out of Tiffany's. He smiled to himself.

'What are you grinning at?' she asked, squeezing his knee.

'You'll see,' he said, smug.

But she didn't. As they pulled out of the gate and turned towards Hampstead, two paparazzi jumped on to a scooter and gave chase. They followed them, right on their tail. So close that Hayden could see the whites of their eyes.

'Idiots!' Laura tutted. 'If I have to brake hard they'll go right over the top of us.'

Seconds later they'd come up on the left side of the car, a dangerous undertaking move, and the guy on the back pointed his camera at the car window. Hayden turned away and lifted his hand to block his face.

'I can't get away from them,' Laura complained.

The road narrowed for a speed restriction and she slowed right down. The scooter swerved in front of them and braked hard so that the man on the back could twist to snap them.

'They are a *total* pain in the arse,' she muttered.

Laura had to swerve to miss them as they danced about in front of the car.

'Watch out!' Hayden had shouted. Sometimes he still called it out in his sleep.

He'd tried to grab the steering wheel. But, instead of taking out the scooter, Laura had hit a bollard at the side of the road at a dangerous angle. Before he knew what was happening, the car had flipped on its side, slewing across the road. The windscreen shattered and shards of glass showered over them both. There was a terrible screeching of metal and the blaring of a horn. Hayden crouched down, hands over his head. There was a van heading towards them which also had to swerve to avoid the scooter. He could see the driver fighting to keep control, the panic in his eyes. It was too late, there was nowhere for him to go and, in awful slow motion, he'd hit them head-on. The noise was terrible, it sounded like a bomb exploding. There was a ringing in Hayden's ears and then he felt a thump in his chest as his airbag went off and all of his breath seemed to leave his body.

Laura wasn't so lucky. Her airbag failed to inflate and he heard her blood-chilling scream as she was thrown forward, slamming into the steering wheel at full force. Then, when all the sounds of metal on metal stopped, there was nothing. Just a terrible, eerie silence.

He was unaware at the time, but the photographers had fled the scene, leaving the stricken van driver to call for an ambulance while Hayden cradled Laura. Blood was pouring from a gaping wound in her chest. It covered his hands, spilled on to her clothes, on to the floor of the car. It seemed like the emergency services were taking an age to arrive and every time he asked, the van driver told him they were on the way. Hayden talked to Laura the whole time, held her to him.

'Hold on, sweetheart,' he murmured softly. 'Not long now.' He'd stroked her face, her hair, wiped the tears from her eyes.

'I'm going,' she said.

'No, no, you're not,' he insisted. 'You'll be fine. Absolutely fine.'

Desperately he tried to keep her spirits up, keep her with him, but her face was becoming paler and paler. Her eyes seemed to glaze over and dim. There was a bubbling sound in her breathing and her lips were turning blue.

'I love you,' he whispered. 'Don't leave me. We're going to have such a long and happy life together.'

As he heard the ambulance sirens approaching, Laura turned to him. Light came back into her eyes. Her mouth opened, but he could tell she was struggling to find the words. He put his face close to hers.

'I'm sorry,' she whispered, barely audible. Her hand had reached up to touch his face and he'd held it there, tightly. 'I love you.'

Then she'd slipped away from him. He'd watched as the life drained from the love of his life and there wasn't a single thing he'd been able to do to stop it. All the money in the world couldn't bring her back. Every day he knew that he would have given up everything – all his worldly goods, all his money, all the trappings of fame – for just one more hour with her. None of them meant anything to him now.

Hayden pushed his memories aside and, once again, the reality of being all alone hit him hard. He put his hands to his face and found it wet with tears. The pain of that moment never went. It gnawed in his heart like a voracious parasite. The light in his life had gone out that day. He'd turned his back on the music industry and had never played nor sung a note since. He'd never wanted to. Laura was gone. She was never coming back and nothing could change that.

He'd buried his reason for living in a dark, damp grave on an obscenely sunny day. The beautiful engagement ring that she'd never known about was on her cold finger.

The paparazzi who caused the accident got off lightly. When the police had eventually tracked them down, the photographer on the back hadn't been charged with a single offence. The man in control of the scooter had been charged with death by careless driving. He'd pleaded guilty and been given a paltry twelve-month custodial sentence and a two-year ban from driving. He was free again six months later and back in his old job harassing celebrities. Not much in the way of punishment for

102

robbing someone of their life, which only added to Hayden's pain. He wondered if either of the guilty men woke up drenched in cold sweat in the middle of the night, reliving the accident in their dreams, as he did.

'What ifs haunted Hayden both night and day. What if they'd gone somewhere else? What if he'd been driving? Would Laura have survived? What if he hadn't dismissed the security team? Would they have been the ones to have taken the brunt? If he could turn back the clock, could he have prevented it in any way?

Climbing off the bed, he went to wash the tears from his face in the en suite bathroom. If only he could wash the tears from his heart as easily.

He stared at the thin, pale face that looked back at him. Laura would be cross with how he was dealing with this. He knew that. He just couldn't help it. She'd want him to be out there, living his life. Until this evening he'd thought he could quite happily stay in this room for ever. Now what? Tonight something inside him had shifted, and he wasn't sure what.

With that simple singing of 'Happy Birthday', was there suddenly a glimmer of hope around the corner? Whenever he'd tried to sing before, the words had jammed fast in his throat. Yet today the sound had flooded his chest with a feeling that he thought had been long gone. He felt the notes resonate in his blood, his muscles, his heart. And that was a couple of lines of the worst, dirge-like song on the planet. He tried to imagine what it would be like if he tried to sing a whole song again, something that he loved. One of his own. Could he do it? These days he was so unused to even speaking to people that he often found a few sentences of conversation quite taxing. Would he be able to manage a whole song? The thought both frightened and thrilled him.

And what about his new lodger? Ayesha Rasheed. Yesterday

he hadn't given her a second glance. Had written her off as a plain, mousy little thing. But tonight ... What had happened there? She looked so different. Like a dull, desiccated moth transformed into a vibrant, pretty butterfly.

When he looked at her, his mouth had gone dry and he could feel his heart banging inside his chest. It was all he could do to take his eyes off her. And it wasn't simply the fact that she'd put on some make-up or prettier clothes. It was as if years of pain were starting to lift from her face and he knew how that felt.

When she looked back at him, she still seemed so frightened. From what little Crystal had said, the woman had been through an awful time. Plus she had a traumatised kid in tow. In one way or another they were all damaged people, and it would serve him very well to remember that.

# Chapter Twenty-one

I'm beginning to feel more comfortable with the music, enjoying the unaccustomed loosening of my body. I twirl around, almost carefree. Then, out of the corner of my eye, I see the silhouette of a man framed in the doorway.

My heart leaps to my throat. For a moment I wonder if it's Suresh come to take me home and I'm rooted to the spot with terror. But as the man steps forward from the shadows I realise it's Hayden Daniels. However, his face still looks dark, menacing in the low light, and I feel myself shrivel in front of him.

'What do you think you're doing?' he says tightly.

'I hope you don't mind me using the living room,' I answer, struggling to find my voice. 'Crystal seemed to think that it would be all right.'

'The music.' He nods to the iPod. 'What are you doing playing my music?'

'It was quiet,' I offer. 'And I was feeling a little lonely.' My heart is beating nervously and my mouth has gone dry. I've made him angry. 'It's a beautiful song.'

At once he strides across the room and reaches out. I fear

that he's going to strike me and instinctively I drop to the floor and curl in on myself as I've learned to do. When the blow comes it will first hit bone rather than soft flesh. Ashamed of my weakness, I cower against the leg of the piano. If I could, I'd crawl under it.

Instead the music clicks off and, though I brace myself for a punch or a kick, it doesn't come.

Hayden stands over me. His eyes glitter in the darkness and I hide my face again. 'Why are you on the floor?' he says, astounded.

He reaches for my arm and I flinch away from him.

'Ayesha.' He speaks softly now. 'Ayesha, get up. I'm not going to hurt you.'

How many times have I heard this promise? I stay where I am.

'Please.' He sits down next to me on the floor and leans against the piano stool. I hear his breath in a ragged exhalation. 'I'm sorry. So sorry.'

Slowly dropping my hands from my head, I risk a glance at him. He looks wretched.

'I didn't mean to shout, or to frighten you,' he insists. 'I was just shocked.' Another uncertain breath. 'I *never* listen to my own music. I can't bear it. I haven't since ... since a long time ago.'

'Since your girlfriend's been gone.'

'Yes.' I see the pain written on his face. 'More than two years ago.' I see the glisten of a tear on his cheek. 'It doesn't seem to get any easier though.'

Hesitantly, I uncurl and sit on the floor next to him, hugging my knees to me. Hayden doesn't look as if he'll be violent. He seems to be a man who's sad and deflated. He must have loved her very deeply. 'I'm very sorry that you're so unhappy.'

'*Unhappy*.' He gives a hollow laugh. 'Understatement of the

106

century.' Hayden shakes his head. 'I'm like a man drowning and I don't know what to do.'

'But you have so much to live for. All of this.' I sweep my hand to encompass all that I can. 'And your beautiful music. It's wonderful. It's the first time I've heard it.'

He laughs again, but it sounds less troubled. 'You must be the only person on the planet who hasn't.'

'I wasn't permitted to listen to music,' I venture. 'I've missed a lot.'

'I've always taken it for granted, I suppose. Then I couldn't face it. There was too much emotion in the songs. When I joined in with the singing earlier, it's the first time I've done that since Laura went.'

'Crystal told me that.'

Hayden risks a smile. 'Good old Crystal.'

We sit in a silence marked only by the sound of us both breathing in and out.

'You have an incredible voice,' I offer eventually. 'I'm so sorry that you no longer feel able to sing.'

'Perhaps I've turned a corner. It felt good,' he admits. 'To hear it again.' His breath is shuddering and I feel it's an effort for him to talk. 'First, when Laura went, I didn't *want* to do it. As time went on, I didn't know if I *could* still do it, and then that scares you even more.'

'It must be very frightening.'

'Yes.' He sounds unbearably sad.

'I wonder if this is how my daughter feels.'

'It must be very worrying that she doesn't talk.'

'I'd very much love to hear her voice again. That would mean the world to me.'

'It's not impossible,' he says. 'If an old fool like me can turn it around, then I have every hope for your lovely child.'

I smile at him. 'I hope that you're right.'

'So, Ayesha Rasheed, are we going to sit on the floor all night or should one of us get up and make a cup of tea? That's actually what I came downstairs to do.'

'I'll make it,' I say. I feel that I want to offer this broken man what small comfort I can.

He stands, then reaches out to take my hand and helps me up from the floor. For a moment, he holds it tightly as we face each other. 'While you live here, under my roof, you and Sabina have nothing to fear.'

'Thank you,' I say. I would like to believe that. Really I would.

# Chapter Twenty-two

I make a pot of tea and bring it back to the living room along with two mugs. Setting it down on the coffee table in front of Hayden, I fuss with pouring it. I'm uncomfortable being alone with a man, as I'd never have been allowed to do this in my previous life, but I'm trying to fight the feeling. I'm not that person now, I assure myself. I have my hair loose, I'm wearing modern clothes, and now it's just Hayden and me together. I feel both proud of myself and anxious. Change, in my case, is of course for the good, but possibly I'm doing too much too soon.

Hayden picks up the book I've left beneath the reading lamp and studies it. 'Bridget Jones?'

'I hope that it's all right for me to borrow this book.'

'It was Laura's favourite,' he says, turning it in his hands. 'She used to sit here giggling away.'

'It's a funny book?'

He looks up at me. 'You haven't read it?'

I hang my head. 'No,' I admit. 'I don't read or write very well, but I'm trying to learn along with Sabina. I can happily read books for her age. We help each other.'

He waves *Bridget Jones's Diary* at me. 'This might be a big step up.'

'I'd hoped to find out about modern women.'

Hayden laughs, but it's not a cruel sound. 'I'm not sure you'll want dear old Bridget as your role model, but I think the book will make you smile.'

'I hope so.' I feel that I'd like some lightness in my heart.

He looks as if he's weighing something heavily before he speaks. 'I could help you too,' he says. 'We can read it together in the evenings. If you like.'

The thought makes my heart quicken and I'm not sure whether it's with anxiety or anticipation.

'I'd like that.' I'm hesitant. 'But I may be embarrassed by my lack of education.'

'If we work on your reading and writing, then you won't have to be.'

'Although I'm very good at both reading and writing in my native tongue,' I add hastily, in case he thinks that I'm simple.

He looks at me with sadness in his eyes. 'It won't make me think less of you, if that's what you're worried about. In fact, I consider you a very brave woman to be striking out on your own.'

'I feel brave,' I tell him. 'And also very frightened.'

'You're among friends now, Ayesha. I hope you know that.'

'I don't think that Joy likes me.'

'Joy doesn't like anyone,' he says wryly. 'She's been through some tough times. Now she's damaged like the rest of us.'

'This is a house of broken hearts.'

'Perhaps we can all help each other to mend.'

I nod.

'Did you have a tough time with your husband?' Hayden takes his tea. 'Tell me to mind my own business, if you don't want to talk about it.'

110

So I put some more bread in the toaster. Next to come downstairs is Joy. She looks surprised to see the kitchen so busy, but it's clear that she feels that she can't back out now.

'What are you doing down at this time of day, Hayden?' she asks.

'I had a great night's sleep,' he answers, sounding surprised. 'I feel as if I could take on the world today.'

'Well, that's nice to hear.'

I'd second that, but I think it's better for me to keep my opinion to myself. Instead I say, 'Come and sit down, Joy. What can I get you?'

'Has this place suddenly turned into a café?' she mutters. 'I only have a bit of yoghurt and fruit. I'm perfectly capable of getting it myself.' However, she sits down next to Hayden, which I take as my cue to get it for her.

Sabina looks at her shyly from under her lovely dark lashes.

'How are you today?' Joy asks.

Sabina holds up a hand to high-five her and, with a confused laugh, Joy high-fives her back. I glance at Hayden, grateful that he's given her this small method of communication. It's clear that Sabina finds it amusing and I hope it will increase her confidence to connect with her world once more.

Hayden's toast pops up. I butter it, pour him some fresh coffee and deliver it to the table.

'Thank you.' He bites into the toast, grinning. 'You know, I think I'm going to like you living here, Ayesha.'

Flushing, I then bustle to find Joy's yoghurt and fruit in the fridge.

Last night Hayden and I spent an hour or more in the living room, starting to read *Bridget Jones's Diary* together. Already, I think I'm going to like Bridget. She's a very funny lady and I haven't found the book as difficult to read as I'd imagined.

Though I've learned some saucy English words that I never knew I would say!

I'm making slow progress, but Hayden seems to be a patient teacher and helped me to form the words that I didn't know, like when I show Sabina. He seemed to find it all very amusing, but he never once made me feel silly or stupid. I hope that we'll read some more together tonight, but as yet he's not mentioned it and I don't like to broach the subject.

'There's some stewed rhubarb in there,' Joy says. 'I'll have that with the yoghurt.' She tuts crossly. 'You know, there's really no need for me to sit here like an invalid. I always get my own breakfast.'

'I'd like to spoil you,' I say. 'For making my daughter and me very welcome.'

She purses her lips at that and I see Hayden suppress a smile. 'Humph,' Joy says.

I warm the rhubarb in a pan and resist the urge to add some ginger or cinnamon, if I could find any, to liven it up.

'Is this from the garden?' I ask as I set it down for her.

'Yes. I've got a raised bed and like to keep it going for as much of the year as I can.'

'I'd like it very much if you'd show me around the garden,' I say to her. It looks abundant with greenery and reminds me of the small patch my parents tended at home, which was lush with plants and fruits. 'I'm not a gardener, but I have a keen interest in cookery. We could work together to make the best use of the produce. If you'd like that.'

Amazingly, she looks quite taken with the idea. 'Often, when we have a glut of things, I have to give produce away. It makes me a very popular lady at the WI and the day centre that I go to,' she says with a proud smile. 'But it would be nice to be able to use more at home.'

Perhaps Joy, like me, is searching for approval.

'Then we'll try to do that.'

'Hayden never eats, and Crystal thinks Cadbury's Dairy Milk is a vegetable,' she adds waspishly.

That makes me laugh.

'I can hear you talking about me.' Crystal comes into the kitchen and yawns.

She's barefoot and is wearing a very small dressing gown. There's nothing beneath it but underwear, equally small. No nightdress or anything. I should think that Hayden would be very interested in her appearance, but he doesn't give her a second glance. Whereas I can hardly take my eyes away. How can someone be so comfortable with their body? It's voluptuous and strains against the confines of her clothes. I can't help but glance down at my own boyish body, my small breasts. They are tiny limes compared to Crystal's ripe watermelons.

'Chocolate's made of cocoa beans,' Crystal counters. 'It's a vegetable. True fact.'

Joy rolls her eyes.

Sabina tries out her high five for the third time.

'Wotcha, Beanie,' Crystal says, returning it. 'All right?'

Sabina nods. I may be reading too much into this, but I think there's a light behind my child's eyes that's been missing for a long time. Her face, so often totally impassive, seems a little more animated. I hope it's not simply that I'm wishing it so.

'We could walk round the garden after breakfast,' Joy suggests to me. 'See what there is to pick for a meal this evening. Not much at this time of year, of course.'

'I'd like to cook for you all again,' I say. 'If that's all right.' When I was at home my only solace was to hide in the kitchen and cook. It was the one and only thing I could do to please my husband. 'I don't wish to impose.'

'Sounds good to me,' Crystal says. 'Impose away. I'm going to get as fat as a house with you here.' Though there are plenty

117

of empty seats, she nudges my daughter off her own chair, then pulls her back on to her knee and wraps her arms round her. 'We love your mum's cooking, don't we, Bean?'

Sabina nods vigorously.

'I'm afraid I don't really like foreign food,' Joy says. 'I have a delicate palate.'

'Bollocks, you do,' Crystal says. 'You're just an old stick-in-the-mud.'

'I could try to make a dish that I think you'd like.'

'Well,' Joy says, looking pointedly at Crystal. 'If it's not too spicy.'

'Get some chilli down her neck,' Crystal says. 'A bit of fire in your belly might warm you up, Joy.'

I smile sympathetically at the older lady. 'It's fine to like what you like, I think.'

She looks pleased by that.

Crystal leans in to Sabina conspiratorially. 'Nick a bit of Hayden's toast for me,' she stage-whispers. 'Look, Hayden!' She points to the garden and, obligingly, Hayden swivels his head.

Sabina, quick as a flash, reaches out and steals a slice of toast from his plate. Crystal bites it quickly as Hayden looks back, pretending to be shocked. My daughter covers her mouth with both hands and I hope for a moment that she might burst out with a spontaneous giggle. It's not to be. But we all laugh at her antics and I feel this is a good environment for her. They don't tiptoe around her and treat her as if she's odd or special. They treat her like a normal little girl, and for that my heart is glad.

'What about a birthday tickle?' Crystal says, and launches into a gentle tickling assault on Sabina.

My daughter throws back her head and opens her mouth wide. It's very good to see. For months her face has been solemn, impassive, dead, and it's almost as if I can see her coming back to life before my eyes.

Hayden and I exchange a glance and he gives me a surreptitious wink. He too can see that my daughter will be happy here.

This is a good place for us to be, I think. A very good place.

# Chapter Twenty-four

When I've cleared up after breakfast, Joy folds her newspaper and makes noises to say that she's ready to take me on my tour as I've requested. Quickly I wipe my hands.

'Come with us, my daughter?'

Sabina shakes her head and leans against Crystal. She's happy where she is and that's nice.

Joy leads the way into the garden and I follow close behind. I must be very careful not to step on her toes as this is clearly her domain.

'I like spring,' she says over her shoulder to me. 'When the garden lies dormant, trying to survive over the cold winter, it's easy to forget the gorgeous flowers that bide their time beneath the surface, waiting to surprise you all over again with their beauty.'

'I feel like that myself,' I confess to Joy. 'I've been in the dark and cold, waiting until I could unfurl my petals to the sunshine again.'

'Oh, you darling girl,' Joy says, frowning. 'It must have been a terrible time for you.'

'Yes. Now I hope that there'll be no more winter for us,' I say. 'My dream is that we'll always live in sunshine.'

‘I hope so too.’ Self-consciously, she touches my arm. Then, in a voice that’s not steady, she surprises me by confiding, ‘I’m no stranger to domestic difficulties myself. Of a different nature to yours,’ she adds, ‘but my marriage wasn’t a walk in the park either.’

‘I’m sorry to hear that.’

She waves my comment away with a flick of her hand. I’d thought that Joy was too strong a person to have suffered in this way, but she doesn’t offer any more and I don’t like to ask.

We stand together on the terrace, gazing out over the lawn and the expanse of garden that stretches away from us. ‘It looks lovely,’ I tell her. ‘A credit to you.’

For the moment, she seems lost for words, so I take in the view before me. At the bottom of the garden there’s a variety of mature trees that screen off the surrounding houses. There’s also a summerhouse, but it doesn’t look as if it’s ever used. The borders, to an untrained eye, appear to be immaculately tended. Joy obviously lavishes a lot of love on this garden.

‘There’s a wide variety of herbs on the patio,’ she says, brisk again, and we go to look at the arrangement of tubs sheltered against the wall of the house. ‘Feel free to use those as you will. There’s parsley, sage, marjoram, thyme – three different varieties, including lemon – mint and rosemary. The chives grow like weeds, but they look very pretty with their purple pompoms in bloom.’

I recognise all of these. It makes me think of my daddy, bent over in the sunshine, tending our small patch of garden at home. The things he grew there, you can’t imagine. My grandparents too had lush and productive land that they tended. I’d like to think that green fingers run in the family but, to be frank, I wouldn’t know where to start.

‘When I was a child in Sri Lanka, every year we used to visit my uncle,’ I tell Joy. ‘He lives in a place called Matale, high in the hills near Kandy, and runs a spice farm. We used to love it there. He grows cinnamon, pepper, nutmeg, clove and mace. It's a very beautiful place.' If I close my eyes, I can recall all of the scents, the muskiness of the damp soil and the humid heat of the jungle of leaves, Hinni and me running between the towering trees. It makes me long to go home. 'My mummy taught me how to use all the flavours in her family recipes.'

'I used to enjoy cooking,' Joy says. 'Baking especially. The boys used to love my cakes and biscuits. But there's no point in baking for yourself, is there?'

'Could you show me how to bake, Joy?' I ask. 'I'm good with spicy meals and curries, but I'm not so very good with cakes.'

'Perhaps I could do that,' she says grudgingly. 'Though when I'll find the time, I don't know. Shall we look at the rest of this garden or not?'

I fall into step behind her as she marches past the beds, barking out the names of plants as we go. 'The snowdrops have all gone, but the crocuses add a spot of colour.' She points out some yellow and blue flowers. 'That's forsythia.' A shrub with delicate yellow flowers. 'The spring colours are so bright.'

'That's because they know we need a lift after all the greyness of winter.'

Joy turns to me. 'I've done all this myself. Hayden's not the slightest bit interested. Such a shame.'

'I'm sure he appreciates it.'

'I'm not entirely sure he even notices it,' she counters. 'He rarely comes out of his room, let alone ventures into the garden.' She shakes her head, as if she simply can't understand it. 'You have to be busy in the garden in spring. There's a lot of tidying up, a lot of preparation for summer.' We go through an avenue of eight trees in full blossom, heading towards an area that's been put aside for vegetables.

'Flowering cherry.' Joy points up at their delicate pink

flowers. She plucks a single bloom and hands it to me. 'Beautiful, but one stiff wind and this will all be gone.'

With questions burning in my mind, I risk asking her something personal. 'How long have your children lived overseas, Joy?'

She doesn't look at me when she replies. 'Malcolm, my eldest, he's been in Hong Kong for ten years. He has an English wife, Pat, and two lovely daughters, Kerry and Emma. They're sixteen and fourteen now.'

'You've never been there?'

'No . . . no,' she blusters. 'They ask me. Regularly. It's not for me though.' She examines a bush for some imagined flaw. 'Who'd look after the garden, if I jumped on a plane every ten minutes? It would have gone to rack and ruin by the time I got back.'

I don't point out that, from what little I know about Hayden, I'm sure he could afford to employ a gardener, even on a temporary basis.

We march on to the greenhouse. Inside it's very warm, heady with the smell of damp earth and vegetation.

'Tomatoes,' she says, pointing to some green shoots. 'There's three different varieties – Gardener's Delight, San Marzano and Costoluto Fiorentino. We'll be sick to the back teeth of them in a couple of months.'

'I could make tomato curry and serve it with *pol mallun*, a coconut chutney, and a traditional Sri Lankan dish, string hoppers.'

My companion looks slightly alarmed by this suggestion.

'Soup,' she says. 'They're good for tomato soup. The ones that stay green are excellent for chutney. There's some basil here too,' Joy continues. 'Don't know if that goes into the kind of thing you like to cook?'

'I will try it.'

'Basil's probably more for Italian food.'

'Do you eat that?'

'Oh, no,' Joys says, looking horrified at the thought. 'Too much garlic. Plays havoc with my digestion.' She goes back outside and strides towards a bank of raised beds. I trot behind her.

'I've got potatoes here.' Joy points them all out as she talks. 'And spinach. Cabbage. There's one or two cauliflowers left and a few late beetroots. Some carrots which will be ready soon. The runner beans are getting going in the greenhouse and I'll plant them out here when it's time.'

'I do a nice side dish with beans fried Gujarati-style with chilli.'

Joy wrinkles her nose. 'Courgettes. We'll be eating those until they're coming out of our ears too.'

I'll try to think of interesting ways to present them, perhaps as a curry or as a pickle. 'Already, I'm quite excited about the opportunity to cook with such lovely home-grown produce.'

She beams at that. 'You're in for a treat. You've not seen the fruit yet.'

We pass through an opening in a hedge. Beyond it there are fruit cages and more raised beds. I can tell that this is where the rhubarb came from.

'Apple trees,' Joy says. 'Some bakers, some eaters. Plums and pears, but they've been a bit patchy the last few years. I could teach you how to rustle up a nice crumble. Stephen was always very keen on a crumble.' She smiles sadly. 'He always puts that in his letters.'

'Your other son?' I venture.

'He's the younger one, but he's lived abroad for many years. Likes the lifestyle and the sunshine. We don't get a lot of that here. He's been all over the place. I can hardly keep up. They're all in Singapore now and he's married a girl from there.'

'They have children too?'

'Three. The girls are four and two. They've a new baby boy as well. He's called Jay and must be six months old now.' She turns her gaze on me. 'And, before you ask, no, I haven't been out to see them either.'

'Wouldn't you like to visit your new grandson?'

'Of course I would,' Joy snaps. 'But it's just not possible. I don't fly. I don't eat foreign food. I haven't got that kind of money. I have to be content to wait until they come here.'

'We can do anything that we want to, Joy,' I say softly. 'A few days ago I was a person who dared not speak to her own shadow. I found a way to change that.'

'You're young,' she scoffs. 'You have your whole life ahead of you.'

'I *am* young, but I've wasted many years being scared of life.'

'I know all about that.' She shrugs and her shoulders look burdened. 'All water under the bridge now. Anyway, you can't teach an old dog new tricks. I'm seventy-five. Ancient in today's eyes. I'm at the tail end of my life.'

I take her hand and tuck it into the crook of my elbow as we turn back towards the house. 'All the more reason to enjoy every day and experience new things.'

# Chapter Twenty-five

Hayden felt weirdly energised today. It was as if he could actually feel the blood surging round his veins. Something he hadn't felt in a long time. Every nerve in his skin was alive and zinging. It was as if he'd just bounded off stage at Wembley Arena, high on adrenalin, drunk on the ecstasy of the crowd.

If that's what a good night's sleep and some coffee and toast for breakfast could do, then he needed more of them in his life.

It had felt strangely good to be sitting at the breakfast table with the rag-tag of life that constituted this household. Not that Crystal – or any of the ladies – would be happy to be classed as rag-tag. It was an arrangement that shouldn't work but somehow did. They coped very well with his eccentricities and he with theirs.

He wanted to do something. Anything. He didn't know what. Leap tall buildings with one single bound. Unless he channelled some energy, he'd end up pacing the house relentlessly. Joy and Ayesha had gone for a tour of the garden. He could follow them, he supposed, but gardening wasn't really his thing and he felt as if Ayesha wanted to spend some time alone bonding with Joy. That had to be a good thing.

Crystal had picked up a glossy magazine and was glancing through it with the kid still nestled on her lap. She looked comfortable with the child, and he realised that she really would make a great mum. They were both engrossed in whatever the current gossip was. He couldn't stand to look at the glossies any more, even though the minutiae of his own life no longer graced the pages.

Hayden pushed away from the table.

Crystal glanced up. 'All right?' she asked.

'I'm great,' he said and, even to himself, he sounded perplexed by it.

She grinned back over Sabina's head.

He didn't want to go down into the basement to work out. It was another glorious spring day and he wanted to feel fresh air blowing through the house.

Not knowing what else to do, he made his way into the living room. The cushions on the sofa still bore the indents from where he and Ayesha had sat until late reading *Bridget Jones's Diary*. She'd made small steps forward and her reading wasn't nearly as bad as she imagined. It had been difficult to start with because the book had been one of Laura's favourites. He'd always asked her how she could still laugh at it when she'd read it time and time again. It was a keeper, she'd teased, just like him.

The room was dark and he threw back the curtains on the French doors to the garden. The sunlight flooded in, catching a flurry of dust motes in the air, and he opened the doors wide to let in the day. He watched Ayesha and Joy conducting a tour of the borders and then disappearing down towards Joy's sanctuary, the vegetable plot. He should eat more fresh food, he thought, put some strength back into his body. It was about time he went into the garden too. He couldn't remember the last time he'd been to see what was going on out there. Joy was always busy and he should take more notice of what she did. But then, it was fair to say that he hadn't been interested in very much of anything in recent times.

Ayesha was a nice woman, Hayden thought. Quiet, uncertain of herself on the surface, but he could see that there was an inner resolve, and he could only admire that. For someone so timid on the surface, there was a little bit of feistiness lurking beneath it. Already a few of her questions had left him breathless with their directness. He hoped she would blossom here, lose the fear that obviously stalked her. It had torn him up inside when she thought he was going to raise a hand to her last night. What sort of a bloke had she been married to? If she could fight back from what she'd been through, why couldn't he do the same?

When Ayesha and Joy moved out of sight, he turned back towards the room and the sunlight fell on the piano. He sat on the stool, as he'd done in the moonlight the other night, but this time the energy felt very different. This time he wasn't fearful. There was a trembling deep down in his stomach, but it felt hopeful. Eager.

He let his fingers dance on the keys. Hesitant at first, he tried a couple of classics, nothing too threatening, nothing too emotional. There were a few stumbles, a few halting trills, but it wasn't too bad from someone who was so rusty. He couldn't, however, quite make his voice come again. That seemed to be beyond him. Every time he opened his mouth to try, he could feel his throat tighten, his vocal cords protest, his tongue seemingly grow to twice its normal size.

That was OK. For now. He'd proved last night that his voice was still in there somewhere. Good things came to those who waited. He'd have to be patient and take baby steps on his road to recovery.

Perhaps the next thing to do would be to work through his

own songs, on the piano. He tried some of his album tracks. Songs that he hadn't played for so long, he struggled to remember parts of them. There was a vague attempt to hum along, but even that didn't work. His mouth was too dry, too fearful.

As he was working his way up to trying out some of his better-known hits, a movement caught his eye and he looked up. Standing at the foot of the piano, still and silent, was Sabina. She studied him intently.

'Hey,' he said. 'Have you been there long?'

She nodded.

'I'm a bit rusty. I haven't played for ages.'

The child shrugged.

'I'm going to practise though. Sometimes, if you don't use it, you lose it.' He tinkled the ivories again and she smiled. 'Can you play the piano?'

She shook her head.

'Want to try?'

A nod, but she stayed where she was.

'Come on then.' He waved her towards him and budged up on the piano stool so that there was room for her next to him.

Hesitantly, Sabina inched forward and sat down. There was something about her calm composure that settled him too.

'Right,' he said. 'This is called "Chopsticks".' He played the silly ditty that he'd learned in childhood. The tune that had started him on the road to learning the piano and, ultimately, his love of music. 'Want to try?'

She turned her face to him, her eyes widening slightly.

'OK. A piano keyboard starts at A and runs to G.' He showed her on the keys. 'Like the alphabet. Except it goes A to G all the way along and each group sounds a bit higher.'

He hoped that he wasn't making it too complicated for a kid, but it looked as if she was taking it all in.

'Then, using your index finger on each hand' – he wiggled

them at her to show her which ones they were and, to his relief, Sabina copied him – 'you put them on the F and the G key.' He guided her to the right place. 'All you do now is press them six times.'

She did as she was told.

'Then move your left finger to the E key. Like this.'

He carried on teaching her the rest of the tune and, a diligent student, she didn't put a foot, or rather a finger, wrong. For a young child, her concentration was remarkable and in a short time she'd learned the basics of the melody.

'Now,' Hayden said. 'We'll try it together.'

They started out very slowly and went through the notes several times. 'Now faster,' he instructed, and they picked up speed. 'Faster.'

Up they went again. 'Keep doing the same thing. Don't change.'

So while Sabina played the same repeating tune, he added a second part and some frills and twiddles. Then he ended with a big flourish.

The girl smiled shyly at him.

'High five.' He held up his palm and she met it. 'Well done. That was *totally* cool.'

With a self-satisfied smile, but without a single word, Sabina stood up and walked out of the room. Behind her she left a man grinning like a loon with an unexpected tear in his eye.

# Chapter Twenty-six

When I return to the kitchen, Crystal is still sitting reading her magazine. She has her feet up on the chair next to her and her dressing gown has fallen open, revealing an awful lot of her skin. I try to avert my eyes.

'I've got to get off to the day centre,' Joy says. 'The other old biddies will wonder where I am.'

She bustles out and soon the front door closes behind her.

'She had a slight stroke,' Crystal says, nodding after Joy. 'Not long after she moved in here. She was only in hospital for a week and then I looked after her at home. She was a bloody nightmare.'

That makes me smile. I can imagine that Joy wouldn't be a gracious patient.

'She made a brilliant recovery. There's a bit of weakness in her right side and she limps a bit when she's tired. Amazing really. She still goes down to some sort of day centre place where they sent her for a bit of rehab or something. I don't know what she gets out of it now. I think she just likes to go and boss everyone around.'

Perhaps she simply needs friends of her own age to socialise with. I know that's something I've missed dreadfully over the years and now, suddenly, I have a new friend in Crystal. It's a great pleasure to me.

'Joy said that there'd been difficulty in her marriage.'

'Not in the way you might be thinking. From what I can gather, her husband was ill for a long time. I'm not sure what the problem was, but he was bedridden for years. Joy was his sole carer. It was really hard on her boys when they were growing up. She said that they had to do a lot for themselves as she was so tied in looking after her husband. I don't think he bore his illness well. Awkward old bugger by all accounts. That's probably why Joy's so prickly too. Sad really. The minute their sons finished university they were off and never looked back. I don't think they wanted to come home again to all that illness. That's what Joy implied, anyway. I've never met either of them. I've seen photographs though. Good-looking kids. And they've done really well for themselves. Joy doesn't say too much, but I know she's very proud of them.'

'She must miss them very much.'

'When they went her life got smaller and smaller,' Crystal says. 'Everything revolved round her husband. She rarely went out, never socialised. I think she was so bound to him that she stopped being able to see beyond her four walls. All credit to her, she was dedicated to him until the end, but it meant she lost her zest for life, her sense of adventure.'

'Then he left her without money?'

'He'd made some *seriously* bad investments. They reckon whatever he had might have affected his mental faculties. Could be tittle-tattle though. I don't know the ins and outs of what went on. You know Joy: she gets really tetchy if you dig too much. All I know is that, after a lifetime of working and caring, she's now got jack shit.'

'That must be very hard for her.'

132

'Bloody nightmare,' Crystal agrees. 'God only knows what she'd have done if Hayden hadn't let her stay here. Perhaps she would have had to go to one of her sons then, whether she wanted to or not.'

'That's so sad.'

'We try to look after her, but she's an awkward old cuss. Quite bitter about it too, I think. She's too independent by half as well.'

'That's probably what keeps her going,' I offer.

'You're probably right.' Crystal shudders. 'Anyway, let's talk about something else. All this doom and gloom is bringing me down. Joy will be all right. She's one tough cookie.'

I realise that my daughter's not here. 'Where is Sabina?'

'She went upstairs to get a book,' Crystal says.

I take this opportunity to talk earnestly to my friend. 'Crystal, I need to find a job. Something very quickly. We have little money and I must provide for Sabina. Are there any job vacancies where you work?'

'At the club?' Crystal throws her head back and laughs. 'You want to be a dancer?'

'I'll do anything. I have inadequate reading and writing skills in English, but I can dance a little.' In truth, I've had no reason to dance for a long time. My efforts last night proved that it doesn't come easily to me now. 'In traditional Sri Lankan style.'

'I don't think you know what kind of dancing I do, Ayesha.' Crystal is more serious now. 'All I do is jiggle my tits in the faces of sweaty businessmen.'

'Oh.' I'm taken aback by this. 'Really?' I imagined her in a show or cabaret, wearing a spangly costume, with feathers in her hair.

'*Really*.' She nods and I can tell this is no joke. 'It's a total dump, catering for total sleazebags.'

133

I thought that Crystal would work somewhere wonderful and glamorous. It seems this isn't the case.

'It's a lapdancing club, sweetie.' She pulls a rueful face at me. 'Can you see why I think you're not suited?'

'Yes. I can see.'

'Don't worry.' She pats my hand. 'We'll find you something.'

She must see dejection written on my face as she says, 'You could show me how you dance though. That'd be fun. I'd love to see it. I know nothing about your culture.'

'I have no music.'

'Let's go into the living room, see if we can find a bit of "Jai Ho" on the iPod. Will that do?'

'It's Indian, not Sri Lankan, but it will be fine.' I wring my hands. 'At Sabina's school they did some Bollywood dancing. This song was her favourite and when my husband was out we'd sometimes sneak to play it. She used to sing along at the top of her voice.'

The thought saddens me.

'She will do again, one day,' my friend assures me. 'Just keep believing.'

Crystal takes me by the hand and we go through to the living room. Thankfully, it's deserted. The French doors are open and a lovely breeze blows through the room. Crystal goes to the iPod and flicks through it.

'Here we go,' she says eventually.

While I take my place in the middle of the floor, Crystal curls up on the sofa – my audience of one.

'I'm embarrassed now,' I tell her. 'I haven't done this for a long time.' I remember last night when I was dancing and Hayden came in. I'm ashamed now that I thought he was going to strike me. I have to be stronger to rid myself of those bad memories.

'It's a bit of fun,' Crystal says. 'That's all. I'm not the judge on a talent show.'

134

Just in time for my performance, Sabina comes into the room and snuggles up against her new auntie on the sofa. She expresses no surprise that her mama is dancing.

Crystal presses the remote control and 'Jai Ho' starts up.

We have many different traditional dances in my home country: the Kandyan dances of the hill country; Pahatharata Natum, which is from the low country; and Sabaragamuwa dances, which are a mix of both. Each style of dance has different movements, rhythms and meanings and a special kind of drum is used according to the dance. There's been no reason for me to continue with traditional dancing since my marriage. All this I remember from my childhood, and I'm saddened that my daughter knows nothing of it. She was born in England and has never been home to the country of her ancestors. If I work hard and do well, perhaps one day I may take her to visit her grandparents. They're not getting younger and I hate to think that they'll never see her.

Since I've been here, I've written to my parents to tell them of our circumstances and am dreading the moment they receive my letter. The impression they have of their daughter's perfect life will be shattered for ever. I can only hope that I've managed to convey that, even though our situation is precarious, I'm happier now than I've been for some considerable time.

I think back to the things I did with my parents when I was a small girl. I'd like to take my own daughter to the Temple of the Tooth, and to the ancient ruined city of Sigiriya. She should see the verdant tea plantations which stretch out across the hills of my land, ride on an elephant and drink water straight from the coconut. I'd like her to visit the home of my birth, to feel the hot, white sand beneath her feet and hear the rush of the clear blue Indian Ocean.

Despite the uplifting music, I feel melancholy in my heart. I start to dance, showing some simple, elegant moves. It seems strange to do them wearing my new clothing. My dress feels restrictive, and it makes me think how very comfortable a shalwar kameez is. One day, when I feel safe again, I may wear my traditional dress once more. Though I'll never buy khaki. I'll always wear light and beautiful colours.

Then the sound takes over and my spirit rises. The hands are very expressive in Sri Lankan dance and I twist them this way and that, trying to remember the correct moves. When the song clicks off, both Sabina and Crystal clap enthusiastically.

'Oh, I can't sit here,' Crystal says, jumping up. 'You got to teach me how to throw some of those shapes. Come on, Beanie.' She hustles my daughter up too and presses the remote again. For the second time, 'Jai Ho' rings out.

Crystal and Sabina stand next to me and I go through my little routine again. They try to copy me.

'Bloody hell, woman,' Crystal complains. 'You look like a delicate little bird, and I look like a flipping vulture.'

'Just follow me.'

'I'm trying!'

We start the music again and, though Sabina fares very well, we all end up giggling. Though my daughter makes no sound, she's shaking with laughter.

'I think we'll do freestyle,' Crystal says. 'I'm too rubbish at that.' She cranks up the music and we all hold hands and dance round the living room, skipping in a circle and, two of us, singing our hearts out.

As we are having so much fun, none of us notices that, out in the garden, Hayden is watching us all with a happy smile on his lips.

# Chapter Twenty-seven

I hope that we'll all have dinner together again tonight. With Joy's blessing, I collect vegetables from the garden, taking care to choose the best ones or use things that are coming to an end. I have a small trug which Joy gave me and it's filled with lovely, fresh produce. I have a beetroot, an onion, a cauliflower and some potatoes. I've also picked some mint. They all smell wonderful, of freshness, of earth.

Crystal takes me down to the big freezer in the garage where all the meat is kept and I select a bag of stewing lamb to make into a rogan josh for tomorrow night.

Looking around me, I count that there are three cars parked in here, all under dust covers.

'Does no one drive these?' I ask, feeling as if I must whisper.

'No. Hayden hasn't been out in them for years. He used to have someone ferry him around, but he rarely went out even then. Now he doesn't go out or drive at all.'

'Since Laura?' This seems to have been such a terrible moment in his life that all of his pain stems from it.

'Yeah.'

'He must have loved her very much.'

'He adored her. By all accounts.'

'You never knew her?'

'No. She'd already gone when I met Hayd.'

'She looks very beautiful.'

'A stunner,' Crystal agrees. 'You should see some of the pictures of her in the glossies. Hot!' She makes a sizzling noise. 'When I first met him I think he was trying to drink himself into an early grave. Thank goodness he knocked that on the head. You might not believe it, but he's a lot better now. He's still not the same man he was, though.'

I'd like to ask Crystal what happened to make Laura leave, but I daren't intrude. Hayden would have told me if he'd wanted me to know.

Crystal waves a hand at the unused vehicles. 'The cars sit here in mothballs.' She runs a hand over one of the covers. 'Can you drive?'

I shake my head. 'I'd like to learn. One day.'

'It's a nightmare in London,' Crystal says. 'The traffic's ridiculous and the cost of insurance is sky-high. You might as well get a bus or a tube everywhere.'

It will be a long time before I can afford to run a car anyway, so it's not a pressing problem. But how can anyone have so many cars that are simply unused?

'I think you're good for him, Ayesha,' she says. 'Between us we might make him a fully functioning human being again.'

I'd like to think that.

'Now,' Crystal says. 'Let's get that dinner on before I starve.'

Back in the kitchen, I make some seasonal vegetable dumplings and cauliflower pakora that I'll serve with a spicy *kadhi* yoghurt curry. For Joy, I'll make a cool raita with mint. I'll also make a side dish of saag bhaji with the spinach, and fry some potatoes.

The cupboard is well stocked with spices, but I'm missing some fresh chillies and coriander.

'I'll pop out to the grocers up the road,' Crystal says. 'Shopping I can do. Want to come, Beanie?'

'I'd rather she stay here.' I feel myself panic at the thought of her going out without me. 'If you don't mind.'

'Of course not. But I'd look after her, Ayesha. You know that. I love her to bits.' Crystal squeezes my daughter and then picks up her keys. Sabina looks as if she desperately wants to go with Crystal but, of course, she says nothing. 'I'll be back in ten.'

Sabina watches, chin in hands, while I make puri breads with flour and caraway seeds, which I'll deep-fry before we need them, so they're nice and warm. Then I start to prepare my vegetables.

Before long, Crystal returns with my supplies. 'Good Christ, Ayesha.' She stares at all the food that's now spread out on the counter. 'Have you never heard of the perils of carbs?'

'No,' I say honestly.

'I'm going to have to start working out with Hayden,' she says.

'Did I hear my name?' Hayden comes into the kitchen. He also casts his eye over my ingredients. 'Looks good. What's on the menu?'

I run through my plan and he raises an eyebrow, which seems to be approving.

'Will you join us?'

'Go on, Misery Guts,' Crystal urges. 'That'll be two nights in a row you won't have hidden in your room by yourself.'

Hayden grins at her. 'When you put it so nicely, how can I possibly refuse?'

'Look at this lot.' Crystal waves her arms, encompassing my efforts. 'This is better than toast. We hit paydirt when Ayesha rocked up here,' and she bounds out happily from the kitchen.

'We did,' Hayden says softly and, even though I hadn't planned it, our eyes meet.

It leaves me flustered. 'I'd better get on.' I busy myself.

'I went out into the garden earlier.' Hayden comes up behind me, searching, I think, for something to nibble on, but finds nothing to his taste. I hope it will all be more appealing when cooked. 'It looks great out there.'

'You should tell Joy. She'd be very pleased,' I say.

'I'll do that.' Then he says, 'I saw you dancing. Through the open window.'

That makes me flush more.

'It looked like you were all having fun.'

'We were.'

It seems that I've slipped so easily into my new life. Cosseted within these walls, I feel as if I don't have to look over my shoulder. Here I can pretend all that I've been through simply doesn't exist. My thoughts have turned very little to my husband or what he might be feeling now, and perhaps that's callous of me. My feeling is that if you do not love, then you will not be loved in return. I'm trying to change my ways – to be stronger, more assertive – and my husband must also change his or he'll always be alone. I hope that I'm safe here. How would Suresh begin to find me? Surely there's no way. If I live a quiet and anonymous life, then will I be free of him for ever?

'Do you want to read some more later tonight?' Hayden asks.

'I'd like that. When I've put Sabina to bed?'

He nods. 'I was teaching her to play "Chopsticks" today. On the piano.'

I'm surprised at that because, of course, she didn't mention it. 'Did she do well?'

'Yes. She's a bright child. A very quick learner.'

'Thank you. It's nice of you to take time with her.'

'She's a great kid.' A flush colours Hayden's cheeks, and when I gaze at him he quickly says, 'Can I do anything? Set the table?'

'That would be very kind.' I return to my peeling and preparation.

'You don't have to cook every night,' Hayden says. 'We won't expect it. As Crystal says, until you arrived, we all pretty much lived on ready-meals or toast.'

'But you have cupboards full of lovely spices and a garden filled with fresh vegetables.'

'And all wasted on us. Until now.'

'I was a housewife,' I tell Hayden. 'I had very little to fill my days but cooking and cleaning. I tried to be the very best at it that I could.'

'You never went out with friends?'

'I wasn't allowed.'

'That must have been hard.'

'I suppose that it's something I got used to.'

Then we both run out of words and I return to my preparations. 'You must tell me if you want me to stop cooking,' I inform him. 'I don't wish to offend anyone.'

'Ayesha,' he says. 'You're fitting in here brilliantly. It's as if you've been here for weeks already.'

'Thank you.'

'I hope you'll be able to stay here for a long time.'

I smile at him. 'I hope so too.' With the cameras and the high walls, and the support of my new friends, I feel that nothing can touch us here.

# Chapter Twenty-eight

In another house in another city, Suresh splashed whisky into glasses. It was a supermarket brand, better than nothing but all he could afford for now. All that was about to change though. The three men sitting with him downed the rough spirit in one and he instantly refilled the glasses.

Suresh spread his hands on the kitchen table. 'So no one's seen her?'

They all shook their heads.

Suresh breathed out through his nose. His parents were still insisting that they knew nothing too. He was sure they were lying to him. But what was he to do? Beat it out of them? Some days he was sorely tempted. It was maddening. Ayesha must be somewhere. You couldn't simply fade from existence. 'Smith, you've spoken to all your contacts in the city and there's been no sightings of her or the kid?'

'She's not in Milton Keynes, Suresh. I'm sure of it,' he said in reply. He was in his mid-forties, white and built like a brick out-house. His face bore the marks of someone who had once been a boxer. Suresh had worked with him on many occasions. They'd turned over more than a few houses together in their time, stolen some tasty high-end cars to order. These boys were a good team to bring in when anyone needed money collecting or they wanted the frighteners put on people, and Smith was a useful man to have at your back when things got tricky. He also knew how to teach someone a lesson that they wouldn't forget in a hurry.

It was all small-fry stuff, though, and they needed to move up on to a bigger stage. If they were going to make some serious cash they needed to start playing in the first division. Now was their time. Trust Ayesha to put a spanner in the works by going missing. He could well do without the aggro of getting her back.

Suresh clenched his fists. How could she and the girl simply disappear? He'd offered bribes, he'd dealt out threats and still there'd been no news of her. 'What about you?'

The man next to him pushed Ayesha's picture on to the table. Even looking at her made Suresh's blood boil. Flynn was also a long-standing associate. He could get hold of anything you needed, no matter how hot. 'I took this down to the station and showed it around,' Flynn said. 'Nothing. No one had seen hide nor hair of her.'

Suresh's younger brother, Arunja, piped up. 'You should never have let a woman give you the runaround, Suresh,' he taunted. 'You must be going soft in your old age.'

Suresh fumed inside. Normally Suresh was top dog, and his brother was enjoying his discomfort. His wife had made him a laughing stock in the heart of his own community. That was unforgivable. When he got her back – and he would – he'd make her life a misery.

'I did do better at the Coachway though,' Flynn said. 'One of the staff reckoned she'd been in there. Couldn't be certain, but he thought she'd got the first bus out to Victoria.'

Suresh raised his eyebrows. 'London? She knows no one in London.'

The man shrugged. 'That's what he said. Thought she looked shit-scared, and there can't be many women on their own with a kid catching a bus at half-four in the morning.'

He chewed at his fingernail. So it appeared she might have taken a bus to London.

'What do you want us to do now, Suresh?'

'I'm thinking.'

Smith helped himself to more whisky and passed the bottle to Flynn. 'We could put some feelers out there. Send a few lads down to look around.'

'It's a tough call,' Flynn said. 'You could just let her go.'

'Never.' Suresh took his turn with the whisky. It burned his throat, but not as much as his heart burned with hatred for his wife and what she'd done to him.

'It's going to be a hell of a lot of expense, Suresh. Had to bung a twenty to the bloke at the Coachway to get a peep out of him.'

People always knew the value of information. Suresh opened his wallet, peeled off a note and slid it across the table to him. 'No one will be out of pocket.'

'Thanks, mate.' Flynn palmed the cash and pocketed it. 'It's not just the money though. If you want to get her back, it's going to be a lot of trouble too.'

'There'll be a way,' Suresh countered. 'And I'll find it.'

Arunja tipped his chair back and put his hands behind his head. 'London is a very big place.'

Suresh narrowed his eyes. 'Not big enough.'

# Chapter Twenty-nine

'What's a dildo?' I look up from *Bridget Jones's Diary*.

'Good grief,' Hayden says. 'Don't ask me that. What page are we on?'

Hayden and I are sitting on the sofa together in the living room. Sabina's already tucked up in bed and the night is drawing in. I tell him the page number.

'Oh.' He looks slightly pale. 'Long way to go yet.' He rubs at his chin and I see pink spots bloom on his cheek.

'I've embarrassed you.'

'No. Yes.' He laughs. 'It's a girl thing. You need to ask Crystal.'

'Or Joy.'

'Not Joy.' Hayden shakes his head vigorously. '*Definitely* not Joy.' He points at my page. 'Move on.'

'It's a bad word?'

'It's a word that I think, I *hope*, you don't need to know.'

Something about his discomfort makes me want to smile.

'No laughing at me,' he teases. 'The next book we read is going to be a classic. Jane Austen or something. We'll be on much safer ground with Austen. I'm pretty sure she didn't have ... those things.'

I'm secretly pleased to hear that Hayden is already thinking about a 'next' book.

'We'll skip that bit for now. Pick it up here.' He points to a line and obediently I continue reading.

My reading is slow but I'm very much enjoying it. Bridget is a funny lady, and already I can see why Hayden's girlfriend would have liked to read it over and over.

I'm trying to form each word carefully, in the same way I used to show Sabina. Now she reads her books silently and I don't know what goes on in her head or how she's progressing. At her last school, her teachers always assured me that her schoolwork wasn't suffering, and I can only hope that they were right. I pray, for the millionth time, that one day my beloved daughter will come back to me.

Crystal has already left for work this evening and Joy has retired to her bed. I know that she likes to go upstairs early and watch her own television. It's a lonely life for her, I feel, despite her love of the garden and her trips to the day centre. I'm sure she'd be less grumbly if her family were around her to bring love into her life.

The evening is warm still and the French doors are open in the living room. There's so little air that it doesn't even stir the gauzy curtains. I lift my loose, heavy hair from my neck. Sometimes a plait is a very practical style.

'You hair looks lovely when it's down,' Hayden says shyly.

'Thank you.' I stare fixedly at the page in front of me.

'Now I've embarrassed *you*,' he says, 'when I didn't mean to.'

'I'm not accustomed to compliments.'

'That's a shame.' He lets out a shaky breath. 'Laura had long blonde hair. She was very beautiful. I used to tell her as often as I could.'

'I believe that's her photograph on the piano?'

146

He nods. 'It's the only one I can bear to look at. The others make me too sad. There are so many stored on the office computer. Hundreds and hundreds of photographs of me and Laura together, lying somewhere between reality and cyberspace.'

'One day you'll be happy to look at them.'

'I hope so.' There's darkness in his eyes, but somehow I don't think he looks quite as bleak as the day when we arrived.

'It's nice having a kid here,' he says, as if he has read my mind. 'Even though Sabina doesn't talk, she brightens the place up.'

'I'm glad to hear it.'

'Laura and I wanted to have children together,' he confides.

'I'm very sorry that it never happened for you.' I want to lay my hand on his arm, but I'm afraid to touch him.

'Shall we get back to Bridget?' he says brusquely. 'It's getting late.'

Happily, I read on. The more I practise, the easier I find the words. The chapters are short and I turn the pages quickly until I stumble over a word. 'I don't know this one.'

'Fuckwittage,' Hayden says, clearing his throat. 'That's another one we might well skip over. Don't use it when the vicar comes to tea.' He takes the book off me and closes it. 'I'm beginning to think we should have gone for something altogether more wholesome than Bridget.'

I laugh. 'I think she's fun.'

'I'm sure you do.'

'She's like Crystal,' I say. 'Fearless. I'd like to be more like her.'

'I think you're fine exactly as you are,' Hayden says. Then he laughs. 'Sorry, that sounded like something Daniel Cleaver would say.'

'I think he sounds like a lot of trouble already. Bridget should only go out with nice Mark Darcy.'

'But women don't always choose the nice guy. They like the bastard.'

'Do they? Then they don't know what it's really like to be with a ... a ... bastard.'

'No,' Hayden says. 'I'm sure you're right. Sorry to raise it. I didn't mean to make you think of home.'

'I didn't choose a bad man,' I tell him. 'My mummy and daddy arranged the marriage for me. They thought that they were doing the right thing. Suresh's parents were distant cousins and they'd been told that the family were well connected.'

'But they weren't?'

'No.' I take a deep breath. 'Not really. I think they gave my parents a false picture of their wealth and standing. They had much by my parents' standards, but, as I was to discover, little in Western terms.'

'That must have been tough.'

'Not so,' I say. 'I could have borne that. I'm not a person for whom money is a god.'

'Me neither,' Hayden says. He glances at the grand room. 'Despite all this. So what went wrong?'

'They weren't to know that their son had a dark side.' I can't bring myself to look at Hayden as I speak. 'Suresh was handsome and quite kind when I first met him on his one and only visit to Sri Lanka. I thought he'd be a good husband. I had no experience of men – how could I think otherwise? My mummy and daddy thought that his family would look after me and embrace me as a daughter. But the truth was that Suresh's mother and father couldn't do that either. Though they did try, at first. All they could do, eventually, was cope in very difficult circumstances.' I hear myself sigh sadly. Perhaps I'm telling Hayden too much, but I cannot help myself. I've never spoken like this to anyone before and the words are tumbling out of me. 'By then it was too late. I was married and in England. How could I ever tell my mummy and daddy that they'd made a terrible mistake? That we all had. There would be no end to their weeping. They only ever wanted my happiness and, somehow, they'd failed me. I'd failed myself. Perhaps they'd been too trusting, too naïve. Perhaps I was too taken by the stranger that came to court me.'

'You've been here a long time?'

'Ten years. Which have flown by.'

'What do you miss most about Sri Lanka?'

'The sea,' I say, and I can hear the longing in my voice. 'Our home was right by the beach. Beautiful white sand, swaying palm trees, the Indian Ocean.' I lower my lashes. 'My troubles lift when I think of it. One day I hope that I may see it again.'

'Not quite like the seaside in England,' Hayden laughs.

'I've never been to the seaside here.'

He rocks back at that. 'Never?'

'No.' I shake my head. I don't like to say that my life revolved around my home or rare trips to the shopping centre. All the time I was married I'd never even been on a holiday. 'I'd very much like for Sabina to see it.'

He grins at me. 'Then we'll have to see what we can do.'

# Chapter Thirty

A week goes by and Sabina is, I'm very relieved to say, given a place at the local school. Crystal and I take her to the supermarket to buy her new uniform.

That night, after our dinner, she tries it all on and comes down to show us. There are tears in my eyes as she parades up and down the kitchen, holding out her skirt and smiling proudly. My child is growing up before my very eyes and I'm powerless to stop it. Like myself, I see Joy and Crystal wipe away a surreptitious tear. As she does her last twirl we all give her a round of applause and, now bashful, she flees upstairs.

I follow her and, in the privacy of our own room, I wrap my arms round her and hold her to me. 'This is our new life, my dear daughter. I hope you're pleased with it.'

There's anxiety in her eyes and I'm sure she's worried about her first day at her new school. Of course she would be.

'They know what you're like and I hope they'll help you, but it would be so much better to help yourself and speak out, Sabina. There's no need to be frightened now. We're safe here. Our troubles are all behind us.' I don't say that I hope she'll never have to see her daddy again. Every child should have a good father figure in their life, and it makes me sad to think that Sabina doesn't. 'This is a nice home. Hayden, Auntie Crystal and Joy, all are very fond of you already. That should make you happy.' I step back and appraise her. 'You look so grown-up.'

She clings to me again and I stroke her back. I feel as if I can't bear to let her go, that I want to sit next to her in all of her lessons. But, as much as I want to cosset her and never let her out of my sight, if she's going to learn to speak again then she must surely have to face her new school alone. It's hard, but Sabina will have to learn to stand on her own two feet.

'I'm sorry that it took me so long to leave,' I tell her. 'I promise that I'll always do my very best for you. You're my only child and I love you very much.'

I look at her face and memorise every contour of it, my heart tightening. I stroke her cheeks, her eyelids, her lips that stay sealed, and know that I love her more than life itself. Whatever happens in our future, she'll always be my priority.

'Take off your school clothes now,' I tell her. 'You must have your bath and an early night. I want you to sleep well so that you'll be rested.'

Unpeeling her from me, I tug off her white shirt and grey pleated skirt. She has white socks and new black shoes. Tomorrow I'll buy her an official sweatshirt from the school which is a pretty blue colour.

I stay with her while she bathes. I soap the sponge and caress her tiny back, watching the suds run over her skin. Then I wash her hair, which is as long and as dark as mine, but more unruly. Tomorrow I'll plait it so that she's neat and doesn't look like a ragamuffin. Soon, very soon, she'll be too old for me to care for her in this way.

'I want you to do well at school,' I tell her softly. 'Study hard,

151

be clever. Then you can be anything in the world that you want to be.'

You'll not have to rely on a man to provide for you, to feed you, to clothe you. To tell you what you can and cannot do with your own life.

I dry her gently with a fluffy towel and she slips into her pyjamas. When she snuggles down into the voluminous bed, I lie next to her and together we read her bedtime story. I read the words out loud and Sabina follows with her finger. Crystal showed me where the nearest library is and now we've both enrolled and Sabina has a stack of books to choose from.

Every night I'm still reading with Hayden and we're nearly at the end of *Bridget Jones's Diary*. I'm worried for Bridget as, even though she's sometimes very silly in her behaviour and she smokes and drinks too much, I hope that she gets her man. Like all of us, Bridget just wants someone to love her.

The next morning, Crystal and I both walk Sabina to her school. It's a beautiful, warm day. Fluffy cotton-wool clouds waft gracefully across the sky. Days like this herald that summer is nearly upon us.

My daughter's quiet but happily holds both of our hands as we turn out of our gates and head down the street.

I haven't been out much since I've been here. It's foolish to be fearful, but I can't help looking over my shoulder and I only hope that this feeling will soon pass.

At the school, I introduce myself and my daughter to her new class teacher, who seems to be very nice. When she's settled, Crystal and I leave.

'She'll be fine,' Crystal assures me as she marches me down the corridor to the main entrance. 'Absolutely fine.'

Yet, in the playground, we hold each other and cry.

'I'm traumatised,' Crystal says, dabbing her tears away.

'Look at the state of my make-up. I can't bear to leave her. What must you feel like?'

'I am a little upset,' I admit, when my heart is actually tearing in two.

'Well, I feel like bloody wailing. We need to go and get a coffee. And something chocolate-based.' She links her arm through mine and steers me away from the school. My breathing is tight in my chest as we walk up to the High Street and find the nearest coffee shop.

'You need to get out more,' Crystal says. 'There's no reason for you to hide away in the house now.'

'Old habits are hard to break. I've always had to ask for permission to come and go. It's strange to be able to walk out of the door whenever I choose to with no one asking why.'

'You can do exactly what you like now, so enjoy it.'

How true that is. I'm going to wholeheartedly embrace the simple pleasure of relaxing in a coffee shop with my friend.

Crystal queues at the counter while I find us a seat. I choose a leather sofa near the window so that we can watch the world go by. I like it here. The High Street is always bustling and interesting. It feels like a busy little village tucked neatly inside of London. Some of the shops are very beautiful and a long way out of my price range. But then, even Primark is out of my price range. I hadn't expected to be so lucky to find somewhere to live like this, and I must ring Ruth to thank her for bringing Crystal into my life. The houses on our street must be worth millions of pounds and I don't know how anyone who isn't a pop star can afford to be here. I'm so thankful that Hayden has opened his home to me and my child. Crystal tells me that Hampstead is a favourite place of celebrities and television stars, but I haven't seen any yet. At least, I don't think I have, as I'm not sure that I'd be able to recognise anyone famous. Perhaps Crystal will point some of them out to me. Then I realise that this is what Hayden

153

lives with every day when he ventures out, and I think I'll make a particular point of ignoring any celebrities from now on.

A few moments later, Crystal brings us both a coffee and a chocolate muffin. She curls up on the sofa next to me and picks at her cake. Today she looks very splendid in tight jeans and a bright, flowery jacket, like a colourful parakeet. Her hair is piled up and she wears big dangly earrings. Her lipstick is orange to match her shoes. She keeps her sunglasses on even though we're now inside. I'm wearing the pretty blouse and linen trousers that Crystal chose for me, which have become my firm favourites. They're modern yet demure, I think.

'You've got to come to the club with me one night,' Crystal begs. 'I've told the other girls all about you and they're desperate to meet you. There's a job going too. Not as a dancer, obvs, but there's a vacancy behind the bar and one in the cloakroom.'

'I think I'd be happier in the cloakroom.'

'Come along and see what you think.'

'What will I do with Sabina?' How can I leave my daughter alone in the evening?'

'Joy will babysit her for an hour. She won't mind.' Crystal shrugs. 'She does naff-all else with her evenings.'

'I'll ask her,' I promise. 'I'd like to see where you work and how you dance.'

Crystal peers at me over her sunglasses. 'It will be an eye-opener for you, sweetie,' she says. 'That's for sure.'

# Chapter Thirty-one

The next evening I make an early dinner for us all as I'm sure Sabina will be tired after her first day back at school. I've taken another foray into Joy's vegetable patch and as a result we're having chicken cooked in a rich onion and tomato sauce, accompanied by fried cabbage and carrots Gujarati-style with chilli. I make a separate chicken dish for Joy without spices, and I boil her cabbage in plain water until it looks like soggy mush – exactly how she likes it.

Sabina looked very subdued when she came out of school. I was waiting there to meet her and wanted to scoop her up into my arms. The teacher said that she coped very well, but that her classmates found it a little odd that she doesn't speak. I bristled at that. If they knew what my daughter had been through then they wouldn't find it odd at all.

She's sitting at the table now and is supposed to be doing her homework, but she's mainly staring into space and I can't find it in my heart to chide her into studying.

I haven't seen Hayden all day. Crystal left me after we'd been to the coffee shop and I walked back to the house alone. When I let myself in, Hayden was in the office with the door closed. I could hear him speaking on the telephone, but he didn't come out for lunch at all even though I'd knocked on the office door and told him I'd left some samosas out on the table for him in case he'd like to have them with salad.

After lunch, I cleaned the kitchen and then the rest of the house that's accessible to me. Lastly, I tidied our room. I sat on the bed and looked around me, and I felt so blessed. The gods who brought us here have been very kind. In the afternoon I had nothing else to do but wait until it was time to pick up Sabina and make dinner. I could have read some of my book, but I didn't want to do it without Hayden. So I took the time to write another letter to my mummy and daddy, to tell them that life is so much better now. I explained to them that we're finding our feet and that I'm happy to be a woman alone. Despite the disappointment of my marriage, I think that they'd be proud to see how I've coped with my new circumstances.

Joy breaks into my daydreaming when she comes downstairs. 'Need another eye on your homework, Sabina?' she asks.

My daughter nods and Joy sits down at the table next to her, and together they look at her book.

The next person to come downstairs is Crystal. I wonder if that may be all of us for this evening, but just as I'm ready to serve our meal, Hayden joins us. It makes me feel happy that he's come to be with us again.

'Sorry,' he says as he sits down. 'Been a bit busy today.'

'Doing what?' Crystal wants to know.

He shrugs. 'This and that.'

'Hayden Daniels, man of mystery,' she teases.

'Joy,' I say. 'This is your dish.' I put the chicken casserole in front of her. 'No spices.'

'Thank you, Ayesha.' She flushes slightly and looks uncomfortable when she says, 'This must be a lot of extra work for you.'

'It's no trouble,' I assure her. 'There's some plain boiled cabbage too.'

'I would like to try your food, if I may,' she continues. 'I'm not sure if I'll like it.'

'This korma is very mild,' I tell her. 'But I won't be offended if you don't eat it.'

'Get it down your neck, Joy,' Crystal bellows. 'It's top grub.'

I hold the dish out to Joy and she helps herself to a little. 'Thank you. I'll just taste it,' she says. 'As you've made this casserole for me specially, I wouldn't like it to go to waste.'

Tentatively she tastes the curry, and I have to look away or I will laugh. Her lips pucker and purse. She drinks a lot of water. 'Very nice,' she says, and then coughs a lot.

We all laugh and Crystal thumps her heartily on the back.

'It's nice,' Joy grumbles. 'Don't make a fuss.'

Crystal rolls her eyes at me. When all the dishes are served, I take up my place at the table and help Sabina to some chicken and rice.

'I had a letter from Stephen today,' Joy says. 'They'd hoped to come home next year – the whole family – but now it's not going to be possible. He's very busy at work, and with three children . . .' Her sentence tails away to nothing.

'You're disappointed.' I rest my hand on hers. It feels dry, papery. This is a hand that has worked hard in the soil. When I look at it more closely, the skin is chapped and raw. It's not the hand of someone who's had a pampered life. I'll have to find some Ayurvedic cream for her with camomile, or perhaps marigold, which will soothe it.

'Yes, dear,' she says in answer, her voice constricted. 'Very much so.'

'Perhaps this is your time to visit them,' I suggest.

'Oh, I don't think so,' Joy blusters. 'They know I can't do that.'

157

'Today you've tried a little bit of my curry and found it not too bad,' I note. 'Last week, you didn't think you'd do that.'

'Getting on a plane and going halfway round the world is a whole different kettle of fish.'

'We should all get on a plane and go together,' Crystal pipes up. 'Have you been there, Hayd?'

'On tour,' he replies. 'You'd really like it, Joy. It's very clean.'

She harrumphs at that.

In order to change the conversation, I say, 'I wanted to ask you a small favour, Joy.' I glance at Sabina. 'I'd like to be able to take a job and there's one available at Crystal's club. In the cloakroom. Would it be possible for you to look after Sabina while I go with Crystal for a short while this evening? I'd be very grateful.'

Joy's head shoots up. 'You can't possibly be going to that place.'

'There's nothing wrong with it.' Crystal is suddenly very defensive.

'You *cannot* take Ayesha there.'

'The other girls want to meet her,' Crystal says tartly. 'At the end of the day, a job's a job.'

Joy tuts crossly. 'There must be a million other things she can do.'

'I have no skills,' I point out softly. 'I'm not very experienced.'

'That shows only too clearly, my dear,' Joy puffs. 'You must be *mad* even going near somewhere like that.'

'We've all got to do things in life that we don't bloody like,' Crystal mutters.

'I think Ayesha's had a lifetime of doing things that she didn't like, doing what other people have told her to do,' Hayden interjects. He turns to me. 'If you want my opinion, I don't think it's for you. However, you should be free to make up your own mind.'

'I can't even believe that Crystal has even asked her.' Joy is still on her high horse.

'I'm not ashamed of what I do.' Crystal is all puffed up and I feel that I can't let her down even though I'm now very worried about accompanying her.

'Perhaps you should be.'

I can feel myself getting jittery inside. 'I'd like to go.'

'I'll look after Sabina,' Hayden says. He looks across the table at my daughter. 'Will you stay with me?'

'I'll do it,' Joy counters.

Now they're fighting over her and I find that I really don't want to go at all.

'Can you crochet, little one?' asks Joy.

Sabina shakes her head.

'Then I'll show you how.'

My daughter smiles at that.

'Great,' Crystal says. 'Sorted. You'd better change out of that blouse, Ayesha. Put your maxidress on. You look a bit Pollyanna.'

Hayden's head snaps up and, with more force than I've previously heard him use, says, 'She looks beautiful exactly as she is.'

We all turn to him, mouths open, and he flushes red to his hair roots.

'Well,' he says. 'She does.'

# Chapter Thirty-two

Suresh stared out of the window. Not that there was much to see as Flynn's black Jag was boxed in on either side by lorries.

The four men were in the car on the way to London. It was currently stuck in stationary traffic on the M1 motorway near the London Gateway Services, due to roadworks. Flynn was driving, the radio was playing some inane drivel and Suresh could feel his rage rising. They'd set off later than he wanted to and now they were in danger of getting into town as everywhere was closing up.

'What's the plan when we get there?' Arunja asked from the back seat.

'I want to make sure that Ayesha and Sabina actually arrived in London,' Suresh replied tightly. 'We'll check the shops and cafés at Victoria Coach Station. See if they were spotted by any of the staff there.'

In the rear-view mirror, he could see Arunja and Smith exchange a weary glance.

'They could have gone anywhere,' Arunja pointed out. 'They could have got straight on another coach, to Bristol or Bournemouth.'

'Then we'll try to discover if that *is* the case. I have to do something,' he snapped. 'Would you have her walk away with my child?'

His brother shrugged.

'You're being well paid, Arunja. Don't complain.'

His brother was lazy and it made Suresh furious. His own wife came and went as she pleased. Arunja didn't know where she was half the time. His children were wayward and, what was more, he didn't seem to care. Arunja was too easygoing by half. Well, they might be brothers, but that wasn't *his* way. Ayesha's absence was eating away at him like acid in his stomach and he wouldn't rest until she was returned home.

The traffic inched forward and his temper inched upward. No matter what his brother thought – or Smith or Flynn – he couldn't let this lie. Someone knew where Ayesha was, and he would find them.

'We should make a night of this,' Flynn said, leaning on the steering wheel. 'I know this guy, Vinny Alessi. We used to work the doors together years ago. He's running a lapdancing club now, off the Finchley Road. "Desires" or something. We should go. Pick up some girls.'

'I'm in,' Arunja said.

'When there's easy pussy available, you always are,' Suresh threw over his shoulder.

His brother laughed, the insult bouncing off him. 'I can't see a problem with that.'

To be honest, Suresh didn't see a problem either. It would be good to let off some steam.

'I'll call him,' Flynn said. 'We can drop by later.'

It took another hour or more to get to Victoria Coach Station, and Flynn swung the car into the neighbouring NCP car park. They all climbed out. Suresh handed them fresh photographs of

Ayesha and Sabina that he'd printed from the computer. He didn't remember when this picture had been taken, but his wife and child were staring impassively at the camera. It wouldn't have hurt Ayesha to smile, he thought bitterly.

He nodded to Flynn and Arunja. 'You two go into the station,' Suresh said. 'Ask at the kiosks, the shops, the ticket desk. Try to find anyone who recalls seeing them here.' He turned to Smith. 'We'll ask in the shops and cafés in the surrounding streets. Keep in touch. Let me know any news immediately.'

The men headed across the road towards the station. He and Smith fell into step together and worked their way towards the shops and cafés that bordered it.

'I'll go this way,' he said to Smith. 'You take that street.'

Smith did so without protest. If only his brother could keep his mouth shut in the same way.

Suresh entered the first shop he came to and went up to the counter. He held out his photograph to the woman who stood behind it.

'Hello.' He pasted a smile on his face. 'I'm a police officer. I wonder if you can help me. Have you seen this woman recently? She's missing and we're very worried about her.'

The woman was hard-faced, chewing gum. He knew her kind. She glanced at the photograph. 'No.'

'Thank you,' he said, and he could feel his fists tightening. 'You've been very helpful.'

Back on the street, he moved on to the next shop. It was the same in there. And in the next one. And the next. No one had seen Ayesha. Hoping the other lads were having better luck inside the station, he worked his way along the row, stopping in anywhere that looked likely. He drew a blank in every place. He hated to admit this, but perhaps his brother was right. This could well be a wild-goose chase.

Down the next road he walked into a mini-market, a couple

of cafés and then a deli, where he was met by more shaking heads. The next café he went into was warm, welcoming. The smell of fresh coffee was overwhelming and Suresh thought it was time to get the lads together to have some refreshment. He had to keep them on side, keen.

'An espresso, please,' he said to the elderly man behind the counter.

The man took a cup and set his coffee machine going.

Suresh started his well-worn script again. 'I'm a police officer. Looking for this missing woman and her child.' He held up the photograph. 'Have you seen them?'

The man behind the counter glanced up from his work. His eyes widened. 'Sure,' he said. 'I've seen them.'

Suresh felt his heart thud erratically. 'Recently?'

'A few weeks ago. Maybe longer. I remember the child though. A very pretty little girl. Her mother said she didn't speak.'

Now Suresh's mouth dried up and he struggled to get the words out. It was them. Who else could it be? He tried to keep his face impassive. 'Did they say where they were headed?'

The man pursed his lips. 'She showed me an address,' he said. 'Up near Euston. Drummond Street? I can't be a hundred per cent sure. It was a while ago.'

What the hell could she be doing there?

'Is there anything else?' asked the man.

'No,' Suresh said. 'You've been a great help.' He paid for the coffee and moved away from the counter.

Sitting at a table in the window, he punched Smith's number into his phone. 'We're one step closer,' he said. 'Call in the lads.' Suresh told him the name and directions to the coffee bar. 'I'll see you in five and I'm buying the coffee.'

He hung up and grinned to himself. You might be able to run, he thought, but, my dear Ayesha, you can't hide.

# Chapter Thirty-three

'Be good for Joy,' I tell my daughter. 'Not too late to bed. I'll be home as soon as I can.' Oh, how I hate to leave Sabina in the care of others, but, if I'm to be a working mother, then it's something I'll have to learn to do. I kiss her head, inhaling her sweet scent.

'We'll have fun,' Joy promises. Then she touches my arm, her face concerned. 'Are you absolutely sure you want to do this?'

Joy and Hayden exchange a worried glance.

'Yes,' I say. 'I must.' I've promised Crystal that I'll go with her to the club where she works and I don't feel that I can let her down.

Joy sighs and lets me go. 'Look after this girl,' she warns Crystal, 'or you'll have me to answer to.'

'Take a chill pill, Joy,' she tuts. 'It's a job in the cloakroom. That's all.' She fluffs her hair one last time. 'Come on, Ayesha, taxi's waiting. If I'm late, we'll both be looking for jobs.'

So, reluctantly, I leave my daughter in Joy's care and race after Crystal. My friend's wearing a very short leopardskin-print dress that's cut extremely low at the neck, fishnet tights and heels so high that I don't know how she walks in them. Over the top she slips a light, cream mackintosh and pulls the belt tightly around her.

In contrast, I'm wearing my maxidress as instructed. On top I have one of the smart little jackets that Crystal bought for me.

'I feel very plain compared to you,' I confess as we slide into the back seat.

'You look fine,' she insists.

'Thank you.'

'If you were auditioning as a dancer it would be a different matter. Then they'd want to see some skin.'

'Oh.'

She's put make-up on me again. Much more this time, I think. Strangely, it makes me feel slightly more confident, as if it's a mask I can hide behind. I'm grateful for that, as I believe I'm going to need some help to get me through this evening. Hayden and Joy looked so worried on our departure that I'm now filled with trepidation.

The taxi ride is slow and we spend a lot of time in traffic. I don't know where it's taking us and there seems little point in asking Crystal as it would mean nothing to me. So I'm content to sit and watch the cars go by, while Crystal spends her time chewing gum and texting.

I should buy another mobile phone. One for me and one for my daughter. She should always be able to get in touch with me in case there's an emergency. I think of the phone that I threw away when I first arrived here and wonder if Suresh is still ringing it, trying to catch me out, or if he has given up by now. I've had such a short time away from Suresh, yet for me it feels like a million years. I'm a new person, living a new life. But I'm also like a fugitive, newly escaped from prison, and I can't help but be anxious that there's still someone out there looking for me.

I turn to Crystal and ask anxiously, 'Could Suresh find me?'

'Nah. Anyone can disappear if they want to.' She pauses in her texting. 'Unless you're Hayden Daniels, of course.'

'He's very precious of his privacy.'

'With good reason,' she says. 'You don't bounce back from a blow like he's had.'

'I feel very sorry for him.'

'Me too,' Crystal says. 'By all accounts he's a shadow of the bloke he once was. Used to be the life and soul of the party.'

Perhaps I like him better as he is. Men like Daniel Cleaver are the life and soul of the party.

'He's been different since you've been around,' Crystal adds. 'He never used to come out of his room much. Must be your cooking.' She nudges me and laughs. 'They say the way to a man's heart is through his stomach. I can't even open a tin without having a disaster. That's where I've been going wrong all these years.'

It makes me feel warm inside to think that he's a little better since my daughter and I came to stay, and that it's not simply me hoping it is so.

The taxi stops.

'Shake a leg,' Crystal says. 'We're here.' She gets out of the cab and I follow her. While my friend pays the driver, I look at our surroundings.

We're on a busy main road, closer to the centre of London, I believe. Though my sense of direction may have failed me. The street is full of restaurants and office buildings, but we've stopped outside a doorway with a brash neon sign that says DESIRES GENTLEMEN'S CLUB. There are two burly men in overcoats who stand at the door and, I must be truthful, this doesn't look like the kind of place that a gentleman would visit. Already I wish that I'd heeded Hayden and Joy's advice and stayed at home.

Crystal stands on the pavement and turns to me. 'Right. Don't be shocked. OK?'

I nod. 'I won't be shocked.'

She too now looks anxious that she's invited me. But then she grabs my hand and, before I can think better of it, we go inside.

# Chapter Thirty-four

Hayden sat at the piano and played. It seemed he'd now opened the floodgates, and music flowed from his fingers. They tingled with energy and it felt good. There was, out of nowhere, a nugget of happiness at his centre. That felt good too.

At the other end of the room Joy sat with Sabina nestled next to her. The child was in her pink pyjamas, looking all sweet and cuddly. She pulled a wayward strand of her dark hair across her face and held on to it while she sucked her thumb. Hayden played softly so that he could hear what Joy was saying to her.

'Now then,' Joy said. 'Take your wool like this.' She leaned in to the little girl and Sabina sat up so that she could see better. 'Wrap it round your finger and make a slipknot. Now slide it on to the crochet hook, so, and tighten the wool.' Joy demonstrated and Sabina copied. 'Chain stitch is how we start everything.'

The kid's as bright as a button, Hayden thought. No doubt about that. She was taking in every word Joy said and picked things up in a flash. She was keen to learn, too, which was nice to see. It must be a worry for Ayesha that she didn't speak. Maybe, given time, she'd take her to a specialist again and let them do their worst. The fact of it was, even though she didn't chatter as a child would normally do, Sabina still had the ability to light up a room. Even Joy, who was as grumpy as hell about everything, was warming to her.

He'd thought it was a bad idea for Ayesha to go to the club where Crystal worked. Hayden had never seen it; he'd been to enough of those places in the past to ever want to go again. Also he knew that Crystal was no longer in the West End and hadn't been for a while. She talked about it so little that he was sure the place she worked at now was a long way from the glamorous end of an already tawdry market. He knew without even thinking that it wasn't the kind of place where Ayesha would be comfortable. Still, Ayesha was a grown woman and it was up to her to make informed decisions about what she did and didn't do.

He'd offered time and time again to set Crystal up with something else, but her pride wouldn't let her accept. She had debts that he wanted to settle, but she wouldn't hear of that either. She already took too much off him, she said. Which was nonsense. Crystal had been his lifeline these past few years. It was he that owed her, not the other way round.

'Now we go under, over and pull it through,' Joy continued. Sabina did the same. 'Keep going until we have a chain.'

Sabina concentrated on her work.

'I have lots of grandchildren,' Joy said proudly as she dashed off a chain of stitches. 'When the two oldest girls lived in England, I used to teach them how to crochet and knit.' Joy examined Sabina's first few stitches. 'Very nice. Keep the tension the same all the time. Not too loose. Not too tight. You'll soon get the feel of it.

'I don't see them now,' Joy added. 'All my children live a long way away.' There was a sadness in her eyes. 'I've got one grandchild who I've never even seen. Can you believe that?'

Sabina looked as if she could.

'Oh, but you've never seen your grandparents in Sri Lanka either, have you?'

Sabina shook her head.

'Would you like to?'

The child nodded.

Joy looked thoroughly miserable. 'Life sometimes is very hard,' she said. 'We have to be apart from the people we love. I'd like to be able to show my other grandchildren how to do this too, one day. It's what grandmas do, isn't it?'

Suddenly Joy looked ten years older, sadness weighing heavily on her, and her eyes filled with tears. Hayden was pleased to see that Sabina inched closer in to Joy's side.

'Right,' Joy rallied herself. 'Next bit. Now we go back on ourselves.' She demonstrated to the child with her yarn. 'We miss this stitch and then we do a single crochet into the next one.' Joy wound the wool while her attentive pupil watched closely. 'Under, yarn over. Pull through. Easy.'

The two of them worked together, and Hayden smiled at their heads bowed in concentration. You could keep fame, he thought. This was what he wanted. A quiet, peaceful life. You could keep your red-carpet events. You could keep your champagne. As far as Hayden was concerned, he never wanted to attend another one in this lifetime. In fact, his vision of hell would involve a red carpet.

He looked over at Joy and Sabina. Would he one day have a wife and child of his own who would knit or sew together in the evening while he played the piano? Perhaps they'd move away from London as he and Laura had planned. Buy a small, remote place in the country or by the sea. He glanced up at the photograph in front of him, her smiling face, her flowing blonde hair. She was slowly fading from view. Without looking at her photograph, the contours of her face were now slightly fuzzy in his mind. He couldn't recall every single one of her quirky mannerisms as easily as he used to. Perhaps he was finally letting Laura go. If he was, it seemed as if it was the right thing to do.

Maybe rediscovering his music was starting to fill the emptiness in his heart. He looked up at Sabina and Joy, heads close together. Or perhaps it was something else.

'Just one more line and I think it's time for your bed, young lady. You want to be up bright and early for school.'

As instructed, Sabina finished one more line and then wrapped up her wool and put the crochet hook through it as Joy had done. The child was a delight, no doubt about it.

'Say goodnight to Hayden,' Joy instructed, 'and then I'll take you up to bed.'

Sabina slid down from the sofa and padded across the room to where he sat at the piano. She came and wrapped her arms around his neck. As he held her tiny body against his own, a feeling of great tenderness rushed up inside him and he was overwhelmed by a fierce protectiveness of her, the like of which he'd never known before.

He squeezed her tightly and dropped a light kiss on her forehead. Despite the lump in his throat, he said, 'Sleep tight, Beanie.'

Smiling at him, she returned to where Joy was waiting, hand outstretched, to take her upstairs.

Sabina turned and waved as she went and his heart swelled again. He'd thought he would never feel like this until he had a child of his own. Perhaps this little girl was showing him otherwise.

# Chapter Thirty-five

We pass through a plush reception area, heavy with scarlet velvet, and I note the cloakroom area. A woman with black hair, a black dress and heavy eyeliner is currently standing there. She looks very bored.

Crystal waves to her and she raises a hand in return. 'We'd normally go straight in the back door, but I wanted you to check out the cloaks. If you're interested in the job, that'd be your domain.'

'It looks very nice,' I oblige.

'You could do it in your sleep,' Crystal says. 'The pay's rubbish, but the tips are really good. She doesn't have to put them in the pot either, like the rest of us.'

We reach an ornate, sweeping staircase and Crystal stops before we go down. 'That's where the punters go,' she says. 'It leads down to the main bar and dance area. We'll have to duck through here or I'll get a bollocking from the manager.'

She takes me through a door that's almost hidden, and instantly the velvet disappears and there's nothing but a stark corridor with breezeblock walls. The carpet gives way to concrete.

time that I've known her, she's done so much for me. 'I'd like to stay.'

'Come on then.' She inclines her head towards another door. 'I'll find you a place to watch out of the way.'

Two more girls follow as we head down another grubby corridor past a sign marked TOILETS. I think I would have found them by following my nose.

We pause at a door with a circle of glass in it and Crystal peers through. 'It's still quiet out there,' she says to the other girls.

They tut and go ahead of us into the club. One wears shorts that are entirely see-through, with red stilettos, and the other has a shiny black corset that laces up the back. Her breasts are bare and she's not wearing any pants at all. I feel an anxious gulp travel down my throat.

Crystal puts a hand on my arm.

'I'm thinking Joy and Hayden were right.' She chews her lip. 'Maybe this isn't the place for you.'

'Perhaps not,' I agree. 'But I'm your friend and would like to see where you work.'

'OK.' Crystal shrugs. 'Brace yourself, sweetie.'

As she pushes open the door, I take a deep breath.

# Chapter Thirty-six

The club is set in a basement and here the velvet is all purple. I can see clusters of men in suits, sitting in booths. A few sit at the bar alone.

When we step out into the gloom, I see that Crystal was right to think that I'd be shocked. Around the room there are a few poles which run from floor to ceiling. Already there are girls dancing on them. They gyrate lazily to the pounding music, exposing the intimate parts of their bodies to the groups of watching men.

'Here,' Crystal says as she ushers me out of the way. 'Tuck into this alcove, no one will bother you. Don't talk to anyone. Just shoo any blokes away if they come over.' Then, as she looks around nervously, 'Oh shit. Here comes Vinny.'

A small man in a dinner suit comes up behind Crystal. Without speaking, he grabs a handful of her buttock. He turns her and with his other hand tweaks her rosebud nipple. Crystal tries to stand away from him but he holds her fast.

'Difficult crowd in tonight,' Vinny says. 'Hard to please. You'd better put on some good moves. Get rid of that.' He hooks a finger into the front of her sequinned thong and tugs it down while I look on, appalled.

'Later.' She moves his hand.

'I'm in no mood for stroppy cows tonight,' he says. 'Be good or you'll be out like Kelly.'

He lets her go and marches off, smiling smarmily at the customers as he disappears. Crystal raises a single finger to his back. 'Twat,' she says. 'I told you.'

'Why do you let him speak to you like that?'

'It's his club. He calls the shots.' Her face is dark with concern. 'Will you be all right here?'

I don't think that I will be, but I don't like to say so.

'Look, I'm on now,' Crystal says. 'I'll get one of the girls behind the bar to bring you a drink. I'll come back to you as soon as I can.'

She makes sure that I'm seated and then disappears.

I watch the girls on the poles. They're lethargic, going through the motions. Their hips thrust with angry boredom at the men who sit in front of them and ogle. They have vacant faces and limbs that shout out that they would rather be anywhere else. How can the men enjoy this when the girls look so miserable that they're here at all?

Crystal takes up the empty pole in the middle of the floor and, when she starts to dance, she lights up this sordid place with a vibrant energy that's been sadly missing. Instantly, all eyes swivel to her. The music ramps up and Crystal goes through her moves on the pole: she twirls this way and that and tilts upside-down and, though I can hardly bear to keep my own eyes open, I'm enthralled by the sheer athleticism and skill of her performance. She can really move and seems like a shining star in this awful, seedy place.

'Hiya, love.' A scantily clad woman puts a glass of Coca-Cola down on my table. 'From Crystal.'

'Thank you.' I gulp the drink greedily. I feel hot and my underarms are damp with anxious sweat.

Crystal dances through a few tunes on the pole and, just as I'm beginning to be accustomed to seeing her like this, her manager comes back into view and beckons her towards him. He directs her to a group of rowdy men sitting in the booth next to me and I shrink back into the curtains.

'These gentlemen would like you to entertain them,' I hear him say.

Crystal puts on a bright smile. She gyrates in front of them, holding up her breasts for their appreciation. They look at her with cold, dead eyes like hungry sharks.

One of the men sits forward and it's clear that Crystal is to give him special attention. She straddles his lap and gyrates slowly as he watches, slavering. Then she slides her breasts down the full length of his body until she's swishing her hair in his groin. How can she do this? I wonder. To a man who's a stranger to her? The man makes a grab at her flesh and she slaps his hand away. The others roar and bay with laughter.

These men look as if they want to stick fingers in her, and their private parts. They want to rip her and hurt her, and I feel sick to my stomach that I'm forced to sit here and watch, powerless to help. Crystal isn't smiling now, and tears fill my eyes to see her so abused.

The scantily clad barmaid comes back with a tray of drinks. In one deft movement, Crystal takes off her sequinned thong and bends over in front of the men. The other woman lines up the drinks, carefully balanced on her bottom as if she is nothing more than a human table. I shield my eyes with my hands as I do not think that I want to see my friend used so.

If they knew Crystal, if they'd talked to her, then they'd know what a kind and caring person she is. They'd know that she's funny and a good friend. Perhaps then they wouldn't be able to treat her in this terrible, degrading way. They must have wives themselves, or girlfriends. Maybe some of them are fathers. Would they like it if their women were abused like this? I don't think so.

One at a time, to the cheers of the others, the men take the drinks in their teeth and then knock them back. More drinks are lined up until the tray is empty. The last man takes the drink in his hand and pours it all over Crystal's buttocks. Then he holds her fast with his hands and, as Crystal tries to pull away, slowly laps up the liquid with his probing tongue from the inside of her thighs while the others egg him on.

I can take no more. My stomach heaves and bile rises to my throat. I must get out of here, and fast. As I move, Crystal looks up and catches my eye. I shake my head and mouth, 'I'm sorry.'

Then, as quickly as I possibly can, I bolt for the door.

# Chapter Thirty-seven

I head straight to the toilets, banging the door open in my rush. In one of the cubicles, I drop to the floor and am violently sick into the bowl.

I kneel on the cold tiles, head resting on my arm, sobbing.

A few seconds later, I hear Crystal's voice say, 'Ayesha? Are you in here?'

'Yes,' I manage through sobs.

She pushes the cubicle door open and when she sees me she says, 'Oh, good grief.'

My friend unravels some toilet roll and eases me away from the bowl. 'Hey, hey,' she says. 'Are you all right?'

I nod feebly. She sits down next to me and takes me in her arms. My head rests on her bare breast and I'm even more aware of her nakedness now. She rocks me to her. The pounding music is still a background noise.

The cubicles are all painted black and are scrawled over with graffiti. The light has a dim, red glow, and it's probably a good thing, as it doesn't show this place in its full horror. The floor is dirty, strewn with tissue, and the smell of bleach does little to mask the smell of filth. It's a poor place for a heart-to-heart.

'They treat you so horribly,' I sniff. 'How can you allow them to do this?'

'It's my job,' she says with a weary laugh. 'It's not so bad.'

'It is. It's awful. Those men, they're vile.'

'They pay good money.'

'To abuse women? To humiliate them?' It feels worse than anything that Suresh ever did to me. His violence was born of frustrated anger. But what does this come from? What makes men think that this is the right way to treat women? What makes a lovely woman like Crystal become so immune to the terrible indignity of it? Is the human spirit so debased? I wonder if my husband ever went to places like this when he was out late at night, when he didn't come home at all. Is this how he took his pleasure? I wonder fleetingly what he's doing, what he's thinking without me there.

'No one has made me do it,' she says tightly.

'But you *cannot* enjoy it.'

'No,' she admits flatly. 'I certainly don't enjoy it.'

I clutch her hand. 'You're worth so much more than this,' I tell her. 'You're a bright and caring woman.'

'I've no qualifications,' she says. 'Not a single one. No skills to write home about. I pull in a lot of money doing this, Ayesha, and I've got debts like you wouldn't believe. What else can I do?'

'I don't know,' I admit. 'But I hate to see you like this.'

'Promise me you won't tell Hayden.' She squeezes my fingers. 'He doesn't know how bad this place is.'

'You must confide in him. He would help you. I know it.'

'He already does too much for me. I don't want him to pity me.'

'It wouldn't be like that. I'm sure.'

'Don't say anything. Please. You have to promise.'

'I promise.' I touch her arm gently. 'But you're bright and

funny. You have so much to offer. How can it have come to this?'

Crystal tips back her head and sighs. 'It's not a pretty story.' Her voice wavers as she starts. 'I ran away when I was young. Wanted excitement. My parents were really strict. I couldn't wear make-up, couldn't date boys. I lived in a small town and was bored to death. I wanted to do it all. Throw myself at life. Couldn't wait. Look where that got me.'

'I didn't know.'

She shrugs. 'I left for the bright lights of London when I was seventeen. Bought into the whole streets-paved-with-gold thing. I had twenty quid in my pocket and not a qualification to my name. That's how I ended up doing this. To be honest, I didn't mind it at first. I tried to kid myself that it was liberating and empowering. What bollocks. The other girls were great, though. We were like a little family. That's when I met Ruth, from the women's-aid charity you first went to. We've kept in touch over the years. Sometimes I help her out if there's a girl in trouble. She got out of this game quickly. It messed with her head. I thought I could cope with it. More fool me.' Crystal smiles sadly at the thought. 'I took some drugs to help me through the worst bits. Most of the girls do. I even believed, for a while, that I was having a high old time. The dancing paid the rent. Kept me in weed.' She gives me a rueful glance. 'All things considered, I did all right for myself. When Hayden and I first met, I was dancing in a decent club. Classy. One that all the celebs go to. I made a fortune in tips and there was no ... well, none of that stuff you saw out there. It was just dancing.' She looks worn down. 'I'm getting on, Ayesha. I'm pushing thirty from very much the wrong side. The clubs want fresh meat. Younger, tighter bodies. At my age you end up working in worse and worse dives, having to do more extreme stuff to earn the same money.' Her eyes fill with tears and she tries to blink them back.

'Now you've made me cry and my mascara will run. I'll have to go back to the dressing room and put some more slap on before I go out there again.'

'Don't,' I beg of her. 'Please don't do this. You have a beautiful soul and this will destroy it.'

'A beautiful soul? I'm not sure I have one left at all.' Now the tears roll silently down her cheeks and she looks wretched. 'I've done this for years. What else can I do?'

'I don't know, but we can find something together.'

She laughs wetly and a bubble of snot erupts from her nose. I hand her some toilet roll and she wipes it.

'Look at the state of us,' she says. 'Sitting on the floor in a filthy loo. And me in the bloody nip. What are we like?'

That makes us both smile for a moment, but then we start crying again.

'What *am* I doing here?' she asks, almost to herself.

'I don't know,' I tell her. 'But I can't bear to see you like this.'

'I'm sorry.' She holds me to her tightly and strokes my hair. 'So sorry.'

Then the door bangs open again. 'Crystal! Crystal!' It's an angry male voice and I can only assume that it's her weaselly manager.

She rolls her eyes at me and shouts back, 'Yes.'

'What the fuck are you doing in here?' he wants to know. 'Get your arse out there now and get the punters spending.'

Crystal goes to move.

'No,' I urge her in a whisper. 'Please don't go.'

She looks torn. 'I have to.'

'Don't,' I beg. 'Please don't. This life will ruin you. If I can change, then so can you. Please, Crystal. Please.'

Then the cubicle door is kicked open and Vinny towers over us. I feel myself shrink back, but Crystal stands up, dragging me with her, and squares up to him.

183

'Get out on the floor, you useless cunt,' he snarls.

Despite being naked and vulnerable, she pokes him in the chest and meets him eye to eye. Her voice is level and calm when she says, 'That's the very last time you ever speak to me like that.'

She pushes him out of the way and tows me behind her.

'Come back,' he says, surprise and outrage on his face. 'You're my best girl, Crystal. The punters love you. You can't just walk out of here.'

'Watch me,' she tosses back.

Then we're running down the corridor hand-in-hand, laughing, laughing, laughing. Crystal is still naked, but her face is flushed, her eyes sparkle and she's giggling. Now she looks free.

# Chapter Thirty-eight

Crystal grabs her belongings from the dressing room and belts her mackintosh over her naked body, and we flee out of the club before Vinny can pursue us. She hails a cab and, as it pulls up to the pavement, Crystal waves to the security staff on the door. 'Bye, lads! You've seen the last of me.'

Jumping into the taxi, we are breathless and giggling.

'Where to, ladies?' the driver asks, and I give him the address of our home.

As we set off, a sleek black car pulls up sharply and takes our place at the kerb. More disgusting men to ogle the women, I think. The doorman steps forward to open the car door and the four men in black leather jackets begin to spill out. I turn my face away; I can't even bear to look at them.

We join a stream of cars and, when I do venture a glance backward, they've already disappeared into the club.

Crystal punches the air as she flops back. 'This feels great,' she says. Then she turns to me and frowns. 'I might think differently when I wake up in the morning and realise what I've done.'

'You won't,' I assure her. 'You'll still feel marvellous.'

'I hope you're right, Ayesha.' The taxi weaves through the

busy traffic. Crystal lets her head rest back and tears slide down her face. 'I feel like a ma*hoo*sive weight has gone from my shoulders. How could I have taken all that shit for so long?'

'We put up with a lot of bad things when we feel that we have no choice.' I think of my own situation, which also went on for too many years.

'You're right,' she says. 'Well, no more. This is the first day of the rest of my life.'

'We'll think of what to do. Together.'

She opens her mac and flashes her breasts at me. 'I bet you've seen more of me tonight than you ever needed to.'

'That's true,' I confess.

'I once turned up at a boyfriend's flat like this. Just a coat with nothing underneath. It's an old cliché but it works. I rang the doorbell and stood there flashing my wares. Except this time his wife opened the door.'

I shake my head. 'You're a very different woman to me.'

'Not so much.' She links her arm through mine and I feel her start to relax. 'I've never had a decent relationship.' Crystal looks for my reaction. 'Who wants to get serious with a lap-dancer? Whenever they found out what I did they'd either run for the hills or get all weird on me. I might be able to get a nice guy if I'm on the straight and narrow.'

'You might,' I agree.

'I want to be loved,' she says sadly. 'Is that too much to ask?'

We hug each other. 'No,' I say. 'I think not.'

The taxi pulls up outside the house and we jump out. Crystal pays the driver.

'I think it may have worked out to be an expensive evening, taking me with you.'

'What price self-esteem?' Crystal says. Then she hugs me tightly. 'I'm glad you came. Whatever the cost.' She punches the code into the gate and then waves at the security camera as she

186

opens it. 'I wonder if Hayd is still up. He'll be surprised to see us back so early.'

Hayden is, indeed, still awake when we go back into the house. He comes out of the living room when he hears the front door open.

'What are you two doing back here so early?' he asks.

'I've quit my job,' Crystal informs him with a grin on her tear-stained face. 'I'm feeling quite giddy.'

'Wow,' he says. 'I think that's cause for celebration.'

'Let me go and get some clothes on first, then we can crack open a bottle,' she says. 'I ran out of there in the nuddy!' She treats Hayden to a flash, as she did me.

He rolls his eyes as she disappears, then says to me, 'Is she all right?'

'I think so,' I tell him. I'm sure there are tracks from my tears in my make-up too, but I don't care. 'It wasn't a pleasant experience, but Crystal is a survivor.'

'As are you.'

I shrug. 'Only time will tell.' I take off my jacket and suddenly weariness overwhelms me and I want nothing more than to see my daughter. 'Is Sabina in bed?'

Hayden nods. 'She went up about an hour ago.'

'Was she a good girl for Joy?'

'Ayesha,' he says, 'your child is adorable. She's no trouble at all. They sat and crocheted together and then Sabina went to bed without protest.'

'I'm glad to hear it. I'll go to say goodnight to her.'

'Are you coming back down?'

'Yes.'

'I could open a bottle of champagne.'

'I don't drink alcohol,' I remind him. 'But I'd like a cup of tea.'

'Your special black tea or my very own builder's tea?'

I smile at that. I've bought some black tea and am trying to encourage my housemates to drink a good blend. With little success, it must be said.

'Tonight I think calls for builder's tea.'

Hayden grins at that. 'I reckon I can organise that.'

So I climb the stairs, my legs feeling tired and heavy after our emotional evening. Slipping quietly inside our room, I'm relieved to see that Sabina is sleeping soundly in our big bed. Lying down next to her, I stroke her hair. I hope that when she's older, I can spare her all the pain that I've been through, that women like Crystal go through.

All I want to do is get into a hot bath and scrub away the terrible feelings, the stink of that seedy club, and then crawl into bed next to my child. But I've said to Hayden that I'll go downstairs for a cup of tea and I don't like to disappear without explanation. I wash my hands and face, which helps a little.

Taking off my jacket, I slip on my comfortable cardigan instead. The night is warm and still, but I feel chilled inside.

Downstairs in the kitchen, Crystal and Hayden are already sitting at the table, nursing cups of tea. There's a mug on the table that I assume is for me, so I sit in the place next to my landlord. Crystal is wearing a tracksuit and her face has been scrubbed clean of make-up. Her hair is pulled back in a scrunchie. She does look so much younger and prettier like this, and I long to tell her.

'I would never have had the courage to walk out if Ayesha hadn't been there,' Crystal is saying. She looks at me fondly.

'You have so much more to offer,' I assure her.

'Who to?' she asks. 'I'm going to have to find something else to do and I'm clueless.'

'Tomorrow we'll put our thinking caps on.'

'I like the sound of that,' she says.

'For what it's worth, I'm glad you've got out of there too,' Hayden says.

'Yeah. Me too. Now all I've got to do is find a real job.'

'I've told you before, I'd love it if you became my assistant.'

'You don't need an assistant,' Crystal puffs. 'You don't *do* anything.'

Hayden purses his lips. 'You could run the house, take over any administration. You know I hate doing it.'

'What if you get bored of me?' she says. 'Or find someone else and move on?' Crystal glances surreptitiously at me.

'That would never happen.'

'I don't want you to pity me.' Crystal glares at him.

Hayden laughs. 'I'm trying to be nice.'

'I want to make my own way,' she insists. 'I must be good at something other than waggling my booty in businessmen's faces.'

We all laugh at that.

'We'll all put our heads together,' Hayden says. Then he pushes back from the table. 'This is a momentous occasion, I can't toast it with tea. We have very little to celebrate and I think this is a time when we need to break out the fizz.'

'Like I'm going to stop you,' Crystal says.

He disappears to the garage and returns with a bottle of champagne, which he pops open. Crystal jumps up and gets tumblers for us all.

'I don't drink,' I repeat.

'A tiny drop. Just a few bubbles to say what great gals we are.'

I shrug and Hayden splashes out half a glass for me too. As he hands it to me our fingers touch, and we both jump at the contact. My cheeks flush and Hayden moves away hastily.

'To us,' Crystal says, and we clink glasses together. 'To a sparkling bright future.'

'To us,' we echo.

I can feel Hayden's gaze on me and I lower my eyes.

Crystal crushes me to her. 'I love it since you've been in the house, Ayesha.' She knocks back her drink. 'To Ayesha!'

'To Ayesha,' Hayden agrees.

I smile shyly and raise my glass again, sipping the champagne. The bubbles fizz against my nose and lips and I like it.

'Promise you won't ever leave us,' she says.

I shake my head. 'Never.'

# Chapter Thirty-nine

Crystal and I walk Sabina to school. When we reach the play-ground, I like the fact that my dear daughter hurries towards her new friends as we leave her.

'She's settling in well.' Crystal links her arm through mine.

I've never said that I'm nervous to walk Sabina to school on my own but Crystal has hauled herself out of bed, put on dark glasses in lieu of make-up and has accompanied me. For that, I'm very grateful.

'I'm pleased. Her teacher says that she's doing very well.'

'As if there were ever any doubt,' Crystal says. 'She's brainier than the rest of us put together. That kid will end up being an astrophysicist, or prime minister.'

'I just want her to be happy.'

'I want her to be happy and make a ma*hoo*sive amount of money so that she can keep her old mum and her favourite Auntie Crystal in the style they'd like to become accustomed to!'

'In the meantime, we must find ourselves jobs.'

'Ah, yes,' Crystal agrees. 'That's exactly what we're going to do the minute we get home.'

That puts a spring in our step and we head back to the house, drinking in the day as we do.

As soon as we're back home, Crystal throws down her bag and declares, 'Right! Now to get cracking on some blue-sky thinking. We need a notepad, pens and lots of tea.'

'I'll start with the tea.' I offer to do this menial task as I'm not exactly sure what 'blue-sky thinking' involves. So I head to the kitchen while Crystal goes into Hayden's office.

A moment later she reappears, armed with a pad and pen. 'It's such a glorious day, we could do this outside.'

'Joy is already in the garden.' I can see her pottering in the vegetable patch. 'I'll make her some tea too.'

Crystal goes on to the patio and yells, 'Joy! Tea's up!'

The old lady raises her head and then I see her putting down her spade.

I take the tray loaded with tea and biscuits outside. Briefly, I wonder where Hayden is. He didn't come down for breakfast this morning and I hoped that when we returned he'd be here to help us.

I'm becoming used to his company and I'm not sure that's a good thing. I've relied on a man before and it was the wrong thing to do. All I should concentrate on now is making a future for myself and for Sabina. It would be wrong to even think of having another man in my life. Not that I am.

Joy comes to join us at the table. 'This is very kind,' she says.

Crystal gives her one of the cups and pushes the plate of biscuits towards her.

'Thank you for looking after Sabina last night.' I pour tea for Joy. 'She was very pleased with her first attempt at crochet. She showed it to me before she went to school.'

'It was my pleasure. She's a very clever little girl.'

Crystal takes a biscuit from the plate. 'One more benefit. Don't have to watch my figure now,' she says as she bites into it.

'Better still, no one else will be watching it either,' I tease, and she laughs at that.

'I packed in my job last night, Joy. With Ayesha's help.'

Joy's eyes widen. 'Really?'

'Told them where to stick it,' she adds proudly.

'I'm very pleased for you, Crystal.'

'Yeah. Me too. Downside is that now I need to find something else to do.'

'You could take the opportunity to retrain,' Joy suggests.

'I'll have to,' Crystal agrees. 'I can't do anything else. Ayesha is looking for something to do too. I thought we'd have a little brainstorming session and see what we can come up with. Preferably, we're looking for a job that we can both do. Right, sis?'

'Yes, indeed.'

She looks up at me, pen poised in one hand, biscuit in the other. 'OK. You kick off. Hit me with your talents.'

Of course I instantly dry up. What can I do that would be useful in a workplace?

'Er . . . er . . .' I rack my brain but nothing will come. I've never actually had a job other than looking after the home. I've no formal qualifications and my reading and writing skills are woefully inadequate for the world of commerce. 'I . . . er . . .'

Think hard as I might, nothing useful comes to mind.

When I singularly fail to offer any insight into my skills, Crystal says, 'You're kind. You're caring.' She scribbles these qualities down on her pad in a determined manner.

'You're an excellent cook,' Joy chips in.

Almost as soon as we've started, we run out of steam. I gaze round the garden searching for inspiration, but none comes.

'There must be something,' Joy says, exasperated. 'Can you sew? Can you drive?'

'Joy,' I lower my head as I admit, 'I'm barely literate.'

'But you speak so beautifully,' she says. 'Answering the telephone. Receptionist.'

Crystal scribbles again and then there's a long pause when we drink our tea and eat biscuits, but no one can think of any more talents for me.

'Let's do me,' Crystal says.

'You're very loud,' Joy throws in.

'Thanks for that, Joy. I don't want to be working on a market stall. Think of something else.'

'You're confident. Very beautiful,' I offer.

*Confident. Beautiful*, she writes down with a flourish. 'That's better than *loud*, Joy. And I've got a great body.'

'May I remind you that you've just got out of an industry where that was the only requirement,' Joy says.

Crystal sticks her tongue out at Joy, who counters the gesture with a disdainful face.

'Nursery-school assistant,' Joy suggests.

Crystal looks appalled. 'With my childcare skills? You're joking.'

'I was thinking more of Ayesha,' Joy admits.

'We want to do something *together*,' Crystal reminds her. 'Strength in numbers. I need a job where I won't get my nails broken either.' She holds out her splendid, manicured talons for us to admire. 'I'd have some kid's eye out with these.'

'Manicurist,' Joy tries.

Crystal's mouth drops open. 'Omigod,' she breathes. '*Omigod*. You genius, Mrs Ashton. You might have discovered my dream job! *Squeee!* Manicurist!' My friend looks as if she might hyperventilate. 'Do you fancy that, Ayesha?'

I shrug. 'I don't know. I've never had a manicure.'

My friend feigns a swoon. 'I keep forgetting you've lived in the Dark Ages. We need to get you one. Today. Now.' She picks

194

up her phone and punches in a number. Seconds later, I'm booked in for my very first manicure.

'I'll get Hayden's laptop and we can have a look for training courses. I bet there are masses.' She dashes off.

'I'll put the kettle on again,' I say to Joy.

She examines the soil beneath her fingernails. Joy holds out her hands to me. 'Perhaps I should be your first customer.'

I take her fingers in mine and hold them gently. 'They are the hands of a busy person.'

'Well, the devil makes work for idle hands.'

'He certainly does,' I agree.

Joy stands up. 'Don't let her bully you, Ayesha. You've made your escape, now you must do what *you* want to do.'

I nod. 'I've had enough bullying in my life. I'll be my own woman from now on. But I like Crystal. It'd be nice for us to train to do something together. She has an energy that I wish I had, and she gives me courage. She's teaching me how to have fun when I had quite forgotten how.'

Joy pats my arm kindly. 'That's good to know.'

'Thank you again for looking after Sabina. She was very close to her grandmother and, though she doesn't say, I'm sure that she misses her. It's nice that you've taken her under your wing.'

'My pleasure.' Joy picks up her trug. 'What do you want me to pick for dinner tonight, dear?'

'What would you like to eat?'

'I enjoyed that korma you made,' she says, not quite meeting my eye. 'It was creamy. Not too spicy.'

'Then that's what I'll do. Pick whatever there is, and I'll make some side dishes to go with it.'

'Right-oh. See you later.' Joy waves as she heads back down to the working end of the garden.

I smile to myself as I watch her walk away. I will have her eating the hottest vindaloo and devilled food yet.

195

# Chapter Forty

'We can do a basic manicure course and then, when we're *completely* brilliant, we could do acrylics, gels. Then we could go on to do make-up – weddings, proms, all that stuff. It's big business.' Crystal scans the online brochure. 'What about offering spray-tanning too? Body wraps for fat bits? We could rule the world!'

My friend is giddy with excitement. She claps her hands in glee and I find that I'm caught up in her enthusiasm.

'The college isn't far from here either,' she adds. 'We could walk up there. Win-win.'

'It's all very expensive.' I try to interject an element of practicality. I'm not sure that I have the money to match Crystal's ambition.

'We can start small,' she assures me. 'I don't know why I didn't think of this before. It's perfect.' She pushes the laptop across the table to me. 'Have a look at this. See what you think. I've got to run out for an hour, but I'll be back to take you for your manicure. OK?'

'Yes. Thank you.'

Crystal kisses my cheek and dashes off.

Angling the laptop so that I can see the screen better in the sunshine, I scroll slowly through the programme and the different courses on offer. I'm still doing my reading lessons with Hayden, though we haven't done so for a few nights now as we're ready to start a new book. We've finished Bridget Jones's very excellent diary now. Who, thank goodness, has finally seen that Mark Darcy is a better bet than the very naughty Daniel Cleaver. Poor woman. I was very worried for her.

On the screen, I stumble over words like 'extensions', 'technician' and 'aromatherapy'. It takes me an age to peruse the brochure. I have to read and re-read many of the sentences to make sense of them. If I'm struggling to understand this, then how will I manage with my studies? Surely there will be manuals to read, written work to complete? How will I cope?

For the first time, my stomach chills and I feel myself tremble with fear. I've never really had to fend for myself before. I went straight from living at home to my marriage. Suresh may not have been a good husband, but he dealt with all the money, all the bills. I know nothing of that. What if I can't find a job? What if I'm unable to provide for Sabina? Running away seemed to be the best idea I ever had. What if it wasn't?

I wish to be strong, but I feel tears stream down my face. I'm receiving benefits from the government now, which are topping up my small amount of hidden money, but these courses are expensive. Each module costs more money. Will Crystal and I have to offer many services before we become a viable business, or can we start small as she hopes? I don't know, and I'm finding it too difficult to think about.

'Hey.' I look up to see Hayden stepping out into the garden. 'Great day.'

Quickly I wipe away my tears. 'Yes. Very lovely.'

He drops into the chair next to me. 'Everything all right?'

I want to say, 'Yes. Perfectly.' But I can't find my voice.

197

Then he sees that I'm crying and he tenderly lays a hand on my arm. 'What's all this?'

I sniff back my misery. 'Crystal has found us some lovely courses. We had hoped to train to do manicures together, but I'm having great difficulty even reading the brochure. How will I be able to learn?'

'You're doing really well with your reading,' Hayden says encouragingly. 'You whipped through *Bridget Jones's Diary*. We can start something else as soon as you're ready. Maybe even tonight. It's only a matter of practice. I can help you. Crystal will help you.'

That makes me cry more.

'Remember that you're not alone any more, Ayesha,' he says softly. 'We all care for you here. You *and* Sabina. I'll do everything I can to help you build a future. I'll pay for the courses. If you want to, we can get a private tutor in so that you can go at your own pace. Whatever it takes.'

'I couldn't accept that.'

'I have more money than I know what to do with,' he insists. 'It would give me great pleasure to help you and Crystal find something you'd like to do.'

'I've never even *had* a manicure,' I confess. Perhaps it's a silly dream to think that I can do this.

'I'm sure if you speak to Crystal, then she'll sort it out.'

'I'm booked in at the Highly Polished nail salon at two o'clock,' I tell him with a watery laugh.

'There you go,' he says. 'Already on your way.'

'Thank you, Hayden. I appreciate your help.'

'We should get back to reading together tonight,' he offers. 'Make it our priority. If you want to.'

'I'd like that very much.'

'You're doing well. Don't be so hard on yourself. Rome wasn't built in a day, and neither is a new life.'

'I'll make some builder's tea,' I say. 'I think we need it.'

'Sounds like a great idea,' Hayden agrees.

I'm heading back towards the kitchen when a thought strikes me, and I turn back to Hayden. 'Would you like to walk to the school with me to collect Sabina? Crystal and I need to leave here at three-fifteen. We'll come straight back after my manicure. She'd like it if you did.'

I see anxiety cross his face.

'It's five minutes down the road.'

He wrings his hands.

'If I can do these things, then so can you,' I tell him.

'You're right.' He sighs. 'I'll come.'

# Chapter Forty-one

Crystal and I walk up to the High Street. Summer has given us a tantalising taste of things to come with a beautiful, warm day. Perfect for a pleasant stroll. My friend links her arm through mine, chattering all the way there, and I'm happy to be by her side, just listening.

A few minutes later we push open the door to Highly Polished. A little bell rings on our arrival. It's an oasis of whiteness and calm. Soothing music greets us. The beaming receptionist takes our jackets and shows us to two tidy nail stations next to each other.

'This is very nice,' I whisper to Crystal excitedly.

'It could be us next,' she says. 'Watch out, world!'

'Would you like some tea, or wine?' the receptionist asks.

'Glass of white would go down a treat,' Crystal says.

'I'll have tea, please.'

'Daytime blend, Earl Grey, rooibos?'

'Do you have any builder's tea?'

'Of course, madam.'

I sit down and a young girl comes to sit opposite me. 'Good

afternoon, Mrs Roberts,' she says. 'What am I going to do for you today?'

'I don't know,' I admit.

'Do you want a basic manicure, French manicure, reverse French, funky French, American polish? We also do shellac, acrylic, gel powder and bio-sculpture gel.'

'Oh.'

Crystal leans over. 'She'll have a French manicure, please. Can you use this pale pink?' She points to a colour.

'Yes, of course, Ms Cooper. No problem.'

So I sit there, trying to keep as still as a stone while my nails are filed and shaped. Then the girl paints on white tips followed by a transparent pink colour. She asks me all about my daughter and where I'm going on my next holiday while she does it. When I tell her that I've never been on a holiday, the girl looks as startled as Hayden did and spends the next ten minutes telling me how much she enjoys Greece.

During this time my tea is delivered, but I'm too terrified to move and drink it.

'There you are,' she says when she's eventually finished. 'They're lovely.'

I hold up my hands to admire them. They do look prettier than they ever have before.

'You should go to Greece one day,' she advises.

'Perhaps I will.'

Crystal downs the last of her wine and I take a few hurried sips of my tea. 'We'd better get a move on if we're to pick up Sabina.'

I'm very careful with my nails as I shrug on my jacket. It would be terrible to spoil them after they've had so much care and attention. 'I've asked Hayden to walk with us this afternoon.'

'And he said yes?'

201

'He did.'

'Wow,' she says. 'You're deffo a good influence on him.'

I'm bashful now. 'I don't think so.'

We go to the desk to pay and the receptionist looks up at us and smiles. 'Your account has been settled, Ms Cooper. A treat from Mr Daniels.'

'Hayden paid the bill? Cool.'

'That's very thoughtful of him.'

Crystal looks at me carefully. 'He's a catch,' she says. 'There aren't many men like him around. Just remember that.'

'I think that he's still in love with Laura,' I say. 'Perhaps he always will be.'

Crystal sighs. 'I think you're probably right. It's time he let her go, though. That man *seriously* needs to move on. It's not as if she's ever going to come back.'

'Perhaps he hopes that she will,' I offer. 'One day.'

'That's never going to happen, is it?'

'Sometimes these things have a way of working themselves out.'

Crystal looks at me, surprised. 'Laura's dead,' she tells me. 'You didn't know?'

I reel and have to hold the reception desk to steady myself. 'No one told me.'

'I'm sorry,' Crystal says. 'What an idiot I am. I assumed you knew. Hayden doesn't like to talk about it, but I thought he would have said *something*. You do seem to have a lot of cosy chats.' Crystal raises her eyebrows.

'I thought she'd left him.' I assumed that she tired of the relationship or had met someone else. The usual things that happen.

'God, no. They were totally loved up, about to get engaged. But they had a car accident. A terrible one. Laura was driving when they were chased by paparazzi. I don't know exactly what

202

happened, but something they did caused Laura to flip the car. Hayden walked away without a scratch. Laura didn't.'

'How terrible.' He might have escaped without major injury, but there's no doubt that his pain continues daily.

'Laura's gone for good,' Crystal continues. 'I hope one day Hayden can accept that and learn to love again. God knows I've tried my best.' She slips her arm around me. 'Perhaps, my little friend, you'll have better luck than me.'

# Chapter Forty-two

At three-fifteen I'm reading, and waiting in the hall for Crystal and Hayden to walk up to school to meet Sabina. Hayden is the first to arrive. He's wearing a black wool hat pulled right down over his ears and brow. It's so low that it's touching the dark glasses he's also wearing. He has on a jacket with the collar flipped up.

'It's very warm outside,' I say to him. What I really want to do is reach out and touch him, tell him that I now understand his pain.

'Photographers,' he says. 'I don't want anyone taking a photograph.'

'Oh.' I hadn't thought until now how much of a trial this might be for him. My new knowledge puts a different slant on everything. 'You don't have to come.'

'I'd like to,' he says. 'Old habits die hard, though.'

'I don't think that there are any photographers outside,' I offer.

'They're everywhere,' he tells me.

'Oh.' I don't know how to make this better for him. Yet I have to risk a glance at my watch. Soon I must be going or

Sabina will be out of her class and she'll be left by herself waiting for me.

At that moment, Crystal sticks her head out of Hayden's office. 'I'm stuck on hold on the phone to the college,' she says. 'Can you two go without me?'

'Yes, of course.' I turn to Hayden. 'Is that all right with you?'

'Fine,' he says, but his face seems to turn pale.

'Sure?'

He nods and we go to leave. But at the threshold, he stops and holds on to the frame. 'Wow,' he says. 'This is a little harder than I thought.'

For a moment, I think he might faint.

'Perhaps I should go back inside,' he says.

Now it's my turn to panic. 'I don't like to go alone.'

'What a pair,' Hayden says. His breathing is shallow. 'We can do this. We can do this.'

It makes me realise that in all the time that I've been here, I've never actually seen Hayden go out of the house at all. He might wander occasionally into the garden, but no further. I might know why now, but that still can't be a good thing.

'There's nothing to worry about,' I tell him. 'If you'll be there for me, I'll do the same for you. Sabina will be so thrilled to see you.'

His hand goes to his heart. 'I think my chest might explode.'

'Then we'll take it slowly. Small steps.'

I link my arm through his as Crystal does to me.

'Small steps,' he echoes.

So we go out into the sunshine, me with my newly painted nails, Hayden with his woolly hat on.

At the security gates he pulls up again. 'I haven't been outside of these for a very long time.'

'The walk to the school is very pleasant. It only takes a few minutes.'

205

He nods at me and gingerly we inch forward.

Hayden looks both ways, up and down the road. When he's satisfied there are no photographers around, together we venture out on to the pavement. We fall into faltering steps beside each other.

'That's not so bad, is it?' He's like a man who's walking on the edge of a cliff.

'No,' he says, but his teeth are gritted.

'Thank you very much for paying for my manicure.' To distract him, I hold up my hands for him to see.

'Beautiful,' he says, and the word catches in his throat.

I blush. 'It was very kind.'

'Just a little treat.'

'I feel very glamorous.' Not like Crystal, but in my own way.

Eventually the school comes into sight and I give his arm a slight squeeze. 'We made it.'

He smiles, but there's sweat on his top lip when he says, 'That wasn't too bad.'

As we go through the school gate, some of the mothers turn to look at Hayden. He puts his head down and studies the ground, but they continue to stare at him and nudge one another. A titter goes round the group. I wonder if they recognise him, or if they're simply excited because he's tall, muscular and handsome and very few men like that wait at the school gates. Whichever it is, I can tell that he's uncomfortable and I wish they'd leave him in peace. This is trial enough for him.

Not a minute too soon, the children run out of the door and I feel Hayden relax slightly. When Sabina sees us she dashes towards us, heading towards Hayden first. He catches her at full tilt and swings her high up into the air. I can barely believe my own ears, but a little squeak of delight escapes from her throat.

Hayden and I exchange a careful glance. My eyes fill with tears. It may not seem like much, but it's the first sound of any kind that I've heard from my daughter's lips in a very long time. I know now that her voice, although locked up, is still inside her, and I hope beyond hope that one day it will be free again.

'You weigh a ton, Little Bean,' Hayden says, tossing her in the air as if she's nothing but a feather. He swings her back to the ground. She's breathless and smiling.

'And a kiss for your mama?' I say.

Her sweet lips brush my cheek. Hayden and I take a hand each and we walk her away from the playground.

Over her head, we exchange another glance. This time, Hayden tips down his sunglasses and winks at me. I wink back.

# Chapter Forty-three

Crystal ambushes me the minute we walk through the door. 'I've booked us on a course,' she says. 'Manicurist. Just two days.'

'Really?'

'Next week. A hundred and fifty quid each.'

I reel at that. 'I don't have that amount of money to spare,' I tell her. 'I can't do it.'

'The course at the local college is heaps cheaper, but it doesn't start until September,' Crystal says. 'I can't wait until then. This way, we can be out and working as soon as possible.'

My heart sinks. What can I do now?

'I'll pay for it,' Hayden says. 'For both of you.'

'I can't accept,' I tell him. I don't even need to think about this. There's no way that I can be beholden to a man again. Even this kind one.

'Call it a loan,' he says. 'You can pay me back when you get on your feet again.'

'I'm not so sure,' I admit. 'It's a big commitment.'

'Think about it,' Hayden says. 'There's no pressure.'

Crystal shuffles her feet. 'Er ... actually there is. I've already booked for us and paid on my credit card.'

'Oh, Crystal,' I say. 'You shouldn't have done this without my permission.'

'Don't look at me like that,' she says, pouting. 'It will be *totes* fabulous fun!'

'This is supposed to be the start of me running my *own* life.'

'Oh,' she says. 'Didn't think of it like that.'

I sigh, when really I feel like crying.

'Can't you start running your own life *after* we've done the course?' Crystal cringes apologetically.

'Go,' Hayden intervenes. 'Enjoy yourselves. I *insist* on paying.'

'How will I collect Sabina from school?' Now I'm thinking of all the obstacles.

'Hayden will go and get her,' Crystal says. She looks at him. 'You're not doing anything else?'

'I don't know if that's a good idea,' I interject. It was so difficult for him today that I don't know if I could ask him to go through that again.

'Crystal's right,' he says. 'I can pick Sabina up from school both afternoons, if you're not back in time.'

'Are you sure? We could ask Joy.'

'She'll be at her day centre,' he points out. 'No need to drag her back. I can do it.'

I must still look uncertain as he adds, 'I *can* do it. I promise. You won't mind that, will you, Beanie?'

My child shakes her head and smiles shyly. I think she's taken quite a shine to Hayden and he seems to be very patient and caring towards her.

'The course will be good for both of you,' Hayden adds.

Feeling myself weaken, I can't help but break into a smile. It seems like it would be a soothing job, something that I could do. I like to care for people, and this is a nice way to do it. If we can find work, I could perhaps fit it around Sabina's school hours. 'I'd very much like to take the course.'

Crystal pounces on that. 'Fab! There's all kinds of other modules, but this will teach us the basics.'

I turn to Hayden. 'But I'd very much like to pay for it myself. That's important to me.' I still have several hundred from the money I brought with me, but I want to keep it for emergencies. What if I have to leave this house?

He shrugs. 'I can understand that.'

'However, can I please accept your offer of help with any written work and to collect Sabina?'

'Of course. It would be my pleasure.' He smiles at me. I want to have his respect. I want to respect myself.

Crystal hugs me tightly. 'I'm so excited,' she says.

'Me too. I hope it will be lots of fun.' I've never taken a course in anything and it feels as if a whole world of possibilities is opening up to me. But, first things first. I'll soon have a lot of hungry friends. I slip off my jacket. 'Now I must start dinner or we'll all be eating at midnight. Sabina, do you have homework?'

She nods.

'I'll do it with her,' Hayden offers.

'Thank you.'

They sit at the table together and I listen to Hayden as he patiently goes through a list of spellings with her. I try to repeat them in my own head.

I chop and fry the chicken and leave it to cook in a sauce of spices and coconut milk. Joy has left a selection of vegetables on the counter and I set to peeling them.

I'm thrilled and anxious about the manicure course next week. I should feel very grateful to Crystal for organising it, as I wonder if I would have had the courage to book it and go along by myself. I realise that if I'm going to make it out there in the big wide world, then I have to be more assertive.

Hayden looks up and smiles at me as if he's reading my thoughts. 'We're nearly done here,' he says.

'Dinner will be a long while yet. Why don't you play the piano?'

'I might just do that.' He turns to Sabina. 'Fancy another "Chopsticks" duel?'

She nods enthusiastically.

I watch as he takes her by the hand, and together they go off towards the living room.

I'm lucky, so lucky, to have landed up here on Hayden Daniels's doorstep, but this place is a bubble. I feel protected here, as if it's a halfway house to real life. After this, it's going to be very difficult to step out on my own.

# Chapter Forty-four

The trail had gone cold again. Suresh stared at his laptop screen and pushed his fingers through his hair. He'd scoured the internet and had found the name of a women's-aid charity that had offices in Drummond Street. Maybe that was where Ayesha had gone. Trust her to want charity. Now everything about her sickened him.

He'd tried to find out by ringing them direct. Despite a dozen increasingly irate telephone calls he'd got nowhere with them. In the end he'd resorted to threats, but still to no avail. They were tough bitches. If she had been there, they were saying nothing. 'Client confidentiality,' they kept spouting. What lies. All they were doing was keeping husbands from their wives and fathers from their children. He'd told them as much.

Suresh had been down to London again, twice more. Both times on his own. Even the lads thought he was becoming obsessed and his brother took every opportunity to tell him so. He could do without that. He'd driven round in his car, walked the streets, hoping for a glimpse of her. Ayesha couldn't just fade into the background. Sometime soon she'd make a mistake and he'd be there, looking over her shoulder, breathing down her neck, waiting, waiting.

He spent day after day searching the internet for some mention of her, some clue to give him an idea of what to do next. It was time he could ill afford and that made him even more angry with her. There was a big job coming up with Flynn and Smith. Bigger than anything they'd done before. It was time they stepped up a league. They'd be rich men if they could pull this off, but it was taking a lot of planning. Every night they gathered in his kitchen to go over the details, fine-tune them so that nothing could go wrong. Yet this business with Ayesha was distracting him.

His mother came over with a cup of tea for him. Her movements were slow now, laboured. She seemed to have shrunk into herself, diminishing in size since Ayesha and Sabina had gone, and that riled him. She put the tea down next to the computer.

'Not there,' he snapped. 'What if it spills?'

His mother slid it further away on the table. Before she could move from him, he grabbed her by the wrist. It was thin, papery, it would snap so easily. She was frail. Her grey hair sparse. His father was no better. All he did was sit in his chair for hours on end, talking about the good old days.

'You're hurting me, my son.'

He let go and she nursed her arm against her body. 'Have you heard from her?' he said. 'No secret letters? No phone calls that you've forgotten to mention?'

'No,' she answered. 'Nothing.'

'I don't want you contacting her parents.'

'What would I tell them?' his mother said. 'That your wife and child have run away into the night and we don't know where they are? They would be beside themselves with worry. I wouldn't wish to bring that on them.'

'She will try to speak to you,' he said. 'I know these things. You would tell me, wouldn't you?'

There was a slight hesitation that told him all he needed to know. His mother turned her face from him.

'I won't stop looking,' he warned. 'When you *do* speak to her, you tell her that.'

'She won't get in touch with us,' his mother said sadly. 'We've lost her. She's taken our grandchild and gone for good.'

'You say that as if it's my fault.'

Again, the telling hesitation.

'You must look into your heart, Suresh. Were you a good husband to her?'

'She had everything she needed. A roof over her head. Food on the table.'

'All anyone ever needs is love,' his mother said.

'Duty,' he countered, stabbing his finger at the table. 'That's what this is about. She should do her duty.'

'Do you miss her?'

He looked up, surprised. 'What's that got to do with it?'

His mother shook her head and left the room.

'She'll be back,' he spat after her. 'Mark my words.'

# Chapter Forty-five

The following Monday morning, Crystal and I are scrubbed, polished and ready to take on the world of manicure. I'm wearing my floral blouse and white linen trousers. They get dusty very quickly and I'm having to wash and iron them every few days. Being more stylish is time-consuming, but I'm determined to try. Crystal has put a little make-up on for me so that I look groomed. Her word, not mine. Crystal is wearing a tight white T-shirt and equally tight white jeans.

'Are you sure you're happy about walking Sabina to school?' I say to Hayden. My heart is fluttering in my chest. What if he gets halfway there and feels that he can go no further?

He glances at Sabina with raised eyebrows. 'Are we sure?'

My child nods. It doesn't look as if her heart is troubled.

Hayden turns to me. 'We're sure.'

'And you'll be there on time to pick her up this afternoon?'

'On the dot,' he assures me.

'I've told the school that you will be collecting her.'

'Good.'

'If it rains, take an umbrella.'

'I could have worked that out for myself,' he tells me gently.

215

He makes me realise that I'm being ridiculous. Hayden has promised me that he'll do it and I must trust him. I want to tell him that I know about Laura, that I understand why this is so very difficult for him, but I don't know how to find the words. 'I'm sorry. You're a responsible adult.'

'Of the very best quality.'

'I'm worried. I don't want this to be an ordeal for you.'

'You have no need for concern.' Hayden puts his hands on my arms. 'Really. I *will* do this. Have a great day. Concentrate on your studies. Learn lots. Don't fret about Beanie.'

I nod.

'We're going to be late if we don't get a move on,' Crystal says.

Hayden kisses her cheek. 'You have fun too.'

'I intend to,' Crystal says.

Then, unexpectedly, he reaches down and brushes my cheek with a kiss too. It's all I can do to stop myself from reaching up to touch where his lips have been. I can feel my skin burning there, but not in a bad way.

'Have a good day, ladies.'

Bending down to Sabina, I hug her tightly. 'Be a good girl for Hayden and Joy. Wait for Hayden in the playground. Don't leave with anyone else. No one. Do you understand?'

Sabina nods solemnly.

'I'll see you later.' I help her to slip on her jacket and then Hayden holds out one of his big, strong hands for her. My daughter's tiny one is enveloped by it and I feel my eyes brimming with tears.

'None of that,' he chides. 'Not today.'

I gulp them back.

Crystal grabs my hand. 'Come on, dilly-dolly woman, let's get our swag on.'

So, waving goodbye to Sabina and Hayden, we rush out of the house.

The Hampstead Beauty School is at the bottom of Rosslyn Hill and it takes us about fifteen minutes to walk there. I never fail to be impressed at how Crystal manages to stride out in her teetering heels. Even in my sensible flat shoes, I struggle to keep up with her.

Inside, it looks as if we are to train in a marshmallow, as everything in the school seems to be white and sugar-pink. Even Crystal looks slightly anxious now and we cling together as we're asked to fill out details on forms. Surreptitiously, Crystal helps me with my writing and I manage to complete mine without problems.

There are two other women here for the training who look older than Crystal and me. Then there's a young girl who's on her own, and I'm pleased to see that the class is small as I feel less intimidated.

Thankfully, Crystal and I are paired together and, without further ado, we're given our own nail station and are set to work. Crystal's eyes light up like a child's in a sweetie shop when she scans the rainbow array of nail polishes.

'Look at these!' she breathes in awe. She picks up a little pot of sparkles and shows them to me for approval. 'Jewels!'

'Very pretty.'

'I can't wait till we do this.'

Throughout the morning, we're shown how to treat neglected cuticles and shape the nails in a variety of popular styles. I've never done anything like this before and I find it absorbing. I feel very proud of myself for being able to keep up. This afternoon, the tutor tells us, we're doing polishing and basic decoration. Tomorrow we'll learn hand massage.

'So,' Crystal says as she starts to file my nails. 'Where are you going on your holidays this year, Mrs Roberts?' Which makes us both giggle and we get a stern look from the tutor. When Crystal has finished, we change places and I do hers.

217

At lunchtime we're given an hour's break to go and get a sandwich. The room is chilled with air-conditioning and it feels nice to have the sun on my skin as we walk along the High Street, which is bustling as usual.

Crystal links her arm in mine. 'I'm glad we're doing this together. It makes it more fun, doesn't it?'

'Yes.'

'You know that Vinny's not stopped texting me asking me to go back to the club?'

'Really?'

'Yeah.'

'You never would?'

Crystal sighs. 'No. Never. Can't say I'm not missing the money though. I've got a bit saved up, but it won't last for ever and there's still a ton of stuff on my credit card. I'll have to get a regular job pretty soon. There's plenty of money to be made in a nail salon, but I'm under no illusion that it will be as much as wiggling my bum in someone's ugly mush.'

I laugh at that.

'Still, thanks in no small part to you, I'm out of there now.'

'You feel better?'

'Yeah. Heaps. I didn't realise how low that stinking job had brought me. Now I feel I could take on the world.' She high-fives me. 'I owe you one.'

I stop and turn to her. 'You don't. It is I who owe you. I want you to know that I'm very grateful for all that you've done for us. For me and for Sabina.'

'Go on with you.' She nudges me. 'We're mates. We look after each other. Promise me: wherever you go, whatever you do, we won't lose touch. Promise we'll always be friends.'

'I promise.'

We hurry to eat our lunch together on a bench outside the deli before rushing back for our next lesson.

In the afternoon, we learn how to apply nail varnish with a variety of techniques. Crystal, with more experience of polishing nails than me, has a steadier hand, whereas I seem to put more of it on my skin than my nails. I'll need to have more practice.

When it gets to three-fifteen, I look at the clock. I hope that Hayden has remembered to collect Sabina. I hope that he hasn't found that he's unable to go beyond the gates of the house. I'm worried that she'll be waiting there alone. I'm worried about a thousand things that I cannot easily speak about.

'She'll be fine,' Crystal says, even though I haven't voiced my concerns. 'Hayden won't let you down.'

'I know. I can't help it. I hate having Sabina out of my sight.' As the time goes by, I'm becoming more convinced that we have escaped from Suresh's clutches. But there's always a small part of my mind that wonders whether we are yet truly free.

# Chapter Forty-six

Hayden felt completely paranoid, but he was sure as he'd walked Sabina up to school that morning that someone was watching him. The old feelings of panic started to set in.

Now, at the allotted time, it was all he could do to put on his hat and sunglasses and go out of the door to collect her. He stood at the door, his heart pounding. His upper lip was sweating profusely. Under his hat, his scalp prickled with it. He could do this. He *had* to do this. He'd promised Ayesha.

At the gates, he paused again. As far as he could tell, there was no one around. Perhaps the press had forgotten about him after all. Goodness knows they had enough celebrity fodder to fill the glossy mags, the online star sites and the red-tops.

Walking up to the school, he forced himself to stride out. After a few minutes, his legs loosened and the tightness went from his jaw. It was good to be in the sunshine, beyond the confines of the gates, and he wondered if he could ever go back to a time where he was of little interest to people. What if he wanted to make music again? Would that mean putting up with all the other crap that went with it? He didn't know if he could ever face that.

Up at the school, he leaned against the railings, keeping his head down. There was only five minutes to go before Sabina would be let out. He could tell that some of the mums were looking at him. They were giggling and nudging each other, as they had this morning. Perhaps even more overtly now. He busied himself with a bit of fake texting, a technique he'd used more than once, with mixed success.

Then, out of the corner of his eye, he realised that this was going to be one of the less successful occasions.

'Hello.' A small blonde woman had crossed the playground to come and stand in front of him. She fiddled with her hair. 'I'm a big fan of your music, Hayden. I've got all of your albums. I wondered if I could have my picture taken with you?' She brandished her mobile phone at him.

They were the invention of the devil, Hayden thought. It meant that no one was ever without a camera these days.

'Would you mind?'

Now he was torn. He'd rather have his eyeballs poked out, but if he said no then he would be branded as rude and she'd tell all her friends what a stuck-up knob he was. The trouble was, these days, it would be all over Twitter and Facebook within seconds.

'Sure,' he said, wishing she'd go away and leave him alone.

She stood next to him and held out the camera at arm's length. Click. And it was done. It made him feel sick to his stomach.

He hoped Sabina would hurry out, otherwise the rest of them would be over in a minute and he'd be mobbed. It had happened enough times over the years for him to know the inevitable pattern.

Thankfully, at that very moment the school's doors opened and disgorged its precious cargo of children. They streamed out towards their mothers, and the woman who'd photographed him said thank you and blended back into the crowd.

Tomorrow, he might have to ask Joy to do the school run. He wasn't sure he could cope with it if word got around that he was there.

The child rushed out to him, and once again he scooped her up. He had an overwhelming urge to put her on his shoulders and take her home that way, but it was probably unseemly. Instead he dropped her to the floor and high-fived her. Solemnly, her palm touched his.

'Had a good day?'

She nodded. Her big brown eyes gazed up at him. Those eyes would break hearts one day, just like her mother's.

'Did you learn anything new?'

Sabina shrugged.

'Want me to teach you another song on the piano?'

She smiled and his heart melted.

'OK.' He took her hand in his and they started the short walk home. 'Let's do it.'

By the time they got back indoors, Hayden was starting to sweat, and he was glad to be out of the sun and in the cool of the kitchen once more. Walking back with Sabina had calmed him, but more than once he'd turned round to check that they weren't being followed. He'd have to conquer these feelings though, otherwise he'd soon find he didn't have a choice whether he went out or not.

Sabina sat at the table and he poured her a glass of milk. Then he found two chocolate-chip cookies in the biscuit tin for her. He decided to join her and did the same for himself. He sat down opposite her.

'Got spellings to do?'

She nodded.

'Let's do those first.'

So she opened the Hello Kitty backpack that she was so

attached to and fished in it until she pulled out her homework. Sabina worked through them in silence, sipping her milk as she did.

Was this what it would be like to have his own child? he wondered. This charming little girl had certainly worked her way into his heart. He looked at her with a paternal tenderness and protectiveness that he'd never known was possible. She might not speak but she was brimming with personality and she was razor-sharp. One day, he thought, he'd like a family life. If he kept living in the past, brooding on what might have been, then he was going to end up alone. He couldn't expect Joy or Crystal or even Ayesha to be around here for ever. Though, looking across at Sabina, he couldn't bear the thought of any of them going. It was in many ways a dysfunctional little unit, but somehow it worked.

He looked at the counter. Joy had left a pile of vegetables there, as she'd taken to doing. Perhaps he should start to prep them, help Ayesha out as she'd have had a busy day. They'd fallen into the routine of eating together every night, which was nice.

Ayesha was a fantastic cook. She'd even got Joy eating some spicy dishes. No mean feat. He'd started to work out harder since she'd arrived, otherwise his waistline would have begun to thicken. In fact, he could really do with starting to run again. He could feel the need to pound the pavements itching in his feet, but that would mean him going outside on a daily basis and he wasn't sure he was quite ready for that. When he thought about it, Ayesha had a lot of qualities. It stirred feelings inside him that he'd thought were too deeply buried to ever come to the surface again. He wasn't sure he was ready for those, either.

When Sabina had finished, she turned the book and pushed it across the table for Hayden to check. While he was busy, she nibbled daintily at the cookies, dropping crumbs all over the table, and he realised that he should have given her a plate.

'Very good,' he said, impressed. 'Ten out of ten. There were some hard words in there.'

She smiled shyly, a glimmer of pride peeping through.

'Ready to play the piano?'

More nodding.

'Go and wash your hands.' She jumped down from the table and went to the sink. When she'd dried them, they went through to the living room.

Hayden threw open the French doors, letting the sun flood into the room, and they took up their places on the piano stool, side by side.

'Do you know "Mary Had a Little Lamb"?'

Sabina shook her head.

'Let's get started then.'

# Chapter Forty-seven

I've thoroughly enjoyed my day learning how to be a manicurist, but now, I have to confess, I can't wait to get home and see my child. It's so hard to leave her and I wonder how difficult it will prove to be a working mother. I will, at times in the future, have to leave her in the care of strangers, which pains me more than I can say. Yet this is the price I have to pay for my freedom.

Crystal is totally hyper, or 'totes hype', as she would say. She's loved our day too. In fact, the tutor nearly had to manhandle her out of the door as she didn't want to go home. I think it's fair to say that Crystal has found her calling.

I make Crystal hurry home as fast as we can and when I burst through the front door, the very first thing that I do is shout out my child's name.

'Sabina! Sabina!' Sometimes I forget that she won't shout back, but it doesn't stop my heart from longing.

'In here!' Hayden's voice comes from the living room. I throw down my bag and rush to see them.

They're both sitting at the piano and Sabina is beaming.

'Hello, my darling,' I say. She jumps down from the stool and runs to embrace me. I inhale the beautiful scent of her hair as I hug her to me. 'Have you been good today?'

She nods.

'Did you enjoy your course?' Hayden asks.

'Very much so. I'm looking forward to going back tomorrow.'

'Any homework you need help with?'

I grimace. 'Diseases and Disorders of the Nail.'

He laughs. 'Riveting. We'll have to put our more entertaining reading aside for the night.'

'I fear we will.'

Sabina unwinds herself from me and goes back to the piano stool.

'Want to hear what we've been doing?' Hayden asks.

'I'd very much like that.'

My child settles herself and, when Hayden nods, together they play a delightful little tune. It brings tears to my eyes to see her concentrating so hard.

When they finish, I clap my hands together. 'You are both *so* clever. That was lovely.'

'She's picked it up really quickly,' Hayden says. 'I think she has a natural talent.'

'Thank you for taking the time with her, and thank you for collecting her from school.' I know how difficult that must have been for him.

'The pleasure's all mine.'

'I'd better start our dinner.'

'I'll come and help.'

We exchange a shy glance. 'Thank you.'

I make dinner, something quick and easy so that we can eat soon. Hayden helps me by preparing vegetables and Sabina sets the table. For the first time in my life, I have to watch my fingernails while I work.

When Joy and Crystal join us, I serve. There's a hearty vegetable curry, all made from Joy's wonderful produce, and plenty of plain boiled rice. There's a salad of grated carrot with chilli, lime and coconut to go with it.

When we're ready to eat, Hayden raises his glass. 'To Ayesha and Crystal. Wishing them every success in their new career.'

We toast with some lemonade that Joy has made.

'I'm going to need a bit of practice,' I confess. 'Crystal had no trouble at all, but my polishing skills are very wobbly.'

'That's because you've led a very unglamorous life up until now,' she says.

'I'd offer to be a model,' Joy says, 'but it would be pointless. Tomorrow I'll be digging up potatoes again and that will ruin all your hard work. Once upon a time, I did have very beautiful nails.'

Hayden holds up his hands. 'Don't look at me.' He laughs. 'I don't mind going through Diseases and Disorders of the Nail with you, but I draw the line at practical help.'

'You could come in to my day centre, if you like,' Joy offers. 'I'm sure the old dears wouldn't mind you practising on them. In fact, I'm certain they'd absolutely love it. They like a bit of fuss.'

I turn to Crystal. 'We could do that.'

She's busy spooning more vegetable curry on to her plate. 'Don't see why not.'

'Could we come in next week when we've finished our training?'

'I'll sort it out when I go in tomorrow.' Joy helps herself to curry too.

How exciting! It looks as if we may have our first customers. I believe wholeheartedly that this is the right thing to do. Suddenly, the future is beginning to look very rosy indeed.

# Chapter Forty-eight

Desires Gentlemen's Club. Suresh had been there twice more on his visits to London. After a day searching fruitlessly for Ayesha, he needed something to cheer him up, and watching the girls put out for the punters warmed his blood.

This time it hadn't worked. He'd taken one of the girls back to his hotel behind Euston Station and had paid too much for too little enthusiasm. He'd been on top of her when suddenly Ayesha's face had appeared in a blur before him, and he put his hands round her throat and felt his fingers tighten. He wanted to squeeze and squeeze, see the life go out of her. Then he'd realised that the woman beneath him wasn't the woman he wanted to punish, and he'd pulled himself back from the brink.

He'd stopped in time, but the temptation to give the hooker a backhander or worse had been almost overwhelming. Instead he'd thrown her out of the room as soon as she'd finished, and good riddance to her.

Shaken at what he could so easily have done, he hadn't wanted breakfast in the hotel, which seemed to be full of noisy Chinese tourists on a coach tour. They were heading off to

Bicester Village, a designer shopping centre, for the day, he heard. Madness. Why come all the way to London and then go shopping? he wondered. Suresh, on the other hand, had decided to head into the thick of the tourist spots. Maybe he'd be more likely to find her round there. It would be just like her to take Sabina out for the day.

Plus, he'd got to the point where he didn't know what else to do. Flynn, Smith and Arunja had quickly grown tired of him banging on about her, so he kept his own counsel now. He hadn't asked them to come down with him again and none of them had volunteered. Not even his own brother. But none of his friends understood how deep this went. It was as if she'd carved out his heart and now there was nothing left in its place. He'd never expected a woman to do that to him.

First he headed up to Covent Garden, grabbing a bacon sandwich which he was charged a fortune for as it was on ciabatta rather than sliced bread. But it tasted good and, two cups of strong coffee later, he was fortified for the day.

He wandered the streets, taking in the performers, who were starting up early, going through their well-worn routines for the smattering of morning tourists. By the afternoon this place would be unrecognisable, heaving with sightseers and pick-pockets.

A few times he turned sharply, thinking he'd seen her out of the corner of his eye. But each time he was disappointed. They were never as pretty as Ayesha, never as delicate.

He took in some of the places he'd lived as a child, before his parents had been lured by the empty promises of life in a vibrant new city and they'd moved out of London. Pacing the streets of Brick Lane brought him some familiar comfort, but still no sign of his wife.

By the evening, he'd worked his way through Soho and back to Leicester Square. He was footsore and angrier than he'd ever been in his life. For her, he'd trailed all over London, and it had brought him nothing. Nothing but more pain.

They were setting up for a film première at the main cinema, the Odeon. The barriers were already in place. The picture of the impossibly handsome film star was twenty foot high and dominated an entire wall. It was someone that Suresh had never heard of.

Along one side of the square there were groups of young women gathering to wait until their idol appeared. It was warm still, but rain was threatening and yet they wore little clothing. The sleeping bags at their feet showed that they had been here since yesterday, prepared to wait hours and hours for even a glimpse of some man they worshipped. Some of them looked as if they should still be in school.

This was the sort of shallowness that life was about now. What had this bloke done to deserve their adulation? He was a man, nothing more. Women wanted more than a good, reliable husband. Much more. They wanted money, diamonds, fancy cars, designer clothing. That's what they wanted, and he despised them for it.

There was an agony building inside of him that wasn't physical, but he didn't know how to release it. He flicked open the Swiss Army knife in his pocket and let the fleshy pad of his thumb tease the blade.

The rain started now, intermittent hard splashes that made the young, inadequately dressed girls squeal. Some of them ripped open plastic bags and held them above their heads. Their shrieking seemed to pierce deep into his brain until it felt like it was he who was screaming.

The torrent increased now and the girls scattered, running into shop doorways and cafés. Suresh remained where he was and tilted his face to the clouds, letting the water run down his face. He was soaked, soaked through to the skin, but the water didn't feel cleansing as he'd hoped it would. It only made the pain intensify.

He took the knife and pulled it slowly across the palm of his hand. The cut was shallow, but it released his agony. He held his hand up to the grey, unforgiving sky. The blood seeped out, mingled with the rain and flowed on to the pavement.

Suresh threw back his head and cried out, 'Ayesha!'

# Chapter Forty-nine

Crystal and I finish the course and both pass with flying colours. My friend's forte is decorating the nails and adding a multitude of sparkles. I enjoyed learning how to massage the hands and found it very soothing to do. We both have bona fide certificates to prove our worth, and we're both thrilled with ourselves.

Joy has arranged that on Monday we'll go into her day centre to give manicures to the ladies. We bought some necessary equipment from the college, so that was a little more expense that I could have done without. Hopefully, now that I can work, I'll be able to start to recoup some money.

It's Saturday and Crystal has gone out shopping with a couple of her friends from the club. She can't wait to catch up on the gossip and see what's been said about her shock departure. Buoyed by our small success, I know that she also wants to try to persuade some of the other girls to leave and try different career paths too. She tripped out of the house all excited just as Sabina and I were getting up, and that's most unlike her.

It's not yet nine o'clock, but it's already mild in the sunshine and Sabina was wriggling in bed, so it was better to get up or I'd have had bruised shins. We're having breakfast in the garden, and once again I think how lucky I am to be here and to be safe. The weathermen have said that the weekend ahead will be very hot and it's nice to feel the heat through my blouse, warming my arms.

As I'm making more tea, Hayden joins us.

'You're awake early,' I note.

'Couldn't stay in bed on such a beautiful day,' he says. 'The sun was streaming through the window. Have you been up for long?'

'I couldn't stay in bed because my dear child is a terrible fidget,' I tell him.

'Take another bedroom,' Hayden says. 'There are at least another couple empty on my floor. We'd need to clear some junk out, I guess, but I want you to be comfortable here. You and Sabina could have separate rooms if you want to.'

I shake my head. 'For all she disturbs me, I want to be near her all night. I don't think I'd sleep at all otherwise. Perhaps when she's a little older, I must do that.' I lower my eyes. 'If we're still here. But not now.'

'I hope you'll both be here for a very long time,' he says softly.

My cheeks burn and I busy myself at the counter. 'Can I get you some breakfast?'

'Toast would be great.'

'Go and sit down. I'll bring it to you.'

Hayden heads out towards the garden to sit with Sabina but before he steps out of the French doors he turns back. 'Have you got any plans for today?'

'I'd hoped to do some laundry, but nothing more.'

'Can the laundry wait?'

'I should think so.'

'Fancy going to the seaside? The three of us.'

233

My heart pitter-patters. 'Today?'

'Now,' he says. 'This minute. As soon as I've eaten my toast.'

'Oh, yes!'

'Beanie,' he shouts out to my daughter. 'Want to go to the beach?'

She nods so much I fear her head may fall off.

Hayden grins at me. 'Carried unanimously. The beach it is.'

# Chapter Fifty

When he'd thrown a few spare clothes in a bag, Hayden went down into the garage. It was so long since he'd been in this place, he'd almost forgotten what it looked like. There were three cars housed here and, to his eternal shame, a raft of others stored at a ludicrously expensive garaging facility somewhere in south London that hadn't been used in years.

Hayden wasn't even sure what was still here. He cast his eyes over the shrouded cars and felt sick to his stomach just looking at them. Now he'd promised Ayesha and Sabina a day out and there was no going back. So, bracing himself, he pulled off the first dust cover, and discovered a Porsche that he'd actually forgotten he'd bought. How could he forget that he'd bought a car? What kind of wanton extravagance had there been in his life? It was a nice one, granted, but it wouldn't be much good for a family day out.

The next car he uncovered was a Mercedes coupé, also a two-door sports model. Not much use either. He'd obviously been going through an impractical-car phase. Some of these could be sold. Tracking down the paperwork for all the cars he owned should be high on his list of Things To Do. Someone

235

else could make better use of them. It was such a terrible waste to have them all sitting here, idle and rotting away.

He desperately hoped the final car didn't have only two seats, or he'd be left with egg on his face and two very disappointed ladies.

Swishing the cover aside revealed, thankfully, a Range Rover. It was the same type of car that Laura had been driving when she'd been killed, and he felt a tremor of dull pain work its way through his body at the thought. Had he owned this one before she died, or was it a replacement? He didn't know. However, it was this or nothing and now he was committed.

Hayden folded the dust sheet and opened the car door. The keys were already in the ignition and he hesitated, taking a deep breath, before he was able to sit in the driver's seat. The other thing that he hadn't considered when making this rash and spontaneous decision was that he hadn't been behind the wheel of a car since Laura had died. The image of her lying, bloody and dying, in his arms flashed to the front of his mind. He'd have to get a grip or they'd not get down there today at all. If only he'd thought this through rather than getting caught up in the moment, but it was out of his mouth before he'd even weighed up the implications. He could have booked a driver for the day. There was someone who used to come in and drive him around London when it was necessary – before it had become easier to stop going out at all. Ayesha would understand if he pulled out, but how would he explain that to Little Bean? He couldn't bear to go back and tell her that he'd made a bad mistake. It would have to be someone with a harder heart than his to want to see that face disappointed. The kid deserved some fun and, come hell or high water, he was going to give it to her.

There was nothing for it. He had to do it. Hayden clicked the fob that operated the electric garage door and, despite not having been troubled for years now, it slid effortlessly open. His

236

palms were sweating just sitting there, and he wiped them on his jeans. He wanted to feel safe doing this, confident. There was no way he wanted to put either Ayesha or Sabina in danger. He knew what a lethal weapon a car was and he had to be sure he was in control before he'd risk it.

Taking a few deep breaths to steady himself, he gunned the engine and slipped the car into gear. It felt alien, almost unreal, to be back behind the wheel again. His legs shook slightly as he eased the car out on to the drive.

Ayesha and Sabina were waiting for him, eager smiles on their faces, and it bolstered his courage. When he jumped out of the car, his legs no longer trembled.

'We don't have to do this.' Ayesha touched his arm. In her eyes there was such compassion that it nearly had him undone. 'I'll understand.'

So it looked like Crystal had told her what had happened with Laura. 'I'm fine with it,' he said, and deep down he knew that he really was.

'Good.' She smiled again, and it sent feelings through him that he'd thought were always going to be denied him. 'Shall I quickly make a picnic?'

'No, definitely not. I want this to be a day off for you too. Sling your gear in the back.' He did the same with his own bag.

'I've left a note for Crystal and Joy to tell them where we are,' she said. 'I hope that Crystal won't be cross that we're going without her.'

'She'll be fine,' he said. 'We'll take Crystal and Joy another time.'

It was a glorious day, the sun already putting on its best show. The sky was azure-blue, cloudless, like a Mediterranean sky that had wandered unwittingly into north London. He wondered if they'd have a good summer this year. It was certainly overdue.

237

Ayesha and Sabina both hopped into the car and he made sure they were buckled up. He was sure that he could remember the route, but he programmed the satnav nevertheless. Then he put on his dark glasses and pulled down his hat. His mouth was dry as the gates swung open and they drove out into the street. He got a flashback to a bank of cameras clicking every time he drove out of the gates, and relief swept over him when he realised that today there were no photographers lurking in wait.

By the time they'd hit the motorway and were heading out of London, Hayden had started to relax.

'Where are we going?' Ayesha asked.

'Wait and see,' he said. 'It's one of my favourite places. We always used to go there for family holidays, and I looked at buying a house in the area a few years ago.' He waited for the familiar stab of pain to come as he talked of something that he'd done with Laura, but it didn't. It was a fact, nothing more.

They could have gone to Brighton, Bournemouth or somewhere on the east coast. There were other beach resorts that were a lot closer. But they were overcrowded, and Brighton was always full of people looking for a photograph as there were so many celebs living there. This place was more low-key and, if he went about his business quietly, everyone left him alone. He was sure Ayesha would appreciate that too.

If it was to be their first taste of the British seaside he also wanted somewhere that was still as unspoiled as it had been when he was a boy. And this place was as close as it got.

He'd thought that the world and his wife would be on the road today, heading for the coast, but it wasn't too bad. As it was still early, the traffic was relatively light and it was only a few hours before he was seeing signs for their destination.

They'd not talked much, but had listened to music all the way down, nothing too emotive, and had stopped once for coffee at a service station while Hayden filled up with petrol. Both Ayesha and her daughter were easy, undemanding company. There was a DVD player fitted in the back of the car and he'd have to get some DVDs suitable for little girls, if they were going to do this again.

Soon they were turning off the main road and making their way down towards the coast. The road got smaller and smaller until it became a single track, banked by high grass verges. Hayden took great care as he wound the car carefully through narrow lanes, passing tiny thatched cottages and a picture-perfect church. He'd always thought that he and Laura might marry there, and he blanked off the image that came to him. Today was a day for fun and happiness, not sadness and regret.

'This is so very pretty,' Ayesha said next to him. 'I've never seen England like this.'

'I thought you'd like it.' He grinned across at her.

On the road down to the centre of the little village, they glimpsed the sea sparkling invitingly. Hayden pulled over to the side of the road and looked out to the horizon.

'Oh, look, Sabina! The sea!' Ayesha pointed out beyond the headland, smile wide.

Her daughter sat up in the car and peered out of the window, excitement shining in her eyes.

Something inside his heart settled and, watching the gentle rhythm of the waves, a peace that he hadn't experienced for some time washed over him. This might not be the Caribbean Sea or the Indian Ocean, but there was an old-world charm about an English coastal resort that nowhere else on the planet could match. The sheer beauty of Lulworth Cove in Dorset was also one of the best examples he could think of to introduce someone to the seaside.

'We're here,' he said unnecessarily. 'This is Lulworth Cove.'

The rays burned pleasantly on his pale, sun-starved arm as he rested it on the open window. A comforting warmth flooded his body, which had felt chilled to the bone for so long. To his embarrassment, he felt like weeping with a mixture of relief and delight.

This had been a good idea. A very good idea.

# Chapter Fifty-one

We park up on a hill overlooking the village and Hayden goes to buy a ticket from the meter. I make myself useful by lifting the bags out of the back of the car. As it was all done in such a rush, I didn't really have time to think what to bring. There are some towels, some spare clothes, but not much else. I haven't got sunscreen for Sabina and we have nothing for her to play with on the sand. She doesn't even possess a ball yet.

When Hayden comes back, he takes the bags from me and slips his free hand under my elbow. 'We'll go straight to that shop by the heritage centre,' he says. 'We can stock up on sun-tan lotion and buy Beanie a bucket and spade.'

'I was thinking that myself.'

'While you choose some bits and bobs, I'll find us some lunch.' Hayden hands me some money. 'Here, take this.'

'I have money,' I tell him.

'I have more,' he teases. 'Take it. This is my treat.'

So I buy a purple bucket shaped like a castle and a pink spade for Sabina and, by the time we've paid, Hayden has appeared bearing a carrier bag filled with piping hot pasties, sandwiches and soft drinks.

'I think we're all set for the day now,' he says.

As the weather is very fine, the resort is busy, and we head down to the beach through the pretty main street with a steady trickle of excited families laden with deckchairs, sunshades and picnics.

As we step on to the sand, I have to stop and marvel at the view. It's as different as possible to the magnificence of the Indian Ocean, but this has a homely beauty all of its own. The cove is almost a full circle of sand, banked by sheer grassy cliffs, with a narrow exit that leads out to the sea beyond. The sea is turquoise, as still as a millpond, and looks so inviting.

'This is truly beautiful.'

'It is,' Hayden agrees, and he fills his lungs full of tangy sea air.

Lulworth Cove is obviously very popular with families, who are already spreading out towels, staking their claim to a stretch of beach. So we walk along the pebbles until we find a spot further away from everyone else where we can settle. We find a place over by the cliffs that looks just fine.

'Here?' Hayden asks.

'Perfect.' And it is. I've never seen anywhere nicer in my life. I feel lighter simply looking at it.

'Isn't this beautiful, Sabina?'

She nods her agreement, and I can tell from her beaming smile that she's as happy as I am.

Hayden deposits the bags on the sand and I shake out the towels and set them down side by side. While we fuss in the way that adults do, Sabina has already kicked off her shoes and run down to the sea. She lets the water wash over her feet as she holds her arms outstretched above her head, welcoming, embracing the sun.

Hayden flops down on to a towel. He pulls off his woolly hat and the sea breeze ruffles his blond hair. He tries to smooth it down and fails. For the first time in my life, I want to run my fingers through a man's hair. I want to smooth it down, only to muss it up again.

Catching me looking at him, he says, 'What?'

'You look very relaxed. The sea air must be good for you.'

He stretches out on his back, arms flung above his head. 'This is the life.' Then he turns towards me. 'I sometimes think about getting away from it all. Coming to somewhere like this, blending into the background. Who would find me down here? Who would even care?'

Sitting down on the towel next to him, I pull my knees into my chest and hug them. 'You wouldn't miss London?'

'I hate London,' he admits.

'Then why stay there?'

He shrugs. 'I stay for Crystal, for Joy. Because I don't know what else to do with myself.'

'You'll find your way,' I assure him. 'It just takes time.'

'Maybe I need to come here more often, to sit and think.'

'That would be a very good plan.'

Sabina comes back to us. Her face is glowing, happy. I wish she would speak out, tell us how she feels, thank Hayden for bringing us to this wonderful place. But she doesn't.

Instead, I speak for her. 'Hayden, we're both very grateful for this outing.'

'It's my pleasure,' he says. 'We should do more of this.'

'I'd like that very much.'

'I'm starving,' Hayden says. 'Let's open that bag.'

So I spread out what we've got and we eat the pasties while they're still hot and watch the world go by.

'I must put some sunscreen on my daughter.' Her arms and legs are mostly covered, and I look at the other children and see that many of them are similarly protected. I think it's a bad thing to let your child be caught by the sun these days,

243

but I wonder should I allow her more freedom? She's a child and shouldn't be self-conscious about her body. Would it be a bad thing for her to have the sun on her skin, her arms? I smooth the cream on to her face. In the shop, I bought her a cotton sunhat, which I fix over her hair.

'Now I'm going to teach this young lady how to make *the* best sandcastle the world has ever seen,' Hayden declares.

Sabina grins at him and coyly picks up her spade.

He kicks off his flip-flops and unbuttons his white linen shirt. The wind lifts it and flares it open, exposing a chest that's pale, hairless, but strong and defined. I want to touch his skin, see how my dark hand looks against the snowy whiteness. The thought makes me flush.

I've bought a wide-brimmed straw sunhat too, which I put on, then I settle myself on the towel in the sunshine. I watch Hayden and Sabina play together in the sand, marvelling at his patience with my child. He's a kind man. A good man.

How I wish my marriage could have been like this. With a man like Hayden I could have been a different woman. A happy woman.

# Chapter Fifty-two

We spend the day on the beach, eating ice-cream, making sand-castles, paddling in the sea. We all hold hands and walk the length of the cove in the edge of the sea. My feet sink into the sand and Hayden holds my hand tightly so that I keep my balance. I like how it feels. I like it very much. He says that he'll teach Sabina to swim if I'd like him to.

I look at him, his face soft and golden in the sinking sun, and think that he's a very beautiful person. The things that he says make me believe that he wants us to be in his life for a long time. I can only hope that I'm right.

Lifting Sabina from the sea, he swings her into his arms and carries her back to our towels. Her T-shirt and trousers are wet through, but I've taken the precaution of bringing spare clothes for her. It's nice to see her so free and unburdened.

'We should find somewhere to eat,' Hayden says as he folds up his towel. 'I bet Sabina is hungry.'

'What time must we leave?' I ask.

He stops what he's doing and turns to me. 'We don't have to go back tonight,' he says. 'The forecast for tomorrow is good too. We could find a hotel and stay overnight. There's another place that I'd really like to show you. I think Sabina will love it as well.'

'We have no things with us. No overnight clothes or toiletries.'

Hayden shrugs. 'We can buy whatever we need. Have you anything to get back for?'

'Well . . . no.'

He grins at that. 'Then you'll stay?'

'If that's what you wish.'

He puts his hands on my arms. 'It's what *you* want that's important. Would you like to spend the night down here?'

'Very much,' I say.

'Then that's settled. I'll ring Crystal so she doesn't worry, and then we can drive a little bit further down the coast and see if we can find some accommodation.'

My heart lifts. This feels like an excellent adventure.


We drive for about half an hour along the coast and then Hayden spots a white house high on the cliff above the beach. The sign says VACANCIES.

'Look OK to you?' he asks.

'It's fine.'

He swings into the drive and parks up. 'Give me a minute. I'll see if they've got two rooms,' and he sprints away.

A moment later he comes back and says, 'We're on. It's really nice. The rooms overlook the sea.' He lifts our sandy bags from the boot and carries them into the house. We follow Hayden inside and up the stairs.

'Here you go. This is you and Sabina.' I'm relieved to see that I'm sharing with Sabina. I was uncertain what the arrangements would be and I didn't like to ask.

It's a big room with one double bed in the middle and a

single under the window. The wallpaper is pretty, sprigged with pink flowers, and the bedspread is a cheery pink and white stripe. There's a glass coffee table that has a quirky base made from driftwood, which is flanked by two cream linen armchairs. French doors open out on to a small balcony, and beneath it the garden of the house stretches out to the edge of the cliff, with the beach beyond. It's surrounded by fields and sand dunes on all sides. I open one of the doors and can hear the rush of the waves. I turn to Hayden. 'This is very lovely.'

'That's Lyme Bay.' He comes behind me and, resting a hand on my shoulder, points into the distance. 'It's beautiful, isn't it?'

'Very.' The sun is golden across the water. What few clouds there are in the sky are tipped with raspberry and apricot hues.

'Glad you like it,' Hayden says. 'I'm right next door. It's an adjoining room.' He points to a white door that I hadn't noticed. 'The key is on your side.'

'Thank you.'

'I'll be back in a second. Just let me dump my stuff.' He disappears into his own room.

I go to the door that separates us. There is, indeed, a heavy key in the lock.

Moments later he returns as promised. 'Let's run to the nearest supermarket and grab some supplies.'

So we drive out through the pretty countryside until we find a small supermarket where we buy toothpaste, toothbrushes, clean underwear and cheap T-shirts for us all.

'You realise that Crystal would have had to buy an entire new wardrobe *and* a suitcase full of make-up,' he jokes as we queue to pay.

'I've discovered from Crystal that I'm very low-maintenance,' I quip in return.

'You are,' he says. 'Nothing wrong in that.'

I get a pang of regret that my dear friend isn't with us. Though I must confess that I'm enjoying my time alone with Hayden.

Back at the house on the cliff, we deposit our new clothes.

'The owner told me there's a lovely café just below us on the beach. They close quite early, so we'll have to go straight down there and see if they can fit us in for dinner.'

So that's exactly what we do. We walk across the fields and then make our way down a steep path worn into the cliff until we're on the beach. There are still a lot of people walking dogs along the edge of the sea, and a handful of fishermen cast their rods into the edge of the waves. The sun is lowering steadily as we make our way towards the café.

'This is part of the Chesil Bank,' Hayden says. 'It stretches for eighteen miles along the coast.'

'You know a lot about this area.'

'We often came here as a family when I was younger. It was our favourite spot.'

'Where are your family now?'

'I don't see much of them,' he admits, pursing his lips. 'It's probably eighteen months since I last visited. My mother and father live in Oxford. Still in the same house I grew up in. I should see them. Call them, at least.'

'That's not far from London.'

'No,' he agrees. 'Not in miles.'

I find it odd that his parents live so close to him and yet Hayden doesn't see them. Why? I wonder. I'd give anything to spend time with my mummy and daddy again.

When we reach the café, it's bustling and we're seated under a plastic awning adorned with fairy lights. A heater above us takes the chill from the ocean breeze and the encroaching evening. The people who were walking dogs in green wellies, come in too. The dogs sit obediently under the tables while they all order champagne and cocktails and talk in loud voices.

We have a hearty dinner made with local ingredients. Hayden and I share a hot shellfish platter piled high with Burton Bradstock lobster, West Bay crab, langoustines and local hand-dived scallops, steamed with chilli, ginger, garlic and cream. Sabina has home-made fish fingers with chips. Hayden orders two glasses of champagne for us too, and I throw caution to the wind and drink it all.

Afterwards, with tummies full and my head a little bit swimmy, we walk down to the beach again. It's dusk now. The light has all but gone and the tide is coming in. We sit on a low wall and watch as the red ball of the sun sinks slowly below the horizon. I feel such peace in my heart that I don't want this day to end, not ever. It's been perfect. I don't have to mind who I am when I'm with Hayden. I don't have to watch my words carefully in case they should ignite his anger. There's not a band of tension constantly squeezing my chest. I can be myself.

I look at him, his handsome profile in the shadow as the sun falls to the horizon, and I realise for the first time in my life that I'm in love. I want to reach up and touch his face, feel the graze of his stubble beneath my fingers. I want to feel his mouth on mine, hot and searching. I'm surprised by the force of my feelings but, for once, not frightened by them.

The sun finally disappears and, without meaning to, I shiver slightly.

'Cold?'

'A little,' I admit.

Casually, as if it means nothing, Hayden puts his arm around my shoulders and moves closer to me. I can feel the warmth of his body against mine, and a feeling of belonging right here floods through me. I should like to tell him at this moment that I have fallen in love with him, but I find that I simply can't.

While I'm fighting my reticence, Sabina yawns sleepily. 'I should put her to bed now.'

So we walk back along the beach to the house and Hayden's arm stays around my shoulders. We clamber up the steps of the cliff and through the dark garden. He picks Sabina up and carries her in his strong arms. She falls asleep instantly against his shoulder.

When we get to the bedroom, he takes her straight to the single bed and lowers her on to it. Softly he drops a kiss on Sabina's forehead and tenderly brushes her hair from her brow. Her eyes flicker, trying to fight sleep and failing. Hayden smiles to see it. 'Night-night, Little Bean.'

Then he turns to me. 'Night, Ayesha.'

'Goodnight, Hayden. I can't thank you enough.'

He presses a finger to my lips. 'It's good to be here with you. I think it's done us all a world of good.'

'I think so to.'

'If you need anything call me,' he says. 'If not, I'll see you in the morning. Breakfast at nine?'

I nod my agreement. 'Goodnight,' I say again.

Without warning, his tender kiss touches my lips. Then he's gone, into his own room, and I stay in mine as he closes the door behind him.

# Chapter Fifty-three

I would have liked to bathe Sabina but I don't wish to wake her from her deep sleep, so I simply cover her and leave her be.

Instead, I fill the bath for myself, and even treat myself to some of the scented foam that's provided for guests. It smells of vanilla and anise. I lie back in the water and let the aroma soothe me. My mind fills with thoughts of Hayden and I wish I'd had the courage to ask him to stay longer in our room.

As I dry my skin, I look at myself in the full mirror. My breasts are small, dark; my hips boyish. I'm not comely, voluptuous as Crystal is. I wonder would Hayden really like a woman such as me, when he's had a woman in his life like that? Laura was such a beauty too, and I know that I could never compare to her. It's sad to think that although I'm a married woman of ten years, I know little of love or how to please a man. With Crystal's experience, I should imagine she's fun, abandoned in bed. I don't think I'm like that at all. With my husband, physical love was always done for duty, not for my pleasure. There's a longing deep inside me as I wonder how different it would be with Hayden.

Hanging on the back of the door there's a white dressing

gown, and I wrap myself in it. The waffle material is slightly rough, abrasive on my skin, which seems suddenly to have a heightened sensitivity. Is it from the sun or has the unaccustomed alcohol made it so? Or is it from the thought of Hayden sleeping in the very next room with nothing but a door to separate us?

Sitting on the edge of the bed, I wonder what to do now. It's not late, barely past nine. Sabina makes wet, snuffling noises in her sleep. I go to the connecting door and press my ear against the wood. If I strain to listen, I can hear Hayden moving about his room.

Feelings stir inside me that I've not experienced for a long time. A mix of anxiety, excitement and desire. There's an ache in my heart and in my body. I'm yearning for Hayden and I don't know what to do.

What would it be like if we became lovers? Would it make the situation at the house more difficult? I love to live there. Already, in the short time that we've been residents, I view it as our sanctuary. I feel so safe. I couldn't jeopardise that for Sabina, and I don't know how we would find somewhere even a fraction as nice on the small rent that we pay. Is becoming closer even a possibility, as he's still so in love with the memory of Laura?

If Hayden and I were ever to take our relationship to a more intimate level, would it change things? What if I were terrible? I have nothing to measure it by. If something I did failed to please him, what then? Or what if it was marvellous and then Crystal became jealous of our relationship and stopped being my friend? I couldn't bear that either. What if he used me and then moved on to someone new? I don't believe that he'd do that, but I couldn't be sure. Whichever way, my situation would be untenable.

I hear him move next door and my heart and my stomach

lurch. Is he, right now, on the other side, feeling the same as I am? What would Crystal do in this situation? She'd be bold and would knock on Hayden's door wrapped only in this dressing gown. It would drop open slightly, showing him that she was wearing nothing underneath. She would lie with him, make love to him. She wouldn't fear the things that I do. I press myself against the cool wood, wishing that I was Crystal. Wishing that I had the courage to go to him. Wishing that I knew what it was like to lie with a man that I loved with all of my heart and soul.

But I'm not Crystal. I am me and I don't have the courage. Instead, I slide down until I'm sitting on the floor, my head resting against the door. Closing my eyes, I wrap my arms around myself and picture Hayden only a few metres away from me, lying alone on his bed. I imagine him waiting to take me in his strong embrace. I imagine him above me in the darkness, his body inside mine. I imagine a life where I love him wholeheartedly and he loves me. I hold myself tightly and I stay here and do nothing.

# Chapter Fifty-four

After breakfast they loaded up the car and Hayden headed for Lyme Regis. He had great memories of sunny childhood days spent here, and now, all these years later, it didn't look so very different.

He parked up at the top of the town and they all took the zig-zag path down through the park to the seafront. Hayden had an overwhelming urge to show Ayesha and Sabina this place, and it startled him as he'd felt exactly the same way at the start of his relationship with Laura, that urge to share what he'd loved as a child.

Yesterday had been about getting away and relaxation. Today was all about fun. He took Ayesha's hand and they walked down to the harbour, the famous Cobb. The view of the bay was spectacular. The sea sparkled, blue and inviting, in the sunshine. The tang of salt from the sea sharpened his senses. Seagulls wheeled overhead, calling out. The smell of freshly cooked fish and chips from the cafés on the seafront held its own inimitable allure. Despite having just eaten breakfast, his stomach answered with a longing rumble. Perhaps they could sit out here and eat later, if Ayesha and Sabina wanted to, as he'd done as a boy. He could almost taste the crisp golden batter, the fluffiness of the chips. It was good that some things in life never changed. A contented breath escaped his lips as he said, 'I think this might be my favourite place on Earth.'

'Then it will be mine too,' Ayesha said, nestling in close to him. 'It's lovely.'

It was strange that he felt closer to his parents down here than he ever did in London. Why was that? In the years since Laura had died, he'd gradually drifted away from them. His mother and father were worried about him, he knew that. The problem was, every time he saw them or spoke to them on the telephone, they tried to jolly him out of his misery. And, to be honest, he'd been content to wallow in it. Soon it was easier not to hear how he should move on, how Laura would want him to enjoy life. They were pointless platitudes and he'd wanted to be left alone to grieve. He realised now that they were simply trying to do their best for him in the only way they knew how, and he was ashamed that he'd distanced himself from them. Perhaps it was time to build bridges.

He looked across at Ayesha. She was a calming influence on his soul, and he was more comfortable in her company than he could ever have imagined. She put no pressure on him, wanted nothing from him. Last night it had been very hard to say goodnight to her. He'd wanted nothing more than to take her to his bed, love her and wrap her in his arms. She was so fragile though. Would it have frightened her away completely if he'd made any kind of move on her? He hadn't even dared try.

He was out of practice. Terribly so. Laura had been his one, his only love. They'd grown up together, learned together. When he was on the road, his band would disappear with the inevitable gaggle of groupies, but that wasn't for him. Laura had been the only woman he'd ever needed. For someone who'd once been classed as a heart-throb, the ways of women were a total mystery to him. What if he'd got it horribly wrong with Ayesha? He couldn't risk a clumsy manoeuvre as it could all end in disaster. What they both needed was to take it slowly, very slowly.

They walked past the families playing on the beach and Hayden felt pleased that someone might look at them and think they were a family too. He was wearing his hat today, and sunglasses, but no one was giving them a second glance. If anyone was turning heads it was Ayesha and Sabina, people astonished at how pretty they both were. In a ridiculously old-fashioned way, he felt proud to have them both on his arm.

Soon they were out on the high sea wall which curved round the harbour. It was broad enough for them all to walk along side by side and they joined the other day-trippers as they promenaded. Spray from the waves showered over them. The sun caught the droplets and made rainbows.

'A book was set here,' Hayden said. 'And a film. *The French Lieutenant's Woman*.'

'Is it good?'

'I've never read it,' he admitted. 'But I think we've got a copy at home. Perhaps we should read it now that we've finished with Bridget.'

'I'd like that.'

They went into the small marine aquarium that had been there as long as he remembered. The grey mullet were tame and could be hand-fed. Sabina wrinkled up her nose as the fish softly sucked the proffered food from her fingers. They stroked a giant lobster and watched a bad-tempered crab with one claw scuttling along the tank and trying to nip the other fish. It took him back years in time, to a place before anything bad had happened in his life. He got a sudden urge to reconnect with that. He should call his parents. Before too long.

Sabina was overjoyed to hold a starfish in her hand.

'I think you should make a wish,' Hayden said.

The child closed her eyes and screwed up her face in concentration. When she was finished, she looked first at Hayden and then at Ayesha. She might not be able to speak, but there was no doubt what her wish had been.

Ayesha flushed.

'Let's have lunch,' he said. So they went back out into the sunshine and found a table at a café right next to the beach. The fish and chips, when they came, were every bit as good as he'd hoped. The girls tucked in too. Considering they were both so tiny, they certainly enjoyed their food.

Afterwards they all walked hand-in-hand along the front. Ayesha popped into one of the little boutique shops and bought a lavender cream that she said would help Joy's chapped hands. He picked up sticks of sweet, stripy rock for them all.

A game of crazy golf on the hill above the bay finished off the day. Sabina was good at it, as she seemed to be at everything she turned her hand to, and Ayesha was unexpectedly competitive. It was only by the skin of his teeth that he beat them with a last jammy shot through the windmill.

Too quickly it seemed the sun was lowering in the sky and they'd yet to tackle the long drive home.

'Let's not go back,' he whispered to Ayesha. 'We could run away from it all. Make a new life down here away from all our troubles. Let's stay here for ever. Just you, me and Beanie.'

'We can't.'

'What's stopping us?'

'Sabina has school. And what about Joy and Crystal? We can't leave them.'

'But we could,' he said. 'One day?'

'I'd like that very much,' she conceded. 'One day.'

'Ayesha . . .' he breathed deeply.

'Yes?'

He wanted to tell her that he loved her. The words were on the tip of his tongue. The moment was right, he was sure. But what if he frightened her off? It might be too soon for her. She'd only just escaped from one relationship, so, despite the signs, maybe she wasn't ready for another one. The last thing he wanted, after the wonderful time that they'd had together, was to come on too heavy.

She frowned at him and he wanted nothing more than to smooth away the worried furrows in her brow. 'Is everything all right?'

'It's fine,' he said. Then he chickened out completely. 'I only wanted to say that I've had a great time.'

# Chapter Fifty-five

On Monday morning at nine-thirty sharp, Crystal and I are both waiting for Joy at the foot of the stairs.

It was a long drive back last night and when we returned home we went straight to bed. I found it very hard to say good-night to Hayden and let him climb the stairs to his own room. It was a weekend that I never wanted to end.

While I was away with Hayden, Crystal has been very busy. She's assembled a vast array of nail polishes and equipment that she insists we can't live without.

'Have you seen these sparkles?' she says to me, showing me a sheet of pink diamanté decorations. Her voice is breathless with awe.

'They're very pretty,' I tell her. 'Do you think the ladies will like them?'

'What's not to love?' Crystal says.

As we're organising ourselves to leave, Hayden comes down the stairs. My heart starts up an erratic beat when I see him. He looks as if he's just woken. His eyes are heavy with sleep, he's unshaven and his hair is very messy, but he still looks beautiful to me. 'I wanted to wish you both good luck.'

I missed him so much at breakfast today. After our weekend together, I wondered whether things might have changed between us, but I don't think that they have. Apart from the briefest of kisses on Saturday night, there was no intimacy between us at all.

Crystal greeted us at the door last night, brimming with excitement about today's visit to the day centre. Although she winked at me once, she didn't have the opportunity to quiz me about the weekend. I'm sure she will today.

'Why don't you take the car?' Hayden suggests.

'It's only a short walk away,' Joy says. 'Fifteen minutes at the most.'

Hayden nods at the pile of equipment at Crystal's feet. 'Have you seen all the stuff they've got? You'd need a dozen sherpas.'

Joy frowns.

'We want to do the job properly,' Crystal says. 'I've got pink sparkles and everything.'

Now Joy rolls her eyes towards the heavens, which makes me smile.

I admit that I'm quite nervous about my first day at work. The ladies will only be paying us a small amount for a manicure today, to try us out, but if they like what we do, we're hoping that it will be a regular booking.

'Will you be back in time to collect Beanie?' Hayden asks me.

'I should be.'

'If there's any problem, just call. I'm happy to walk up to the school for her.'

'Thank you.'

He and I exchange a shy, warm glance and I wonder if it's right to say that nothing has changed between us.

'Let's get a move on then, girls,' Joy says.

Hayden tosses the car keys to Crystal and she catches them deftly. 'I promise not to wrap it round a bollard.'

His face darkens.

'Sorry.' She tuts at herself. 'That was a twattish thing to say.'

'Be careful. Please. Now you've got me worried sick. Perhaps I should drive you.'

'We'll be fine,' she insists, scooping her box of nail polishes into her arms. 'You fuss too much. I'll bring Ayesha safely home to you.'

'I'd be very happy if you'd do that.'

'Laters!' Crystal waves at him over her shoulder as she heads for the door. I pick up a pretty pink holdall that contains I-don't-know-what and wave in the same manner.

'What have you got in here?' Joy mutters as she picks up yet another box. 'The kitchen sink? You're doing a few manicures, Crystal, not moving in.'

'Chill out, Joy. I used to be a Girl Guide. I need to be well prepared.'

'If you were ever a Girl Guide, I'll eat my hat. You obviously never got your cookery badge.'

'I was off that day,' Crystal retorts.

Hayden steps forward into the bickering. 'Here, let me give you a hand.' He lifts the last of the bags, carries it out to the car and helps us to load up the boot.

Finally, we're all bundled in too. Crystal's driving, Joy's in the passenger seat and I'm in the back.

'*Please* drive carefully,' Hayden reiterates. '*Please.*'

Crystal kisses him through the open window. 'You worry too much. I'll look after her.' Then she puts the car into gear with an unnerving crunch, and we swing out of the gates. As they close behind us, I turn to wave at Hayden again.

He looks so forlorn standing there by himself, and I wonder how he is going to fill his hours without us.

*

The Constance Fields Day Centre is a short drive away on the other side of the Heath, and Crystal gets us there without incident. The building is low, squat and unattractively plain. We unload the car and carry our wares inside. There seems to be a lot of equipment and, despite my training, I don't know what any of it is. I'm only hoping that Crystal knows what she's bought.

The centre is alarmingly hot inside and smells of artificial air freshener in a scent that may be pine, or a spiky attempt at lavender. Joy leads us through into the large day room, where old-fashioned upright armchairs are arranged in groups. The carpet is highly patterned, as are the curtains, and there's a slight air of neglect. But the room is bright and sunny due to a large wall of windows facing the well-tended garden. Outside tells a completely different story, and I wonder if Joy helps them out here too, as the borders look as if they're as meticulously maintained as those at Hayden's house. I'm sure I can see her deft touch here.

The other people who are arriving seem to be just as sprightly as Joy, and the living room is soon filled with the sound of happy chatter.

'You're lovely ladies,' one man comes to tell us. 'You'll brighten up our day no end.' He nods at Crystal. 'You look like that Katie Price, love.'

'Cheeky bugger.'

'She does, doesn't she, Ted?'

Another elderly gentleman joins him. 'Aye, she does. If I were twenty years younger . . . !'

'Make it fifty and we'd be talking,' Crystal teases.

Even if we're not a hit with the ladies, Crystal already has her fans among the men.

'You two reprobates leave young Crystal alone,' Joy chides. 'Make yourselves useful and go and get that tea urn on the go.' She rolls her eyes at us as they go off giggling like naughty schoolboys. 'Too much Viagra,' Joy says tightly. 'I bet there are many women who rue the day that was invented. I'll make everyone a cup of tea.' She disappears in the direction of the kitchen.

'Look what lovely jubbly stuff I got for us,' Crystal says as she unpacks little boxes to reveal pretty nail varnishes and accessories. 'I found a local beauty warehouse online and shot up there yesterday while you were gallivanting at the seaside with Hayden.'

'I do not think that I was gallivanting,' I counter.

'And *I do not think* that you're going to get away without telling me all about it, miss,' she mimics. 'Here, have a gander at this little beauty.' Crystal opens a sizeable box and slides out a portable manicure table. 'This will make life easier for us. Forty quid apiece. Cheap as chips.'

That may be, but the cost of this venture is steadily mounting. My heart flutters with anxiety. Soon I'll have very little of my savings left.

'Don't stress about the money,' she says as if reading my mind. 'I've got it covered.'

'I can't let you pay for everything.'

'I've battered my credit card. Let's sort it out when we start earning.'

So we set up the nail bars side by side and Crystal tops them with a selection of rainbow-coloured nail varnishes. She hands me a roll of manicure tools and a new fluffy towel in the palest pink.

'This is all lovely. You've done very well.'

She waves away my compliment. 'Quick, before we start, you need to give me the low-down. Did it go well at the weekend with Hayd?' she asks me quietly. Or as quietly as Crystal can.

'Yes,' I say. 'It was a spur-of-the-moment decision for us to go. I'm sorry that you couldn't come with us.'

'Yeah. Like I want to play gooseberry to you lovebirds.'

I laugh. 'It wasn't like that. We sat on the beach all day on Saturday and on Sunday we went to Lyme Regis. Sabina loved it. This was her first ever trip to the seaside.'

'Oh, bless. I *do* wish I'd been there.'

'We'll go again. Hayden promised. All of us.'

'It's nice to see you out and about. Both you and Hayd.'

'I'm very glad that we went.'

'Sleeping arrangements?' Crystal says. 'I need to know.'

'We didn't plan to stay over. It was a last-minute decision.'

'I don't care about that bit.' She pulls an exasperated face at me. 'I want details. Nitty-gritty. Did Hayd have his wicked way with you?'

'Separate rooms,' I confess, casting my eyes down. 'All night long.'

'Really?' Her face falls. 'How very bloody disappointing.'

I laugh at her cheekiness and I don't tell her that, in my heart, I feel the same.

# Chapter Fifty-six

Joy brings us tea, which calms my nerves, and we sit at our pristine nail bars, ready for our first customers.

'I'm going to get us some matching polo shirts,' Crystal whispers. 'Pale pink. That'll look cool.'

Crystal, as always, is groomed within an inch of her life, immaculate. I do feel as if I'm letting the side down and, if they have us back, I'll try harder to look as if I'm a proper beauty professional.

A smart lady with grey hair and a string of pearls sits down in front of me and I check the paper that Joy's given me. 'Hello, Mrs Hill.'

'Hello, dearie,' she says. Her smile is kind, but her eyes are tired. 'I've never had my nails done before. I'm looking forward to it.'

'You're my first customer,' I admit. 'Please be patient with me as I'm rather slow and want to make a good job.'

'I'm in no rush,' she says. 'I'm retired, you know. I've got all the time in the world.' Mrs Hill holds out her nails for inspection and her hands are frail, spotted with brown patches of age. I go through all that I've been taught at the college with as much precision as I can.

Crystal has no such qualms. She's already whizzing away with her nail file, chatting animatedly with her client.

I work my way quietly along Mrs Hill's fingers and then ask, 'What polish would you like?'

'Oh, I don't mind. Nothing too bright.'

'Can I try a French manicure please? I'd like to try to improve my techniques.'

'I've no idea what one is, but you do what you think, dearie,' she says.

I can see Crystal painting furiously. She already has the sheet of sparkles out. As I watch her, she looks up and winks at me. My friend gives me the thumbs-up and I return it.

'We trained together,' I tell Mrs Hill. 'This is my first ever job.'

'Then you're doing very well,' she tells me kindly. 'You've a very relaxing personality.'

Crystal finishes her client and starts on another one. The first lady wanders over to my station.

'Look at this, Agnes.' She proudly holds out her fingers. Her nails are shocking pink and encrusted with diamanté.

'Oh, my word,' Mrs Hill breathes. She examines her own nails, which look very plain in comparison.

'I can ask Crystal to put some more decoration on them if you wish,' I say. 'I'm not yet confident enough to do this.'

'Oh, no,' she says, a trifle too quickly. 'I like them just as they are.'

So I dry them off to finish and then Mrs Hill is replaced by another lady.

We work all morning, then Joy makes us a sandwich. We go out into the garden and the sunshine to eat it.

Crystal sits on one of the benches and instantly attracts a crowd of elderly gentlemen around her. I wander off and leave them flirting with her.

'Show me the garden,' I say to Joy. 'Do you help out here?'

'Yes,' she says. 'I keep trying to persuade them to try a few vegetables, but to no avail. They're all flower people.'

'You're quiet today?'

She purses her lips and I can see a dark shadow cross her face. 'Had some bad news,' she says. 'I hoped both of my sons might come home for a visit this year. It appears neither of them can.'

With that she starts to cry, and I put my arm around her, steering her to a nearby seat. We sit down and I offer her the clean tissue I have in my pocket. I notice that Joy's hands are shaking as she wipes her eyes.

The seat is white wrought iron and is shaded by a rose arbour, which means we're out of sight of the other guests.

'They're busy,' she continues, sniffling. 'They both have very demanding jobs. I know that. I'm very proud of them. Really, I am. But it's been so long. I barely know Stephen's family. My own grandchildren. I haven't even seen baby Jay, and I wonder now when I ever will.'

'You could go to them, Joy,' I suggest softly when her tears have abated.

'I don't think so.'

'At one time I thought I was trapped for ever in a loveless marriage, but I found the courage to leave.'

'I hate to fly. I've never been on a plane in my life and I don't intend to start now.'

'It would take you to your family,' I remind her. 'In less than a day, you could be there to see them all. How lovely would that be?'

She crumbles again. 'I do miss them so terribly.'

'You mustn't be frightened to do this, Joy.'

'I'm not getting any younger, am I?'

I shake my head. 'None of us are.'

Patting my hand, she says, 'I'll think about it.'

'Am I going to do your nails today?'

'Look at my hands,' she says. 'They're full of soil and the cuticles are ripped to shreds.'

They look sore and neglected. 'I've learned to do massage too,' I tell her. 'I bought some lovely lavender cream for you in Lyme Regis which will soothe them. I could file them and then give you a gentle massage. That would be nice?'

Some of the pain in her face recedes. 'You're a very considerate person, Ayesha. I think I'd like that.'

'Then I will consult my very busy diary,' I tease, 'and find you a special appointment.'

# Chapter Fifty-seven

When we get home, Hayden is waiting at the door for us. He rushes out to help us carry our bags in from the car, and I wonder if he's been lonely while all three of us have been out all day.

Crystal swung by the school and we picked up Sabina on the way home. She rushes into Hayden's arms as soon as she sees him.

'Good day at school, Beanie?' he asks, and my daughter nods.

We go inside and dump all of our manicure and nail-painting paraphernalia in the hallway.

'I've made dinner,' Hayden says. 'It's not up to your standard, Ayesha, but there's a lasagne waiting to go in the oven.'

'I didn't know you could cook,' Crystal says, surprised.

'That's about the extent of it,' Hayden admits. 'And it's been years since I even did that, but I enjoyed it.'

'It's a very nice thought,' I tell him. For once, I don't feel like putting on my apron and peeling vegetables, so this is very welcome. Then, 'Sabina, have you homework to do?'

She shakes her head.

'I could paint your nails if you like,' Crystal says to her. 'That would be all right, wouldn't it, Ayesha?'

My daughter turns pleading eyes to me.

'As long as it's something very, very discreet. No pink sparkles. I don't want Sabina being told off by her teacher.'

'We'll sit at the kitchen table,' Crystal says. She glances at me and Hayden. 'Why don't you two go for a walk on the Heath? I'll put the lasagne in the oven a bit later. I bet you haven't ventured out of the house all day, Hayd. A bit of fresh air would do you the world of good.'

He looks uncertain. Crystal's right. He's probably closeted himself away in our absence.

'It's lovely out there,' I urge, and all the time I've been here, I've been too afraid to take Sabina out on to the Heath. This weekend, spending time on the beach, laughing together, has given me a further taste for freedom. We've all been hiding away behind tall walls for too long and I'd like to explore my surroundings more. 'It would be nice if you showed me the Heath.'

'Go on,' Crystal says. 'Don't be so miserable. We'll be all right here, won't we, Bean?'

I think Hayden senses that resistance is futile, as he shrugs his acceptance. 'OK. Let's take a turn in the park.'

'Be a good girl for Auntie Crystal,' I tell Sabina. Not that she's ever naughty. Sometimes I wish I could tell her off for being noisy or unruly. It's the only sadness in my heart.

Hayden and I walk to the front door and, before we leave the house, he covers his blond hair with his customary woolly hat and puts on his sunglasses. He's wary as we turn out of the gate, but there's no need as we're quite alone in the street. A short walk and we cross over to the entrance to the Heath. It's a pretty expanse of parkland and we stroll together along the well-trodden path. A few dark clouds are gathering in the sky that seem to have come out of nowhere. The air is heavy, tangible. Perhaps the heat has built up too much, too quickly, and needs to break.

We fall into step together, and after a few moments Hayden reaches out and takes my hand. It feels warm and strong and I take great comfort from it.

'I've missed you today,' he says. 'After such a great weekend, the house seemed really empty.'

'We had a lovely time,' I tell him. 'The British seaside is very beautiful.'

'I could buy a house down there,' he says. 'We could go regularly. If you'd like that.'

I hesitate. It seems so easy for Hayden. Just like that he can buy another house if it takes his fancy.

'You're not keen?' His face is worried. 'I'm rushing you?'

'No, no. It's not that.'

Hayden stops and turns to me. 'Do you think we can be together? I know that we've both got . . . well . . . baggage. For want of a better word. But I think we could be good for each other. I know my life's been a lot brighter since you came into it. And I love Sabina. I adore her. Almost as much as I adore you.' His finger lifts my chin. 'I hadn't planned to say so much, but, now you know. That's how I feel.'

I'm about to speak when Hayden spins round. 'Fuck,' he says. 'Photographer.' Instantly he turns his back to the man and his body shields mine.

I glance past his shoulder, and sure enough, there's a man standing some distance away. There's no doubt that his camera with its large white lens is trained on us, and he's snapping away.

'Quick. In here.' Hayden grabs my arm and pulls me into the trees. 'We'll have to stay hidden for a bit before we can make our getaway.' With me in his wake, he works his way deeper into the undergrowth until soon we're in a dense thicket. Stopping, he leans against a towering oak tree and pulls me to him, sheltering me in his arms. 'I don't think he'll follow us in

271

here.' He glances anxiously along the route we've just come and listens for footsteps. I can hear nothing.

Hayden's heart beats erratically in his chest.

'How did you know?'

'I'm not sure.' He lifts his sunglasses; now it's gloomy in the trees and the sun has disappeared. His blue eyes are dark and troubled. 'Built-in radar, or simply years of practice. By some sixth sense, I can usually tell when there's a camera around.'

It must be awful for him to have lived his life like this. 'I didn't understand how bad it was.'

'I'm worried for you,' he says. 'I hope he didn't get a good picture of us together.'

My heart sinks. 'You'd mind that?'

'It could be all over the internet tonight and in the newspapers tomorrow. Next week it will hit the gossip mags. What if by some chance your husband sees it?'

'Oh.' I hadn't considered that. I thought that *he* wouldn't want to be seen with *me*, not the other way round.

Rain starts to fall. Big, fat spots that bounce angrily on the leaves.

'There's nothing we can do but wait. I might be old news. They might not run it.'

I don't know who 'they' are, but I can only hope that he's right.

'I'm sorry,' he adds. 'If this blows your cover then I won't forgive myself. I should have chased after the bloke and made him delete the picture.'

'There's nothing we can do now?'

'No. We'll just have to sit tight. I'll buy all the papers tomorrow.' Hayden strokes my face. 'I'm sorry. So sorry. I've compromised your safety.'

My throat tightens, but I say, 'I've never felt more safe than when I'm with you.'

He pulls me into his embrace and I press my body against his. Hayden's lips, when they find mine, are warm and searching. It feels as if there is a world of sadness and pain in them. We cleave together against the trunk of the oak, under the shelter of its leaves. The rain is heavier now. His hands rove across my body and I want to lie down on the carpet of wet leaves and have him make love to me.

He breaks from me, putting my face away from his. 'You're getting soaked through.'

My thin blouse is plastered to my skin. 'I don't mind.'

'We should get back,' he says tightly. 'He won't follow us in this. He won't risk getting his damn camera wet.'

There's a bitterness in his tone that I've not heard before. He's clearly angry that this man's camera will be more precious to him than our privacy and the harm that he could do in exposing us.

So, with one final kiss, Hayden takes my hand and leads me out of the woods.

# Chapter Fifty-eight

'Oh, you're half drowned!' Crystal says as we appear in the kitchen. 'We heard the rain, didn't we, Joy? Guess you didn't make it to shelter.'

'We were hiding in the woods when it started,' I tell her, dripping on the kitchen floor. My hair is in rat's tails, and water drips from the hem of my trousers, which are blackened with dirt. I fear my summer sandals may be ruined. Suddenly, I feel like crying.

'You poor things. Let me get you both towels,' Joy says, and hurries out of the kitchen.

Hayden looks wretched. He pulls off his sodden hat. 'Some good this did me,' he grumbles as he tosses it into the sink. 'We were papped, Crystal. Just as we got on to the Heath.'

'After all this time?'

'They're sharks,' he spits. 'Always circling.'

Crystal looks anxiously at Sabina. 'They got a shot of both of you?'

'I don't know.' He rakes his hair.

I want to be in his arms again, yet I don't know how to cross the void between us.

274

'I'll up the security on the house.' Hayden paces the kitchen. 'Perhaps Sabina should have a bodyguard.' He looks at me, eyes bleak. 'Or you should get away from here. Leave altogether.'

I swallow deeply before I say, 'I do not wish to do that.'

'Of course she doesn't. Calm down, Hayd,' Crystal says. 'Let's wait and see what happens. It might be a storm in a teacup. If Lady Gaga flashes her boobs or Cheryl Cole falls out of a nightclub in nothing but her knickers, they might not be interested in you.'

He looks slightly mollified by that, but says, 'I don't care about *me*. I'm worried about Ayesha.'

'She'll be fine,' Crystal says. 'She's got us looking out for her now.'

'How can you say that when I've steered her straight into the path of the paparazzi?'

'It might be a one-off, Hayden,' she assures him. 'Let's not go overboard.'

Joy returns with two towels. She hands one to Hayden and then starts to dry my hair with the other, fussing over me. I feel miserable, bereft. Just when I thought everything was going so well. I should have known that it would be too good to be true. What if my photograph is in the newspaper? What if Suresh sees it? He'll surely come after me, come after Sabina.

'Dinner will be ready soon,' Joy says. 'That'll warm you up again.'

'I'm not hungry,' Hayden says. 'I'm going to have a hot shower.'

With that he leaves and disappears upstairs. I want to rush after him, cradle him to me. I want to feel the comfort of his arms once more. Instead, I stay rooted to the spot.

'Don't worry about him,' Crystal says lightly. 'Give him a few hours and he'll be fine. He takes everything to heart.'

But I know that it's because of Laura. He's thinking that what happened to her could happen to me, to my daughter.

'Go and get yourself into some dry clothes,' Joy says. 'I'll serve dinner in five minutes.'

'Thank you.'

I go upstairs and strip off my wet things. When I've towelled myself down, I pull on my maxidress and a little cardigan. The warm, dry clothes against my chilled skin are soothing. I think about climbing the stairs to see how Hayden is, but I don't want to incur his wrath. I feel that I encouraged him to go on to the Heath, and if it wasn't for me, there'd be no photograph.

I stand at the bottom of the staircase, looking up, straining to hear any noise, but there's nothing. After a few moments I tiptoe back downstairs.

Joy is lifting the lasagne out of the oven.

'Let me,' I say.

'Sit yourself down, miss,' she instructs.

I do as I'm told and take the chair next to Sabina. My daughter's face is so sad, and I slip my arm around her. 'Don't worry, little one. It will all be sorted out. You've nothing to fear.' I can only hope that I'm right.

Hayden's lasagne looks very appetising as Joy cuts into it and I wish that he was here to enjoy it. Joy passes the plates around.

'If you want some good news,' Joy says, 'all the folk at the day centre loved you. They definitely want you to come back next week and they're happy to pay a good price for your services too. They'll still want a discount, obviously, as they're not charging you for the facilities. But I thought that was promising. I need to check with Edgar. He's the new manager of the centre, who's been brought in to be a bit of a new broom for the place. We've got some lottery funding to give it a revamp, and Edgar wants to bring in more outside speakers and services to jolly us all up. This should fit in nicely. If he says it's all right, we're hoping you can make it a regular booking.'

'Wow. That's great,' Crystal says. 'I'm definitely going to get those pink polo shirts now. I could take some make-up in next week too. A few of the ladies asked about that.'

'Thank you,' I say to Joy.

'It's not going to pay your bills, but it's a start.'

Sabina holds out her tiny fingernails for me to examine with a proud smile. They're painted with the palest of iridescent pinks, which makes her nails look like mother-of-pearl. 'Very pretty. Do they remind you of the shells on the beach?'

She nods and a lone tear slides out of her eye to run down her cheek.

'Tell me how you're feeling, my child,' I urge her. 'Please.'

But I know that she cannot or will not.

# Chapter Fifty-nine

I tuck Sabina into the big bed and then decide to get in next to her. It's still quite early in the evening, barely eight o'clock, but I'm weary to my bones.

Next to me Sabina is hot and restless. Her legs fidget and she throws the covers back and forth as she tosses and turns in troubled sleep. I stroke her hair and offer soothing words. Eventually her breathing changes and she falls deeper into slumber.

Lying on my back, I stare out of the window. I've not closed the curtains and I watch the trees as the summer breeze wafts branches gently across the street lamp outside to make the shadows shift in our room.

I like this place and I don't wish to move on. I'm frightened to move on. I like being here with Crystal and Joy and, more particularly, Hayden. What will I do if my whereabouts are exposed in the national press? Is that really possible? If it is, surely word will then get back to Suresh? In my heart I know his stubborn pride will mean that he'll not let me get away from him.

Resting my head on the cool pillow, I try to think of what I'll do, but no cohesive thoughts will come. They're all a jumble and make no sense to me. I don't want to spend my life running from Suresh, always having to look over my shoulder. It's been so easy to forget his presence while I've been cosseted here, while my life has been changing so much. I could pretend that he didn't exist. Yet he's a lurking presence to me, as much as the photographers are to Hayden. We're both people who are pursued, hunted. All we both want is to be left alone in peace. Is that too much to ask?

When I fall asleep my dream isn't pleasant. In it I'm chased by a dark figure, through dense and unfriendly woods with trees that catch and scratch at the shalwar kameez that covers my arms, ripping it away from me, exposing my skin. I'm trying to hold my clothes to me and run for my life when a hand reaches out from the blackness and clutches my hair with steel fingers. It stops me in my tracks and then I'm pulled to the ground. I feel the hair tearing from my scalp and I cry out but there's no one to hear me.

A noise drags me from my dream and I sit up, panting heavily. My body is drenched with sweat. The lamp from the street shifts the shadows again and there, in the corner of my room, a man is standing. I want to scream, but my voice is knotted in my throat and won't come.

He moves towards me, and finally I manage to call out. A scream starts in my throat.

'Hush, hush.' It's Hayden's voice. Relief floods through me. 'It's only me. You scared the life out of me. I heard you shouting and thought something was wrong.'

He comes to sit next to me on the bed and I put my hand on his arm, glad to feel the solid reality of his body.

'You must have been having a bad dream.'

'I was,' I say. 'Someone was chasing me through the woods.'

'Did he have a camera?' he asks, trying to make light of it.

I laugh softly at that. 'No. He didn't.'

'Do you want me to go downstairs and make you a cup of tea?'

I shake my head. 'Stay here with me. I don't want to be alone.' My body gives an involuntary shudder.

'You're cold.'

I don't know if I'm cold or if I'm hot, but tenderly he wraps the cover round me, as I do to Sabina.

'I'm frightened,' I tell him.

'Do you want to come up to my room?' he asks. 'We can talk without disturbing Sabina.'

'I wouldn't like to leave her. She was having troubled sleep too.'

'Poor love.' Hayden reaches across and strokes her hair. He gazes at her as a father would at his child. 'I want to protect you both, and yet all I've done is make your situation worse.'

'We don't know that yet,' I remind him.

'We'll find out soon enough,' he says, 'and then we can decide what the damage limitation needs to be.'

'I can face anything with you.' I run my fingers along the contours of his cheek. He's a very beautiful man.

Hayden lies down beside me and I curl into his arms. He plants soft kisses on my hair. Sabina sighs in her sleep and nestles in towards me. And, despite all our troubles, we're all soon asleep.

# Chapter Sixty

We wait and wait. Two weeks spent on tenterhooks, scouring the internet and the tabloids each day, and all to no avail. There's no picture in the newspapers or the gossip magazines.

'Perhaps he didn't manage to get the shot,' is Hayden's conclusion. 'Or it was too blurry.'

'Maybe we turned quickly enough and all he saw was your back?'

He shrugs. 'Could be.'

Whatever the cause of its absence, I'm very pleased. Hayden, on the other hand, seems both more relieved and more anxious.

'One thing this has shown me is that I don't want to spend all my days cooped up here,' he adds. 'I have a right to a life as much as anyone else does. But if I'm going to venture out into the world again, I'll have to put more security measures back in place. This guy might not have been able to sell his photograph, but once they get a whiff of the scent they'll be back at the door, as sure as eggs is eggs. I'm only amazed they're not camped outside already.'

That brings my skin out in gooseflesh. I don't like the sound of that at all.

Today we're going back for our third visit to Joy's day centre and, as she promised, Crystal has bought us both a pink polo shirt to wear as a uniform. They're very pretty, in the palest of pinks. Mine is loose-fitting and buttoned up to my neck and she's bought me a long-sleeved white T-shirt to go beneath it. Crystal's is very tight and is opened as far as it will allow, to show off her impressive cleavage. I hope that none of the elderly gentlemen in her fan club has a heart condition.

We load up Hayden's car again. Yesterday evening I baked a few batches of samosas and some pakoras for the day-centre visitors to try. Joy, to my great surprise, has been telling them what a marvellous cook I am. Wonders will never cease!

I hate to leave Hayden behind. In the fortnight since our trip to Lulworth Cove and Lyme Regis, our relationship has grown. Since the night he came to wake me from my nightmare, he's been sleeping in our room. When Sabina is asleep, he comes to our bed and curls up beside us. Every morning I have a blissful moment when I wake and find myself in Hayden's arms. I watch him, his face relaxed in sleep, until his eyes open.

Then we kiss quietly, shyly, and Hayden slips away before I have to wake Sabina. I'm sure she wouldn't mind finding him there, but the less she knows of these things the better. We've told neither Joy nor Crystal of our growing fondness, but I'm sure that they can tell from the warm looks and glances we exchange.

'I'll be fine,' he says as he sees me hovering.

'We'll collect Sabina on the way back,' I tell him.

He nods and then stands back to wave us away. I watch as he turns back into the vast house alone. Crystal swings the car out of the gates and I see the security camera swivel after us.

*

I'm sure there's a change of atmosphere at Constance Fields. There seems to be more of a spring in the step of some of the regulars. The ladies look like they've dressed up a little and I'm sure that the men, too, are looking more spry. Some of the windows are thrown open to let in fresh air, and it makes me happy to see it.

When we're setting up our stations, Joy comes over. 'Can I introduce you to the new manager, ladies?' she says. 'This is Edgar Janson.'

Crystal and I look up. Standing beside us is a tall, dark and very handsome man. My friend's smile brightens instantly and I do believe that her eyelashes actually flutter.

'Well, hello,' she says.

Edgar Janson takes her hand and shakes it. 'Thank you for coming in to our centre,' he says in heavily accented English. 'Our clients are enjoying it very much.' Then he grins at her. 'Now I can see why.'

Crystal flushes and giggles girlishly.

'I'm Ayesha,' I say. He takes my hand too, but he doesn't hold it for a long time, as he did with Crystal.

'I hope I will have a chance to talk to you later,' he says. 'Perhaps over a cup of tea.'

Crystal watches with open admiration as he walks away down the corridor. 'Phwoar,' she says to Joy. 'Where did he come from?'

'Latvia,' Joy says, ever practical.

'You know what I mean, Joy,' Crystal says crossly. 'You're not that dried up that you can't spot a looker. Why didn't you tell us about him before now? Is he not as fit as you'd like?'

'He's very attractive,' I agree.

'Hands off. You've got your own,' Crystal says. 'Don't think I haven't noticed those longing glances between you and Hayd. He's had puppy-dog eyes since the day you moved in.'

I flush and she winks at me.

'Don't rule out getting a new hat before too long, Joy,' Crystal says, flicking her head in my direction.

'I am actually already married,' I point out.

'Details,' she counters with a dismissive wave. 'Right, we'd better get started. If this lot all want to look like Joan Collins before teatime we've got our work cut out.'

Joy rolls her eyes at me, but Crystal does make me laugh.

At lunchtime Crystal and I sit in the garden to eat a sandwich, as has become our custom. I've handed round my samosas to the ladies and gentlemen and they seem to be enjoying them. Our clients are divided into two camps and they're instantly identifiable. All of Crystal's ladies are sporting little rainbow-coloured faces with matching rainbow-coloured nails. My customers, on the other hand, have pale pink or peach polish with the barest shimmer of matching lipstick. My massages are very popular too. A number of men with arthritic fingers have joined my appointments list – though I'm sure they'd be happier if I wore my polo shirt like Crystal. Despite their advancing years and failing eyesight, they're very taken with her.

'Don't know quite how to tell you this,' she says, when she's finished her sandwich. 'Don't be mad.'

'Of course not.'

She chews her lip anxiously. 'I've got myself a full-time job.'

My heart plunges to my boots. 'Not back at the club?'

'No, you dozy woman! What do you take me for?'

My smile comes back.

'At the nail bar on Rosslyn Hill.'

'Really?'

'Start next week.' She studies me closely. 'You are OK about it?'

'I'm delighted,' I tell her. 'Of course you must do this.'

'My day off is probably going to be Monday, so we can still come along and do this together if you want to.'

'You mustn't think of that, Crystal. You'll need some time for yourself. I can carry on here.'

'I'll ask them if there are any more jobs coming up for you as well. If you want me to. We can work at Highly Polished together.'

I shake my head. 'I don't think it's the right place for me.' Looking around at the garden, at the lovely people who come here, I feel at home. There's a calmness in the atmosphere that soothes me, and I like listening to the wisdom of the older people as they chat to me. I wouldn't like to give this up now. 'This place suits me. I think I'd like to do more massage, more caring rather than just nails.'

'I want to keep coming here because I fancy that manager,' Crystal intimates.

'Edgar?'

'He's gorgeous.'

'He is.'

'I've never been able to keep a man,' Crystal says quietly. 'Well, not a nice one. When I had my job at the club no one was interested. They all wanted to get a good look at my noo-noo, sure enough, but they didn't want to take me home.' The hope in her eyes tears at my heart. 'Perhaps it will be different now.'

We lean together and Crystal puts her head on my shoulder. Together we enjoy the sun on our faces. 'I hope so, my friend,' I say to her. 'I do hope so.'

# Chapter Sixty-one

Later in the afternoon, before we leave, Joy comes to sit at my nail station. I soak my cotton-wool pad in varnish remover and gently take the polish off her nails.

'Although we live in the same house, we don't get very much time to sit and talk, do we?' I say to her. 'There's always so much to do. This is nice.'

'I feel you're fighting a losing battle with my nails,' she notes. 'I should wear gardening gloves.'

Every week there's soil beneath her nails and her cuticles are torn. 'You are a lady who likes to feel the earth beneath her fingers.' I smile up at her. 'Your garden is all the better for it. Besides, I like a challenge.'

Joy offers a smile too, but it doesn't reach her eyes.

'There's something wrong?'

'I've got a lot on my mind,' Joy admits. 'I didn't sleep very well last night.'

I wait to hear what's troubling her, but she volunteers no more. So I pick up my file and move on to shaping her nails. They're dry and cracked, her fingers quite raw and red. She also, I think, has some arthritis in her hands. The joints of her fingers are gnarled and twisted like the roots of a tree. I'm sure that she likes the massage part of her treatment more than her nails looking nice and, as she's my last client today, I'll spend a little extra time on them. I use the lavender cream that I bought in Lyme Regis to gently rub them. Her hands are tight with tension.

Joy's not getting any younger and I wonder who'll look after her when she's older. She seems to have a lot of acquaintances here, but not one close friend. Will Crystal and I still be at Hayden's home when she starts to need our care? Would she even be happy with us doing it? She's a woman who likes her privacy, and it's a worrying thought.

When I look up, I see that her eyes are filled with tears. I stop my massage and simply hold her hand, waiting until she feels able to speak.

'My son phoned me last night, after dinner,' she says, wiping her eyes. I hand her a tissue. 'Stephen, the one in Singapore.'

'That's nice.'

'He was on the phone for an awfully long time. I felt quite exhausted by the time he hung up.' She lets out a ragged breath. 'They've asked me to go and live with them. My other son, Malcolm, and his family will be moving there next year too and they're going to look to settle near Stephen. It's a chance for us all to be together again.'

'Oh, Joy. Won't that be lovely?'

'I'm frightened,' she admits. 'I've always had my independence. They've said they'll build a separate annexe for me in their garden, but I don't know if I like the sound of that. I'll have my own bedroom, my own living room. But they won't really be my own, will they?'

'Your family will be right on your doorstep. Surely you like the sound of that?'

'What if they get fed up of me?' she says. 'They're young.

They have their lives to live. What happens if I become ill? I'll be in a foreign land, in a foreign hospital, and they'll be stuck with me.' Joy lowers her voice although there's no one near us. 'I had years and years of looking after my husband when he was ill and housebound, I know what it's like. It blighted the boys' lives when they were growing up too. I know that when they went to university they couldn't wait to escape it. They don't need any more sickness. I couldn't burden them with that.'

'They're older men now, not impetuous youths,' I point out. 'Now that they have children of their own, they'll appreciate more what family means.'

She gazes round her, at the other people of her age gathering together, chatting, in this room. 'I'd have to leave everything I know. I don't suppose any of this lot would miss me. Not really. But I'd miss them. I don't make friends easily, Ayesha. Here I'm busy. I have lots to do. The garden to look after. In Singapore what would I do with myself all day?'

'There'll be a garden there too. Think of it as an adventure, Joy. How many people get a chance in their life to do that?'

She doesn't look convinced. 'Then there's you and Sabina. And Hayden. Even Crystal. We're a funny old bunch all thrown together, but it works, doesn't it?'

'Everything changes, Joy. I wouldn't want you to pass up this chance because of us.' I don't like to tell her of Hayden's yearning for a quieter life by the sea.

'I've only met Stephen's wife, Ling, a couple of times. She seems very nice, of course, but will she really want me under her feet?'

'You should talk to her about that, Joy. It might make you feel better if you get all of these things out in the open.'

Slowly, I continue to rub the nourishing cream into her hands, working on each finger individually, taking care to massage each ageing knuckle, each tired joint. Joy sighs with relief.

'They're really aching today,' she admits. She watches as I work my thumbs across the back of her hand. 'That feels very nice.' Joy sighs again. 'What would you do? In my situation.'

'I would go,' I tell her honestly. 'It won't all be plain sailing, I won't pretend that.' I remember when I set out on my own journey to a strange land, leaving all that I loved behind. How hopeful I was then.

'It didn't work out well for you,' Joy notes.

That makes me smile. Trust Joy not to miss a trick. 'That's true, but I was leaving my family to come and live with a husband I didn't really know. I put my trust in him and I was wrong to do so. You'll be going to people who love you very much and want you to be with them.'

'Hmm,' she says.

'Decisions should never be rushed,' I tell her. 'Take your time. Do what's right for you.'

'At least, having eaten all your spicy food for the last few weeks, I know I won't starve now.'

'Your daughter-in-law might be very happy to turn her garden over to your care. Think of all the exotic vegetables you could grow.'

Joy harrumphs at me. 'You're wasted as a manicurist, Ayesha,' she says wryly. 'You should be a bloody peace ambassador.'

# Chapter Sixty-two

Hayden was playing the piano when he heard the front door open. He glanced at his watch and couldn't believe where his day had gone. When he'd sat down this morning, the music had simply flowed out of him, just like the old days. It felt good. He felt strong inside. Happy.

'Hello.' Ayesha popped her head around the door and his heart soared some more. 'I'm not disturbing you?'

'No,' he said. 'Good to see you all back.'

Beanie pushed past her mother and ran to him instantly. She threw herself into his arms for a hug and then sat down on the piano stool next to him. He budged up to make more room for her. With a nod from him, they launched straight into their 'Chopsticks' duet and, when they'd finished, Ayesha clapped with delight.

'Shall I make some tea?'

'That'd be great,' he said, and she disappeared towards the kitchen.

Hayden started to play again. Softly this time. He turned to Beanie. 'These are some of my old songs,' he told her. 'You probably won't even know them.' He let the tune slide into 'My For

Ever Love'. 'This was my biggest hit. It was number one all over the world.' His fingers moved over the keys, automatically remembering the haunting melody. 'I've managed to sing some of my songs today. One or two. But I can't get close to this one. It's about a friend that I liked very much but now she's gone.'

He carried on to the refrain, when he tried to hum along, but after a few bars his voice wouldn't comply. 'See,' he said. 'Just stuck.'

Then, to his utter shock, Beanie took up the tune. Her voice was soft, barely audible, but there was no doubt that it was there.

'*You are my sun, my light, my life. My for ever love,*' she sang.

He forced himself to carry on playing, act as if there was nothing untoward. But his heart was beating madly against his chest and silently he was screaming for Ayesha to hurry back.

Sabina's voice got stronger as she continued to sing. '*You are my day, my night, my hope. My for ever love. My for ever love.*'

He tried to join in with her, but his voice was more clogged up with emotion than ever before and he couldn't get a single note out.

Moments later, when he was trying to work out how to keep the song going so that Sabina wouldn't stop singing, Ayesha came back bearing a tray of tea and biscuits for them.

He looked up and caught her eye. She stopped still and he saw her rock back when she realised that Sabina was singing. How she kept hold of the tray, he didn't know. He saw the mugs rattle and the tea splash out of them though.

She stood transfixed in the doorway as Sabina continued, the child seemingly unaware of the affect she was having on them both. Tears, he could see, were streaming down Ayesha's cheeks. He had to admit that he wasn't far from weeping himself. Sabina had lived here for weeks and in all that time he'd only heard one tiny little noise from her, barely a squeak. Now her

291

soft, childish voice singing his most emotive song was in danger of breaking his heart.

They came to the natural end of the song and his fingers stumbled on the keys. Sabina gave him a reproving look.

Ayesha quickly put down the tray and clapped. 'Very pretty, darling,' she said, a tremor of excitement, relief and nerves in her voice.

He couldn't imagine the emotions that must be going through her head. Saying that she'd be absolutely thrilled didn't seem in any way adequate.

'I didn't know you knew that song,' she added.

Sabina said nothing.

'Shall we sing it again?' Hayden suggested in the most casual way he could manage.

The child shook her head and went over to the tray. It seemed as if the song had unlocked her singing voice in some way, but she still wasn't going to speak. A glass of milk and a biscuit was obviously more attractive. Ayesha hugged her daughter to her, looking as if she never wanted to let her go.

'Well done,' she said to her. 'It was so very lovely to hear you sing.'

Over her daughter's head, she mouthed to him, 'Thank you.'

# Chapter Sixty-three

The pub was crowded, the band playing too loud. Suresh stood leaning on the bar next to Flynn, Smith and Arunja. He couldn't even hear himself think, let alone tell what they were saying, and they had a lot of planning to do tonight.

Suresh leaned over the bar and spoke to the landlord. 'Can we use the room upstairs for an hour, Cav? We've got a bit of business to do.'

'Sure. No problem.'

'Get us another round in then.' He nodded to the other men. 'We can go upstairs. I can't concentrate with this racket.'

So they waited until their glasses were refilled and Suresh had paid, then pushed through the crowds of youngsters until they reached the stairs. Suresh unhooked the rope that barred the way and they followed in line up the narrow stairs.

It was a room they'd used many times before. The pub landlord, Pete Cavendish, was a useful bloke to them. Sometimes, if they had gear with a dubious provenance to shift, they moved it through the pub, with a tasty cut for him, and he could be relied on to keep his mouth shut.

'It's as hot as hell in here,' Flynn complained as he walked into the room. 'It's a night for a barbie, not sitting roasting our nuts off indoors.'

Smith threw the window open, but it did little to freshen the sour-smelling space. There was an all-pervading reek of damp walls, stale food and old carpet.

'The quicker we get through this the better,' Arunja said.

'Have you got something more important you need to be doing?' Suresh asked tightly.

'It's not that—' his brother began.

Suresh cut across him. 'If anyone doesn't want to put the time into the planning, then it's fine by me if you drop out now. You're either in or you're out. This is too big to fuck up. One wrong move and we'll be enjoying an extended stay at one of Her Majesty's hotels. I don't know about you gentlemen, but I want to be taking my holidays in the Caribbean after this.'

Flynn and Smith pulled up chairs and sat at the table in the middle of the room. After a moment's hesitation, Arunja did the same.

This *was* going to be a big job for them. A step up from the piffling little stuff they'd handled before. The stakes were higher than they'd ever been and, as it had been his idea to try for the big time, Suresh wanted nothing to go wrong.

There was a new jeweller in the town, a smart, upmarket store right in the heart of the shopping centre. It sold to the luxury end of the market, none of your cheap crap in there. Even snatching a tray of Rolexes would net you a couple of hundred grand. He was tired of doing small jobs. They took up a good deal of time and the rewards were disproportionately low. You had to keep the turnover high to make a good living. He wanted to be out of the shitty estate where his parents lived, in a home of his own again. One of those penthouse flats over-looking Campbell Park would suit. Three beds, two baths. Roof terrace, too. That was the sort of place he wanted.

They were planning to do a smash-and-grab raid. Risky, as it was always busy in the centre no matter what time of day. The element of surprise would be essential. Nothing as audacious as this had been attempted before. Someone who worked in the store had told Suresh that security was lax at best. There were hundreds of thousands of pounds' worth of watches and jewellery all there for the picking. And they had his name on them.

They were tooling up for it too; Smith was getting the guns. 'Find the persuaders yet?' Suresh asked.

Smith nodded. 'Yeah. No probs. I can pick them up next week. We just need to sort out the cash.'

Suresh nodded. 'I've got it for you.' He undid his laptop bag and handed over the money he'd squirrelled away for the job.

Smith quickly counted it and folded it into his inside pocket. 'As soon as we've got them, we're almost good to go.'

They'd all been in separately to look at the place and had paid the snitch employee handsomely for information. They had overalls, masks, holdalls. Everything was coming together nicely.

'We'll strike as soon as they open, catch them unawares,' Suresh said. He unfolded the plan he had in his pocket and spread it out on the table. 'We need to get the motorbikes.'

'That's easily enough done,' Flynn said. 'Are you sure you don't want to do it by car? We can get in a professional driver. We could be in and out quicker on foot. A lot more could go wrong on a bike.'

'With every extra person we bring in, the more we have to split the money, and the bigger risk there is of someone grassing on us. I say we keep it in-house. With the bikes we'll take them by surprise.' It would be audacious this way, intimidating. He could almost see the newspaper headlines. 'We can ride right up into the store. No one will expect it.'

'I can't wait to get on a bike again.' Arunja put his hands behind his head and sat back. 'It's years since I've ridden.'

'That's why Flynn and Smith will be up front,' Suresh said. 'You and I will ride pillion.'

'I can do it,' his brother told him testily. 'I can. I used to be a great rider and know this city like the back of my hand. I'm the best man to ride.'

'No,' Suresh said firmly. 'You'll go behind Smith. I'll be behind Flynn. We'll be first off the bikes.'

Arunja sulked and Flynn looked only partly placated, but it was Suresh's job and he'd run it as he saw fit.

Doing this had taken his mind off Ayesha too. Everything he'd tried had led to a dead-end. She was gone and it didn't seem as if she was planning to return any time soon. She probably thought she was free of him. He'd show her how wrong she was.

It had gone beyond getting her back. This was now war, and he wanted them both wiped off the face of the Earth. He looked at the faint wound across his palm. It would leave a scar, and that was all he wanted left to remind him of her. He wanted a fresh start, unencumbered by an errant wife and a silent child. This raid would make him a rich man. What would he want with a woman like Ayesha when he could have the pick of them? He could have a wife like Arunja's on his arm. A woman who wore too much make-up and too little clothing. Women like that appreciated a rich man.

He may have failed to track his wife down so far, but that wouldn't stop him trying. In the depths of the night, when he couldn't sleep, he trawled the internet, looking for clues. One day Ayesha would make a mistake. A silly mistake. And he'd be waiting.

# Chapter Sixty-four

Summer's at its height now. The days are long and hot. Everyone has forgotten the cold damp of the winter and complains about the heat. But I've nothing to complain about. All in my life is well.

Sabina has sung three more times with Hayden while they've been at the piano. I could sing from the rooftops myself to hear her sweet voice again. When I watch her, I sit as calmly as I can so that I don't frighten her into silence once more.

She still hasn't spoken at all, but I feel with hope in my heart that words are just around the corner.

Joy is happy in the garden. The borders are in full bloom, with roses of every colour and bright pink peonies. Fat bees labour in the lavender bushes and the heady scent of sweet peas fills the air. We're gorging ourselves on runner beans, courgettes and tomatoes.

Crystal has now started work at the Highly Polished nail bar in the High Street and has already attended another specialist course on gel nails. I do believe that she's found her true calling. She never mentions that horrible club any more.

I go along to Joy's day centre twice a week now. On Mondays

Crystal and I go together as it's her day off. We arrive in a whirl-wind with all our nail equipment and the names fill up our appointment sheet instantly. The hand massage goes down very well, and I'm thinking I'd like to learn to do Indian head massage. I can't afford to do another course yet, but perhaps I'll be able to borrow a book from the library to help me. I think the people here would enjoy that too. They're all elderly and many of them are alone. All they want is a little human contact, some gentle caring.

I also go in on Thursday every week by myself. The calm atmosphere here suits my soul. The ladies and gentlemen fuss around me like a mummy and daddy would, and I realise that I've missed my own parents' care very much.

In the morning, a small group of us tuck ourselves in an alcove by the window and I read out loud to them, and they help me with any words I stumble over. Sometimes one or two of them doze off, but I leave them be. I can still speak above the snoring.

Currently I'm working my way through *Pride and Prejudice* by Jane Austen with them, and I'm finding it very enlightening. How very different things were in those days. Perhaps my sensibilities would have been more suited to those times. I also bring my new friends Sri Lankan savouries to try – vegetable samosas, deep-fried potato patties and lightly spiced flatbreads – and I never have to take any home.

Hayden is playing the piano every day, and he was over-joyed to tell me that he's writing songs again. When the phone rings now, he doesn't shy away but answers it. He says that Sabina and I have unlocked his heart, and I can't express how glad that makes me feel. I believe that he's unlocked my own heart too.

Today, Crystal is beside me at the day centre and I'm happier for that.

'Look at you,' she says. 'Positively glowing. You make me sick.'

I giggle at that.

'No good laughing,' she says. 'It's all right for you to be loved up, but we've got to find a nice man for me.'

'I thought you already had your eye on one,' I tease. She's been chatting and flirting with Edgar for weeks now, but to no avail.

'If I flutter my eyelashes any flipping harder, they'll drop off,' Crystal counters crossly. 'He's immune to my charms.'

'I don't think so,' I assure her.

'Well, he'd better get a move on,' she says, 'otherwise I'll be so desperate, I'll resort to copping off with one of these old boys.'

I'm scandalised. 'Crystal, you wouldn't!'

She chuckles at me. 'I might do. Ted there has his eye on me.' Crystal winks at a smart man in a cardigan who must be eighty if he's a day. He winks back. 'See.'

'Then you must make your intentions very clear to Edgar.'

'Do you think I should open some more buttons on this top?'

'There are no more buttons to open,' I tell her. 'Besides, you don't want Ted to have a heart attack.'

'True dat,' Crystal says.

'Look.' I glance up. 'Here comes Edgar now.' Indeed, the centre manager is ambling towards us. He seems like a man who's never in a hurry. Perhaps this is why he's being so slow with regards to my dear friend.

'Oh, look at him,' Crystal sighs.

He's a very handsome man, and surely he must be a kind, caring person to work here. His dark hair flops over his brow in an appealing manner. He's slender in a boyish way, all hips and elbows.

'He's much younger than me, isn't he?'

'Not so much,' I tell Crystal. Edgar looks as if he's in his late twenties. 'Perhaps he likes a lady with a little experience.'

She gives me a sideways glance. 'What about a lady with a *whole* lot?'

I giggle at that too.

'There's always a bit of his shirt untucked,' she notes in a breathless way, 'as if he's a naughty little boy. I'm never sure whether I want to tuck it back in or rip the whole thing off him.' She lets out a longing sigh as he nears our stations.

'Ladies,' he says. 'How very nice to see you here again this morning.'

Crystal's eyelashes go into overdrive.

'I have good news for you.' A beaming smile spreads across his face.

'Really?' Crystal leans on her elbows and gazes at him. He seems momentarily distracted by her cleavage, and I feel myself flush.

'What was the news?' I ask.

'Oh, er . . . ' He drags his attention back to me. 'I didn't want to tell you before now, but I have a little surprise for you. Can you come with me while I gather everyone around?'

We follow Edgar into the centre of the room. He claps his hands. 'Attention please, everyone! Ted, Lillian! Joy, are you here?'

Joy pushes her way to the front. Crystal and I stand to one side of Edgar. I make sure she's next to him. She has on a lot of fragrance today and perhaps the scent of it will lure him in.

'Can everyone hear me?' He pulls a piece of paper out of his back pocket. 'We have a little announcement.' Edgar clears his throat and turns to both Crystal and me. 'Everyone has been so delighted with the contribution that you've made to the centre, haven't we, ladies and gentlemen?'

A ripple of applause goes round the room and I feel myself

300

becoming very self-conscious. I don't know where to look or how to hold my hands. Even Crystal looks slightly abashed.

'You both really brighten the place up,' Edgar continues. 'But it's more than that. Much more. You've brought some glamour and fun into our lives.' He looks embarrassed as he says it. 'Your kind and caring manner has really made a difference. Everyone looks forward to your weekly visits. In the short time we've known you, we've all grown to love you.' Edgar gives a little self-conscious cough. 'So, with that in mind, we had a talk among ourselves and we entered you into the annual Community Awards, sponsored by the *Ham & High* newspaper.'

Crystal and I look at each other, baffled.

'I'm very pleased to tell you that you've been shortlisted in the Caring for the Community category.'

Now there's much clapping and grinning.

'There's a cheque for twenty-five pounds for each of you for reaching the finals, and next week we'll find out who is the winner. There'll be a ceremony at the Town Hall that we'd like you to attend.'

'Wow,' Crystal says. She looks quite moved. 'I've never won anything before. That's really nice of you.'

'Yes,' I agree. 'Thank you so much. It's very kind.'

'Nonsense,' Edgar says. 'We all love having you here, don't we?'

A cheer goes up.

'Now we must keep our fingers crossed for the big prize,' he finishes.

Everyone comes to hug and congratulate us. I'm feeling very thrilled as I, like Crystal, have never been put forward for an award before. It's a very big honour for me.

'Well done, my lovelies,' Joy says, and she kisses us both. 'I think I should get the tea urn going.'

'I think we should open a bottle of fizz when we get home,' Crystal says.

'Why don't we have a barbecue tonight? That would be nice.'

'Great idea,' she says. 'I'm up for that.'

'Edgar,' I say to the manager, 'would you like to come to our home tonight for a small celebration? While the weather is fine, I thought we'd have a barbecue.'

'I'd like that very much, Ayesha. Thank you.'

'Crystal will text you the address.' My friend stands there, looking stunned.

'I look forward to it. Here's my number.' He reels it off while Crystal rushes to tap it into her mobile. Then he grins at Crystal and moves away. 'See you later.'

When he's out of earshot, I turn to Crystal. 'There you are. That wasn't so hard.'

'You beaut!' Crystal pinches my cheeks. 'What a result. A date with the delectable Edgar. That's better than any naffing "community award".'

# Chapter Sixty-five

'We've won an award,' I tell Hayden when we get home. We're sitting together in the garden with a well-earned cup of tea. 'Well, we've been shortlisted for the finals. But it's still nice and, even if we don't win overall, both Crystal and I get a cheque for twenty-five pounds.'

'Well done.' He comes to hug me and I enjoy the warmth of his body against mine. 'Haven't you got a clever mummy?' he says to Sabina.

My daughter is at my side colouring in a book with pencils that Crystal bought her as a treat. My friend was so thrilled to learn that my daughter is able to sing, but she's not yet heard her.

'I hope you don't mind but I invited Edgar, the manager from Constance Fields, to the house for a small celebration this evening. Crystal has a soft spot for him and I thought it would be nice for them to be able to spend some time together, to get to know each other.'

'Matchmaking, eh?'

I smile. 'Maybe a little bit. Can we have a barbecue?'

'Great idea. It's a fabulous evening and it'll be nice to have some more testosterone here for once.'

I think back to a time, not so long ago, when I wouldn't have dared to breathe, let alone invite a male friend around for dinner or organise an impromptu barbecue. Now, not only can I do that, I also have my very first award. A small recognition that I'm a worthy part of society. I'm growing as a person and I think that I rather like it.

'I've written a song today,' Hayden says. 'It's rough, but I think it could be a good one.'

'I'd like to hear it.'

'Not yet,' he says. 'But soon. You'll be the first to hear it, I promise.' He levers himself from his deckchair. 'I'll get the barbecue going.'

'Edgar's coming at six o'clock.'

'We'll not see Crystal before then,' is Hayden's assessment. 'She'll be too busy preening herself.'

'I heard that. Cheeky bugger.' Crystal comes out of the kitchen. 'I'm actually coming to pimp the garden. Thought I'd open up the summerhouse.'

'Hayden's going to light the barbecue. I'll make some side dishes.'

'Can we have something that doesn't involve Joy's tomatoes? I'm going to look like one soon.'

'Only a few tomatoes,' I concede.

'I'm quite nervous about Edgar coming,' she admits. 'What am I going to say to him?'

'I'm sure that won't be a problem, Crystal.'

'You're not normally lost for words,' Hayden chips in.

'Shut up, you two,' Crystal complains. 'You're not helping. This is important to me. He's a nice guy.'

'You'll be fine,' I assure her.

'I hope so,' she mutters and wanders off down the garden.

Hayden and I exchange a glance.

'He *is* nice,' I say. 'You'll like him.' If Hayden feels strange about Crystal bringing a potential date back here then he doesn't say so.

'I'll get some sounds rigged up out here too,' he offers. 'An evening like this is perfect for a party.'

'I'll go to help Crystal before I start on the food.' I don't like to see her so anxious and I follow her down the garden, enjoying the feel of the grass on my bare feet.

The warmth of summer is held in the garden, embraced by the high walls. The scents are heady in the early evening, richly perfumed roses mixing with sweet peas and lavender. Pretty butterflies flit among the thick purple blooms of the buddleia. A large willow tree, in full leaf, hangs low to the grass.

Crystal has opened the doors to the summerhouse and is brushing away cobwebs with her hand. 'It could do with a good clean,' she says. 'It's a shame it's never used properly. I had to give the doors a good yank to get them open at all. Looks like Joy's been using it to store overflow garden equipment and plant pots.'

Sure enough, there's an assortment of spades and forks leaning against the walls. A tall stack of terracotta pots that tilts like the Leaning Tower of Pisa graces one corner.

'We could get rid of this stuff. Put it back in the shed,' Crystal suggests.

'Joy won't mind?'

'Of course she will. She grumbles about everything. Wouldn't Beanie love it as a playhouse?'

'I'm sure she would.'

Together we pull out some fading striped deckchairs and dust them down.

'There's some bunting too.' Crystal pulls out a tangled string of fabric flags made from all different kinds of floral fabric.

'This is very pretty.'

'We can hang it between the trees. Give me a hand, Ayesha.'

She drags a small stepladder from the summerhouse and I help her to tie the bunting on to the branches until it criss-crosses the bottom of the garden. 'Fab,' Crystal says as she admires our handiwork. 'We should leave it up all summer. It brightens up the garden no end. Wish we had some lights too. Perhaps I'll ask Hayden if we can get some.'

I brush off my hands. 'I'd better go and make a start on the food.'

'Thanks for doing this.'

'It'll be fun,' I assure her. 'Just relax and enjoy it.'

Crystal catches my arm. 'I'm worried,' she says. 'Proper worried. I really like Edgar, Ayesha, but he doesn't know what I used to do.'

'You'll find the right time to tell him.'

'What if he legs it?'

'Edgar's a nice man. I'm sure he'll understand. If he doesn't, then he's not the man we think he is.'

Suddenly her eyes brim with tears. 'I've got so many secrets and I'm tired of them.' Her spirit sags and I look at her with concern. Normally Crystal would bounce back with a witty quip, but she doesn't.

'You can tell me, if it helps.' Instead of leaving, I sit back down in one of the deckchairs and pat the other.

Crystal joins me and we sit silently for a few moments as I wait patiently for her to speak. The sound of someone mowing a lawn in another garden drifts towards us. In one of the trees a bird competes by singing out sweetly.

Eventually she lets out a wavering sigh. 'I had a child, Ayesha. A little boy.' Tears roll down her cheeks. 'I never tell anyone this.' Another shuddering breath. 'He died when he was a few months old.'

'Oh, Crystal. I am so sorry.' I can't imagine what it must be like to lose a child.

'Sudden Infant Death Syndrome. That's what they called it.'
She brushes away a tear, but another is quick to take its place.
'It seems such a cold and clinical title to describe something so
devastating. I felt as if my heart had been ripped out.'

'What was your baby's name?'

'Max. Named for his daddy. Bastard that he turned out to
be.'

'You didn't stay with Max's father?'

'Not for long. If I'm honest, he was never really mine at all.
I met him at the club I was working at. A much more glamorous
one in those days. He was well known, with a high-profile marriage.'

'Oh.'

She raises an eyebrow at me. 'I can always pick them.'
Crystal twists her hair in her fingers and gazes up at the towering tree above us. 'I adored him. Even then, even when I fell
pregnant, I knew there wouldn't be a happy ending for me.'

'You wanted him to leave his wife?'

'Of course. But there was no chance of that. I thought he'd
want nothing more to do with me when he found out about
the baby, but I was wrong on that count. He supported me
financially when Max was born, and he wanted *me*. Yet he
didn't want to see his own child. That much he made clear.
How could someone be so cold towards their own son? It
broke my heart.' She shakes her head sadly at the memory.
'Max's father wasn't even around for the birth. I shared a flat
with a good friend from the club, Billie. She came with me to
the hospital and was my birth partner when the time came.
She helped me so much, but it's not the same, is it?'

'It must have been a terrible situation.'

'It was. I had money enough, but that wasn't what I needed.'
She turns to me and her face is the picture of misery. 'I could
have stayed at home with him, you know. Looked after him like

a proper mum. At least for a short while. I didn't though. I went back to the club pretty much straight away. I exercised like a fiend to get back in shape. You see, it was the only time I saw his father. I thought if I kept the relationship going, then things would change, that he'd eventually come and see Max and fall in love with him. You should have seen my baby, Ayesha.' Crystal smiles at me through her tears. 'He was so beautiful. Perfect in every way. I used to sit for hours gazing at his tiny fingers and toes, his little rosebud mouth. And he'd come from me. That was the most amazing part of all. The biggest fuck-up of all time had managed to produce this amazing little bundle of delight. I swore then that I was going to turn my life around. For Max's sake.' She sags back into her deckchair.

'What happened?'

'One night I was at the club and Billie was babysitting for me. As I said, she was great. She loved Max like he was her own and gave me a hand whenever she could. I came back at three in the morning and was so happy as his father had finally agreed to come and meet him. I knew he'd adore him on sight. We'd had a great night together and I thought everything was going to be all right for once. I was over the moon, I felt as if I was walking on air. The first thing I did was go straight into Max's room to look at him. I wanted him to know that his daddy was finally coming to meet him.'

She hugs her arms around herself. 'I stood there staring at him in the glow of his nightlight, my perfect little cherub fast asleep in his cot. Except he wasn't.' Her words catch in her throat and now I cry with her. 'When I brushed his cheek it was cold, Ayesha. As cold as the grave. When I left to be with his father, he was warm and soft and when I came back he was chilled like marble.'

'Oh, Crystal.' I lean across and hold her while she sobs. Eventually she brushes her tears away with her arm.

'I went to pieces,' she continues. 'Not surprisingly. I couldn't work for ages. I was a total mess. I drank too much and took all kinds of shit to try to block out the pain. That's why I ended up running up so many debts. When I went back to the club, my heart wasn't in it and there were too many scenes in front of the punters. The night I left with Hayden, I never went back to that club at all, never saw Max's father again. When I finally got my act together, they wouldn't take me back. I was too old, a has-been, more trouble than I was worth. The only job I could get was at that rancid club you came to. I took it. At least it helped me to start paying off what I owe. I sort of saw it as my punishment, too. As if I wasn't worthy of anything better.'

'Of course you are.'

'It's wrong to lose a child, Ayesha. Against nature. He was so flawless. Like an angel. He didn't deserve to die like that.'

'There was nothing you could have done.'

'Is that true? I've tortured myself over the years. What if I hadn't gone back to work so quickly? I was in such a hurry to resume my relationship with his father, I didn't really consider the alternatives. In my head, I was doing it for Max. But what if I'd been at home with him that night instead of Billie? Would I have known instinctively that my boy was dying? Mothers know these things, don't they?'

'They do,' I agree. 'Sometimes. However, that doesn't mean that they can always prevent them.'

'I think about him every single day.'

'We can all hurt ourselves with "What if?",' I tell her. 'I wonder, if I'd left my husband sooner, would Sabina still be able to speak? It's my fault that she is as she is.'

'You're doing the right thing now,' Crystal says. 'I'll never have that chance.'

'There'll be other children. They'll never replace Max, but you'll be a mother again one day. I know it.'

'God, I hope you're right. Having Beanie here has been *totes* brilliant. She's a great kid. It's made me realise that I'm broody. I'd love another baby. I'd be a nightmare though! How could I ever let the child out of my sight even for a moment?'

'You'll find a way.'

'I'd like to take you to see Max.'

'I'd very much like that.' Then, a question I have to ask. 'Does Hayden know?'

'Yeah,' she says. 'We used to pour our hearts out together when I first got here. He was the first man after . . . after it happened. We were both in pain. I think that's why I ended up staying here. Two lost souls together.'

'Joy doesn't know though?'

'No,' Crystal says. 'Not Joy. I think she'd disapprove.'

'She wouldn't, you know,' I assure her. 'She loves you very much.'

'Maybe.' She shrugs. 'I feel as if I don't deserve anyone's love. I'm so ashamed of the things I've done, Ayesha.'

'We've all had to do things that we didn't want to in order to survive.' I get a flashback to Suresh striking me, and me bending to his will, whatever it involved. Quickly I push the image away. Both Crystal and I have known pain. 'That's the past,' I tell her. 'Now you're going towards a new future. Take it slowly.'

'I'm not sure there's going to be any other way with Edgar.' She rolls her eyes ruefully.

'That's a good thing. Get to know each other.' I speak from the experience of a woman who married a man that she didn't know. 'You're looking for a husband now, not a one-night stand.'

'You're right,' she says. 'Of course you are. I'm just so used to jumping into bed with someone straight away. But I'm done with that. That was the old me, and I think that sends out all the wrong messages. I want someone to love and respect me for who I am. I'm going to do it differently this time.'

'You and me both,' I confide.

'Thanks. You're a good listener.' She hugs me. 'God, I'm emotionally exhausted.'

'We'll have fun tonight. Laugh with Edgar and see what the future brings.'

'I'll drink to that,' she says.

'We are women on a journey.'

'Yeah,' Crystal agrees thoughtfully. 'We are.' She grins at me. 'And now your journey needs to take in the kitchen, otherwise there'll be nothing to eat tonight.'

# Chapter Sixty-six

The barbecue's hot, the food nearly ready. Hayden's busy at the grill and the scent of sizzling sausages and char-grilled chicken is making us all hungry. Crystal has sworn off alcohol for the evening and has made a punch with fresh orange, cranberry juice and lemonade. She's flitting about nervously, glass in hand. After our talk, she went inside to wash her face and has put on a pretty white sundress and sparkly flip-flops. Her hair is loose and she's wearing very little make-up. She looks so beautiful, and my heart goes out to my friend. I hope that this man will be good to her.

When Edgar arrives he's freshly showered, with clean hair. His face is clean-shaven and shining. Even his shirt is tucked in all the way round. Our guest is holding a bottle of wine and a bunch of flowers that are wilting a little in the heat. He looks every bit as nervous as Crystal when we answer the door.

'Come into the garden,' I tell him. 'Don't be shy. You're among friends.'

'I had not expected such a large house,' he confides.

'Looks can be deceptive,' Crystal says. 'Half the rooms are uninhabitable.'

As we go out to the garden, Edgar gives the flowers to Crystal with an embarrassed smile. When Hayden comes over, he hands the wine to him.

'Nice to meet you, Edgar.' Hayden shakes his hand. 'It makes a change not to be the only man about the house.'

'This is my daughter, Sabina.' I introduce her to Edgar. Solemnly she shakes his hand. 'She doesn't speak.' I tell him. 'Not yet.'

'Very pleased to meet you, Sabina,' he says politely, and she graces him with a shy smile. 'I have a little girl too. Beatrise. She's six.'

'A daughter?' Crystal says. 'You hadn't mentioned her.'

'I didn't?' Edgar pulls out his wallet and shows her a photograph. 'She's the light of my life.'

I peek at it too. She's a pretty little girl with long dark hair and her father's eyes.

'She's beautiful.' Crystal grins at him.

'You like children?'

Crystal's eyes flick to mine and she smiles bravely before she says, 'I love them.'

'I see her nearly every weekend,' Edgar says. 'She comes to stay with me. I live in a small flat above the day centre. It's a very nice place, but not like this.' He looks around at the house and garden, still gaping slightly. 'You must come to see it.'

'I'd like that,' Crystal says.

'Let me take the flowers,' I say. She hands them over to me and I pop inside to find a vase. I arrange them as prettily as I can and then put them out on the table in the garden.

I've made an effort with how I look this evening and am wearing my maxidress. Crystal has piled my hair up for me and it's nice to feel what little movement of air there is on my neck. Joy follows me outside; she's also dressed up, in a floral shirt and white trousers. Her outfit is topped off with a broad-brimmed sunhat.

'The garden's looking lovely, Joy,' I tell her.

'It takes a lot of work,' she says with a weary sigh. 'Sometimes I wonder how long I'll be able to manage it by myself.'

'I can help you,' I offer. 'If you show me what to do.'

'You've got enough on your plate, young lady. You don't want to be tying yourself down to the garden as well as everything else.'

'Perhaps Hayden can get you some help.'

She shakes her head and forces a smile. 'No need to bother him. I'm all right really.'

But I wonder if she should have someone to give her a hand. It's a big garden and a lot of work for her to manage by herself. Maybe I should find a quiet moment to speak to Hayden about it.

I slip my arm through hers. 'Come on, let's join the others. This evening you can relax and enjoy it for a change.'

So we wander over to where Crystal and Edgar are chatting together while Hayden tends the barbecue.

'Where did all this lovely bunting come from?' Joy asks. 'I've never seen it before.'

'It was tucked away in the summerhouse,' Crystal says. 'Don't know what it was doing there.'

'We had it for Laura's birthday the year we moved in here,' Hayden says over his shoulder.

'You and your big gob, Joy,' Crystal tuts.

'Oh, I'm sorry, Hayden,' Joy says, embarrassed. 'Stupid me. I didn't even think.'

'It's fine,' he assures her. 'Really, it is.' He glances over towards me and smiles. 'I'm finally moving on.'

'Great news about the award,' Joy says, hastily changing the subject. 'I'm sure you're both in with a very good chance of scooping the main prize.'

'All we do is slap on a bit of nail polish,' Crystal protests.

'It's more than that,' Edgar says shyly. 'Everyone really looks forward to your visits and you've given our spirits a lift. I only wish I could find a reason to have you in every day.' He blushes as he says it.

'A toast to our lovely ladies,' Hayden says.

We all raise our glasses.

'Lovely ladies!' we echo.

Crystal clinks her glass against mine. 'To us,' she says. 'We're flipping fab!'

'I'd better serve this food before it's all charcoal biscuits,' Hayden says. 'Have you got a big plate, Ayesha?'

'Just here.' I take it over to him and he piles it up with meat, chicken and vegetable kebabs.

We all gather round the table and tuck in. The chatter flows and the laughter is easy and plentiful. Edgar tells us of his life in Latvia and how he came to England two years ago. We hear how he'd been working as a manager in a nursing home before accepting this job. He's a charming and articulate man. I like how attentive he is to Crystal, helping her to salad, making sure that her drink is topped up. He touches her arm, her shoulder, affectionately. It's nice to see and I hope that he stays around.

When we've eaten, I make coffee for us all. Hayden goes into the house through the French doors and sits at his piano.

'Come on, Beanie,' he says, waving Sabina towards him. 'Join me.' Without hesitation, she goes to sit next to him.

They work through their repertoire. First we're treated to a break-neck-speed version of 'Chopsticks', then they play two pretty little tunes together that I don't recognise. It's clear that they've been doing some secret practising together.

Then Hayden moves on to his own songs. He nudges Sabina off the stool as he starts up with 'My For Ever Love', the strains

315

of which even I now recognise. My daughter stands next to him, but faces out towards us.

As he plays, her voice sings out clear and strong. My eyes fill with tears. No longer is she hesitant and unsure. Somehow singing is beginning to unlock her voice once more, and I marvel to hear it. I thought, I feared, that it would be a day that would never come.

I feel the tears roll down my cheeks and, as I glance across at Joy and Crystal, I see that they're both weeping too. Crystal reaches across and surreptitiously squeezes my hand. Joy rummages inside her sleeve, pulls out a handkerchief and dabs at her eyes.

When Sabina finishes, we all clap rapturously. Crystal whistles her appreciation.

'What a voice, Beanie!' she cries. 'You sound better than blinking Beyoncé.'

My daughter grins shyly.

'Shall we do another one, Bean?' Hayden asks. 'What do you fancy?'

She shakes her head and comes to sit next to me. My daughter, it seems, knows her own mind. So Hayden carries on playing and I pull Sabina into my embrace. 'I love you so much, my child,' I tell her. 'You are both clever and beautiful.'

'Just like her mum,' Crystal adds.

'That was lovely, little one,' Joy says, flapping her handkerchief. 'Lovely.'

Edgar looks a little perplexed by the outpouring of emotion, unaware of the significance of what he's witnessed.

As dusk is falling, I shoo Crystal and Edgar to the bottom of the garden. 'Spend some time together while I tidy up,' I insist.

So they sit together in the deckchairs beneath the bunting, Crystal with her legs curled under her. She's timid with him and seems a world away from the woman I saw in that tawdry club, which I think can only be a good thing.

Joy brings some citronella candles from the shed and lights up the garden. The sweet scent carries on the night air.

Sabina yawns. 'It's time for bed,' I tell her. 'School in the morning. Go and get into your pyjamas and I'll be up to read to you in a moment.'

As I start to tidy up, Hayden stops playing and comes into the garden. 'Leave that for a minute,' he says and he draws me down on to his lap, wrapping me in his arms. 'This has been a magical evening.'

'It has,' I say. 'Thank you for taking time with Sabina. I can't thank you enough for what you've done for her.'

'It's of mutual benefit,' he tells me. 'As she's finding her voice again, she's unlocking something inside of me. As are you. We have something special, don't we?'

'I believe we do.' I stroke his face. My hand trembles as I touch him. I'm not a woman who is accustomed to love, but I feel that this is it. I love Hayden with all of my being but I'm too afraid to tell him. Instead I settle on 'I am happy here. So very happy.'

'Then I hope it will never change,' he says.

I rest my head on his shoulder and his solidity soothes me. 'I'd very much like that too.'

In my heart I hope that we can freeze this moment and live our lives like this for ever.

# Chapter Sixty-seven

A week later, we all go along to the Community Awards ceremony at the Town Hall. It's an imposing building and I feel
quite intimidated to be going there. Edgar is holding Crystal's
hand as we approach it. Hayden is coming along too, plus Joy
and Sabina. They'll be cheering us on and it feels good to
know that we have our own support in the audience. Also
Edgar bought tickets for some of the other ladies and gentlemen from the day centre to join us, which is very lovely.

'It feels like a flipping film première,' Crystal whispers to me.
'Closest we'll ever get to one, anyway.'

She's right. It does feel very special and we're being treated as
if we're important people. We're all shown to chairs which have
our names on them, right near the stage, and settle into them.
Soon, alongside us, the dignitaries take their places too. The
ceremony is officiated by the editor of the *Ham & High*, and
the prizes are to be presented by a local resident who's also an
actress in a soap opera that, to my shame, I've never watched.

I'm very tense as I'm unused to being in the limelight and
feel quite uncomfortable with it. I don't really hear what's said
when the rest of the awards for services to the community are

announced. It all passes me in a blur as I think anxiously of when our turn might be. I clutch Hayden's hand tightly, waiting for our big moment of glory or failure. I don't know why, but I really want to win this. It's as if it's some sort of affirmation that what I'm doing is right. It's come to represent more than a local award to me.

'You'll be all right,' Hayden whispers to me, but I'm too terrified, too anxious to reply.

Then suddenly it's time for the final award, for Caring in the Community. The list of finalists is read out and the presenter tells a little of all our stories. There's someone who has helped to create a garden for a nursery school, and surely this is more worthy than our meagre offering? I steel myself for disappointment, sure that I'll let down all of my friends.

Then our names are read out. 'The last names on the list of finalists are Ms Crystal Cooper and Mrs Ayesha Rasheed.'

Crystal grips my other hand and gives a little squeal of delight.

'Ms Cooper and Mrs Rasheed have been singled out for this award due to their exemplary care for some of our elderly residents.'

'He has my proper name,' I whisper to Crystal.

'I told Edgar. If we won, I didn't want them putting a false name on the trophy. I wanted it to be you.' She looks concerned. 'Did I do wrong?'

I shake my head. 'I was just surprised.' Nevertheless, a cold circle of dread has settled in my tummy.

'At the Constance Fields Day Centre Ms Cooper and Mrs Rasheed perform manicure and massage services. Centre manager Mr Edgar Janson has been fulsome in his praise of their work. He says, and I quote, "Ms Cooper and Mrs Rasheed have been a welcome addition to the visiting services at our day centre. Their bright personalities and caring natures have brought warmth and light into the lives of our regular visitors. Their weekly visits are anticipated eagerly as a part of our calendar. Not only do they conduct their services with a professional air, but they also go above and beyond what is required of them. Mrs Rasheed brings in delicious food for our visitors to try and is happy to sit and read to them on a voluntary basis. Ms Cooper always lends a caring ear to anyone with troubles."'

'I like a bloody good gossip, is what that means,' Crystal whispers to me.

On stage, the man folds his notes. 'That, ladies and gentlemen, is the last of our finalists.' The audience clap enthusiastically. 'May the best man or woman win!'

Someone urges the pretty young actress forward.

'So it's with great pleasure that I ask Poppy Valentine to announce the winner.'

The actress rips open an envelope. She leans forward to the microphone. 'The overall winner of the Caring in the Community Award for this year is Ms Crystal Cooper and Mrs Ayesha Rasheed of Constance Fields Day Centre.'

There's a buzzing in my ears as the applause starts up again. I can hear Edgar and Hayden cheering.

'It's us,' Crystal says, already on her feet. 'Come on, woman! Let's go and bask in the glory!'

Dazed, I follow my friend. She takes my hand and we head to the stage. I lift my dress carefully, so that I don't trip and make a fool of myself.

The actress steps forward and hands the award to me. It's a cut-glass bowl engraved with our names. I run my finger over the etching: CRYSTAL COOPER AND AYESHA RASHEED. I smile at Crystal. We did it. We won the award.

The actress gives Crystal an envelope which contains £250 to go with our trophy, which will be so useful in paying for our equipment. Poppy Valentine kisses me on the cheek and offers her gushing congratulations to both of us. Crystal hugs me and we laugh together. Cameras flash and I feel myself recoiling, blinking. My ears are ringing and I can hear the ladies and gentlemen who've come along shouting for us. Moments later, we make our way off the stage and the awards ceremony comes to a close.

We're instantly engulfed by our friends and the kind people from the day centre. I look round, desperately seeking out Hayden. But as I do, a press photographer comes along and, even before he starts snapping away, Hayden grabs my wrist. 'Do you want me to stop this?' he murmurs.

'I don't know.' My heart is beating too quickly. 'I feel I'll let them down if I do.'

'Come on, Ayesha,' Crystal says. 'This is our big moment. Don't be shy.'

Our eyes meet and I nod to Hayden to indicate that I'll go with her. How can I tell Crystal that I don't want my photograph in the newspaper? She's so excited and it means so much to her. It means a lot to me too, but I hadn't bargained for this level of attention. We're to be fêted publicly, and I hadn't quite expected it to feel so threatening.

Instantly Hayden fades into the background. I want to disappear with him, but now the photographer takes my hand and pulls me forward. A second later and he's snapping away, shouting orders to Crystal and me.

The photographer, unaware of my discomfort, gets Crystal and me to pose with Edgar, Joy and the other visitors to the day centre. My mouth goes dry as Crystal and I hold our trophy aloft.

'Smile, ladies,' he says. 'This way. This way.' We turn towards him, but I feel my smile is more false than Crystal's.

'Are you sure you're happy with this?' Crystal murmurs to me.

'Yes.' I nod my consent, but she knows me too well and can tell that I'm nervous.

'Enjoy it,' she whispers to me. 'Don't be so worried. It's only the local paper. Here today and gone tomorrow. It goes to a few streets round where we live. Who'll see it?'

This may, I think, be an optimistic assessment. Perhaps I should heed my own concern, but I don't. I want to celebrate our achievement and I can't disappoint my friends. So, rightly or wrongly, I try to block my concerns from my mind and think no further than that.

# Chapter Sixty-eight

Our beautiful glass bowl is given pride of place in the Constance Fields Day Centre. When Crystal and I arrive for our duties the regulars are clustered around a newspaper.

'What's the deal?' Crystal says as she sets down her bag.

'*You* are,' one of the men replies, and they all part so that we can see what they're looking at. 'You've made the front page, ladies.'

My goodness, so we have. They hand over the newspaper to Crystal and we both peer at it. Splashed all over the front of the *Ham & High* is a photograph of Crystal and me, beaming widely, holding our trophy up to the camera.

'Wow,' she says. 'We're stars.'

'In a very small universe,' I counter.

'But front page, all the same.'

'Inside too,' one of the ladies points out. 'You're right across the middle pages as well.'

Crystal whips open the newspaper. There are photographs of the other contenders too, but right across the centre there's another picture of Crystal and me flanked by members of the day centre with Joy and Edgar. Hayden, quite sensibly, is nowhere to be seen.

I'd thought there'd be a small column covering the event and that there might not have been room for a photograph, but the newspaper has really gone to town on this. I'm both secretly delighted and terrified at the same time. I'm glad that I will, for the rest of my life, be able to look back on this moment with pride. But what if Suresh somehow sees it? Surely by now he'll no longer be interested in the whereabouts of his runaway wife and daughter.

Edgar comes into the room. 'Lovely piece,' he says. 'Very well deserved.' I notice his hand touches the small of Crystal's back and she smiles.

They've seen each other every day since the evening of the barbecue, and I do believe that my friend might be in love. Crystal hasn't yet met Edgar's daughter, but I don't think that it will be too long before she does.

'I've got copies for both of you,' Edgar says. 'They're in my office. It should be framed and put on your wall.'

Joy had gone straight out into the garden when we arrived, to put a new trowel that she'd bought into the shed. Now she comes into the day room.

'Look, Joy,' I say to her. 'We've made the newspaper.'

She pops on her reading glasses. 'Well, look at that. How lovely. Well done, girls.'

'We'd better get cracking with our manicures,' Crystal says, 'or you'll be snatching the award back off us.'

While Joy takes the newspaper and goes to show it to some of the other members, Crystal and I go to set up our nail stations. As we do, I give voice to the dark thought that crossed my mind a moment ago. 'You don't think that Suresh could see this, do you?'

'No.' Crystal gives a dismissive shake of her head. 'It's a little local paper. No one reads it, anyway. Unless your husband happens to be in Hampstead this week, he'll never know. How could he?' Then she frowns. 'He doesn't come to London much, does he?'

'I don't know.' I never knew what my husband's movements were even when I lived with him. Inside, I shiver with apprehension. I wouldn't like to think that he, or someone he knows, will see me. 'I don't think so.'

'You look different too,' she offers. 'I bet he wouldn't even recognise you. You're smiling, for a start. Look at that cheesy grin.'

I smile again, though I believe my lips are actually sticking to my teeth in terror.

'You didn't do much of that when you first came to the house.' Crystal chews anxiously at her lip. 'I wish we'd used your fake name now though. But I didn't want it to be wrong on the bowl though. You've worked too hard for the credit to go to someone fictitious.'

'I'm sure you're right. It will all be fine. Nothing came of the photograph that was snapped of Hayden and me.'

'And that was much more risky,' she notes.

'Yes.' But deep down, there's a knot of disquiet in my soul.

'You're safe with us,' she reassures me. 'Hayden would never let anything happen to you. The house is like bloody Fort Knox too. No one could break in there. There's really nothing to worry about.'

I am worried though. Perhaps I should have done the same as Hayden and faded into the background, let Crystal take the glory by herself. I was too full of my own pride and, against my better judgement, wanted to have my picture in the local newspaper. I wanted people to see that I was a good person of some worth. Plus I wanted to appear grateful to the people who'd nominated me. What would they have thought if I'd shied away from the press and gone to hide?

But what if, in putting these things first, I've placed Sabina and myself in danger?

'I should be more concerned than you,' Crystal says. 'The club was only down the road. What if this lot find out that I was a lapdancer? It could give some of them flipping heart failure.' She nods towards one of the elderly men. 'Ted would be a prime candidate.'

I giggle when I shouldn't. 'You are terrible,' I tell her.

'You know it's true.'

'Have you told Edgar yet?'

'Sort of,' she says evasively. 'I'm edging towards it. I've told him that I have a dark and murky past. Just not the details.'

'He still seems keen.'

Her face softens and she smiles. 'He does, doesn't he? I really like him, Ayesha. *Really* like him.'

'There's a lot that's likeable about him.'

Then we notice some of the ladies glancing at their watches. 'This lot are champing at the bit,' Crystal tuts. 'We're in demand now that we're famous. Are we ready?'

'Yes,' I tell her. 'I'm ready.'

'Perhaps we can put our prices up now that we're "award-winning manicurists".'

I laugh out loud.

'That's better,' Crystal says. 'I don't want you fretting about this.'

'No,' I tell her. 'I won't.'

However, try as I might to be jolly, there's an underlying gnawing of doubt in my mind. I wonder how long and how far I'll have to run from my husband to be certain that Sabina and I are safe. Will part of me always wonder if he's suddenly going to come to take us back?

If Suresh were to see this, then surely he wouldn't trouble to find us. Too much time has passed. I hope in my heart that he will have let us go.

# Chapter Sixty-nine

It was two in the morning and Suresh's eyes were gritty with sleep. He'd been staring at the plans of the jeweller's shop for the last hour, making sure they were imprinted on his brain. Everything was in place now. Smith had got the hardware. They'd got two fast motorbikes with false plates which Flynn and Smith were going to ride, with him and Arunja as pillion.

The bikes were now stashed in a lock-up garage in Netherfield. This raid was going to be daring, audacious, the most exciting thing he'd ever done. It would elevate him to the status of folk hero. No longer would he be a nobody. He'd have more money than he'd know what to do with, and he could get out of this hovel and into his own place. Not a modest little terrace. Something big and flashy that told the world to fuck off. His parents would finally give him the respect he deserved rather than always seeing his waster of a brother as the favoured son. He'd get himself a modern, British woman who wore tight clothes and plenty of make-up. He was done with mousy women from some godforsaken village. He'd thought that was the kind of woman who'd admire him, and look where that had got him.

All they had to do was settle on the date for their raid. He wanted it to be as soon as possible. His whole body was itching for it to be done. There was nothing more he could do now without talking to Flynn, Smith and Arunja, so he folded the plans away and pulled the laptop towards him. Adrenalin was pumping through his veins and he knew sleep would be impossible. Pouring himself another glass of whisky, he clicked on to Google. His parents had long gone to bed and there was nothing to bother him at this hour. The house was quiet, still. It was a good time to watch porn undisturbed. Before he did, he'd take a minute to look at one more thing. He'd put a Google Alert on Ayesha and Sabina's names and every night he checked what the search had thrown up. Every night it came back with nothing.

He should move on. He knew that. So what if she'd gone? He wasn't any worse off without her. Better, if anything. When he came home late at night, or not at all, he didn't have to look at her reproachful face or endure his sullen, silent child. No, he thought, they were better off gone. He didn't want her back. Now he was free to find a woman who could love him in the way he thought he deserved. A woman with scarlet-red lips, big breasts and willing eyes. Women like the ones he watched dance in those dark clubs like Desires that Arunja liked so much, like the ones on the porn sites. Those women would do anything he wanted.

The words blurred before his eyes as he scrolled down the page. Then, just as he was about to give up and click to something more satisfying, there it was in black and white.

*Ayesha Rasheed.*

Suresh could hardly believe his own eyes. But it was right there in front of him.

*Ayesha Rasheed.* His Ayesha?

He hit the link and waited impatiently until the article appeared in full. There was the prickle of anticipation in his blood and his palms grew damp. It was from the online site for the *Ham & High* newspaper, and Suresh blessed his good fortune.

It was her. And his heart raced.

There was a picture of his wife and another, tarty-looking woman holding up a glass bowl. He peered closely. Ayesha looked different. Her hair was loose and she was smiling broadly for the camera. She was beautiful, he thought. How long had it been since he'd noticed that?

He read through the piece, his heart pounding in his chest. So she was working at some old persons' day centre and she'd won an award. It looked as if she was finally trying to make something of herself. Well, he'd soon put a stop to that.

Before they did the job at the jeweller's, he'd have to sort this. The boys might not be happy, but it needed to be done. When this was finished, when his wife and his daughter were gone for good, he'd be able to think straight again.

The article gave the name and address of the day centre where she was working. Constance Fields. How convenient. That would make it easy enough to track her down. He shook his head with incredulity at the simplicity of it after all this time. He'd get Flynn to follow her to where she lived. Now he had to decide what to do.

Suresh rubbed his hands together, grinning to himself in the darkness. He topped up his whisky again and gave a solitary toast to his luck. He'd known that one day she would slip up. And she'd done just that. Now he had her.

# Chapter Seventy

I curl in to Hayden's side on the sofa. Every evening, when Sabina has gone to bed, we read *Great Expectations* by Mr Charles Dickens, and it's a very gripping story. My heart is in my mouth as we learn about the fate of poor Pip and Estella and the horrible Miss Havisham. My soul aches for the bullying that Pip has to endure, and I can only hope that he'll triumph at the end. I'll read it again to my friends at the day centre as I'm sure they'd like it too.

As we finish the chapter, I glance up at the man by my side. I don't think that I've ever been as contented. If this is love, then I never knew it could be so beautiful, so gentle. My fingers stroke his cheek and I notice that he's frowning. 'What is it?'

'I've been thinking.' He turns my hand and brushes a soft kiss against the palm. 'I should go to see my parents. It's been too long and they're not getting any younger.'

'You should. It's not good for families to be apart.'

'You miss your mother and father?'

'Very much. I'd love to see my parents again,' I tell him. 'I worry about them all the time. Mine are halfway across the world, yet yours are so close. It's wrong not to speak to them.'

'I know,' Hayden agrees. 'It's really bad of me to have left it so long and I want to put it right as soon as I can. I thought I'd drive up to their house at the weekend. Will you and Sabina come with me? I really want you to meet them.'

'I'd like that.' Although I'd feel quite anxious about meeting Hayden's parents.

'They're nice people,' he says. 'There's nothing to worry about. I'm the one who's at fault.'

'You should call them first. Make your peace.'

'Yes,' he agrees. 'It wouldn't do to turn up unannounced. Not after all this time.' He kisses me again and pulls me closer. 'They'll love you and Sabina as much as I do. You'll see.'

'I don't want them to think she's simple.'

'Of course they won't. Anyone can see she's quick and clever. You mustn't worry too much about her. She *will* talk again one day. When she's ready. I'm sure she will. In the meantime, you've got a lot to be thankful for. Beanie's healthy and happy. She's doing brilliantly at school and she's a natural on the piano.'

'I don't know where she gets that from. There are no talented musicians in our family, but thank you for encouraging her.'

Sabina and Hayden play together nearly every afternoon when she comes home from school, and he's gradually teaching her more complex tunes. Often now she sings along with him. But as yet that's done nothing to unlock her speaking voice. For the moment, I'm happy to listen to her in whichever way she chooses. It gives me hope that, one day soon, we'll be able to talk like mother and daughter again.

'You're not worried about the piece in the newspaper now?' he asks.

'No,' I tell him. 'Not now. Weeks have gone by and nothing has happened. I don't know how Suresh would have seen it. You were right all along and I was worrying unnecessarily.'

'I can put some extra security in if you'd like. It's easily done.'

'There's no need.' Already there are tall gates, an intercom system and CCTV cameras. Apart from assigning personal bodyguards to us, I don't know what else Hayden could do.

'I want you to feel completely safe.'

'I do.' My head rests on his shoulder. 'When I'm here with you, I've never felt more secure.' We fall into silence again, but the frown doesn't go from Hayden's brow. 'Is this all that's troubling you?'

'I had an unexpected call this afternoon,' he tells me. There's a long pause before he continues, as if he's weighing the words. 'It was the producer of *The Fame Game*. The talent show I won, which got me started in the music business. They want me to go on it as a judge.'

'You're pleased by this? Is it what you want?'

'I don't know,' he admits. 'I thought I'd done with all that, but I've started writing again and some of the songs I'm churning out are good. I want people to hear them.'

'I'd like to hear them too. You said that I'd be the very first.'

'Not yet,' he says, too fast. Then, more softly, 'You'll definitely be the first though when I'm ready. I still feel nervous about anyone hearing them.' Then he sighs wearily. 'The question is, do I want a wider audience for them? There's no doubt my fans still want me to do more, but I can't forget there's a price to pay. If I were to go back into the public eye again, what would that mean for us?'

If I'm honest, I don't like to consider it.

He must see the frightened expression on my face because he quickly says, 'I'm only kicking thoughts around, Ayesha. It's nice for me to be asked to go back into the spotlight. A stupid part of me is grateful that I haven't been forgotten, but that's a long way from wanting all the madness again that goes with it.'

He takes my hand in his and toys with my fingers.

'Whatever happens, it has to be the best for you and Sabina. You mean more to me than anything. You know that.' He looks deep into my eyes. 'Tell me what you're thinking.'

'You must do as you wish. Music makes your heart come alive. Even I, who can't play a single note, can tell that.' I return his gaze steadily. 'If you want to sing again, then you mustn't deny it.'

'I do,' he says flatly. 'There are songs swirling inside me where once I was empty.'

'That's a good thing.'

'I won't let anything bad happen like it did before. I promise you that.'

But how will he stop it? I wonder.

# Chapter Seventy-one

Today we're due to go to see Hayden's parents, but Sabina isn't well. My daughter's been up all night with a tummy bug and, this morning, is listless and tired. She needs to rest and be quiet to regain her strength. It's not the day for travelling a long way in a car and then meeting important new people. Hayden wanted to cancel his trip and stay here, but I've told him he mustn't do that. He's made tentative contact with his parents and he shouldn't let them down. It's more important that he builds bridges with them, and to cancel his visit today would be a mistake.

'I'll miss you,' Hayden says. We're standing in the hall by the front door and he's ready to leave, but still reluctant to go without us. He wraps his arms around me and pulls me close. 'As soon as I get there, I'll call you to see how Sabina is.'

'She'll be fine. The worst is over, I'm sure. All she needs is rest.'

'And plenty of fluids.'

I nod my agreement. At one o'clock this morning I shooed him back to his own room as I didn't want him driving a long way after a disturbed night. 'I'm so sorry that we can't come with you,' I tell him. 'I hope that it all goes well with your parents. I'm sure they'll be very happy to see you.'

'It seems ridiculous, but I'm a bit nervous,' he says. 'I could have done with you for moral support.'

My lips brush his. 'You'll be fine. You're their son and they love you. They'll be so happy to see you again.' While I wouldn't have chosen for Sabina to be ill, part of me thinks that this is a journey Hayden needs to make on his own. We should meet his parents together when their relationship is repaired. They'll have a lot to talk about and it's better, I feel, that Sabina and I aren't under their feet.

'I'll be back tonight,' he says. 'I'll try to get home in time for dinner.'

'You must take as long as you need,' I tell him. 'There's no rush. We're going nowhere. We'll be here waiting for you.'

He gives me a final, deep kiss. 'I count on it.'

I watch him go out of the door and get into his car. The security gates swing open and I wave as he pulls out into the leafy street.

Back in the kitchen, I make tea and take a cup to Joy, who's been up and about for hours. She's in the garden, pottering around in the greenhouse.

'Some tea.' I put the mug down on her bench.

She smooths a strand of hair from her eyes and leaves a smut of soil on her cheek. I brush it away with my thumb.

'Thought you were off to Hayden's parents today?'

'Sabina's unwell. She was up and down all night with a poorly tummy.'

'Poor lamb,' Joy says. 'I didn't hear a thing. I slept like the dead. Hayden's gone on his own then?'

'Yes. He was a little nervous, and I'm worried about him,' I confide. 'I hope they'll be reconciled.'

'I'm sure they will,' Joy says. 'Families, I've found, are end-lessly forgiving. Poor Hayden's had a lot to cope with in the last couple of years. It's nice to see him slowly coming back to his

335

old self. That's largely down to you. Crystal and I tried to chivvy him along, and failed miserably. It's good to see him emerging into the world once more.'

'I love him very much,' I tell her. 'Is that wrong of me, when I'm still a married woman?'

'It was hardly a good marriage, was it?' she says. 'If you ask me, I don't think you owe that husband of yours any loyalty whatsoever.'

'I like to be a good person and I don't feel that I am at the moment.'

'Away with you. You're a wonderful woman,' Joys says. She's normally an unemotional lady, but tears spring to her eyes. 'We're all happier for having you here.'

'That's very kind of you to say so.' I give her a hug and she lets me.

'You and Hayden must grab what comfort you can while you can.' She pats my back tenderly, like a mother. 'Time and tide wait for no man.'

'I think perhaps you're right.'

'I'm much older and therefore much wiser than you. Of course I'm right.'

I laugh at that. 'What are you doing today, old and wise one?'

'Just pottering,' she tells me. 'A little bit of this and that. I've got some winter vegetables to plant out – cabbage and cauli-flower. A few leeks. I'm having to water like mad in this long dry spell, or everything starts to wilt. Me included.' She laughs. 'How would I manage in Singapore with the heat, I ask you?'

'Everywhere is air-conditioned now,' I tell her.

'Not the garden though.'

'No,' I concede, 'not the garden. Have you given it any more thought?'

Joy sighs and sips at her tea. 'I've thought about nothing else, my dear.'

'But you haven't talked it through with your son?'

She shakes her head. 'I need to be clear in my mind what it is that *I* want to do. He's told me to take all the time I need, but he's also told me they're looking for a house that has a separate annexe.'

'They must be very keen for you to go.'

'Is that enough to make me?' she asks.

'Only you can decide that,' I tell her. Then, 'Can I help you with your planting? Sabina's fast asleep now, so I must pop back and check on her in a little while, but I've nothing else pressing to do.'

'That would be nice.'

So, when we've finished our tea, we work together in the garden and Joy shows me what to do. The soil is rich and black and we plant out in tidy rows together, not talking much. I can tell that Joy is a lady with a lot on her mind, but I don't pry further. Instead I concentrate on the planting, and keep my mobile phone close to hand in case Hayden should call.

Sometime later, when the sun is high in the sky, Crystal comes into the garden. She's wearing a white vest with cut-off shorts and is yawning tiredly. Last night she was out with Edgar until very late.

'What are you two up to?' she says, propping herself up on the trellis that divides the vegetable plot from the rest of the garden.

Joy leans on her spade. 'I'm teaching Ayesha how to knit a jumper.'

'Sarcasm is the lowest form of wit, Joy.'

'Planting cabbages,' I say with a smile. 'Want to join us?'

'Nails, darling, nails.' She holds out her hands for me to inspect her immaculate manicure. Today Crystal's nails are painted pure white, set with pink sparkly diamanté. 'These are *not* working hands.'

'They are not.' Crystal, it is fair to say, has found her true vocation at Highly Polished. Already she's the most popular manicurist, and her appointments book is always full. I don't think that she misses her job at the club at all and I'm truly glad to see her blossoming. 'Did you have a nice evening?' I ask.

'Yes,' she sighs happily to herself. 'Did I wake you up coming in?'

'No. Sabina's unwell. I was already up.'

'Oh. Is she OK now?'

'Tummy upset,' I say. 'I think she's picked it up at school.'

'They'll be breaking up soon, right?' Crystal says.

'Yes. Next week.'

'It will be fab if this summer continues. We can go for days out and stuff. Picnics. I love a picnic. Do you, Joy?'

'I do,' she says.

'There you go. The whole summer can be picnic a-go-go.' She yawns again. 'I'm starving. I need a carb boost. Anyone fancy some toast?'

'I could do with some more tea,' I say. 'This is thirsty work. What about you, Joy? Time for another little break?'

'I think so.'

I don't like her to be working so hard in this heat.

'I'll do it,' Crystal offers. 'I wouldn't like to think we'd run out of cabbage in November if I stopped you.'

Joy tuts at her.

'Perish the thought,' I tease.

'I'll give you a call when it's ready.'

So Crystal flip-flops away in her high sandals and Joy and I plant out the last of the cauliflowers and leeks.

Straightening up, Joy rubs her lower back, just as Crystal shouts to us from the French doors.

'A very timely cup of tea, I think.' I slip my arm through Joy's, and together we walk back towards the house.

# Chapter Seventy-two

Before I drink my tea, I go upstairs to see how Sabina is. I find her sitting up in bed, reading her latest book.

'How are you, my sweet?' I ask.

She smiles at me, a little wanly, but swings her legs out of bed.

'Do you want to come downstairs now? It's a lovely warm day and Auntie Crystal is making toast for us all. Maybe you could manage a little?'

My daughter nods at that.

'Pop on your dressing gown and you can dress later, if you feel better.'

She does as she's told, as always, and belts her little pink dressing gown around her – another gift from Crystal, who loves to spoil her.

As I take her hand she feels a little wobbly on her legs, but, other than that, seems much better. Her long sleep has done her good. Perhaps by tomorrow she'll be well again.

'Here she is!' I say as we go into the kitchen. 'The patient's getting better.'

'Bless you.' Crystal kisses the top of Sabina's head. 'We can't be having you poorly. Want a little piece of toast, Bean?'

Sabina nods.

'No butter,' I say. 'We have to see how settled your tummy is.' I dilute some juice for her to drink, anxious to put some fluids back into her body. Her cheeks are brightening by the minute, and it's a relief to see.

'Go into the garden, both of you.' Crystal ushers us towards the door. 'It's lovely out there. I'll bring your toast out in a minute.'

'Where's Joy gone?'

'She's popped back down to the greenhouse. She's picked some veg for tonight's dinner and wants to bring it into the cool before she forgets.'

I take Sabina outside and fuss with her. 'Sit in the shade. Here on the deckchair under the tree.' I pull it into the dappled shade for her. 'It's be too hot for you on the terrace. I don't want your temperature to rise too much, so you must be still. I'm going to help Auntie Crystal, but I won't be long.'

Sabina settles back and closes her eyes.

'She looks a little bit peaky,' Crystal says when I go back into the kitchen, 'but she seems OK.'

'She does,' I agree. 'I think she's over the worst. I just need to keep her cool and rested.'

Crystal starts to load up two trays with cups of tea and a plate piled high with toast, the butter dish, a selection of jams and honey, plus crockery and cutlery for us all. It looks as if there are ten of us eating.

'Bloody hell,' she tuts. 'I've snagged the end of my nail. Look at that.' She shoves her nail under my nose. 'I'll get my file from my bag, otherwise it'll drive me potty. If you grab one tray, I'll take the other. Won't be a sec.'

Before I can do that, I hear my mobile phone ring in the

distance. 'Oh. I've left my phone upstairs and that's probably Hayden.' No one else has the number except the people in this household.

'Quick,' Crystal says. 'Run and you'll catch it.'

So I dash up the stairs as fast as I can, watching Crystal as she follows me down the corridor and heads into the living room to look for her handbag.

My phone's on the bed in our room and the number is Hayden's. I snatch it up on the last ring before the voicemail can cut in.

'Hello?'

'Hi,' Hayden says. 'How's Sabina?'

'She's much improved,' I tell him, still slightly breathless, and I hear him sigh with relief. 'She's just got out of bed and has gone into the garden for some fresh air.'

'That's good to know.'

'How are things with you?'

'Fine,' he says. Hayden lowers his voice and I assume that his parents are nearby. 'They're so pleased to see me, and it's so good to be home. I can't believe I've left it so long. I won't ever do that again. I've promised I'll bring you both to meet them as soon as possible.'

'That'll be lovely.'

'I'll be home soon,' he promises. 'Missing me?'

But before I can answer, I hear a high-pitched scream coming from the garden. It splits the warm summer air and my blood turns instantly to ice. It's not Crystal or Joy. It's Sabina. That's my daughter's voice crying out.

'Mama!' I hear her scream. 'Mama!'

Throwing down the phone, I bolt for the door. Taking the stairs two at a time, I fly towards the kitchen. At the French doors, I reel with shock and every ounce of breath feels as if it's been punched out of my body. Sabina is still screaming.

In the garden, I see two burly men. Despite the hot weather, they have balaclavas over their faces and I know instantly that this isn't good. Bile floods into my mouth. This is my very worst nightmare come true. Suresh has found us.

The gate at the side of the house, usually locked, swings open freely and that's obviously where they've gained access. At the bottom of the garden there's a third man, and already he's fast approaching Sabina, who is backed into the corner by the summerhouse. Dark spots swim in my eyes and my mind is struggling to take it all in. I want to collapse to the floor in terror, but I have to stay in control. There's no one who can save my child but me.

'Mama! Mama!' she cries out again.

'Sabina,' I scream as I race outside towards her. 'Run! Run as fast as you can.'

But where to? All around the garden is a high wall. Our sanctuary has suddenly become our prison. How can she escape them? My only hope is to stop them.

I see my daughter dodge one man as he lurches to grab her, making a break for freedom, but her legs are weak and she stumbles. Quickly, I look around for a weapon to grab. What can I possibly do? There are three of them and just one of me. Then, behind me, I hear Crystal run across the terrace to join me.

'Fuck,' she says, grabbing my arm. 'What's going on?'

'I don't know. There are men, they're trying to take Sabina.'

'Over my dead body,' she says.

'And mine.'

'Any of them your husband?'

'No,' I say. It's hard to tell with their face masks. 'I don't think so.' But surely Suresh must have sent them.

Together we run towards them.

At the same time, I see Joy out of the corner of my eye. She's

342

lying beside the terrace on the other side of the garden and there's blood coming from a wound on her head. Nausea consumes me. It seems that she's already encountered them.

'I can't let them take Sabina,' I say to Crystal. 'What can we do?'

She turns to me, eyes bleak. 'We've got to fight for our lives.'

I see Joy crawling along the side of the garden, unseen by the men. When she nears the vegetable plot, she drags herself up and staggers behind the hedge. I can only hope that she has her phone down there and is able to call for help.

Never in my life have I felt so very useless. Crystal charges at one of the men and he grabs her, but she manages to keep one arm free and pulls at his balaclava. Somehow she gets underneath it, and rakes deeply at his face with her long nails.

'You bitch,' he spits and pushes her aside.

'Knee him in the bollocks!' I shout out.

Crystal looks at me agog, but flies back at him immediately. Before he knows what's happening, she's kneed him in the private parts and he falls to the ground, clutching at himself. While he's down, she kicks him in the ribs and he doubles up again, gasping in pain.

Now I know what I must do too. Sabina has tried to run, but already the man at the bottom of the garden has grabbed her and she's tossed over his shoulder like a sack. My daughter is kicking and screaming like a demon and I run towards them with a speed I didn't know I possessed.

Taking Crystal's lead, I launch myself at him and jump on to his back. In shock, he staggers forward and drops Sabina like a stone while I continue to slap and scratch at him with all my might. I tug at his balaclava and also manage to dislodge it. The man has a ponytail and I hold on to it while he tries spinning round and round to dislodge me.

'Run,' I shout to Sabina as I cling to him with the tenacity of a wasp. 'Run away. Lock yourself in the bathroom.'

Sabina scrabbles on the grass, but then I see her heading back towards the house. I'm being shaken like a rag doll and I don't know how much longer I can cling on to this bear of a man. Should I leave him and run after my daughter, or continue to fight? The next thing I know, Crystal has joined me. She too grabs hold of the man's head and tries to pull him over. Together we circle around and around until I'm feeling dizzy.

'Scratch him,' Crystal shouts. 'Bite his ears!'

I do as she says and feel his flesh tear beneath my finger-nails. I clamp the top of his ear in my mouth and sink my teeth in. For my effort, I taste his blood. He shakes and shakes me and I feel my brain rattle in my skull. But still he stays upright.

We're losing and I don't know what else to do. Then the man lets out a terrible cry. Finally he falls to the ground beneath me, clutching his leg. Behind him I see Joy. She has blood pouring down her face from her head wound and her eyes are wide, staring. It's a terrifying sight. In her hand she's holding a spade and she has it held high, ready to swing it again.

'Not his head!' Crystal cries. 'You'll kill him!'

Joy lets fly with the spade and smacks the man soundly on the bottom with it. He shouts out in pain.

'In the summerhouse,' Joy gasps out, continuing to belt the man on his bottom. 'There's a fork and a rake.'

Joy drops her spade and I see her pick up her wooden trug. The dazed man tries to struggle to his feet and, as he does, Joy swings her trug with both hands and hits him soundly on the head. The man sways slightly on his knees and then falls flat, face-first on the ground. I swear that it reverberates under my feet.

Joy manages a grim smile at us. Stunned out of our shock,

Crystal and I run to the summerhouse and pull open the door. We arm ourselves with the gardening equipment.

'Do you think that Joy has called for help?' I ask.

'No,' Crystal says. 'She'd have said. I think we're entirely on our own.'

I don't like the sound of this. The men are big bruisers, and it looks as if they're well used to brawling. Beneath my raging anger, I feel near to tears. Why have they come to take my daughter? Why can't they leave us in peace?

'Come on,' Crystal says. 'We've not got a moment to lose.'

We go back out and join Joy, ready to face our aggressors. Joy is breathing heavily but there's a determined and slightly mad glint in her eye.

'Let's take these bastards down,' she says.

# Chapter Seventy-three

I can only see one man but, before I can scan the garden for the other, he charges us, letting out a blood-curdling cry. Surely one of our neighbours will hear the commotion and call the police? I can only hope so.

The man barrels into us, sending me and Joy sprawling to the floor. It knocks the wind from my body. Crystal, however, withstands the force and flings herself on to his back, holding the handle of her rake across his throat until he makes choking noises.

'We need to tie him up,' Crystal says, panting. 'Have we got any rope?'

'The bunting!' Joy says. 'Use that.'

So I pull down the pretty floral flags that we strung up between the trees for the barbecue.

'Tie him up tight,' Crystal instructs me.

I bind the man's hands behind his back, and then his ankles, trussing him up with the bunting. He's swearing at us, using very bad words. Worse words than even Bridget Jones uses. He's writhing across the grass, trying to get away from us. I raise my fork high and he screams as I bring it down, full force.

The prongs go right through the material of his trousers and pin him to the ground.

'Good grief!' Crystal holds her heart. 'I wondered what you were going to do for a minute there, Ayesha.'

'It will keep him there while we go to get Sabina,' I tell her. I'm worried that it's taken all three of us to bring these men down and I can't see Sabina anywhere.

Together we rush back to the house. As we reach the French doors, the last man is coming through the living room. He has Sabina gripped tightly by her arm and is dragging her along as she tries her best to struggle against him.

'Mama! Mama!' she cries when she sees me.

My daughter's face is tear-stained, distraught, and my heart is ripped into a million pieces. I haven't rescued her from her father's temper for it to come to this. He'll have to kill me first.

Out of the corner of my eye, I see Joy moving to the side of the doors. She signals to me what I must do and I convey the message to Crystal with my eyes.

'Back off, ladies,' the man snarls, 'and no one will get hurt.'

'Leave my daughter alone,' I warn him.

He laughs at that and keeps advancing. Crystal and I back away on the terrace, giving him room to come outside.

As he emerges from the door, he doesn't notice that Joy has climbed up on the low wall beyond the doors. She's holding a plant pot high above her head and, as soon as she has a clear shot, she brings it down on his head with all her might.

The pot shatters, showering him with soil and a yellow chrysanthemum.

The man is dazed enough to let go of Sabina, and she flies to sanctuary in my arms. We're both trembling with fear and I hold her to me tightly, kissing her precious head. This is the last time that I'm ever letting her out of my sight.

347

'You stay right where you are,' Crystal snarls at the dazed man. 'The police are on their way.'

That's obviously a step too far for our would-be abductor as, still covered in soil, he picks himself up and bolts for the gate. He collects the first man on his way and they help each other out.

'Shall I chase after them?' Crystal says.

'No. I don't want you getting hurt too. Let them go. We still have one.' But even as I say that, the last man remaining rips his trouser leg free of the garden fork. My binding is clearly not as strong as it might be, as he loosens his bunting bonds and flees after his associates.

Crystal, heedless for her own safety, races after him, but before she can catch him he's out through the gate.

'Let him go!' I shout to her but she pays no attention.

I hear the slam of a car door and the screech of tyres and I assume that they've gone.

Moments later, Crystal comes back and she's shaking with rage.

'I didn't even get their bloody registration number,' she spits. 'They sped off in a big black van. It was too fast for me.'

'I know who did this,' I tell her. 'The details make no difference.' The only surprise is that Suresh didn't come himself. But then it's perhaps more like him to send other men to do his dirty work.

My legs feel wobbly as I kneel down in front of my daughter and wipe her wet cheeks with my cuff. 'They've gone now. All gone. We're safe again,' I coo as I stroke her face and her hair soothingly. 'Are you all right, my child?'

'Yes, Mama,' she says in a voice that's strong and clear.

Then it's my turn to break down and cry. I sob against her tiny shoulder. When I look up, Joy and Crystal are crying too. They come to join us in a huddle and we all hold on tightly to each other.

This has been a most terrible and terrifying experience, but they say that every cloud has a silver lining, and this one has brought my daughter's sweet voice back to me.

Her trembling body clings to mine and I thank whatever gods are listening that she's safe and can speak again.

# Chapter Seventy-four

We all help Joy into the kitchen. She's bleeding steadily from the wound on her head. Her hands are dirty and cut too.

'You were so brave.' As I sit her down, I can feel her shaking. Perhaps I've underestimated how much she's been injured. 'What would we have done without you?'

'I couldn't let them take our little Sabina, could I?' She chucks my daughter under the chin.

Sabina throws her arms round Joy's neck and kisses her. 'Thank you, Auntie Joy,' she says softly. 'You got the bad man.'

And that's enough to bring on all our tears again.

'The surprise plant-pot move was sublime, Joy,' Crystal says as she cuffs away a tear. 'I think we're going to call you Rambo from now on.'

'You'll do no such thing, young lady,' Joy warns.

I smile to myself, as it's nice to see that she's still feeling feisty despite her injuries.

'It's a shame they all got away,' Crystal says. 'Bastards. Oh, sorry. Better mind my language now that Beanie can speak again.'

'She's always been able to hear you,' I remind her.

350

'Oh, yeah.' Crystal wags a finger at my child. 'Never, ever repeat what I say.'

Sabina risks a smile. She unpeels herself from Joy and goes to hug Crystal too.

'Were you very frightened?' Crystal says.

'Yes,' she whispers in reply. 'I thought they'd take me away from you.'

'Well, you're safe now.' Crystal looks over Sabina's shoulder to where I'm tending Joy. Her eyes say that she's worried for our safety, and I am too.

Now that Suresh knows where we are, we'll never be safe. I'd hoped that he'd forget us, leave us to quietly live our new life. Now I know for sure that he will not. I'm also certain that he didn't simply intend to take Sabina. It horrifies me to think what our fate might be if we're returned to him, and terror grips me inside.

'You should phone Hayden,' Crystal says. 'He'll be out of his mind with worry. Here.' She presses his number on her phone and passes it to me.

My fingers tremble as I hold it.

He answers immediately. 'Are you all right?'

'Yes,' I say, my voice shaky. 'Yes, we are.'

'What happened?'

'Some men came and tried to take Sabina.'

'They didn't succeed?'

'No. No. They didn't. She's safe.'

'Thank God for that.' He lets out a relieved breath. 'I knew it had to be something awful, so I called 999 straight away and asked the police to attend.'

'No one came,' I tell him. 'But we managed to scare them off.'

'I'm on my way back right now,' he says. 'I jumped straight in the car. It won't be long before I'm there.'

351

'Thank you,' I say, feeling as if I could weep. 'Hurry home.'

'I will.' Then there's a catch in his voice. 'I couldn't bear it if anything happened to you. I love you, Ayesha.'

'And I love you too,' I tell him.

This is the declaration that I've longed to hear, the one that I've longed to speak. Today, it feels almost overwhelming. Emotionally exhausted, I hang up and give the phone back to Crystal.

'Is he OK?' she asks.

I nod. 'He's on his way back now.'

'Good.'

'Before we do anything else, I must tend to your face, Joy.' It's stained with dried and fresh blood. There's more blood and dirt caked in her hair.

'I do feel a bit of a mess,' she says with typical British under-statement.

So while Crystal cuddles Sabina, I get a clean face cloth and a bowl of warm water to bathe Joy's head. There's a nasty cut along her hairline which is starting to swell into a bump. 'I'd like to take you to the hospital. Only to make sure that you're all right. That cut may need a stitch or two.'

'No, no.' She bats my hand away. 'I'm fine.'

At the very least, she needs to relax in a warm bath or she'll be stiff tomorrow, but I don't want to let her out of my sight.

'Will you let me bathe you, Joy? And then go for a sleep?'

'I'm not a baby,' she says crisply, but I can see that she's wavering. 'All I need is a cup of tea.'

'I'll get the kettle on,' Crystal says. 'I don't know about you, but I need a tot of brandy too. I'm all of a quiver inside.'

'That might be a good idea,' Joy says. 'Make mine a double.'

Crystal disappears into the living room and reappears with a dusty bottle of brandy and three small glasses. 'Must have been a long time since we had an emergency.' She sets the glasses on the table and fills them. Not forgetting Sabina, she pours her out a glass of juice.

Crystal hands Joy a tot of brandy and then offers one to me. I'm about to remind her that I don't usually drink alcohol, but I believe there's a time and a place. So I take it without protest.

She raises her glass and Joy and I do likewise. We touch them together.

'To us,' Crystal says. 'We are fabulous and fearless.'

'I was very afraid,' I admit.

'We all were. It doesn't bear thinking about.' Then she laughs. 'But where on earth did you find that language, lady? "Knee him in the bollocks"?'

'Bridget Jones,' I tell her, and we all chuckle together.

'And Joy,' Crystal enthuses. 'You were a star, striking the killer blow.'

Joy raises her glass and accepts the praise.

'We might have been terrified. We might be the fairer sex. But today we were all-conquering,' Crystal continues. 'We were borderline ninja. Despite our knocking knees, we saw off three *mahoosive* blokes. They ran away with their tails between their legs and that deserves a toast.'

'To us,' we all agree and clink our glasses. 'Fabulous and fearless!'

'They've gone,' Crystal says triumphantly. 'Let's hope they never darken our door again.'

But as the brandy burns a pleasant track down my throat, I think we both know that they will.

# Chapter Seventy-five

Before we can do anything else, there's a sharp knock at the door and we all gasp.

'I'll go,' Crystal says, glancing anxiously at me. 'You stay here.'

I think about grabbing a knife from the block, but Sabina comes to sit on my lap, burying her face in my shoulder. I wrap her tightly in my arms. They'll have to cut me away from her to take her. Joy moves to stand in front of us.

Moments later, Crystal comes back with two uniformed police officers. They explain that they've had a call from a Mr Daniels.

'You're a bit bloody late,' Crystal says to them as they come into the kitchen. 'The blokes are long gone.' So she tells them what's happened while they make notes and sympathetic noises.

I explain my situation and tell them that I believe the men have been sent to take my daughter, and possibly myself, by my husband. They say that they'll speak to Suresh and take his details, but I wish they wouldn't as it will only inflame him more. They say that we'll be protected by the weight of the law. Yet I know that these things so often go wrong.

The policemen look at Joy and are concerned about her injuries. They also try, without success, to get her to go to the hospital. She's shaking now and her face is pale and I think that shock is starting to take hold. I help her into a chair again as she's swaying on her feet. She was so tenacious and bold, but I'm sure that the effort must have taken it out of her.

The policemen look in the garden and at the broken gate. The CCTV cameras at the front of the house have been smashed or shot out with air rifles, they say, and it seems that the men managed to scale the tall gates to gain entry. Whatever Hayden thinks he can do, it will never be enough to stop a man determined to do harm.

After half an hour the policemen leave, saying they'll send in another team to take fingerprints and the like. In my heart, I wonder if there's any point. I know who did this and I know that nothing will stop him.

Crystal shows the officers to the door and, as she sees them off, Hayden pulls in to the drive. 'Hayden's home!' she shouts.

Sabina and I jump up and I think that we're both equally anxious to see him. In an instant, he's in the kitchen, his face stricken. He gathers me to him. 'This is all my fault,' he says.

'It's not,' I assure him. 'How could it be?'

'I should never have left you alone.'

'We weren't alone. We were with Joy and Crystal. Behind a big wall with CCTV. You thought we'd be safe. We all did.'

'Tell me exactly what happened.'

I give him the details, filling him in on how heroic Joy and Crystal have been. Without them I would have been lost. A shudder of fear goes through me again as I recount the story. 'I knew something terrible had happened when I heard Sabina screaming.'

He looks from me to her and back again. 'She screamed?'

'I had to,' my daughter pipes up. 'I was very frightened, Hayden.'

'Oh, God.' He drops to his knees in front of her. His face lights up. 'Say something else!'

She laughs and goes all coy. 'Don't be silly.'

'If there's anything good to come from this, it's that my child has found her voice again.'

'Amen to that,' Joy adds. When I turn to smile at her, I see that her face is ashen. 'You must rest, Joy,' I tell her, placing my hand on her arm. 'Please let me help you to have a bath and then go to bed for a little while. I really think that it would help.'

To my very great surprise, she puts down her brandy and says, 'Come on then.'

'Will you look after Sabina for me?' I ask Hayden and Crystal. 'Please don't let her out of your sight.'

Hayden sits on a chair by the table and lifts Sabina on to his lap. 'I don't intend to. I'm going to find out all about this little lady,' he says. 'Now that she can tell me herself.'

'I'll be back very soon.' But I don't want to rush Joy. I'd like to give her the attention she so very badly needs.

Taking Joy's arm, I lead her from the kitchen and help her to climb the stairs. She's not too steady on her feet and I'm worried that the injury to her head was worse than we realised.

I take her into the main bathroom of the house and she lets me without protest. This is a big room, with a large, claw-footed bath in the centre. There are uplighters set into the bleached-oak floor and a squashy armchair in the corner.

When I close the door behind us, Joy sits down on the edge of the bath. Her hand goes to her forehead and she says, 'I do feel a little bit wobbly.'

'I don't want to leave you on your own, Joy. Are you happy for me to stay with you?'

She nods her acquiescence. So I turn on the taps to run the bath and then I help her out of her dirty and bloody clothes.

'My very bones feel bruised.' She moves gingerly to unbutton

356

her blouse, but she cannot steady her fingers enough, and instead I do it for her. My friend normally looks so strong and robust, but now her back is bent and she seems so weary.

'You put a lot of very strenuous effort into fighting for my daughter,' I say. 'I can't thank you enough.'

'Go on,' Joy counters. 'Anyone would do the same. That little girl's worth a good fight.'

I'm frightened that my husband clearly feels the same.

Joy starts to cry, and I hold her close. 'I thought they'd take her,' Joy says, sobbing. 'I didn't think we could stop them.'

'But we did,' I say. '*You* did.'

'It's only afterwards that you think of what might have happened.' She fishes for a handkerchief and, when she can't find one, I give her some toilet roll instead. Joy wipes her tears. 'Silly old woman,' she admonishes herself.

'It was scary for everyone. I wouldn't like it to happen again.' A second time we may not be so happy or so lucky with the outcome. How can I protect Sabina in the future? It's a terrible worry.

'Your bath's nearly ready,' I tell her. 'You'll feel better for it.'

'I'm not sure I could feel much worse,' she admits.

Joy steps out of her shoes and I assist her with her trousers. She fumbles with her underwear and I help her with that. I've never seen her look so vulnerable and it's sad to see. My heart goes out to her. Beneath her sturdy shoes and sensible blouses, she's a frail old lady. Quickly I wrap her in a warm towel and sit her in the armchair until the bath is filled.

When she climbs in, I hold her steady. Joy sinks into the water with a welcome sigh. I've put in lots of bubbles to preserve her modesty. Taking the sponge, I gently wash her arms. She sits forward a little while I wash her back. Then I hold her head as tenderly as I can and shampoo the blood from her hair, which makes the water run pink. Her hair is fine, fragile, and her scalp white with age. No wonder the blow has torn the skin so cruelly.

Sitting in the armchair, I watch her while she closes her eyes and relaxes back, letting the water soothe her. I think she'll be stronger after a sound slumber.

When she's ready, I help her out again and dry her down. I towel her hair and, in the cabinet, find a plaster to put over her cut which, thankfully, seems to have stopped bleeding. Wrapping her in a clean towel like I do with Sabina, I take her up the stairs to her bedroom. She sits on the edge of her bed and gives out a tired sigh.

'Where are your nightclothes, Joy?'

'In there.' She points to a drawer and I pull out a clean nightdress and help her into it. Pulling back her covers, I ease her into her bed and tuck her in. She looks so small and fragile in the bed and it tugs at my heartstrings: I've never seen her like this before. It's all the worse as I know she's like this because of her efforts on my behalf.

'Shall I stay with you until you sleep?'

'No,' Joy says. 'You'll be worried about Sabina. She needs you more than I do.'

'I'll bring you some soup to eat later.'

'That would be nice.'

I kiss her forehead and pull the covers round her shoulders. 'Thank you, Joy.'

She grips my hand. 'No. Thank you, Ayesha. We're all better for having you in this house.'

My eyes fill with tears because, if I'm very honest with myself, I don't know how long I can stay here now that this has happened.

'Sleep tight, my friend,' I tell her.

I tiptoe to the door and, by the time I'm softly closing it, I believe that sleep has already found her.

# Chapter Seventy-six

We're all truly weary by the evening. I'm even too tired to be interested in what terrible things Mr Charles Dickens has in store for poor Pip, although Hayden and I are very nearly at the end of the tale.

Instead, we're lying together on the sofas in the living room. Hayden, Sabina and I are on one, all squashed up in a huddle. Crystal and Edgar are on the other. She has her head on a cushion on Edgar's lap and he's stroking her hair lovingly. We're all wearing pyjamas and this is the first time that I've ever done this. I feel it's a small comfort that I've previously missed in life. Crystal has made hot chocolate for us all and we have nice biscuits. On the television there's a film about penguins who dance, but none of us is really watching it. My mind is filled with worries, but I'm trying not to show it. I rest my head on Hayden's shoulder and he kisses my brow, which feels hot and bothered.

Since he's been home, he's not wanted to let me out of his sight. We've talked briefly of his reconciliation with his parents and he says that it went well. I'm only sorry that he had to dash away prematurely on our behalf.

Earlier, I took Joy a small bowl of home-made chicken soup

and she ate it with some enthusiasm. It was a relief to see that she looked much better but she's decided, I think wisely, to stay in bed and doze again.

'If Joy isn't fully recovered tomorrow, I think we should try to persuade her to see a doctor.'

'I've got a private GP,' Hayden says. 'I'll ask him to call in. I'd be happier if he checked her over too.'

'I feel that'd be wise. You can't be too careful.' Again my stomach lurches at the thought of what might have been. Any one of those men could have seriously harmed Joy, Sabina, Crystal or me. What if they'd come armed with knives, or even guns? What if they do so next time? Then who or what will save us?

'She'll be all right,' he assures me. 'Don't you worry. I'll make sure she is.'

'Thank you.' I pat his hand.

I too have bruises and scratches. I hoped that I'd seen the last of those on my body, but they're superficial injuries compared to what I've suffered in the past. It's only the memories that trouble me, not the physical pain. Sabina too has a darkening imprint of a hand on her arm where the man dragged her, and I'm so relieved that it's the only harm she's come to. In reality, it could have been so very much worse. I'm replaying the incident constantly in my brain, and not even dancing penguins can drive it away.

We watch the film until it finishes and then Sabina yawns.

'We could all do with an early night,' I say.

'I'm dead on my feet,' Crystal agrees, and cuddles in to Edgar.

He's proving to be a strong man for her and I'm pleased to see it. She's now found the courage to tell him of her past and yet he's still here. I didn't think otherwise, but I'm glad to see that my faith in him wasn't misplaced. I see nothing but tenderness in his eyes for her, and it warms my heart. He'll love her and protect her, I'm certain.

But what of me? I've no doubt that I am loved, but who will protect me? Can Hayden or anyone really keep Suresh from finding me and his child? There's a cold ball of dread settled in my stomach and not even the warmth of the hot chocolate can soothe it.

Hayden turns off the television and we all head up to bed. Edgar doesn't have his daughter this weekend, so he's staying with us. We kiss them both goodnight and they go up to their room, as do we.

Sabina looks so weary that I allow her to go to bed without her bath. She'll have to shower before school tomorrow instead.

We climb into the big bed together, Hayden on one side, me in the middle, Sabina on the other. 'Goodnight, my beautiful child,' I say to her.

'Goodnight, Mama,' she says, and once again I feel I could weep for joy. There were times when I feared I'd never again hear those sweet words from her lips, and now she's simply speaking as if she never stopped.

Hayden leans over to kiss her as well. 'Goodnight, Little Bean. Love you.'

'Goodnight, Hayden. I love you too.'

His eyes fill with tears and he brushes them away.

My daughter lies down, slips her thumb into her mouth – which I don't chastise her for – and within moments her breath has deepened and she's happily in the land of dreams.

Hayden lies on his back, arm thrown over his head. I curl towards him and rest my head on his chest. His skin's warm, soft, and I can hear the steady beat of his heart. It does little to quell the unease inside me.

'Her voice is so beautiful,' he says, and I can hear that he's choked.

'It sounds like music to me.'

'Is she all right?' Hayden asks, voice low. '*Really* all right?'

'I think so. As far as I can tell she seems unscathed by her ordeal,' I whisper back.

'And she's *speaking* again. I can't believe it.'

'I'm more relieved than I can ever say.' It's a miracle, indeed. 'It's no small thanks to you. She has surely benefited from all the time that you've spent with her, encouraging her to sing, to unlock her voice.'

'I love her,' Hayden says. 'It's as simple as that. As much as I love you. In the short time you've both been here, you've saved my life. I was totally lost and I feel like you've guided me back. I'm writing again. I'm even thinking about going back into the big, bad world.'

The world *is* big and bad, and I don't like to think what the implications are for our privacy.

'I know what you're thinking.' He holds up a hand. 'The very first thing tomorrow morning, I'm going to call in the security company I use and get them to see what they can do to beef up the protection here. Promise me you won't worry. Let me do that for you.'

'I promise.' Then a shiver of terror grips me. 'Hold me tightly, please.'

His arms enfold me and I wish I could stay here, unmoving, for the rest of my life.

'I don't ever want you to feel unsafe here,' Hayden says.

But I do. And I cannot deny it.

# Chapter Seventy-seven

In the morning, Joy is in the kitchen before all of us. She now has a big, burgeoning blue bruise on her forehead which is quite shocking to look at. I can see that she's changed the plaster which covers her cut for a clean one, but there's still blood oozing through it. She's picking at a piece of toast and the honey pot is on the table in front of her.

'I was just going to bring you breakfast,' I tell her. 'What are you doing up and about already?'

'I'm feeling much better,' she insists. 'No need to fuss.'

'You should take it easy today, Joy. That was quite a blow to your head. I don't want you rushing about as you usually do. You could make yourself dizzy and have a more serious fall.'

'I don't want to miss going to my day centre. I can simply sit there and chat with my friends. If I stayed at home, I'd only go into the garden and tidy up.'

'The policemen told us that we must leave it as it is until they've thoroughly checked it.' Outside the French doors I can still see the shattered plant pot, the shower of soil and Joy's blood on the paving. I turn my face away.

'That's exactly why I'm better out of the way. I'm going to ask Edgar if he'll drive me in though.'

'That's a good idea. Come right home if you feel at all tired or weak. Hayden wants his doctor to give you a check-up.'

She waves a hand at me. 'You youngsters worry too much.'

It's nice to see Joy back to her robust self, and I hope that she really is feeling perkier and isn't simply putting a brave front on it.

Sabina's in the shower, so I make her breakfast. When Hayden comes down a few minutes later, he's already dressed and looks as if he's set to rush headlong into the day. 'How are you, Joy?'

'Doing OK,' she says. 'I won't be needing your doctor.'

Hayden looks at me for support, but I shrug.

'If you feel that anything's not quite right, you must tell me straight away,' he insists.

'I will,' Joy says.

Hayden looks smarter than normal. He's still in jeans and a T-shirt, but they're a little jazzy, I think. They're both baggier, edgier. I think Crystal would call them more 'hip'. He's already wearing his wool hat, his sunglasses perched on top. He looks more like a pop star than I've ever seen him and suddenly, that makes me anxious. 'You look as if you're in a hurry.'

He purses his lips apologetically. 'Forgot to tell you that I'd arranged a meeting for this morning. With my old management team. I thought about cancelling it—'

Before he can complete his sentence I say firmly, 'You must go.'

'I don't want to leave you alone. Come with me.'

I shake my head. 'This is your work. It's not my place. You'll have important things to talk about.'

'I do,' he admits. 'I won't be long, though, and I'll tell you all about it as soon as I'm back. The security company are coming at two o'clock to have a look at the set-up here. I'll be back in plenty of time.'

'Will you have some breakfast before you go?'

'A quick coffee. Nothing else.' He smiles, and there's an unfamiliar radiance in his eyes that I haven't seen before. He's excited, alight inside. 'I feel a bit nervous, if I'm honest.'

It makes me worried too. Something inside me feels as if he's slipping away from us.

Still, I push the thought aside and pour Hayden a coffee. He drinks it while standing up, gulping it down. Sabina comes in as he's leaving and he sweeps her into his strong arms.

'See you later, Little Bean,' he says. 'Look after Mummy for me.'

'I will,' she says.

'See you later, alligator.' Hayden high-fives her.

'In a while, crocodile,' she finishes.

He kisses me briefly and says, 'Wish me luck.'

'I'm sure you won't need it.'

Then, while I'm still filled with disquiet, he heads out of the door.

Edgar and Crystal appear, arms wrapped around each other.

'Morning!' Crystal says, throwing herself into a chair at the same time as taking a piece of toast from Joy's plate. Which earns her a slap on the hand for her cheek.

'Hey,' Edgar says. He looks bashful to be joining us for breakfast for the first time.

'Where was His Nibs off to in such a rush?' Crystal asks as she tucks into Joy's toast.

'He has an important meeting with his management company,' I tell her.

She tuts at that. 'Nothing good can come of it,' she concludes. 'He's only just getting his act back together. What's he thinking of? He doesn't need this.'

'I think perhaps he does,' I venture.

'Then he shouldn't. He should be concentrating on you and Bean.'

'Coffee? More toast?' I offer in lieu of anything else to say.

'Both,' she says. 'Tons of it. All this brawling has made me starving.' Crystal grabs my hand and pulls me to her for a hug. 'OK today?'

'Yes. I'm fine.'

'Not fretting?'

'No. No.'

'Liar,' she says, but she turns to Sabina and hugs her too. 'How's my best girl?'

'I'm happy,' Sabina says.

'Good to hear. What are your mates going to say when they hear you talk for the first time? You'll blow their socks off!'

Sabina grins. I think she likes the idea of doing that.

'I'll walk to school with you two today,' Crystal says. 'If that's all right. You're not doing anything this morning?'

'No.'

'I've got something I want to show you, then I'll walk up to work.'

'I was wondering, Edgar, if you might give me a lift into the day centre?' Joy asks.

'You should be in bed, woman,' Crystal says. 'Tell her, Ayesha.'

'I *have* told her.'

'There's absolutely no reason to cosset me. I'm fine,' Joy insists. 'You're all making a fuss about nothing.'

'Don't let her out of your sight today, Ed,' Crystal says, wagging her toast at Edgar. 'I'm holding you responsible for her.'

'I will care for her to the best of my ability,' Edgar assures us.

'You're all talking about me as if I'm not here,' Joy complains. 'I'm perfectly all right and I haven't gone deaf.'

'It's because we love you, you silly old bat,' Crystal says, stealing another piece of her toast. She wrinkles her nose. 'I hate honey. Why can't you have jam like normal people?'

'Honey's good for you,' Joy says.

'So is staying in bed when you've been donked on the head by a baddie,' Crystal says, 'but you don't do that.'

I deliver coffee and their own toast to Crystal and Edgar. 'Five minutes and then we must leave for school,' I remind her.

'I'm on the case,' Crystal says. 'Can't have Beanie being late for school.'

She bolts her breakfast, kisses Joy on the cheek and Edgar more fulsomely.

'Sabina,' I say. 'Put on your shoes now.'

Obediently she drinks her milk and jumps down from the table.

If I'm completely honest, I don't want my child to go to school. I want her to stay at home, here, behind these four walls. I'd only imagined danger coming directly from my husband, but now I know that it can come from any quarter. I don't ever want to have to walk past a stranger in our street and wonder if they've been sent by Suresh. I want the CCTV trained on us the entire time and burly bodyguards at the gate. Then and only then will I feel that it's safe here once more. But what way is that to live? I want her to return to normality as soon as possible

'I'm ready, Mama.' Sabina has on her shoes. Her Hello Kitty backpack is slung over her shoulder. Her smile is shining, innocent. Already, it seems, she has forgotten the trouble from yesterday.

But I, unfortunately, have not.

# Chapter Seventy-eight

At school, I accompany Sabina into the classroom and speak to her teacher. I tell Mrs Baranek the bare details about what happened yesterday and explain that I'm anxious for Sabina's safety. I insist that no one must collect Sabina from school other than myself, Crystal or Hayden. She's very understanding and also thrilled when I tell her that the trauma has, by some miracle, unlocked my child's voice.

Finally I can delay no longer and must leave Sabina in their care. She appears untroubled, babbling away like a little brook to her friends who seem unfazed by this new chatterbox in their midst.

I rejoin Crystal in the playground and she links her arm in mine.

'Chin up,' she says as we emerge on to the street. 'She'll be fine.'

'I'm worried,' I admit. 'I can hardly bear to leave her. Perhaps I should have kept her at home this week, until they've apprehended the men who did this.'

It's the last week of term and I didn't want Sabina to miss any school, but I feel that I may have rushed her return. Would it have mattered for her to miss a few lessons? I wanted her to get back to normality as quickly as possible, but now worry that I've been too hasty.

'Chances are they won't ever catch those scumbags,' Crystal says. 'Besides, we know who was behind it. *He's* the one you're going to have to take down.'

'I know.'

'Shall we send Joy round to flowerpot him?'

I manage a laugh at that. Yet I know that the only chance I have of stopping Suresh from coming after us is to do it legally, through the courts. But I'm sure even that won't halt him. He's not a man who takes heed of the law. If he wants to have me and Sabina back, then he will.

As we're walking away from the school, a sleek car with blacked-out windows comes down the street. It slows as it nears us and my heart leaps to my mouth. Fruitlessly, I try to peer in the windows. I stop and grip Crystal's arm.

'What?'

'That car. Were they looking at us?'

'I don't know,' she admits. 'I don't think so.'

What if it's someone who's come after Sabina again? What if they try to snatch her from the school playground at her break time?

'I'm sure I've seen it outside the school before,' Crystal adds. 'Isn't it Whatsit's mum?'

Then the car slows further and I'm on the verge of sprinting back to my daughter when the door swings open and a little girl in uniform jumps out and runs to the gate.

'She's very late,' I say and my heart pounds with relief.

'Five minutes, picky,' Crystal says. 'You can't wrap Sabina in cotton wool every minute of the day, Ayesha. She needs to have a normal life. If you jump every time you see a shadow, you're going to make the kid a nervous wreck. Plus if you carry on like this you're going to give yourself a coronary. You need to be strong for her.'

I can feel perspiration on my upper lip and under my arms. A bead of cold sweat trickles down my spine and I'm almost paralysed with fear.

'What can I do?' I ask my friend. My palms are damp with terror.

'We'll sit down later with Hayden and formulate a plan,' she says. 'Don't you worry. We won't let anything happen to either of you.'

But I'm still concerned as we walk away from the school. I have to resist the urge to turn around every few moments.

'It's quite a walk, this thing I have to show you.' Crystal says. 'Are you up for that?'

It's a beautiful, sunny day and the sky is untroubled by clouds. I feel it would do my heart good to stride out and clear my mind. 'Yes. A walk will be nice. Where are we going?'

'You'll see,' she says enigmatically.

So we stroll along on this fine summer's day and must look to strangers as if we haven't a care in the world. We cross over Rosslyn Hill and make our way through the back streets. As we do, we talk about Edgar and the chance that Joy has to go to her sons.

Then, after about half an hour, Crystal stops at a set of tall, ornate gates. 'We're here.'

I look up and see the sign. HAMPSTEAD CEMETERY.

She sighs and says, 'I thought I'd introduce you to Max Junior.'

Our eyes meet as we turn into the pathway and I give her an encouraging squeeze. Arm-in-arm we walk through the well-kept grounds of the cemetery. It's lush and green and I'm sure Joy would be able to tell us what some of the splendid trees are.

'This is a restful place,' I say.

'Yeah,' Crystal agrees. 'Might seem weird, but I like coming here. Sometimes I just sit and talk to Max. Tell him all that we could have been doing together.'

Eventually we turn down a leafy walk, and after a few metres Crystal slows. 'Here he is. My baby.'

There's a small white headstone with a teddy bear carved into it. The name reads MAX COOPER, and beneath it are the dates of his too-short life. There's a bunch of white carnations on the grave and Crystal fusses with them as she coos quietly to the little boy who's resting there. My eyes smart with unshed tears.

'I bought the flowers a few days ago. Thought they might have wilted in the heat, but they don't look too bad, eh?'

'They're lovely. I would have brought some too, if I'd known.'

She takes my hand and we sit on the bench opposite Max's grave, under the dappled shade of a mature tree.

'I didn't want to make a fuss,' she says. 'Just thought you'd like to come. I've been telling Edgar all about him, so he's on my mind. Not that he isn't always.'

'You'll have other babies, Crystal.'

'Hope so,' she says. 'No one will ever replace Max, of course. But it would be nice to have a brother or sister for him.' She gives me a little hug. 'Perhaps you'll knock out another few as well. We'd be as happy as pigs in shit, wouldn't we, knee-deep in dirty nappies?'

'I'd have liked another child, but it didn't happen for me.'

'Probably just as well,' Crystal says. 'You might never have got away with two kids in tow. You could have been stuck there.'

I shudder at the thought.

'It might be different with Hayden. You never know. I bet you'll be up the duff in five minutes. Look at the state of him, he's bound to have fantastic sperm.'

Scandalised, I can't help but giggle at that, even though we're in a cemetery. 'Crystal. You are a *terrible* person.'

'It's true,' she says. 'Don't tell me you haven't thought about it either. I've seen the way you look at him, you little minx.'

'I'll be happy if my only child is Sabina. I feel blessed to have had her. She's the one good thing that has come from my marriage to Suresh, and for that I'll always be grateful to him. She's my life.'

'Treasure her,' Crystal says. 'There's nothing worse than losing a child. I didn't know how I'd carry on without Max. But you do, don't you?'

'You'll have happiness again with Edgar. I'm sure.'

'I hope you're right. O wise one,' she teases. 'I do hope so. And you will with Hayden.'

Yet I don't know if that's possible. He's starting to want things that I don't have a part in. If he takes up his old life, will Sabina and I always be at risk of exposure? I can't risk putting Sabina in danger for any man, not even Hayden. She's my absolute priority and I must sacrifice everything else to protect her. Yet I'm in no position to ask him to give up his fame and fortune for us, to carry on living the life of a recluse as he has. He says that he feels he has his life back. Who am I to take it away again?

Crystal closes her eyes and lets her head rest back. The breeze in the shade cools us. I keep my eyes open and look to the distance, as if I'm trying to see my future. For a moment, I catch a glimpse of it. And, if I stay with Hayden, there are parts of it that frighten me too much.

Then it comes to me in a moment, and I know exactly what I must do.

# Chapter Seventy-nine

We stay by Max's little grave for an hour or so, then Crystal has to head off to work. Together, we walk back to Hampstead High Street, eventually stopping outside the door of Highly Polished.

'You've got your overall?'

'In my bag,' she says. 'I'll quickly change.'

'Thank you for taking me to see Max.' I can't begin to tell her what a profound effect it's had on me, for so many reasons. I think of having to look at my Sabina in the cold ground as Crystal does with her child, and I wonder how I'd ever breathe again.

'He's a part of me,' she says, 'and so are you and Sabina now.'

My voice is stuck in my throat.

'Whatever happens in our lives, we'll still be friends,' she adds.

'We will. Let's never forget that.' I throw my arms around her and hold her tightly.

'Hey,' she says, studying my face. 'Are you sure you're all right?'

'Yes.' I bite down the tears that so want to come.

'We'll talk later.' She strokes my cheek and I hold my hand over hers.

Crystal is probably the best friend that I've ever had. She's more like a sister to me, and I can only hope that she'll forgive me for what I'm about to do.

'I'd better go. The boss really gets her knickers in a knot if you keep any customers waiting.' She kisses my cheek. 'Laters.'

'Laters,' I echo. 'I love you.'

Crystal frowns at me. 'I don't like to leave you like this. You're not you.'

'I am,' I promise her. 'This is just the sad version of me.'

'Shall I call Hayden, get him to come home early?'

I shake my head. 'No need for that.'

'I'll bring us cakes home,' she promises. 'That'll cheer us all up. I hope Joy hasn't keeled over during the day. That would put a downer on things.'

'Oh, Crystal.' I very nearly say that I'm going to miss her.

She looks over her shoulder into the nail salon. It seems as if she is in two minds whether she should leave me and go into work or not.

'Really, I'm fine,' I assure her. 'You should go.'

'Don't worry. We'll sort it. You have to trust Hayden. He'd never let anyone hurt you.'

So I stand and watch as she walks away from me. When she turns back, I wave at her through the window of the salon and pin on a smile. And, when she's out of sight, I walk as quickly as I can back to the house.

Taking our small holdall from under the bed, I open it. Inside is the remainder of my money, still curled into rolls. Quickly I count it out. Thankfully I still have enough left to take me to where I want to be. I tuck it down into the corner at the bottom, as I did on that dark night when I stole away from Suresh with the hope that I could leave him behind for ever.

Well, despite my best efforts, he's followed me and has found me. So, once more I must move on.

Taking the holdall to the dressing table, I start to empty in our belongings as fast as I possibly can. I put in most of the lovely clothes that Crystal has bought for both Sabina and myself, but there isn't much room. I have to be away from here before anyone returns. If I see Hayden or Joy or Crystal, I know that they'll stop me. They'll beg me to stay and I won't be strong enough to resist because, in my heart, I don't want to leave at all. But what else can I possibly do?

Sabina and I are in grave danger here. Suresh now knows where we are. What is there to stop him sending more men? Perhaps men who are stronger, more ruthless. Men who are not easily thwarted by three ladies, one of them elderly. Next time they might have knives or guns. We were lucky this time, I know that.

The longer I'm here, the more trouble I bring to the house. Hayden doesn't need this. He has his life back. He's singing, playing, writing. The world is opening up to him once more and it's a delight to see. It's also clear to me that he needs music in his life more than he needs us. Performing is like breathing to him: it's necessary for him to exist. Yet Sabina and I can't live in the spotlight with him. It would be far too dangerous. So, if we can't be with him, then what are we to do?

I must hide Sabina away. I can't risk harm coming to her or to anyone else. We must live a quiet, anonymous life, and then perhaps we'll be free of my husband for ever.

Crystal will be furious with me. I know she will. She'll think that I'm cowardly, running away, and I can only hope that one day, perhaps far in the future, we may be reunited. That we all will. As I'll miss them all so very desperately. I'm happy that she has Edgar now. He'll do more than fill the place in her heart that my leaving will cause.

Glancing at the clock, I realise that there's no time for hesitating. I catch sight of myself in the mirror and Crystal is right. I'm not me. Staring back at me there's a wild-eyed, frightened creature. I thought I'd left her behind. But no, here she is again.

I cram the clothes haphazardly into the bag. I even take the shabby shalwar kameez that I first arrived in. How long ago that seems now. I've been happy here. So very, very happy. But now I must move on again. It's the only way.

Sabina will be distraught, I know. How she'll cope without Hayden, I have no idea. He's been more of a daddy to her in these few shorts month than her own father ever was. She'll miss him terribly. As I will. It makes me sick to my stomach to think of it. I can only pray that this won't cause her to be silent once more. If that happened, it would break my heart into a million pieces. But I'd rather have her alive, unharmed and mute, than missing – or even worse. So I force the possibility of her return to silence to the back of my mind and press on with my plan.

I take one last look around the bedroom and my heart twists with pain. Rushing downstairs, I go into the living room. On the coffee table, where we last left it, lies the copy of *Great Expectations* that Hayden and I have so enjoyed reading together. How sad that I won't now finish it with him. My stomach heaves with nausea. My knees almost buckle, and already I feel the emptiness like a physical pain. I think of the hours that he's spent with me, patiently, diligently teaching me how to improve my reading, to be proud of myself. To me, that truly says what a kind and caring man he is. It shows me how much he loves me.

What if I never see him again in my lifetime? The thought hits me as hard as a physical blow. Perhaps I'll catch a glimpse of him on television every now and again, and think that I was lucky to have known him, to have been loved by him.

Too many of my loved ones have already been taken from me – my sister, my mummy and daddy, now Hayden. Yet I know that I have to sacrifice my own happiness for the sake of Sabina's safety. I'd never be happy with him again if I stayed and someone took Sabina from me. Seeing little Max's grave today only served to hammer that home. Crystal has somehow recovered her life. She's gone on to be a strong, funny and lovely person. I don't think that I could do that. I'm not as strong, as resourceful as her. Without Sabina I'd be an empty shell.

And so I must leave.

I take a pen and paper from the table and write out very carefully, in my best handwriting, *I am so very sorry. Please let me go. Ayesha xx*

# Chapter Eighty

Walking up to the school as quickly as I can, I force myself not
to look back. When I'm there, I explain to the secretary that I
need to take Sabina out of her lesson and we head along the
corridor together, me wishing that she'd hurry more.

I wait outside the classroom and, minutes later, Sabina comes
out. We go to her locker and collect her bag.

When the secretary has left us, she says, 'What's wrong,
Mama?'

'We must leave,' I tell her. 'Like we did before.'

'On a bus?'

'Yes.'

'Is this because of the bad men?'

'Yes.'

I lead her out of the school and across the playground. At the
gates, she pulls up and looks back towards the house.

'Is Hayden coming with us?'

My voice almost refuses to come. 'No. I'm afraid that he
can't.'

Her tiny face is anxious. 'But if we leave him behind, he'll
become sad again.'

I kneel before her. 'Sometimes grown-ups have to be sad. That is the way of life.'

'You were sad with Daddy, but I know that you'll be sadder without Hayden.'

I fight down the tears that threaten with all my might. I must be strong for my child. Suresh knows where we are now and we simply can't stay. 'You must trust me on this, Sabina. It's the only way.'

'But he loves us,' she pleads.

'I know.'

She looks as if she's desperately trying, in her childish way, to think of another solution. But, like me, who should have the answers for her, she fails.

'We must hurry.'

'Auntie Crystal and Auntie Joy won't want us to go,' she says. 'They could scare the bad men away again.'

How do I explain that, next time, we may not be as fortunate? I don't wish to frighten her, but I believe with my whole heart that we're in grave danger. Suresh won't take this failure lightly. He is not a man to be thwarted. Next time he will come himself, and he will make sure that he doesn't fall short.

'Will we never see them again?'

'I hope that we will see them very soon.' But I can't bring myself to tell her that we may not. That I can't risk contact with the people who we've both come to love most dearly.

Then she cries. Tears of terrible unhappiness course down my daughter's cheeks and I hold her to me tightly.

'I don't want to go,' she sobs.

For a fleeting moment, I wish that my daughter could not speak again. I wish that I didn't have to hear her voice her pain. I wish that she would stand in accepting silence while I destroy all that we've struggled to build. Her words stab agony into my soul.

'For now, it must be just me and you,' I whisper. 'Do you understand that?'

'Yes.'

She looks at me, eyes filled with sorrow, and I know that I'm breaking her heart. I can only hope that one day she will fully know my reason for doing this and that she'll forgive me.

# Chapter Eighty-one

Suresh burst through the front door of the house. Alarmed, his mother came shuffling out of the front room.

'Stay in there,' Suresh barked. 'Both of you. Now. Don't come out until I tell you to.'

His mother retreated, a look of fear on her face. Suresh smirked to himself. Soon he wouldn't have to feel their reproachful gazes on him ever again.

He ushered the lads into the kitchen and closed the door behind them. His heart was still pounding as he found the whisky bottle and four glasses even though it was still early in the day. The lads were laughing, relieved, adrenalin-filled, as high as kites, giddy with euphoria. They'd done it. They'd *actually* done it. The raid had been such a success, Suresh could hardly believe it.

Splashing some of the amber liquid into glasses, he held his high and proposed a toast. 'To us,' he said. 'To audacity. To money.'

He downed his shot and felt the alcohol go some way to calming him inside. Another would surely help. So he refilled his glass and gulped that down too.

They each tipped out the bag that they'd crammed with their haul on to the kitchen table. The raid couldn't have gone better. It was textbook-perfect. Just as he'd planned. As *he'd* planned. No one else. They'd blasted straight into the shopping centre, ridden along the shiny concourses, got in early before many people were about, while the shops were still rubbing their sleepy eyes, waking up. He laughed to think of the faces on the staff in the store when they'd seen two motorbikes roaring straight through the door. They'd nearly crapped themselves. And the feeling when they'd smashed the windows, the display boxes, and helped themselves to whatever they wanted! He'd never experienced such ecstasy. There was nothing in the world like it, and he knew he wanted to do it again. Soon.

'Nice work, lads,' he said as he looked down at the glittering pile of jewellery on the table.

There were fat, sparkling diamond rings, bracelets, necklaces. He'd gone straight for the watches – Rolex, Tag Heuer, Cartier, Breitling. Each tray they'd bagged had netted them over a hundred grand. He looked at the heap of watches. There were plenty to spare, enough that they could each take one, two even, for themselves. And gold. The table was dripping with gold. Suresh heard a giggle, and thought it might have come from his own lips. He'd keep some gold too. Heavy chains for his neck, his wrist. It would be a magnificent reminder of how well this job had gone. That was down to him and no one – not Arunja, not anyone – could take that away.

There was only one cloud on his horizon and that was that the other job he'd planned hadn't gone so well. The lads laughed raucously and raked their hands through the pile of loot, but he couldn't join in with them. The thought of that failure had left him with the taste of bile in his throat and a bitterness coiled in his stomach.

He should have gone along himself to see it through, but he'd wanted to keep his distance. That had been a mistake. The men he'd paid to take Sabina and Ayesha had messed it up completely. He'd thought he could trust them, that they were professionals, but he'd been wrong. They'd been defeated by a few women, one of them an old lady, by all accounts. What a fuck-up. Next time he *would* do it himself. Finish them off once and for all so they wouldn't be lurking in his life like some terrible spectre sent to haunt him. They'd be gone and he could move on, get another wife who he would shower with diamonds, who would be grateful, compliant, and would open her legs without turning from him in distaste. A woman like that would give him a dozen healthy sons.

He would bide his time. Ayesha would be frightened now. She knew he was coming for her. And she'd realise that they had no place to hide.

# Chapter Eighty-two

Hayden's meeting had taken longer than he expected and now all he wanted to do was get home. He'd had to cancel the appointment with the security firm, but he'd still be in time to walk up to the school with Ayesha to collect Sabina, bracing himself to run the gauntlet of the giggly mums.

The meeting had gone brilliantly. Considering how long he'd been out of the game, his management team were still filled with enthusiasm. They all wanted him back out there on top form. The cynic in him said, Why wouldn't they want their major cash cow to come out of hiding and get the money flowing for them again?

They'd loved some of the new songs he'd played to them, and had big plans. Which was great. He'd come out of the office buzzing. But now, if he was completely honest, there was a kernel of disquiet at his core.

Taking himself off the scene for the last few years had pretty much stopped the media madness. If he put himself out there again, he'd be reopening Pandora's box, and this time he'd be in no doubt about what would come out. He might try to convince himself that he'd manage it better this time, but could he? Was anyone really able to tame the rapacious predator of the paparazzi? Many celebrities had tried and failed. Why should he be any different?

What would that mean for Ayesha and Sabina? Whatever happened, he'd put them first. He certainly couldn't consider a return to the limelight while they were still running from Ayesha's husband. This business with Suresh Rasheed would have to be sorted. They could take out an injunction against him, but someone like that would never pay any attention to it. Perhaps he could pay him off. Hayden didn't know why he hadn't considered it before. Ayesha would probably resist, but what else could they do? He sounded like a bloke who would sit up and listen when money talked. Sabina's safety was paramount. He couldn't bear it if anything happened to either of them.

He swung into the drive and the gates closed behind him. Until yesterday, he'd thought they were high enough and secure enough to keep anyone out. Looked like he was wrong. It worried him that the security cameras had been taken out so easily. Still, the security company were coming along soon to see what else they could do.

They could move to the country. Stay out of London. Whenever he was on tour he could take them with him. Other bands managed to take their families on the road with them. But he had to admit that it wasn't the best deal for the kids. It was disruptive, and what child didn't function better in a settled environment? He couldn't see Sabina thriving if she was dragged around the world on a series of buses and planes.

The more he considered it, the more ridiculous an idea it seemed. He'd hated everything about the music business, except for the performing. Why was he even thinking about going back to it when it had already robbed him of so much? He must be totally mad. There was no way he could put the two most important people in his life at risk. He'd seen the anxiety on Ayesha's face this morning as he left the house, but stupidly he'd chosen to ignore it, caught up in his own excitement. How ridiculous it seemed now. How shallow. Now he couldn't wait to get back to her and put her mind at rest. While she was with him, he never wanted her to worry about another thing.

With all these thoughts flitting through his brain, Hayden jumped out of the car and let himself into the house.

It all seemed unusually still and he called out, 'Ayesha!'

There was no reply, but it was a fine day and she might well be out in the garden. He remembered that Crystal was at work and Edgar had taken Joy to the day centre. They had the place to themselves for an hour or two, which would be nice.

Hayden went through to the kitchen but there was still no sign of Ayesha. He shrugged off his laptop bag and put it on the table, then helped himself to some chilled orange juice from the fridge. Smiling to himself, he realised it was the first time the house had been so quiet in months. Strangely, he'd grown to like their new busy, bustling life much better.

Out in the garden, he enjoyed the sun on his face. The offices at his management team had been chilled to Arctic levels and it was good to feel the heat on his skin. If Ayesha hadn't planned anything for tonight, perhaps they'd have a barbecue again. He was getting to be a dab hand at not incinerating sausages. They could get Edgar round too. It was a change not to be the only male in the place, and Edgar was a decent bloke. He and Crystal seemed really happy together. Perhaps it was time both he and Crystal found happiness again.

'Ayesha,' he called out. 'Ayesha! Where are you?'

He wandered down to Joy's vegetable patch, but there was no one there either. Maybe he could get more interested in what went on down here. He'd never taken much note of what Joy got up to in her potting shed or greenhouse, but he might find it relaxing and, in a weird way, he felt that he'd like to spend more time with Joy. Seeing her washed out and frail yesterday had made him realise that she wasn't always going to be around and that he should appreciate her more.

Hayden felt himself frown. Ayesha must have popped out for a while. Which was unlike her. Even after all this time, she didn't generally go out on her own, and after yesterday he thought she'd have stayed very closely to the house. He called her phone, but it went straight to voicemail.

They should get away for a while. Have a holiday in the sunshine. He wondered if he should suggest that they all go back to Sri Lanka. Ayesha, he knew, would love to see her parents again and it would be great for Beanie to meet her grandparents for the first time. They'd have to organise passports as he was pretty sure they didn't have them.

Back in the house, he wandered aimlessly through the kitchen again and into the living room. It was amazing how quickly he'd got used to having people around. He couldn't imagine going back to the days when he stayed in his room all the time, barely came out, barely spoke.

He could spend an hour on the piano, try out some new ideas. That would pass the time until everyone came home.

Then he noticed the scrap of paper on top of the copy of *Great Expectations* that they'd been reading. He picked up the note and, scanning it, felt his stomach churn. The very last thing he'd expected was a goodbye note.

# Chapter Eighty-three

'She can't have gone,' Crystal said.

Hayden handed her the brief farewell note that Ayesha had left. 'I think that's pretty clear.'

*I am so very sorry. Please let me go. Ayesha.* The words were burned on to the back of his eyes.

'Is this it?' she asked.

Hayden nodded. 'Looks like it.'

Crystal passed the note to Joy, who frowned at it and shook her head in disbelief.

'Where could she have gone?'

'That, I don't know.'

The three of them were sitting at the kitchen table. No one had thought to make tea.

Crystal punched Ayesha's number into her mobile. 'She must have had a rush of blood to the head. I thought she was acting a bit funny when I left her this morning.'

'Then why did you leave her?' It came out more crisply than Hayden meant it to.

'I had to go to work, Hayd,' Crystal snapped back. 'I offered to ring you and get you home early, but she wouldn't hear of it.' She clicked off her phone with a tut. 'No answer.'

'I've tried already.' He'd tried a million times, if truth be told. It was clear she didn't want to speak to him.

He raked his hands through his hair and let out a weary sigh. Perhaps she blamed him for not protecting her enough. Goodness only knew, he blamed himself.

'You don't think someone's forced her to do this?'

'No,' Hayden said. 'I checked her room. She's packed all her clothes. If it had been her husband, he'd have simply grabbed them. I phoned the school and they said she'd seemed quite calm when she picked up Sabina. We just have to accept that she's chosen to leave.'

'Well, *I* can't just accept it! You have to go after her, Hayd,' Crystal said. 'You *have* to.'

'She doesn't want me to,' he replied flatly. 'You can read that yourself.'

'She doesn't mean it though,' Crystal countered. 'Not really. Women always say what they don't mean. You *have* to find her. How will she manage?'

'I can't hound her like her husband has,' Hayden said. 'I won't have her looking over her shoulder for *two* people. If I follow her then she's always at risk. I could expose her at any time. She's better off without me.'

'You're such a twat,' Crystal muttered. 'Of course she isn't better off without you.'

'Then why has she gone?'

'She's terrified. She's panicked. Now more than ever, she needs us.'

'She's gone,' Hayden said. 'We should let her go.'

'*No*,' Crystal said vehemently. 'You might be prepared to give up without a fight, but I'm not. She's my friend. The best friend I've ever had. She got me out of that shit-hole club and I

389

owe her. She's given you your life back, Hayden. You were rattling round here like a pathetic shadow until she came. You owe her too.'

He hung his head. Some of what Crystal said rang true, but he didn't want to chase after her. If Ayesha felt she needed to disappear for Sabina's sake, then he should respect that. 'Don't I owe her enough to respect her wishes too?'

'Not when she doesn't know what's good for her,' Crystal cried in frustration. 'Men! You're bloody hopeless. You could pay for a top detective to find her and bring her back.'

'Then I'd be no better than her husband,' he pointed out. 'She wants her freedom, Crystal. I don't want to tie her here.'

'Tell him, Joy. What do you think?'

'Hayden,' Joy sighed, 'I think you're a twat too.'

That night Crystal made dinner, and it was terrible. It was supposed to be macaroni cheese. Even though it had come out of a foil supermarket carton, it was like a solid lump of beige stodge, and the table shuddered when she shook it off the spoon on to the plate.

Joy took one look at it and burst into tears.

'Oh bollocks,' Crystal said, tearful too. 'I take it you're not crying about the state of my mac and cheese, Joy.'

Joy dabbed at her eyes with her napkin and shrugged off Crystal's attempt to comfort her.

Hayden could feel her pain. It radiated from all of them like toxic waves. They sat forlornly at the table, all of them feeling the absence of Ayesha and Sabina keenly.

'This just isn't right, is it?' Crystal said.

He hadn't wanted to come downstairs at all, but Crystal had insisted. His appetite had deserted him and there was no way he could eat this heavy lump of congealed pasta. It would sit like a stone in his stomach.

'You're going to have to get her back, Hayd.' Crystal stared disconsolately at her culinary efforts. 'Or we're all going to starve to death.' She pushed her fork through it in dismay. 'What did we do before Ayesha came?'

He'd lived on sandwiches or fresh air. He'd locked his emotions up tight where he couldn't access them. He'd given up his music and retreated into silence. He'd let no one and nothing touch him. He didn't know about the others, but already he could feel his old life calling him. The hollowness that had been at the centre of him had returned with a vengeance. When he thought he'd banished it, he was wrong. It had simply been waiting, just around the corner. If possible, he felt even more empty, more bereft than before.

Ayesha and Sabina were gone, and the sooner he got used to that the better.

# Chapter Eighty-four

A month had gone by and there'd still been no word from Ayesha. Yet the space she had left in their world was no less gaping.

Joy spent most of her time in the garden and, when she did come into the house, she moved about like a ghost. Crystal's cooking hadn't improved and now she didn't even apologise for the incinerated ready-meals that she plonked in front of them. They all ate without enthusiasm anyway.

Hayden had returned to his old habits and now spent most of his time in his room – except for night-time. When it turned midnight, one, two, three, and still sleep eluded him, he was back down in the basement, working out to try to exhaust his body into oblivion.

It was no use. There was no way of obliterating Ayesha from his mind. If he was awake he thought of her. If he was asleep he dreamed of her. Everything that happened was referenced back to her and he could see no end to it.

His management team, so buoyed by his unexpected re-appearance, had accepted his equally speedy disappearance, and after a week or two had stopped calling. The contract to become a judge on *The Fame Game* remained unsigned on the desk in his office.

The security around the house was now so strong that even to him it felt like a prison. A gilded cage from which he had no particular desire to escape. They would have been safe here, but they would have been suffocated too. Just as he was.

He sat at the piano, fingers poised, but he couldn't make them move. The music that had briefly bubbled up inside him had gone again. Love, it seemed, was the only inspiration he needed, and that, it appeared, was the one thing that eluded him.

Joy came in through the French doors and peeled off her gardening gloves. 'Cup of tea?'

'I'll make it,' Hayden said. 'You sit down.'

She looked tired, and had done since the day Ayesha left.

They went through to the kitchen together and, on autopilot, Hayden flicked on the kettle and made them both tea.

'Still no word?' she asked as she sat at the table.

He shook his head as he put mugs down in front of them both.

'I miss her,' Joy said. 'I miss her and Sabina.'

The words 'Me too' wouldn't even grace his throat. Missing them felt like having ice round his heart, like a sword stabbed into his ribs, like a vice on his brain. The pain was physical and real. A permanent torture.

'It makes me realise that I miss my own grandchildren too,' she continued. 'You get used to them not being around, but that doesn't mean it's for the best. I should go to see them. If it means getting on a plane, then I should just get over my fear and do it. I don't want them growing up not knowing me.'

'You could go on an extended holiday,' Hayden suggested. 'See if you like it out there.'

'I'm frightened,' Joy admitted. 'But I've been thinking of it more since the day the men came here for Sabina. If they'd been more determined, I could have been a goner. None of us like to stare our mortality in the face. If I'm going to do this, I must do it now, before I run out of chances.'

Hayden gave her a sideways glance. 'Do you want me to book you a ticket on the internet?'

'I'll phone my sons. See when they're available.'

'We can Skype them.'

'We could,' she said, much to his surprise. 'Let's do that. I'll comb my hair and put a clean blouse on.' She smiled at him. 'There's one advantage with the telephone: they can't see how very scruffy I've become.'

Hayden put his hand over hers. 'I'm sure they'll be happy to see you at all.'

Crystal breezed in and threw her bag down on the table. 'What am I missing? You two look like you lost a fiver and found a pound.'

'Joy's considering going to Singapore to see her sons on a long holiday.'

'Great idea,' Crystal said. 'But that means you're going to leave me here alone with Misery Guts?'

'Not for too long,' Joy replied. 'I'm thinking a month at the most.'

'Thank goodness for that.' Crystal emptied the dregs of the tea from the pot.

It would be stewed and cold. Ayesha would never have stood for it. She'd have jumped up and made a fresh one instantly. Now none of them could be bothered. Crystal grimaced as she downed it.

Hayden closed his eyes. He had to stop thinking of every little thing in terms of how Ayesha would have done it. That wasn't going to bring her home.

'I'll be back in five minutes,' Joy said and she tripped out of the kitchen, leaving them together.

Crystal stared hard at him.

'Say nothing,' Hayden warned. Every time they were alone, Crystal pushed him to look for Ayesha. She had done for the last month, and it was clear she wasn't about to stop now.

'I'm worried about you,' she said. 'You're back to how you used to be. You never come out of your room.'

'I'm out now,' he said.

'You know what I mean, clever dick. You stay holed up there for most of the day and come out at night when you think Joy and I have gone to bed.'

'I need some time to myself.'

'You don't,' Crystal insisted. 'You need to find Ayesha. She's out there waiting. I know she is. She hardly had a penny to her name, Hayden. I'm worried about her. I've called and called, but she's not answering. She's my friend. Why doesn't she talk to me? What if something's happened to her?'

If he ever thought about that, he made himself physically sick.

'What about Sabina?' she pressed on. 'Even if they're OK, she'll be missing you terribly. You must have some idea where she's gone?'

But he didn't.

'Don't you want to see that child grow up?'

'Of course I do.'

'Then find them.'

'It's not that easy.'

'You're making me want to bang my head on the table, Hayd. You're making me feel bad about myself. I'm all loved up with Edgar, we should all be going out together, drinking cocktails, dancing the night away and having fun. Doing what young – *ish* – people do.'

Hayden didn't point out that it was the last thing on earth he'd want to do. He'd never been happier than when he'd been curled up on the sofa with Ayesha, reading together, or showing Sabina a new tune on the piano. That was what he wanted in his life.

'I don't want to be here babysitting you.'

'You don't have to.'

'But I do.' Crystal tucked her hair behind her ear and stared fixedly at her mug. She cleared her throat before she spoke. 'You know I've always loved you, don't you?'

He swallowed hard before he answered. 'Yes.'

'Then set me free, Hayden. Set me free to love Edgar. Go and find Ayesha.'

# Chapter Eighty-five

The need to do this had been burning in Suresh's veins for weeks, and now the moment was finally here. Most of the haul from the last raid had been sold on – the watches had been particularly easy to move. Who didn't want a flashy designer watch at a knock-down price, no questions asked? He would target more specifically this time to fill what was a big demand. It had been too long since the last job. The tension had been building up inside him and he wanted to get this done. He wondered if this was what junkies felt like when they needed their next fix.

Flynn and Smith had already arrived and they were waiting for Arunja before heading to the lock-up to get the bikes. It was pushing eight o'clock in the morning and his brother should have been here by now to go over last-minute details, but he wasn't. This was so typical of Arunja's couldn't-care-less attitude. Well, if he didn't buck up, Suresh wouldn't use him on the next job. That might make him think more clearly.

Arunja might be family, but that didn't give him a reason to treat Suresh like dirt. He was the brains of this operation. When he said, 'Jump,' he wanted them to say, 'How high?' He'd had enough of people thinking they could walk all over him. Well, that was all about to end and he certainly wasn't going to let his little brother get away with disrespecting him.

'We need to be making a move, Suresh.' Flynn glanced at his watch, irritated. 'Call Arunja. If we wait much longer we're going to miss our window of opportunity. There's no way I want to be heading into the shopping centre when it's starting to get busy.'

'We need to be there as soon as they open,' Smith agreed.

Suresh muttered a curse under his breath. As he was about to punch the number into his mobile, the doorbell rang and his mother shuffled to the door to let in Arunja. She fussed over his brother as she never did with him.

When she'd eventually finished her ministrations, Arunja came into the kitchen.

'What fucking time do you call this?' Suresh said. 'We were about to leave without you.'

'Keep your shirt on,' Arunja said, unruffled. 'I had stuff to sort out at home. You know what it's like. So I'm five minutes late.' He shrugged his indifference, and Suresh had never wanted to punch him more. 'We know the form after last time.'

'Let's get going,' Flynn said tightly. 'We're wasting even more time listening to you two bicker. At this rate we'll get snarled up in rush-hour traffic. Even on the bikes it'll slow us down.'

Suresh grabbed his bag. That was it. After this one, Arunja was out. They could get someone who was more professional, more committed. They didn't need passengers. The rewards were too high to share them with someone who didn't pull his weight. He pushed past Arunja and went out to the car, seething inside.

Flynn got into the driver's seat next to Suresh. Arunja and

Smith got in the back. They drove the ten minutes to the lock-up in stony silence. The atmosphere could have been cut with a knife.

Suresh seethed. When this was over and he was rich beyond his wildest dreams, he'd cut all the dead wood out of his life: his brother, his parents, and he'd finally see to that wife of his. This time he wouldn't leave the job to amateurs. He'd go himself and he'd cut out her heart. Hers and the kid's too. That would be the end of it and he could move on with his new life. It couldn't happen soon enough.

When they arrived at the lock-up, Suresh opened the door, and instantly his hackles rose.

'Someone's been in here,' he said. Since he'd last come up to the garage, one of the bikes had been moved, he was sure of it.

'That was me,' Arunja admitted. 'I want to be one of the riders. I've taken a bike out a couple of times to brush up my skills.'

'You've what?' Suresh was fuming. 'How could you do that without telling me?'

'What's the problem?'

'Someone could have seen you, identified the bike.'

'They didn't,' Arunja said. 'I was careful.'

'Anything could have gone wrong.'

'Well, it didn't. Chill out, Suresh.'

*Chill out?* Suresh fumed. His brother was an idiot. He took nothing in this life seriously. Well, he'd deal with Arunja later, Suresh thought. He was too full of his own importance and needed to be taken down a peg or two.

Suresh scanned the garage quickly and was relieved to see that nothing else had been interfered with. You had to be careful these days, there were a lot of petty thieves about.

The men changed into their bike leathers, black for all of them. Topped with black crash helmets and mirrored visors, they looked mean, menacing. No one with any sense would want to get in their way.

They picked up their holdalls and checked the guns in them. Last time they hadn't even needed to use them; waving them about in a threatening manner had been enough. Arunja and Smith tucked club hammers down the back of their leathers.

'I want to ride on this one,' Arunja said. 'You said I could.'

'I don't have time to argue with you, Arunja. Just get on the back with Smith.'

'You said I could ride.' He sounded petulant, as he always had as a child.

'Shut up and get on the fucking bike,' Suresh snarled.

'We need to be going,' Flynn said. He looked at his watch again, a Rolex that he'd taken a fancy to from the last raid. He was impatient, agitated.

This time, the jewellery store they were doing was an established one that had recently been given a revamp. The whole frontage was glass, the entrance wide and welcoming. It would be easier to get into but, on the downside, it was deeper into the shopping centre. They'd need to be in and out faster. Also, they had no one on the inside this time, but he and Flynn had been in a couple of times to suss out the layout and it seemed simple enough. This was probably the last time they'd be able to hit this place, as they'd get used to expecting them. Next time they'd move on to another shopping centre, out of their patch, and catch them off guard. The stakes were higher and that was what was giving him the adrenalin buzz, but this time something felt off-kilter.

It could be down to Arunja. He didn't fit in with the team and the vibe was all wrong. He'd get Flynn to draft in someone else as soon as he could, and Arunja would be cut loose. His brother was about to find out that blood *wasn't* thicker than water.

They tooled up, opened up the garage and mounted the bikes. Reluctantly Arunja slid on to the pillion seat behind Smith and, when the lock-up door was secured, Suresh got on behind Flynn. They roared out into the workday traffic and turned towards the shopping centre.

# Chapter Eighty-six

Hayden sat in his office, Joy at his side. He clicked the last few buttons on the page he was viewing on the internet before signing off.

'We're done,' he said to her.

'Really?'

He smiled. 'No going back now.'

'It makes me feel sick just thinking of it,' Joy admitted.

The printer kicked into life and spewed out a piece of paper, which he handed over to Joy.

She looked at it with disdain. 'That's it? No pretty folder and bunch of tickets any more?'

'Nope,' Hayden said. 'That's it. E-ticket. Apparently it's progress.'

Joy rolled her eyes. 'Aren't all the bad ideas in the world? Doesn't seem much for all that money.'

'Nevertheless, it's one return ticket to Singapore. You're on your way, Joy. By this time next week, you'll be happily ensconced in your son's home.'

'I hope you're right about the "happily" bit.'

'You'll love it, I'm sure,' Hayden assured her.

Joy had finally agreed with her sons that she'd go out there for a month to see how she liked it. Hayden hoped that, having made the first step, it would pave the way for Joy to go and live out there with them on a permanent basis.

She stared at the paper in her hand. 'I'm glad it's only a few days away. I don't think my nerves would stand it otherwise. I've got so much to do before then.'

'You need to throw a few light things in a case,' Hayden advised. 'That's all. Anything else you need you can buy when you're there.'

'So says the seasoned traveller.'

'Yeah,' Hayden said. 'I'm the man who went everywhere with a dozen tour buses. That's how I know you can manage without them.'

'I *am* looking forward to it,' Joy admitted. 'That doesn't mean I'm not terrified out of my wits though.'

'Trust me, once you get in the air, the overriding emotion will be boredom. At least in first class you'll have some gadgets to play with, and you've more chance of having a snooze to pass the time.'

'I can't thank you enough for booking this for me.' Joy looked at him gratefully.

He'd paid for Joy's ticket. Why wouldn't he?

'I'd never have dared to treat myself to such luxury. You really shouldn't have.'

'My pleasure. Consider it payment for all the work you've done in the garden.'

'Who'll look after it while I'm gone?'

'I'll give it a go.' Hayden shrugged. 'I'm not exactly Alan Titchmarsh, but I'll try my best.'

'Come out into the garden today,' Joy urged. 'I'll show you what needs doing. We haven't seen you outside for weeks, and it's still lovely out there.'

403

He looked out of the window at the blue sky, the fluffy white clouds, and it seemed like a world that was alien to him. 'Not today, Joy,' he said. 'Maybe tomorrow.'

Before Joy could answer, Crystal's voice came from the hall, shrill and loud. 'Hayd! Hayd! Where are you?'

He and Joy looked at each other and they both rolled their eyes.

'What now?' Joy said to him.

'Hayd! Hayd!'

Hayden grinned. 'Let's go and find out before she blows a gasket.'

So he and Joy went out into the hall, where Crystal was running up and down, shouting and waving her arms. In her hand she clutched a postcard.

'I've been looking everywhere for you. Have you seen this?' She waved the postcard again. 'Of course you haven't. It's only just plopped into the postbox at the gate.'

She handed it over, doing a little dance on the spot. 'Look who it's from!'

It was a postcard from Lyme Regis. Hayden didn't even need to glance at the back to know who had sent it. If felt as if all the breath had been knocked from his body and he held on to the banister so that he wouldn't simply sag to the floor.

He looked at the pretty picture again, the sweep of the bay, the Cobb jutting out proudly into the sea, and his mind rewound to the blissfully happy day they'd spent there together.

Hayden knew that was where Ayesha would be. In his heart he suspected that he'd known it all along. Nevertheless, the confirmation of it made him feel like lying down on the floor and weeping with relief. They were safe, and that was all that mattered to him.

With an unsteady hand, he turned over the card. It simply read *A & S xx*. Even that twisted at his stomach.

'So?' Crystal said, hands on hips. 'Where's the happy dance? Where's the cry of ecstasy? Even a smile wouldn't hurt.'

'I'm glad,' Hayden said. 'Of course I am.'

'Glad?' Crystal tutted loudly. '*Glad?* You should be swinging from the chandelier. She wants you to go to her, lame brain. Why else would she have sent that to you?'

'She wants me to know she's OK,' Hayden agreed. 'This changes nothing. I can't go to her. If I did that, it would only put her in danger again.'

'You're not serious?'

'Deadly.'

'Joy, tell him he's being a pillock.'

'There must be some way to make this work, Hayden,' Joy agreed. 'It does very much feel as if she's reaching out to you.'

'You *cannot* go back to your old life, Hayd. We won't allow it, will we, Joy? All you do all day is sit in your bloody room. You could show a thirteen-year-old how to do a good mope! You're back to square one. You're back to where you were when Laura died.'

He recoiled as if she'd slapped him, but she carried on.

'This is different, Hayd. Ayesha isn't dead. She's still out there and waiting for you to go to her. It doesn't have to be like this.'

'Someone could be watching me,' Hayden said flatly. 'The minute I make a move towards Ayesha, they could be on to her again. I can't risk that. I know she's safe. That's enough for me.'

'You're a fucking machine,' Crystal spat. 'You don't deserve love.'

He stood there and took it. 'You're probably right.'

'Joy, do something,' Crystal begged. 'Get it through that thick skull of his.'

'It's not good to be alone,' Joy concurred. 'Is there *really* no way round this?'

'I don't think so. Ayesha knew she was better off without me. That's why she went. This is her way of telling me not to worry.'

'Call her,' Crystal said. 'Perhaps she'll answer her phone now.'

'I can't do that,' he said. 'If I hear her voice then I *will* want to go to her.'

'That's the flipping point!'

He had to stand firm. If he called her, spoke to her, then he'd be lost all over again. He'd have to go to her, and if he did that, he risked leading Suresh to her. 'You just don't see, Crystal. This is how it has to be.'

'Aaaaaargh!' Crystal cried. 'There was never anyone more stubborn than you. If you don't call her then I will. I'll tell her that you're not coping without her. That you've gone back to living in twilight. I'll tell her you're not eating properly, that I'm slowly poisoning you with my crap food. That'll get her running back.'

'You'll do no such thing,' Hayden said. 'Leave her be. She left us for a reason, all of us. She left us for her own safety and that of Sabina.' These were the hardest words he'd ever had to say, but he believed them and he had to stick by them or he'd go stark staring mad: 'If we love her, we'll all leave her alone.'

# Chapter Eighty-seven

They revved up the motorbikes as they came within reach of the shopping centre, increasing their speed. Suresh felt his own adrenalin surge. His whole being vibrated with the thrill of expectation.

Pedestrians dived out of the way as they turned off the road and rode straight over the paved concourse, skirting the fountain. The glass doors opened automatically at their approach and they accelerated inside, scattering the early shoppers.

The corridors of the shopping centre were smooth and wide. They rode along side by side, splitting only to negotiate the marble planters filled with exotic trees. Due to Arunja, they were here later than they'd wanted to be and there were many more people about even at this hour than there had been last time. It wasn't a problem, though, as they all wisely leapt out of the way as soon as they saw them coming, pressing themselves flat into shop doorways for protection.

On the back of Flynn's bike, Suresh cried out and waved his sawn-off shotgun, enjoying watching people flee in fear. This was the life. This was what he was made for. Some people got their kicks out of doing good. He'd realised that he got his kicks out of doing bad.

Flynn kicked out the bike's back end and, according to plan, he pulled up outside the wide-open frontage of the jewellery store next to Smith and Arunja. Pausing only for a second, Flynn throttled the bike into life again and they blasted through the doorway.

As soon as they were inside, the startled staff ran to the back of the store. Suresh jumped off the bike before it came to a halt and Flynn skidded it sideways into a pristine display case, shattering it into a thousand pieces. Diamond necklaces scattered over the floor.

Suresh brandished his gun at the terrified staff, who huddled together behind the far counter. 'Get back! Get back!'

They cowered in the face of his threats. Who was going to be stupid enough to put their life on the line for minimum wage? None of this lot, that was clear. All of this stuff was covered by insurance anyway. It wasn't hurting anyone.

Flynn scooped the necklaces into his bag while Suresh smashed cabinets filled with watches with the butt of his gun. He grabbed a tray at a time and stashed them in his bag.

Out at the front of the store, Smith and Arunja were smashing windows with their hammers, grabbing what they could. His brother had jumped off the bike and was moving along the windows, staving them in as he went. That wasn't in the plan either. They should have both emptied the windows nearest the bike, for a fast getaway. That was where the most expensive watches were kept. Arunja was smashing the windows just for the hell of it. Suresh cursed his brother's stupidity.

Outside, a crowd was already starting to gather, rubbernecking despite the danger. Suresh's mouth went dry. He realised that the extra half-hour they'd missed due to Arunja's lateness could cost them dearly.

'It's time to go,' Flynn said over his shoulder. He slung his bag on his back and climbed on the motorbike.

'A few more minutes,' Suresh said. They had to make up for the time lost.

'Now!' Flynn barked. 'We've got enough.'

But could you ever have enough? There were trays and trays of expensive watches, glittering diamonds. Ostentatious displays of wealth beyond the reach of ordinary people. They sparkled enticingly in front of him. All here for the taking.

While Flynn kicked the bike into life, Suresh was still smashing cases, scooping their contents into his bag. Hundreds of thousands of pounds, like taking candy from a baby.

Flynn throttled the bike angrily.

'Wait, wait!' Suresh shouted. 'I'm nearly done.' The jewels were so beautiful, shimmering and golden. He couldn't bear to leave a single one of them behind.

'No can do. I'm not hanging around any longer,' Flynn said. 'There's too much heat. You and Arunja can stay if you want to. I'll take Smith.'

Before Suresh could answer, Flynn had roared out of the shop, pausing only long enough to bark at Smith to jump on to the back of his bike.

That left Arunja and Suresh alone, which wasn't in the plan either. How could Flynn have left like that?

Outside the store, he saw Arunja leave the windows, jump on the remaining bike and kick it into life. Suresh saw panic in his brother's eyes as he rode it into the entrance of the shop. He spun the bike around. On his shoulder a bag bulged with stolen jewels and watches. It looked as if he'd done good work.

'Let's go,' Arunja yelled at him. 'I can hear sirens.'

That was Suresh's cue to get out of there. But there was one last display of watches that he really wanted. Among the most expensive watches money could buy – Hublot, Patek Philippe, Jaegar-LeCoultre – they were at the back of the shop and it would be unbearable to leave without them. Not only could he

409

shift them all quickly, but he also wanted one on his own wrist. A trophy for his audacity.

As he moved towards the staff, he brandished his gun and they shied away from him. He smashed the glass of the display and scooped the watches into his bag. As he bent forward to reach further in, one of the staff from the store rushed at him from behind and jumped on to his back. Suresh dropped his bag and bucked as the have-a-go hero tried to wrestle him to the ground. The man was strong, but not strong enough to over-power him. They fell together and struggled on the carpet amid the broken glass and the rings, bracelets and necklaces that Suresh had missed.

Arunja turned round on the bike and pointed his sawn-off shotgun at them. 'Get away, you fucker! Get away!' he shouted.

The man released his grip and held up his hands in surrender. Suresh rolled out of the way, but that didn't stop Arunja from blasting away with the weapon. The shot hit the man in the chest and a flower of red bloomed, staining his crisp white shirt. The rest of the staff started to scream.

'You fucking idiot,' Suresh cried, his eyes wide in disbelief. 'What did you do that for?'

Before Suresh could scramble to his feet, Arunja revved the bike into life. He and his brother looked at each other eye to eye.

'I'm sorry,' Arunja shouted, and then he roared off, parting the shrieking, panicking crowd.

Suresh lay there amid the glittering jewellery, stunned into shock. His stupid fucking brother had gone without him. He'd left him behind. After all he'd done for Arunja, at the crucial moment his brother had abandoned him.

He looked at the man lying next to him. His blood, the life that had seeped out of him, now stained the carpet, and the mangled hole in his chest said that there was no way back from this.

Eventually, Suresh managed to stand, and he shook the glass from himself. There was blood pouring from the cuts on his hands and face.

'Anyone else tries it and they'll get the same,' he said to the cowering staff, but he noticed that his voice wavered.

The staff had backed far into the corner and none of them looked as if they were willing to tackle him. A lesson learned. But perhaps too late. In the shopping centre there was a crowd gathering, and with Arunja gone, he wondered how he was going to make his escape.

Then a loudspeaker crackled out, 'Put the gun down and come out with your hands above your head.'

The police. Now what was he to do? Suresh peered out of the nearest window and all he could see was a barricade of black uniforms. The officers were in bulletproof vests; some had guns, some had riot shields. More were moving through the entrance doors of the mall, scuttling along the walls of the shops, taking up position. They must have been three-deep. The crowd were being hustled away now, out of the main shopping area altogether, clearing the space around the jewellery store.

Suresh laughed to himself. After all his careful planning, it had come to this. He should have listened to Flynn, left when he'd said.

He looked again at the dead man on the floor. Arunja had done this and had then made his own escape, leaving Suresh to take the rap. If he did get out alive, he'd kill Arunja with his bare hands.

He heard the marching of boots on the marble floor. The police were closing in. His palms were sweating, slippery against the cool metal of his shotgun.

This wasn't going to end well. He knew that much. There would be no triumph in this. What could he do? Walk out of here, hands held high in submission, and give himself over to the police? He'd get years in prison. Even longer if he didn't finger his own brother for murder. That would be more humiliation than he could stand. Who would look up to him then? Or he could go out in a blaze of glory, blasting his gun until the end. He looked out from the shop at the police in their riot gear, crouched behind their shields, ready to take him down.

Lifting a handful of glittering diamonds from his shoulder bag, he clutched them in his fist. He opened his palm to gaze on his prize. They sparkled and shimmered at him, mesmerising and radiant under the harsh lights of the store. Had it all been worth it? Perhaps, briefly, it had. Then he let the gems fall through his fingers, showering them on to the floor around his feet.

Suresh looked at the gun in his other hand. What a way to go. But he could see no other viable option. At least this way it was *his* way. The barrel fitted under his chin beneath his motorbike helmet with surprising comfort and then, with a feeling of inevitability, he pulled the trigger.

# Chapter Eighty-eight

'Don't faff, Joy,' Crystal said. 'We've got plenty of time to get you to the airport. If you want to check you've got everything once more, then we can.'

Joy was looking panic-stricken, rifling through all her belongings, checking and double-checking that she'd got her money, passport and ticket.

'Crystal's right,' Hayden agreed. 'There's a three-hour check-in and we're going to be there nice and early. We can even sit and have a coffee together before you go through to Departures if you'd like to.'

'I just want to be there now,' Joy said.

'We should have got you some tranquillisers from the doctor,' Crystal said.

'No, no,' she said. 'I don't take drugs. Besides, I want to be clear-headed and have all my marbles about me.'

'They'll look after you, Joy. I've made sure they will.' Hayden had called the airline VIP service and informed them that Joy was flying for the first time. He'd told them that she was elderly, alone and nervous. After all he'd spent with them over the years, flying back and forth across the globe, they owed him a favour.

He was in no doubt that she'd get very special treatment. He picked up her case while she had one last look in her handbag. 'You'll have an escort from the minute you go through Security until you're safely on the plane. You never know, you might even enjoy it.'

She risked a smile at that. 'Thank you, Hayden. I'm so very grateful to you.' She smoothed down her new blouse. 'Do I look all right?'

'You look fabulous,' Crystal assured her. 'I bet you end up picking up a toy-boy while you're there.'

'You do say the silliest things,' Joy tutted.

Hayden smiled to himself. Joy had reluctantly endured a Crystal makeover. She was sporting a new haircut, had a new capsule wardrobe packed in her case, and had perfectly manicured hands.

'You do,' Hayden told her. 'You look ten years younger. Your sons will be very proud of you.'

The attack in the garden had left Joy more shaken than she would have liked to admit. The cuts and bruises had long since gone, but it had taken its toll on her, he could tell. She was less confident now, more anxious. Hayden hoped this break away would do her good.

They didn't talk much about that day now. The police were supposedly carrying on their investigations, but he'd heard nothing positive back from them yet.

From Ayesha there had been no more contact either. The postcard from Lyme Regis lay on his bedside table. Every night he looked at it before he went to sleep. Every night he visualised where they might be. And every night he fought the urge to contact her.

When he closed his eyes now, though, he could see Ayesha and Sabina on the beach, playing crazy golf, eating fish and chips on the prom. What was she doing now? he wondered. Did she feel able, at last, to stop looking over her shoulder? He could only hope so. He understood why she'd felt the need to put the safety of her daughter before everything else. In her situation, he would have done exactly the same. That didn't, however, make it any easier to bear.

Joy let out a long, shuddering breath. 'I'm ready now,' she said.

'Let's load 'em up then.' Hayden carried her case to the car. Crystal had done well. Everything Joy needed had been fitted into a small suitcase that she could manage easily.

They all got into the car. Hayden hit the remote and the gates swung open for them. There was one lone pap standing there, who quickly raised his camera when Hayden swept past him. They all gave him the finger as he did.

Less than an hour later, they were parked up and in the airport terminal at Heathrow. Hayden checked the departures board. The flight was up there already and looked as if it was on time. They checked in Joy's luggage with ease. This had to bode well.

'Do you want a coffee or do you want to go straight through?' he asked.

'Coffee,' Crystal announced before Joy could reply. She put her arm through Joy's. 'I don't want you to rush off, you daft old bat. I want to say goodbye properly.' Crystal had a tear in her eye. 'I hate airports.'

'Let's sit for five minutes,' Joy said. 'I still feel all of a jitter. It's very crowded here, isn't it?'

'It'll be frantic until you get through Security, Joy,' Hayden warned. 'Then you'll be in the care of the executive lounge, which is an oasis of calm.'

There was a Costa Coffee on the concourse that wasn't too busy, and Hayden found them a table tucked away in the corner. He took their order and went to the counter, leaving Joy and Crystal chatting. They'd both miss Joy more than they cared to admit, he thought. It would be strangely empty at the house without her. It had been bad enough since Ayesha and Sabina had left. What would it be like now, with just him and Crystal rattling around in that huge place? Perhaps he should downsize, move to somewhere smaller. But, if he was honest, he worried about being alone now. He'd got so used to someone always being around that he didn't think he could cope on his own. He might not always want to socialise, but it was good to know there was someone there for him.

He ordered their coffees. Crystal and Edgar were getting along nicely. She seemed to be really serious about him and it looked as if he felt exactly the same about her. That was good to see too. Would Crystal want to move out to be with Edgar? Perhaps, when the time came, Edgar could move in with them too. Or would that be too weird? Sometime he might be forced to let go of Crystal as well, but that was too difficult to even contemplate.

If only Ayesha hadn't felt that she had to go. Life had been so much easier, so much happier, with her and Beanie around. But dwelling on what might have been wasn't going to bring her back.

Taking the drinks from the barista, he headed back to the table. Crystal and Joy were still deep in conversation and Joy was laughing, which made him worry less about her. Crystal was holding Joy's hand across the table and it made him think again what a very good friend Crystal was to have.

He sat down and gave them both their drinks. On the table next to them there was an abandoned newspaper, and Hayden reached over to grab it. He rarely kept up with what went on in the world these days, as most of it was too harrowing to bear. When Laura died, the papers had been filled with nonsense about them both, and he'd hardly ever looked at them since. It was probably weeks since he'd seen a newspaper. The last time he'd looked at the nationals was when he thought the picture of him and Ayesha might appear in them.

This newspaper was a couple of days old, so he assumed a traveller must have dumped it here when he'd finished with it.

It was a red-top tabloid. The sort of rag he hated most of all. The paper was crumpled at the corners, well thumbed, and he flicked it open, leafing through the pages aimlessly. The front-page headline, predictably depressing, was about an armed raider who'd turned his gun on himself during a robbery at a jewellery store. Hayden shook his head.

'What are you looking so glum about?' Crystal said.

'Why are newspapers always so depressing?' He turned the newspaper towards her and she frowned as she scanned the headline.

'"Gunman shoots himself." So what? Good riddance, I say.' Crystal tutted. 'The poor people in that shop must have been terrified.'

Hayden flicked his eyes over the story, not taking it in. He didn't really want to read this stuff. Wasn't there ever any good news that they could celebrate?

Then, as he was about to abandon the tabloid, his eyes alighted on the gunman's name. *Suresh Rasheed*. His stomach churned. That was the name of Ayesha's husband. Surely it couldn't be him.

'What?' Crystal stared at him, concerned. 'You've gone as white as a sheet.'

He passed the paper to her and pointed at the name. Crystal looked closely at it and then gasped aloud.

'That's got to be Ayesha's husband,' Crystal said. 'Hasn't it?' She handed it to Joy. 'The raid was in the shopping centre at Milton Keynes,' she continued. 'That's where she was living before she came to us, wasn't it? It's got to be him. Who else could it be?'

'Wouldn't it be too much of a coincidence for there to be another Suresh Rasheed?' Joy agreed.

'Do you think she knows?' Crystal took the newspaper back and stared at it again, reading further down the article. 'It's him. I know it is. I can feel it in my bones. Ayesha will have seen the paper too, surely? She'll call us, won't she? Is it today's?'

Hayden checked the date. 'Two days old.' He could hear his own blood rushing in his ears. 'Could it really be him?'

'There's only one way to find out,' Crystal said.

He looked up at them. 'What shall I do?'

They both gaped at him aghast, until finally Crystal spoke. 'You should go to her, you bloody idiot. If this is her husband – and why wouldn't it be? – she's free. She's free to be with you. There's no danger for her any more.'

His heart pounded in his chest. Could that be true? Were they really free now to be together? The thought shocked and stunned him. His mind was reeling.

Joy looked at her watch. 'I hate to leave now, but I should be going through to Departures.'

'Yes,' Hayden said, dazed. 'We'll take you to the gate.'

Joy and Crystal cried and held on to each other when they stood at the entrance to Passport Control.

'I'm only going for a month, silly billy,' Joy sobbed.

'I'll have no one to nag me,' Crystal sobbed back.

Hayden had to admit that he had a tear in his eye too. It was a time of change and he wondered if life would ever be the same again for them. Joy was moving on, as was Crystal. Maybe now it was his turn.

Crystal gripped Joy tightly. 'Have a great time. Skype us the minute you get there. Cross your heart and hope to die.'

'Oh, Crystal,' Joy said, exasperated. 'I'm hoping to get there in one piece.'

'I'm going to be frantic with worry until we hear from you.'

'I'll be fine,' Joy assured her, drying her tears.

When she and Crystal finally managed to let go of each other, Hayden took his turn to wrap his arms round her. 'You have a great time.'

'I will.'

'If there's anything you need, let me know.'

'You've done enough for me already.'

He kissed her forehead and let her go.

'Just promise me that you'll go to Ayesha,' Joy said. 'As soon as you can. That would make me a very happy old woman.'

'I will,' Hayden agreed.

He and Crystal waved as Joy went through Passport Control. They stood rooted to the spot until she was out of sight.

'I suppose we'd better go home then,' Crystal said, choked. 'It'll be dead boring with just you there, Misery Guts.'

'And there's Edgar,' he reminded her.

'Yes,' she said. 'I do love him, you know.'

'I know.'

She cried again as they left the terminal and he put his arm around her and held her to him while she sniffled. But, despite his sadness at Joy's departure, there was a lightness at the centre of his being again and a spring in his step.

'I am going to go to Ayesha,' he said.

'Good! I'd only have to kill you if you said you weren't going.'

He laughed at that. 'This is a time of big change.'

'Yeah.' Crystal wiped her nose on her sleeve. 'It's never going to be the same again, is it?'

'No.' Hayden agreed. He took Crystal by her shoulders and looked at her tear-stained face. He didn't know what he'd have done without her, but she was right, he had to let her go. 'We've been good friends, haven't we?'

'The best,' she sniffed.

'I want you and Edgar to have the house,' he said as they stood close together on the pavement, oblivious to the passing courtesy buses and the insistent roar of the planes coming in to land overhead.

'You can't mean it,' Crystal said, taken aback. 'Why would you do that?'

'Do whatever you want with it. If you want the house for yourselves that's fine. If you want to take in other women who are struggling and need some space, then do that too. I don't mind how you use it. I'll leave some money in an account for you to cover the costs.'

In the drab short-stay concrete car park of Heathrow Airport, Crystal cried again. This time it was as if a dam had burst, and the tears flowed ceaselessly. He didn't have a hand-kerchief to offer her, so she wiped her tears on his white T-shirt, leaving mascara tracks down it, and he didn't mind one bit.

'Thank you,' she said when she eventually found her voice again. 'Thank you so much. I'll take really good care of it.' Then she gulped. 'You're not planning on coming back, are you?'

He shook his head. 'No.'

Nothing else mattered now. He didn't care whether he sang another song, played another tune or penned another hit. He'd be happy to sink into blissful oblivion with the woman he loved more than life itself. All he wanted was Ayesha and Sabina back in his world, and he'd get that on whatever terms she needed. He'd buy her a farm, a beachfront house, a cottage in the country. Wherever she wanted to go, he'd go too.

# Chapter Eighty-nine

'I'll make some more vegetable samosas tonight, Ben,' I say as I wipe my hands on my apron. 'We sold out of them at lunch-time.'

'They're really popular, Ayesha,' Ben agrees. 'The customers love your cooking.'

I look again at the new shalwar kameez hanging on the door by the cloakroom. 'I can't believe that this is mine,' I tell him as I nod towards it.

Together we ordered the pretty outfit online and it has only arrived today. I don't think that I have ever owned such a beautiful thing.

'You'll look very fetching in it,' Ben says with a wink.

I think that he's right and I'm longing to try it on.

'The customers will love you more than they already do,' he teases me.

Ben is always very fulsome with his praise and it makes me flush with pleasure.

I've been so very lucky in managing to secure this job soon after I arrived here with Sabina. When we fled to Lyme Regis, we spent one week in a small bed-and-breakfast guesthouse. It was a hard and frightening journey, but now I feel it was worth it.

At first I lay awake at night worrying about what I'd done. Sabina cried in her sleep and nothing I could do would bring comfort to her. My life was so good at Hayden's home. I worried that I'd been far too reckless in throwing that all away. I missed him so desperately, more than I ever thought a person could. In the small hours, I would hold myself and pretend that it was Hayden's arms around me so that I could feel closer to him and not so terribly alone. But the only thing I had to be concerned about was keeping Sabina away from Suresh. That filled my mind. Nothing else mattered.

The next day and the one after, I walked the full length of the promenade and narrow streets of this small town, asking at every café and shop whether there was a vacancy for me. On the afternoon of the second day, I struck gold and was offered a job in this little café. Home Foods has eight tables and the owner, Ben, couldn't be kinder to us.

I'm so very grateful that he was prepared to take a risk on me, despite the fact that I had no experience as a waitress. He told me later that he thought I looked honest and desperate in equal measure. I think that was a fair assessment.

Immediately we fell into a warm friendship. Ben has long, blond dreadlocks which he ties back in a ponytail, and a kind face. When I volunteered to make some of my home-made specialities to sell to his customers, he jumped at the chance. Now I'm well settled in and am doing as much cooking as I am waiting on tables.

Ben has even opened on Saturday night so that we could put on two special Sri Lankan evenings, for which I have cooked all the food. Even though I say it myself, they've been a great success and we've filled two sittings each time. Now Ben is keen to make it a regular feature on the calendar, if I want him to. Which I think I would very much like.

There's another one coming up this Saturday – also full – and I've splashed out and bought a new shalwar kameez especially for the evening. It's the colour of honey and is decorated with caramel and gold beads, which I think will look pretty with my dark hair and skin.

Suddenly, I get an urge that tells me there's something I must do. And I must do it now.

We're past our busy part of the day and it's nearly time for me to leave to collect Sabina from school.

'Ben, I have something I need to do,' I tell him. 'Is that all right with you? I'll be back in two minutes.'

Ben shrugs. 'Sure.'

He's a very easy man to work for, I think, and always tries to help me and accommodate my wishes. So I take a moment to run up the stairs to my little home.

The best thing of all is that there's a small apartment above the café. It had been used mainly as a storage area, but when I told Ben of my plight and that I was looking for somewhere to rent on a permanent basis, he cleared out all of the boxes. Together we spent the weekend decorating it to make it habitable. He charges me well below the commercial rate, I'm sure.

Over the weeks, I've spent a little of my wages on making it quite homely. There's only one bedroom, so Sabina has that while I sleep on the sofa in the living room, but it's very comfortable. We have a small shower room and kitchenette too. If you look out of the window and crane your neck just so, you can even see the sea. All that we need.

Going to our single wardrobe, I take out my old, dowdy shalwar kameez. It seems to symbolise my time as a married woman. It's worn, faded and soiled. I stare at it for a moment, thinking that it feels as if it belonged to someone else entirely. Then, before I think better of it, I rush downstairs with it clutched in my hands.

Back in the café, I say to Ben, 'Do you have the matches?'

'Yes.' Puzzled, he hands them over.

'Come with me,' I say. 'You can be my witness.' I take him by the hand and pull him in my wake.

Together we go out to the backyard of the café.

It's a small area, enclosed by high walls of warm, worn bricks. Ben thinks that he might tidy it up and put one or two tables out here for next summer. I think that would be a lovely idea as it's a warm, sheltered space. A sun trap. For now, I'm doing nothing to spoil it, so I place my shalwar kameez reverentially in the centre of the cobblestones.

'Wow,' Ben says. 'Are we having a ritual burning?'

'Yes,' I tell him. 'I want to watch my old life go up in smoke.'

'Goody.' Ben claps his hands as a child would. 'I'm all for that.'

I strike the match and throw it on to the shabby clothes, which instantly ignite. The cheap material shrivels and burns, smouldering with acrid smoke.

'You should say a prayer or something,' Ben advises, as if he does this every day.

So I close my eyes and pray. I pray that I will always make wise decisions in the future, that I will give my daughter a good life and that I will reach the end of my days knowing that I have been loved.

When I open them again, there's nothing left of the shalwar kameez but charred ashes.

I wish that Crystal, Joy and my dear Hayden could have been here to witness this too, and my heart feels a pang of empty longing for them all.

'That's the last of the old me gone for ever,' I say to Ben.

'Excellent. Then I think we should have a cup of tea and a cake to celebrate.'

I smile at him. 'I'd like that.' There's a calm at the centre of my being that I really like. I like it very much.

So we go back inside and Ben makes tea for us. We sit at one of the tables in the now-empty café, sipping tea and each eating one of the cupcakes he buys in daily.

He raises his cup to me. 'To the future.'

'To the future,' I echo.

Soon he glances at the clock. 'Better get going if you're going to be at the school to collect Sabina.'

'Oh my goodness.' I too look up. 'I hadn't realised the time.' Now I'll have to hurry. Quickly I pull off my apron and slip on my cardigan. It's the end of the summer now and we're slowly sliding into autumn. The air, I've found, is cooler down by the sea and the evenings are chilly. 'I'll see you in the morning.'

'Thanks, Ayesha. Enjoy the rest of your day. Any plans?'

'I might try to spend an hour or two on the beach before we're no longer able to.' It's Sabina's very favourite place, and mine too.

'You might be surprised. The winter here is also lovely,' Ben says. 'Quieter. When all the tourists have finally packed up and gone, the seaside has a different charm in the colder months. You'll see. There's still plenty to do.'

Ben has two daughters, one of them Sabina's age, and they've become firm friends at school. His wife, Megan, has also been so very kind. She passes on clothes that her eldest child, Layla, has outgrown as she's so much taller than my tiny Sabina. I have to put big hems on the dresses, but they're a godsend to us.

I feel as if I've been truly blessed to find this place and I can only thank Hayden for that. As soon as I realised that I had to leave, I knew this was where I would come to. My heart is happy here.

'Don't dilly-dally,' Ben says, 'or I'll find something else for you to do.'

'I'm on my way,' I tell him. So I grab my bags and rush out of the door.

# Chapter Ninety

Sabina's new school is lovely and she's settled in well. It's ideally placed as it's only a five-minute walk from the café and our new apartment. We're making a good, quiet life here. One evening each week Sabina attends ballet classes at the local community centre, which she loves. It's a simple pleasure that, at one time, seemed beyond our reach. Some weeks it's difficult to spare the money, but I so wanted her to have the opportunity, and she's proving to be a dainty dancer.

There's not a moment of the day that I don't think of my life in London; and Hayden, in particular, is never far from my thoughts. I thought the pain would lessen as the weeks went on, but as yet it hasn't felt eager to leave me at all. I miss them all so terribly. Despite the difficult times we endured, they brought fun and love into my life again and I'm poorer for not having them by my side.

Sabina talks about them constantly – When will we see them? Can we call them? – and I've had to fend off all her questions with vague responses. She misses Hayden terribly. Sometimes I catch her singing his songs and my heart contracts in my chest. The pain of my yearning is palpable. When I'm feeling down, I think of them at the piano together, laughing, and how he would look at her with the love of a father.

As I walk, I tap Crystal's number into my phone. I haven't yet spoken to her as I didn't know how to apologise for leaving in such haste and didn't dare contact her for fear of somehow being discovered again. Now I must redress that. I can only hope she understood why I needed to go and is still my dearest friend. I'm sure that she'll know my news by now. I hesitate to call it good news, as the death of a person can never be called that. But, for me, finding out about Suresh's death brings nothing but a sense of overwhelming relief. It means that at last I am a free woman.

My heart is pattering with excitement to speak to Crystal, but the call goes straight to her voicemail.

I take a deep breath and launch in. 'My dearest Crystal,' I say breathlessly. 'This is your good friend Ayesha here. I would so love to talk with you again. I miss you terribly. I will call back very soon.'

I hang up, a little disappointed to find that she's not available. I wonder where she is, what she's doing. I can picture her working at the nail bar and think fondly of that time. I'm hoping that Joy, Crystal and perhaps even Hayden will soon, very soon, come back into our lives.

Striding out now, I hope that I'll not be late for Sabina and hurry as fast as I can. I don't like her to be waiting outside the school for me. Even though I know that Suresh can no longer touch us, it will take the anxiety a long time to leave me.

As I reach the gate, I see my child coming through the playground. Every single time I look at her, my soul soars on light wings.

'Mama!' She breaks away from her little group of friends and runs the last few metres towards me. I hug her tightly to my chest.

'How is my beautiful child? Did you have a good day?'

'Oh yes,' she says. 'I've three new books to read.'

I'm so proud of her because she's clever in class and at home she's a dutiful daughter. Well, mostly. But I love the times when she raises her voice to me in defiance. It makes me smile to myself. My daughter is no one's fool and I hope that I have, in the last few months, taught her that too. Sabina is her own person. Now that she's found her voice again, she certainly likes to use it, and I take no issue with that.

'They look as if they're most excellent books.' I so miss my reading times with Hayden, and it's in the evening when Sabina is tucked up in bed that I'm at my loneliest. I read to myself then, but often I'll find my mind drifting, going over the times that I shared with him. Sometimes it's so vivid that I can almost feel his kiss on my lips. Sometimes, when I'm sure that Sabina can't hear, I cry for the want of him.

I turn my attention back to my daughter. 'Shall we go to the beach for a little while before we go home for our tea, and then we'll settle to read them later?'

'Yes.' She skips along beside me, chattering all about her day; I never get tired of listening to her.

When I saw the news about Suresh in the paper, it made my heart bleed for him. How terrible for him for his life to end like that. Even now he's dead, it frightens me to think how close he came to getting us back, and I'm so thankful that due to Crystal and Joy we were able to escape.

Yet I wept when I read the story. I wept for the man that I once called 'husband'. I wept for the man he'd become and for the man that he might have been but never was. I wept that he had, through anger or greed, stooped so low in his life. I wept for the man who'd been killed in the tragedy and for his bereaved family. Arunja and two other men, who I'm sure I'd seen at the house, have all been arrested. But for Suresh, the suffering is over.

429

The truth, though, is that, as sad as that makes me, I also know that I can now live my own life out of his shadow, and for that I feel nothing but joyous liberation. A heavy weight has been taken from me and I know now that I'll never have to run away again.

I was so worried about how to break the news to my daughter. There's always the fear lurking in my mind that a shock will take her voice again, but I needn't have been so frightened. Sabina took the news with calm equanimity and hasn't mentioned her father since. I hope that one day, when she's older, we'll be able to discuss more fully what happened.

My daughter has, however, asked about Hayden frequently. More so in recent days. She wants to know where he is, when we'll see him again. I can only tell her that I hope we'll see him again soon. I pray with all of my being that that is the truth.

When I sent him the postcard from our little seaside town, I secretly hoped that he would come to us. When he knew where we were, surely he wouldn't be able to stay away? But that hasn't proved to be the case. I sent it him so that he'd know we were safe and we hadn't, for one single minute, forgotten him. A million times I've thought about picking up the telephone and calling him, but I haven't had the words to say how I feel. Whenever I start to dial his number, my palms grow damp with anxiety and I have to hang up. What if he's angry with me and doesn't wish for me or Sabina to be in his life? What if he's changed his mind about us? Perhaps he's decided to enter the world of music again and sees us as an unnecessary burden. It will be a great sadness in my life, if I've had to forfeit Hayden's love to find peace, but I'll bear it the best as I can. For now, I would rather remain in uncertainty than know the pain of absolute rejection. But I'd so love to hear his sweet voice again.

I hope that Joy is well too. Now that Suresh has gone, I can

430

contact my friends again freely without fear of being found out or of them being hurt in any way. It would be my dearest wish for them to visit me. I've also written to my parents, to tell them of our circumstances, and I've vowed to diligently save some of my wages every single week so that one day Sabina and I may fly home to visit them.

Now I must write again to tell them that my husband is dead, although I'll spare them the terrible details. My last letter will be to Suresh's parents. They've suffered greatly at the hands of their son and they are not deserving of such pain. Their shame will be hard for them to bear. I'll write to them with my sincere condolences, in the hope that they will one day embrace me as their daughter once more. Sabina, I know, would love to see her grandparents again.

My dear daughter slips her hand in mine and we step on to the crescent of sand by the pretty harbour. The late afternoon is cool and I've brought a little sweatshirt for Sabina even though she doesn't seem to feel the cold as I do. She kicks off her shoes and socks.

Despite this being a regular habit, she jumps excitedly on the sand, holding her arms out to embrace her freedom. I lay down our small rug, then, in my bag, I find the shorts I've brought for her. She wriggles them on under her school skirt and then she peels that off to give to me. It's a routine she knows well, as we spend as much time as we can down here by the sea. The manicured beauty of Lyme Regis is so very different from the wildness of my native home, but it reminds me of it all the same. Somehow, across the miles of ocean, I feel connected. I can stand at the edge of the waves and know that, in another place, my sister, my mummy, my daddy will be doing the same thing. They feel so close to me that I could almost touch them.

I stand and breathe in the air. I love the tang of the salt on the breeze, the call of the wheeling seagulls, the way the wind lifts my hair, the feel of damp, scratchy sand beneath my toes. I could be content here for ever.

While I fold her skirt and brush sand from her shoes, Sabina runs up and down on the beach, arms wide, crying out for joy. Unbidden, there's a tear in my eye as I watch her. She's my life, my reason for being. Whatever we go through in our days together, if she is happy and finds love, then it will all have been worth it.

'Come on, Mama,' she calls impatiently. 'Play with me.'

So I brush away my tear and, kicking off my own shoes, I run to her. We hold hands and scamper down to the sea. Together we jump in the waves as Hayden showed us how to do. We laugh as the shocking coldness of the water on our legs takes our breath.

Sabina turns and, as she does, she suddenly lets go of my hand and her mouth falls open. Then she's running, running out of the sea and away from me up the beach.

'What is it?' I call after her, perplexed by her haste.

'Mama!' she cries. 'Mama, it's Hayden! It's Hayden!'

I put my hand up to shield my eyes from the low evening sunshine. She's right. It's Hayden. He's standing there on the beach before me.

When my daughter reaches him, he scoops her into his arms and twirls her round with exuberant delight, holding her tightly. Over her head, he smiles at me.

And I run to him. I run to him with a smile on my lips, the sun on my face and hope in my heart.

# Acknowledgements

Thank you to all the people who helped to make this novel the best that it could be, including the fabulous team at Little, Brown who make an author's life a joy; to my lovely friend Ayesha Bernard and also my dear Lizzy Kremer, who has the most amazing eye for a story. And, as always, to Lovely Kev for many and varied services above and beyond the call of duty.